THE COURTESAN QUEEN

A NOVEL

THE COURTESAN QUEEN

ANNA TRISS

WARM PUBLISHING
El Paso, Texas
www.warmpublishing.com

Original title: *La reine coutisane*
published by Black Ink Édition
La Jarne, France

Copyright © 2021 Black Ink Édition
Copyright © 2024 Warm Publishing

Interior design by Warm Publishing
Cover design by Angela Haddon
Art by Scarlett Lovell
Translated from French by Iris Clark

ISBN: 978-1-958447-05-5

All rights reserved. In accordance with the U.S. Copyright Act of 1976, the scanning, uploading and/or electronic sharing of any part of this book without the permission of the publisher constitute unlawful piracy and theft of the author's intellectual property. If you would like to use material from the book (other than for review purposes), prior written permission must be obtained by contacting the publisher at warmpublishing@gmail.com.

Thank you for buying an authorized edition of this book and for complying with copyright laws by not reproducing, scanning, or distributing any part of it in any form without permission. By doing so you are supporting our French authors and allowing Warm Publishing to continue publishing them.

This novel is a work fiction. Names and characters, places and incidents are either a product of the author's imagination or are used fictitiously. Any resemblance to actual persons, living or dead, business establishments, events, or locales is entirely coincidental.

"Don't be fooled by appearances."

First rule of the Guild of Shadows.

Elemental FUEGIS Clan
King: Sylvan Ren-Fuegis
Elemental Magic: Fire
Season of Influence: Summer
Clan Emblem: Red Sun
City: Astranis
Philosophy: *"The sacred fire of the Fuegis warrior fueled by the blood of his enemies."*

Elemental GLACE Clan
Queen: Alena Kan-Glace
Elemental Magic: Water
Season of Influence: Winter
Clan Emblem: Two Blue Waves
City: Oceanar
Philosophy: *"Facing his enemy, a Glace sheds no tears, and never relinquishes his weapons."*

Elemental STOWNE Clan
King: Idric San-Stowne
Elemental Magic: Earth
Season of Influence: Spring
Clan Emblem: Holm Oak
City: Stalagmis
Philosophy: *"The wrath of a Stowne is more devastating than an earthquake."*

Elemental AERIA Clan
King: Cyriel Ler-Aeria
Elemental Magic: Air
Season of Influence: Autumn
Clan emblem: Silver Feather
City: Eolan
Philosophy: *"While a soul of an Aeria is as light as a breeze, his heart holds a thousand storms."*

The Powerless: the RENEGADES
Chief: Unknown
Elemental magic: None
Season of Influence: None
Emblem: None
City: None
Philosophy: None

PART ONE

CHAPTER ONE
SHARPENING YOUR WEAPONS

I am Alena Kan-Glace, Queen of the Elemental Glace Clan.

These toneless words float in my mind like shrouds of dark mist. I try to hold on to them, but they slip through my fingers, intangible.

I am Alena Kan-Glace, Queen of the Elemental Glace Clan.

Astranis, the immense city of the Fuegis Clan, rises up on the horizon. Its many crenelated towers remind me of columns crowned with red lace emerging from high fortified walls. Behind me, the Fuegis soldiers shout with joy. They laugh, patting each other heartily on the back, excited at the thought of returning home and reuniting with their families after their third military campaign.

As far as I am concerned, the view that looms before me is more than sinister.

Astranis will be my prison for the night.

But more importantly, it will be my tomb tomorrow.

My body feels infinitely heavy. Although significant, it's not just because of the weight of the chains that bind my wrists and ankles.

Nor is it due to the oppressive heat that reigns over the arid lands of my enemies. The setting sun is no more than a timid arc sinking behind the blood-red curve dunes of the Red Desert. This endless scorching day is about to end.

Just like my life.

My last day in this half-ruined world is coming to an end.

I am Alena Kan-Glace, Queen of the Elemental Glace Clan, and at dawn, I will die.

If you have been told that the Glaces do not fear death, you have been lied to.

Yet, I show nothing of it. My face is an impenetrable mask of ice.

The chestnut horse on which I am seated prances impatiently. My chains are attached to its saddle. Its long reins are held by my jailer, who rides to my right on his own steed.

I don't know the name of this giant with a rugged, scarred face, and, and, honestly, I don't care. His contempt for me is obvious: he hasn't spoken to me once all day. His black eyes are filled with repulsion as soon as they meet mine, which is rarely. He only gave me silent orders with nods or hand signals, and occasionally handed me a bottle of water so I wouldn't get dehydrated on the way. It's not f out of kindness: his duty is to bring me back alive to Astranis, and presenting my corpse to their people would probably look bad…

He's an officer of the enemy army. I have no idea of his military rank, as his gear bear no insignias. Like all Fuegis, he has tanned skin and dark hair. His are braided and decorated with wooden beads engraved with traditional runes. His ears are pierced with five gold rings each. The meaning of these jewels is exceedingly morbid: they prove that my jailer is a veteran fighter who has killed at least fifty enemies… because I can't see if he has more piercings like this on his body. The warriors of his people also count their victims through, thin, purple, vein-like tattoos. These trivial practices have always sent a chill down my spine.

He should be dying of heat under his copper armor, with a breastplate bearing the emblematic red sun of his Clan, but all Fuegis are naturally immune to heat and fire. Like his brothers in arms, he hasn't secreted a single drop of sweat today, unlike me, drenched in sweat, with several patches of my fair skin reddened by the relentless sun of their cursed desert. The white clothes that cover almost my entire body have only helped to limit the damage. I can't hardly stand the heat and the sun; I'm not used to it. I almost passed out three times in my saddle today. In my Glace kingdom, the weather conditions are entirely opposite to what I'm enduring now: summers are cool and humid, winters are freezing. The jagged coastline is always windy. Inland, our plains are covered with a blanket of snow eight months of the year.

As we approach within a hundred meters of Astranis's fortified gates, I see a rider galloping in the opposite direction of the soldiers ahead of us. Another officer, no doubt… He comes from the Vanguard. He rides alongside the long column of red metal in motion. He gives a signal to my jailer, who leads my horse in his direction without hesitation. My heart skips a beat as my horse start to gallops, keeping pace with the rider in charge of watching me.

We break away from the main army troops and quickly make our way up the military procession under the curious gaze of the Fuegis infantrymen, who continue to march toward their city.

Being more and more nervous, I repeat to myself over and over, as if to convince myself:

I am Alena Kan-Glace, Queen of the Elemental Glace Clan.

Then I see him.

My worst enemy.

My executioner.

My future husband…

And my future assassin.

Perched on his imposing warhorse, whose fiery coat reminds me of the color of fire, the king of the Elemental Fuegis Clan, the infamous Sylvan Ren-Fuegis, is about to pass through the enormous lapis- lazuli adorned gates of his city at the head of his army of three thousand soldiers.

He will present to his people his war prize and, accessorily, his fiancée.

Me.

The truth is, I don't even know what he looks like because until now, I've always seen him with his terrifying dragon-shaped helmet pulled over his head. Though seated in his saddle and encased in his black and gold armor, his impressive build is evident. He looks almost as tall and muscular as my jailer. He didn't say a word to me either, even when his brutish men captured me in the throne room of Oceanar's palace under his eyes, hidden behind the slits of his helm. His bright red silk cloak rests on his mount's rump like a bloody banner, visible from afar. The ornate gold hilt of his master's sword juts out from his belt.

I viscerally hate the man—or the soulless, heartless demon—who hides behind the metal reflecting the last rays of a dying sun.

And he terrifies me just as viscerally.

My jailer slows down a few feet from his king, forcing my horse to do the same, then bows his head in greeting. I'm vaguely surprised to see Sylvan returns the respectful gesture… before turning his golden helmet, resembling a scaly dragon's mouth topped by a pair of ivory horns, in my direction. Hidden behind his helmet, he stares at me in silence. Frowning, I keep my gaze fixed on the two slits behind which the eyes of the murderous despot scrutinize me… trying my best not to reveal the fear he instills in me.

"Daegan," declares a deep voice, slightly distorted by the helm.

"Yes, Your Majesty?" asks my guard.

"You know what you have to do."

Daegan nods, scowling.

Goddess of the Ocean, I don't like this at all…

My jailer jerks my reins sharply, forcing my horse to come closer to his. I tense up like a bowstring, unable to control the trembling in my legs.

Daegan leans over, extracting a key from his pants pocket, and removes the chains from my ankles, then my wrists. If he were alone, in theory, I could attempt an escape. But he is not. Thousands of soldiers surround me. Fleeing is clearly not an option in my delicate situation.

I rub my sore wrists, chafed by the irons, as soon as he releases me. Well, *release* is a bit of an exaggeration word.

Indeed, I still wear the thick enchanted gold necklace, which has the property of neutralizing my oh-so-dangerous elemental magic! An ancient, legendary, and unique artifact created by a circle of magicians a century ago, lost and forgotten, but supposedly miraculously found by Sylvan during a treasure hunt in a ruinous temple filled with death traps.

I don't believe that story.

He must have stabbed someone in the back to steal that powerful object.

The Fuegis King took certain precautions against me, which was to be expected. He had already used the preventative measure of the collar when imprisoning his previous wives. Lia, daughter of Cyriel Ler-Aeria, and Belise, sister of Idric San-Stowne.

In other words, this lamentable jewelry was worn by two princesses before me. Now dead. This thought alone sends chills down my spine.

Daegan gives me a disdainful look.

"Take off your clothes before entering the city, white slut," he demands in a firm tone.

My eyes widen, stunned by his order.

Revered Goddess, please tell me I heard wrong.

My bewildered gaze turns to my… my future husband. Sylvan watches me from a distance, like a black and gold steel statue glittering under the torches set on the ramparts.

"Obey, or I guarantee you will regret it, Alena," threatens the king of the Fuegis in an icy tone.

Spontaneously, with a vulgarity more fitting for a peasant girl than a queen, I spit in his direction. My slimy offense misses his helmet and lands on his knee—still a small victory.

Daegan lets out an angry roar and raises a massive fist to strike me in the face, but Sylvan stops him in his tracks with a sharp right hand. The fist of my jailer freezes in the air three inches from my face.

"It's strictly forbidden to damage my fiancée before the parade, Daegan!" barks the sovereign wiping his saliva-stained knee with the back of his leather glove. "Don't make me more unpopular with my subjects than I already am."

Unpopular with his subjects? Since when does he care about being popular or not? Everyone in Symbiosis hates him, and with good reason!

"But she's a fury, Your Majesty!"

"I won't lower myself to having a prisoner beaten in public. She's our enemy, but she's also my future queen."

"Your future queen for one night," sneers Daegan, eyeing me maliciously.

"You, however, will keep the intellectual capacity of a cockroach for your entire life," I retort in a harsh voice.

The guard growls, curling his lips in a fierce snarl, like a rabid dog. I give him a mocking little smile.

"Alena, I give you one minute to remove all your clothes," Sylvan calmly orders. "If you don't cooperate, I'll tell Daegan to do it himself, and he won't be gentle, believe me."

My smile fades. anxiety twists my stomach. He's not kidding, obviously.

"What are you… what are you going to do to me?" I ask in a

strangled voice, swallowing to moisten my dry throat.

Rape me in public? Throw me to his men?

He doesn't answer. He taps the pommel of his saddle with a hint of impatience. My anxiety increases a notch.

Unfortunately, I don't really have a choice.

I have some vague notions of combat thanks to my brother, a warrior, but I'm absolutely no match for defending myself against Sylvan and his desert dogs, and I know it.

With a shaky, mechanical movement, I begin to shed my travel rags one by one. I also take off my turban; my silvery hair, characteristic of the Glaces, tangled from the sand, falls to my lower back. I feel Sylvan's gaze but also the lustful eyes of the men around. Laughter and whistles rise behind me. Soon, I am naked as the day I was born on my saddle; my clothes rolled up in a ball in front of me, covering my crotch. Fortunately, my hair is long enough to cover part of my breasts. However, the infantrymen behind me have an unobstructed view of my buttocks.

No matter. It's just a body. A shell. What belongs to me inside is not shown. Who I am is preserved.

My precious secret is intact, buried deep in my racing heart.

I urge myself to ignore the lewd and degrading remarks that greet my stripping among the soldiers. I catch snippets of obscene words here and there behind my back. "Damn, she's got an ass, the bitch!", "I'd like to fuck the Glace Queen!", "Yeah, well, not me, I'm sure her pussy is as frigid as an ice cave." With his fist closed firmly on its reins, Sylvan turned abruptly toward the men who insulted me.

He doesn't even need to call them to order; they fall silent as one, looking away.

The aura of violence and authority emanating from this bloodthirsty man is overwhelming.

Many sordid rumors circulate in my kingdom about him. One of them claims that the king himself beheads the soldiers of his army who contest his orders or disrespect him in public.

As well as deserters. Slackers. Incompetents.

Anyone who doesn't fit his narrow vision of things, essentially.

Apparently, these rumors are true.

"The law of the strongest rules in these burning lands", explained my mother to me at the beginning of the war that started in Symbiosis six months ago. "The Fuegis don't think like us, my dear. They have always been formidable warriors. It's certainly linked to their fiery temperament and the nature of their elemental magic. They live only to fight and destroy. Most Fuegis parents put a sword in their sons' hands as soon as they take their first steps and teach them to master their powers. They are skilled fighters. That's why they, among the four Elemental Clans, were sent to the Forest of Exile to fight the Renegades. Unfortunately, their new king Sylvan Ren-Fuegis has fueled their thirst for blood and death from the moment he ascended to the throne to serve his own thirst for conquest, power, and domination. Let us pray to the Goddess of the Ocean to protect our people if Sylvan and his armies decide to invade us next, my darling…"

Here I am now… Naked in front of hundreds of onlookers and captive of the tyrant who exterminated some of my people. Future ephemeral sovereign of the Fuegis, condemned to death by her cruel husband the day after our wedding, forced into a vile marriage by the tragic events that occurred in my annexed kingdom.

Yet, despite appearances, I'm not entirely resigned to my fate.

Daegan hands over the reins of my horse to Sylvan.

He's going to parade me in before his people like a trophy, I realize, my stomach in knots.

My nudity displayed in front of the entire city is a show of strength.

An execrable method meant to debase, humiliate, subjugate, and strip me of my own power as Queen of the Glaces. By showing everyone my position of weakness, stripped of my regal attire, I am less than a woman, less than a slave, less than an animal: for Sylvan Ren-Fuegis, I am merely an object.

The spoils of war.

To be use as his whim.

To be discarded without a second thought once he has legally acquired the coveted status of King of the Glaces by marrying me.

He was born Prince of the Fuegis. When his father passed away a year ago, as the only son, Sylvan ascended to the throne by blood right.

A young man with a quiet reputation. Thoughtful. Taciturn. Private.

At least, back then.

Then, the mask of propriety fell off, and the bloodthirsty dictator came to light, causing confusion, shock, and horror on our once-prosperous island... Some skeptics claimed he was possessed by a demon's soul, others that he had been struck by madness at the death of his father. Several other theories were spread among the population to explain his radical change of personality: enchantment, curse, corruption...

For my part, I see only the result of his insanity. Wherever he goes, Sylvan leaves behind death, blood, and pain. Desolation and despair.

This man is a living plague for Symbiosis.

He murdered the kings and male heirs of the Aeria and Stowne Clans after attacking their kingdoms. One after the other, he brought the two princess heirs back to Astranis to marry them... before having them executed the next day. Now, thanks to his official marriages, he is the undisputed king of the other three Clans. I am his final stepping stone—or obstacle, depending on one's point of view—to ruling over all of Symbiosis.

The leather of the saddle burns my bare buttocks. The desert wind bites at my sensitive skin. But the most harmful element of my new environment is undoubtedly the inscrutable gaze of my future husband.

The gates of Astranis open before us with theatrical slowness.

On my horse, I hold my chin high, shoulders back, and spine straight.

My gaze fixed ahead.

My expression impassive.

My bearing regal.

Queen or slave, I remain, above all, a Glace.

I will honor the ancestral philosophy of my Clan.

"Facing his enemy, a Glace sheds no tears, and never relinquishes his weapons."

I am Alena Kan-Glace, Queen of the Elemental Glace Clan, and at dawn, I will die...

But I'm determined to fight with my weapons until my last breath.

I still need to find the weapons I can use against Sylvan Ren-Fuegis

CHAPTER TWO

IN THE DRAGON'S LAIR

The glorious flames burning atop the Tower of Eternal Flame dance before us, like the amber glow of a lighthouse lost in the middle of the Red Desert.

The central tower of the Fuegis Palace overlooks the small stone houses of Astranis, which crowd together along the narrow, labyrinthine streets. Scarlet lanterns hanging from the balconies of the buildings, meant to celebrate the return of the troops, add a festive note to the urban landscape. This gigantic city is very different from the capital of my kingdom, and I can't help but compare them. Oceanar is a remarkable fortified city built on steep cliffs at the most rugged part of our island. It's best not to be afraid of heights when you live there because its white houses are perched on the edge of the void. If an earthquake struck the city, many buildings would tumble down and disappear into the Endless Ocean, where foamy waves crash against the rocks. But Oceanar exudes a vibrant and airy atmosphere, whereas Astranis feels stifling and insular.

I'm not accustomed to the exotic scents that fill my nostrils: spices and flowers to which I can't associate any name, citrus, olives, and also a delicious aroma of grilled meat that awakens my appetite despite the critical circumstances.

I've only had warm water today and I'm starving. Will I at least get a last meal tonight?

Sylvan mentioned his unpopularity before entering his dynamic and flourishing city. Now, I fully realize the truth of his comment.

Behind a line of immobile and austere elite guards, the crowd has gathered in front of the house facades along the main artery we walk.

Astranis is supposed to be bustling with life.

The citizens should be cheering for their king and his army.

But they are not.

The silence in the streets around us is incredibly oppressive. Anxiogenic.

A few discreet throat-clearings, scattered coughs, the nervous barking of a distant dog, and the whimper of a baby echo in the twilight heat. They mingle with the metallic clinking of armor and the clopping of hooves on the sandy avenue, raising clouds of orange dust in their path.

Apart from these noises, there are no ovations.

No laughter.

No chatter.

This gloomy atmosphere, contrasting with the colorful clothing of the citizens and the apparent conviviality of their homes, makes me even more uncomfortable than I already am. All eyes are locked on Sylvan and me: the majority of men, women, and children stare at us with the same indifferent expression. Detached and extinguished. Jaded.

However, I do manage to decipher emotions on some of Fuegis's faces.

A flash of hatred toward the monarch in the shadowed eyes of a merchant with clenched fists, barely containing his instinct to rebel.

A worried expression on a scrawny teenager who casts furtive glances at the black and gold-armored sovereign while wringing his hands.

A dirty look from an old man who licks his lips as if I were a prostitute offered on a silver platter.

A pitying expression towards me is reflected on the chiseled face of a mother, marked by dark circles of fatigue, who clutches her sleeping little girl to her breast, pursing her lips. When my eyes meet hers, she immediately lowers her head to stare at her feet.

The silences, as well as the lack of reaction, and facial expressions of the crowd speak for themselves.

People are afraid of the tyrant who is their king. They fear and hate him like the other inhabitants of Symbiosis. As for me, they see me as a lamb to be sacrificed on the altar of his ambition, another victim of his dark madness… or maybe as a foreign queen who is no better than him and deserves the fatal fate that awaits her.

I, too, carry a particular reputation in Symbiosis. My unpopularity is less blatant than Sylvan's — I'm not a mass murderer who sends his army to massacre defenseless villagers and have his wives executed! — but it is true.

I have heard many unflattering descriptions about Alena Kan-Glace in my lifetime.

"A superficial, selfish, and greedy ruler who spends her time partying and strutting before her court like a luxury hen while her subjects starve."

She's so narcissistic that she brings a jewel-encrusted mirror to the latrine to watch herself shit.

A fornicator who corrupts innocent young men of good families.

Prejudices are as tenacious as rumors.

Even if some of the descriptions hold a grain of truth, I can't deny it.

"It's truly delightful to hear the melodious flight of flies in a city that must *normally* be quite lively," I ironize with an artificial calm.

Sylvan slightly turns his head toward me, piercing me with his dark eyes. "You'll have plenty of time to enjoy the soothing silence of my city and the melodious flight of corpse flies tomorrow," he retorts, his voice as sharp as his sword.

I shudder, the hairs on my neck standing on end.

Don't let rattle you.

"With such a dark sense of humor, it's no wonder your people worship you so much, Sylvan Ren-Fuegis," I snap.

This man is not my king. I will never call him *Your Majesty*.

"That wasn't humor, Alena Kan-Glace," he says coldly, turning away. "I'm in the mood to tolerate your sarcasm and insolence. As far as I know, I didn't give you permission to speak. Be silent, or I will gag you myself."

"Yourself? What a great honor, my loving and caring husband," I murmur, unable to stop myself.

Sylvan ignores my insolent jab.

A smug little smile stretches my sun-chapped lips.

If he thinks I'm going to obey all his orders without flinching and place my head on the chopping block tomorrow morning, moving my hair aside to make the executioner's job easier, he's gravely mistaken.

"Fucking big-mouthed Glace aristocrat!" Daegan, who rides behind me, insults. "You forget your place!"

"You too, soldier," I retort over my shoulder. "Besides, why don't you go back to where you were born?"

"And where do you think I was born?" he growls, irritated.

"In the sewers, among the plague-infested rats of your kind."

A short, strange, muffled sound comes from my right.

Sylvan.

Did my enemy just *laugh*?

No, it must be my imagination… or just a simple cough.

"Yeah, keep it up while you still have your head on your shoulders, Glace!" snaps Daegan. "You won't be so smart on the scaffold tomorrow. I can't wait to see the show; I've never had the pleasure of seeing a queen piss on herself."

What a bastard…

"And you never will."

"Wanna bet?" laughs my appointed jailer.

"Sorry to disappoint you. I don't have any money on me."

"Silence, both of you!" Sylvan commands sharply.

I can confirm, the laugh was just an auditory hallucination.

The rest of the journey to the dragon's lair continues in an almost sepulchral silence.

I must concede that in the kingdom of dunes and red rocks, the Fuegis palace is a true architectural masterpiece. I salute the unquestionable skill of the engineer who once designed this sumptuous marvel that inspires dreams, rest, and meditation—nothing like the belligerent mentality of its residents.

Dominated by the Tower of Eternal Flame and the twin turrets that frame it, the palace displays its countless aesthetic assets to the visitor. To mention only these elements:

Three monumental domes of pristine whiteness.

A harmonious fluted colonnade around which carefully maintained cascades of climbing plants entwined.

Gilded bas-reliefs encrusted with rubies represent the God of Fire and his daughter Light, who triumphantly holding the emblematic red sun of the Fuegis between their four united hands.

Graceful arches adorned with geometric designs in blue, yellow, and green mosaics.

An abundance of semi-open galleries, terraces, and circular stained-glass windows that sparkle like multicolored roses.

I can see part of the palace gardens in front of the right wing: a ten feet high marble fountain surrounded by palm trees and flowering bushes that fill the atmosphere with their sweet perfume.

If this palace weren't my future mausoleum, I would be unreservedly awestruck by its lush beauty. But that's not the case.

Sylvan dismounts from his chestnut horse with feline elegance.

"Does your new palace suit you, my queen?" he asks with a touch of cynicism that doesn't get escape me.

I quickly close my mouth and put on a haughty grimace to be more convincing in my denial—a matter of principle and self-respect, you see.

"Calling this hideous building a palace is the sign of a high level of bad taste."

"If I were sensitive to bad taste, I would have demolished Glace Castle stone by stone," growls the king of the Fuegis Clan, handing his reins to a servile groom rushing toward him. "Your people managed the unusual feat of making it an offense to the gods and to nature."

Clenching my fists in my horse's mane, I grit my teeth, swallowing the blasphemy that burns my tongue.

"Instead, you had the kindness to only half-destroy it during the bloody siege of Oceanar," I remark, filled with cold anger.

"I plan to restore it and strengthen its fortifications."

"I'm relieved, thank you," I reply dryly. "It's a shame I won't be able to witness your dubious military masonry skills."

Without a word, Sylvan approaches my horse, removing his leather gloves and handing them to Daegan. My eyes fall on his bare hands.

His fingers are long, thick, and strong, calloused from handling weapons. His tanned skin studded with prominent veins, a few black hairs, and tiny pearly scars. As virile as they are powerful, those hands could crush my bones with a simple gesture.

These are warrior's hands.

Man's hands.

No demon claws, scales, or fur. Beneath his royal armor, Sylvan is a human being.

And all humans without exception have a weakness.

I just hope I have time to find his.

Human hands… reaching out to me.

Instinctively, I pull back, but Sylvan is much quicker. Without hesitation, he grabs me by the waist, lifts me from my saddle, and sets me on the ground in front of him as if I were as light as a feather. The burning contact of his tanned skin against mine sends icy spikes into my stomach and causes shivers of revulsion on my skin. He releases me as soon as my feet touch the ground and takes a rigid step back with a certain abruptness, as if I had just sent a blast of ice into his hands.

Good, I prefer if he's disgusted too. Maybe it will dissuade him from touching me again without my consent.

Indeed, Sylvan Ren-Fuegis is tall. Very tall, even, and I have to lift my chin to look into the slits that conceal the mystery of his eyes. My height is average for Glace women, but he towers over me by at least two heads. Additionally, the athletic build of this brute is intimidating, accentuated by his armor and helmet

I have the unpleasant sensation of being scrutinized by a real dragon that is about to devour me alive at any moment.

If his face is as ugly as his soul, I will undoubtedly have to suppress a gag reflex when I see it…

"Daegan, you and I are going to enter the palace, Alena," he announces in a whisper, so I have to strain my ears to hear him. "The entire Astranis court is gathered in the throne room and waiting for us. But first, a few words about the Fuegis protocol. Pay attention; I don't like to repeat myself." His voice takes on a stern tone. "You will walk ten steps behind me, closely followed by Daegan. If I slow down, you slow down. If I speed up, you speed up. Always keep those ten steps between us in our sacred palace: it's a symbolic distance that you can only be able to reduce once you become my queen. When I climb the steps to the red stone stage, you'll stop. When I sit on my throne, the entire court will kneel, and you will do the same. You will only get up and speak with my permission, Alena. You will address me exclusively as *Your Majesty*. Is that clear?"

Count on it, you Fuegis bastard.

I give a brief nod, pretending to be reasonable.

"Would you be kind enough to allow me to get dressed before this ridiculous protocol charade, husband?" I murmur.

"No." His helmet gradually lowers toward me. Goddess of the Ocean! Is he looking to my body from head to toe? "Your lack of clothing is part of the performance."

I raise an eyebrow. If I'm reading between the lines correctly, does this mean it's not a public humiliation?

"What do you mean by that?"

"I don't have time to explain here and now. We'll go over these details after the wedding ceremony. As long as you behave yourself. Don't disgrace me, Alena. Show yourself worthy of your rank and your blood. I don't want to have to put chains on your wrists and ankles like a wild animal. Behave like a queen, not a wench."

Out of sheer defiance, I'm tempted to act like a *wench* by spitting on him again to show what I think of his sharp recommendations and his stupid protocol. This time, given our proximity, I won't miss his damn helmet!

This time, however… I don't dare.

With a snap of his scarlet cape, Sylvan turns on his heel and strides into the vestibule of his palace with a smooth, confident gait.

Ten steps behind him, I follow hesitantly, Deagan at my heels.

Am I still Queen Alena Kan-Glace within this enemy palace?

All of a sudden, I'm not quite sure anymore.

CHAPTER THREE
THE FACE OF DEATH

The vast hypostyle throne room is as grim as the rest of the palace is enchanting. And for a good reason: the murals of the battles that decorate it make my stomach grow sick.

Massacres.

Fires.

Rivers of blood.

They depict fierce Fuegis in red armor fighting the Renegades, the Powerless.

The elemental magic of Symbiosis manifests at puberty, usually between the ages of twelve and eighteen. Most of the time, children born into an Elemental Clan inherit the powers of their ancestors. Rarely does a child reveal elemental magic different from their Clan. I once knew a young girl, a pure Glace, who had powers related to the elemental magic of Fire. She was separated from her family by the High-Glaces and sent without trial to the Fuegis Clan.

Also rarely happening a Symbiote reaching adulthood without revealing any powers at all.

On their twentieth birthday, if they are classified as Powerless, they find himself banished from their Clan and forced to join the Forest of Exile where the other Renegades are cloistered. The outcast is strictly forbidden from returning to their home kingdom—or any of the other three, for that matter. They are condemned to a difficult and tormented existence until their death.

I have always found this thousand-year-old law absurd. The Renegades didn't choose to be what they are. In my opinion, all natives of Symbiosis should have equal rights and be allowed to live in the kingdom they desire.

Naturally, the Renegades rebelled against this outrageous treatment. Over the centuries, they have risen up multiple times to try to get revenge on the four Elemental Clans.

Each time, they were defeated and pushed back by the Fuegis warriors, the so-called *protective* army of Symbiosis. Each time, they retreated back into their dark and hostile forest at the center of our island, tails between their legs, suffering heavy human losses.

However, the people of Symbiosis realized far too late that the enemy most to be feared was not the Renegades, but the valiant soldiers meant to defend them: the Fuegis.

Therefore, we were all shocked on the tragic day when Sylvan's army besieged Eolan, the homeland of the Aeria Clan, spilling the blood of innocents in the streets of the city built on the side of the Ancestor Mountains.

By starting this cataclysmic war, King Sylvan betrayed our nation and shattered its ancient foundations. Unity and peace no longer exist within Symbiosis. The alliances between the Glace, Aeria, and Stowne Clans are weakened.

Everyone's freedom on the island is now threatened by his military and political supremacy.

Mine is nothing but a chimera.

My thoughts are reinforced by the menacing omnipresence of dozens of veterans from the royal guard, who line the walls in front of the murals, wielding sharp spears and halberds. Large Fuegis banners are plastered on the red stone columns. The atmosphere of the throne room is aggressive in many ways.

I let my gaze wander over the Fuegis nobles crowded around us, scrutinizing me from head to toe.

The few smiles I catch in passing are far from curious or friendly; they are sardonic or lecherous. The women's eyes show contempt, annoyance, or envy. However, the men's gazes disturb me the most:

the majority of these vultures assess me as if I were particularly appetizing livestock.

I'm convinced I have no allies here.

In their eyes, darkened by vice, I am a freak. As soon as my head is severed from my body, these vultures will forget me and move on to another corpse to feast upon.

With their dark hair gathered into sophisticated buns and eyelids dusted with gold glitter enhancing their naturally tanned complexions, the women are dressed in sumptuous silk or satin gowns in shades of vermilion. They display flashy gold jewelry set with amber and rubies, flaunting their wealth. They are all rather tall and slender.

Their sensual beauty is striking, as is their pride. Here, even the mature women are stunning: the authority and poise they exude give them an undeniable charisma. They proudly wear their wrinkles like precious ornaments. I've heard that the most popular and attractive courtesans in Astranis are between thirty and fifty years old. It's not the young women who have the power in this palace: discreet, they respectfully stay in the wake of the older courtesans who influence the High-Fuegis by whispering sweet words in their ears in the intimacy of a bedroom.

The men, with their stocky builds and stern expressions, sport velvet doublets in shades of orange and shimmering golden capes. Medium-length hair, mustaches, and goatees are trendy among the men of the Fuegis court. Piercings, tattoos, and scars mark their faces, necks, and hands: even the nobles are warriors among the Fuegis.

And they all wear the colors of the flames. Their attire resembles costumes rather than ceremonial garments.

The High-Fuegis, who make up the king's council, stand out from the other nobles by wearing black turbans adorned with a long red feather and a central ruby. These are exclusively men, mostly old. I already know by name their figurehead: Leonal Ren-Fuegis, Sylvan's uncle.

Leonal stands on the royal stage, to the right of the imposing mahogany throne carved with spirals. His hands are crossed behind his back, his gaze is on his nephew, and a raptor-like smile is printed on his thin lips. He must be in his forties, and, if I remember what I was told, he's the younger brother of Sylvan's late father, Saradin. He's the only High-Fuegis not wearing a turban: his eminent rank exempts him from it.

His shaved head gleams under the light from the flaming chandeliers hanging from the throne room ceiling. His dark eyes shimmer like a pair of enigmatic black diamonds. Tattooed in the middle of his forehead is the emblem of the Fuegis Clan: a red sun with twisted fire rays. Only members of the royal family display this symbol on their faces. I myself wear the emblem of my Glace Clan on my forehead: two thin, wavy blue lines.

Leonal is almost as feared as his nephew. While Sylvan is a born warrior, Leonal is a brilliant politician. One embodies brute strength, and the other strategic intelligence. The fist and the brain. Together, they form the most formidable power duo in Symbiosis.

Sylvan slows his paces before the stage, and I do the same, with Daegan close behind. I freeze as my enemy climbs the four steps leading his throne before turning to the silent crowd.

"Welcome to Astranis, Your Majesty," Leonal greets him in a honeyed voice, bowing his head. "Did your journey back home go well?"

"It was long and boring, as you can imagine," Sylvan replies, looking around the room as if searching for someone. "We've had some supply issues over the past few days."

Leonal frowns slightly. The red sun tattooed on his forehead deepens into a furrow.

"No one informed me of this."

"I had far more important priorities than wasting time detailing logistical issues in a message to you, Uncle," the king retorts in a neutral tone.

"Of course, Your Majesty," says Leonal with a hypocritical smile that horrified me. His desert jackal eyes turn to me. He scrutinizes me from head to toe, then from toe to head. "Alena Kan-Glace! A prestigious war prize, my king. The rumors about the beauty of the Queen of the Glace Clan are not exaggerated. Indeed, this young woman looks even more beautiful than your two previous wives behind the layer of dirt that stains her. She will undoubtedly be stunning once properly dressed."

Sylvan neither confirms nor denies his uncle's comment. He says nothing. However, I can feel his gaze on me behind his golden helmet. He's analyzing me. It makes me even more nervous.

An uncomfortable silence fills the throne room. All eyes are focused on the sovereign. The vultures disguised as Fuegis nobles hang on the king's not visible lips.

Leonal clears his throat and speaks again.

"The servants are busy in the Palatine Sanctuary at this very moment, finalizing preparations for the wedding ceremony, Your Majesty."

At the word *wedding*, I stiffen.

This cursed artifact around my neck suddenly feels even heavier. It itches me. Burns me. Tears me. Chokes me. Bruises me. I would sell my soul to the sea demons of the Endless Ocean to be able to open it and bury it deep in the middle of the Red Desert.

"Good, Uncle. You are as efficient as ever," remarks Sylvan with formal indifference.

"Thank you, Your Majesty."

The king throws a piece of cloak behind his hip, revealing the hilt of his sword, and sits on his throne with majestic grace.

In an atmosphere thick with solemnity, the entire court, like a human tide stirred by a receding wave. The women lift the hems of their scarlet dresses before bowing. The men drop to one knee, heads bowed. Even the elite guards prostate themselves.

Only two people remain standing.

Leonal.

And me.

Guess *who* immediately becomes the focus of the entire assembly's gaze?

Here's a hint: it's not the High-Fuegis.

"Kneel," hisses Daegan behind me.

"No," I reply very calmly, meeting Sylvan's gaze.

Sylvan stiffens like a wooden board on his throne. I hear buzzing in the crowd around me, whispers of surprise and disapproval. Leonal studies me with a sly smile, one eyebrow raised, before glancing at his nephew.

"Kneel, Alena Kan-Glace," Sylvan orders in a loud voice, vibrating with fury under his helmet.

Don't tremble. Control your fear, I think, mustering my courage.

"A queen kneels before no man," I declare in a clear, resolute tone so that all the Fuegis in the throne room can hear me. *Praise be the Goddess, my tongue doesn't flatter!* "Whether he be sovereign… or tyrant."

At this provocation, the ambient murmurs double. Sylvan's fists clench on the armrests of his throne. His anger is palpable.

"Has the heat of the Red Desert fried your brain, Alena Kan-Glace?" Leonal asks, his face showing a sly amusement.

"What do I have to lose?" I exclaim dryly. "My life? It's already hanging by a thread!"

"Do you not fear suffering?" Sylvan whispers in a dangerously cold tone that sounds like a barely veiled threat to my ears.

A shadow of a bitter smile forms on my lips.

"Suffering doesn't last, Sylvan Ren-Fuegis. But the damnation of the man who sheds innocent blood is eternal."

Behind me, a man cries out in outrage as if I've just blasphemed. A woman hurls an insult at me in her language. Daegan growls in anger. Leonal shakes his head with a caustic smile, but his dark eyes overflow with hatred and disdain.

Sylvan, however, doesn't flinch.

Then, with a motion of his finger, he signals to Daegan.

My jailer straightens quickly and brings his enormous hands down on my small shoulders. Unfortunately, I can't match his physical power: no matter how hard I resist, the Fuegis giant forces me to kneel before the royal stage. He keeps his iron grip on my shoulders, putting a good portion of his weight on me so that I can't try to stand up. I want to at least keep my back straight with some semblance of dignity, but it's hardly possible. His thick fingers dig into my flesh, making my collarbones and shoulder blades crack. I swallow a moan of pain.

He won't have the satisfaction of hearing me scream. Neither he, nor Sylvan, nor any other Fuegis.

A surge of indignant rage explodes within me. I lock my fiery eyes on my enemy's helm, my heart racing and my breath ragged. I'm trembling with all my limbs.

"So, this is how you gain the respect of your people, Sylvan Ren-Fuegis!" I shout with all the fire in my lungs. "This is how you rise above ordinary men! This is how you treat your opponents when you don't murder them! By degrading them lower than the ground! By chaining them like wild beasts! By humiliating them to rob them of all pride! By subduing them with brute force! Only a weak and cowardly man would display a naked prisoner for all to see and present her like a vulgar war trophy! You may constrain my body, neutralize my magic with a necklace, and inflict a thousand sufferings on me tonight before having me executed, but you will never break my spirit! You are not my king. You are not even a *man*. MAY YOU BE CURSED BY THE GODS!"

My unrecognizable voice echoes eerily in the throne room, where a dead silence reigns, like an ominous omen.

The Fuegis are all stunned and speechless.

Including Leonal, whose mouth is open in dismay at my virulent speech.

I would give an arm to see Sylvan's expression right now…

At this moment, I realize that I will die here and now for defying him in front of his court.

It's not so bad after all. Marrying my corpse won't give him the Glace crown!

Everyone without exception holds their breath, waiting for the king's reaction, silent and motionless on his throne.

They await his imminent execution order.

Sylvan raises his hands on his helmet, leans his head forward, and slides the helmet up. A mass of jet-black hair with coppery highlights spreads to his muscular shoulders.

The sight of his features literally takes my breath away.

In truth, I have never seen such a magnificent face. Not even on a woman.

His youth, first of all, hits me like a punch in the stomach. Despite the short black beard that smears his square jaw and the thin, sinuous scar that slashes his eyebrow arch to his temple, this man is barely over twenty.

Beneath the royal tattoo of a red sun on his broad forehead, his sea-green eyes look like clear emeralds in the middle of his tanned face. His lips, almost as full as mine, are not without sensuality. His fine features have a touch of boyishness quality: they make me think of the portraits of languid young gods on the master paintings that decorate the castle of my kingdom. If it weren't for his beard, scar, and physique that make him far more virile, he would probably look like a late-adolescent ephebe. That graceful, attractive face wouldn't reflect an ounce of cruelty or malevolence.

But the hard expression he now wears and the devastating flame that burns in his eyes make all the difference.

No, I won't be fooled by his appearance: King Sylvan is not a gentle-looking lamb.

He's a carnivorous wolf with teeth as sharp as daggers.

A beautiful wolf, but a wolf, nonetheless.

Who is currently *tearing* me apart with his gaze.

I can't suppress a shiver under his scrutiny.

His verdict will fall like a guillotine any second now.

I close my eyes and prepare myself for the sentence.

Decapitation is the most likely option.

"Daegan," Sylvan calls in a deep, penetrating voice.

"Your Majesty?" replies my jailer with perceptible hope.

Oh, yes, this bastard soldier is truly eager to kill me.

"Release her and step back two steps, Daegan."

I reopen my eyes, stunned. Is he setting a trap for me?

"Excuse me, Your Majesty?" mutters the colossus, as incredulous as I am.

"Release her and step back," Sylvan orders firmly.

Despite his reluctance, Daegan obeys. His hands leave my shoulders. I immediately straighten my back and head to regain a posture more fitting for a queen. However, I do not stand up. Still kneeling like the Fuegis, I gaze at my enemy, who sits back on his throne with a displeased expression. His scar and tattoo are furrowed, and his mouth is pinched.

"You're wrong to take me for a fool, Alena," Sylvan says, his cold tone contrasting with his burning gaze. "I see through your game. Your calculated defiance doesn't deceive me: you tremble with fear like a mouse before a lion. Your reputation as a manipulator precedes you. I know what you're trying to do. You aim to push me to my limits with your insolence, hoping I will execute you on the spot. But I won't kill you tonight, Alena. Nor this evening." The courtiers begin to murmur again around us. "We will marry before midnight. You will become my queen, and I will become your king, whether you like it or not. Your skin will be marked with the Fuegis Clan emblem. Your blood will mix with mine. And you will die at dawn, as planned. That is your destiny."

Standing next to the throne, Leonal slowly nods his head to support his nephew's sharp words.

I frown. He's mistaken; I wasn't trying to manipulate him. I let my impetuous heart speak spontaneously.

I open my mouth to reply…

But something happens.

Sylvan's green eyes dart swiftly to my left. I follow his gaze by reflex.

A Fuegis broke away from the crowd. With a fierce and determined expression, the man rushes toward me at full speed, his hand buried in his orange tunic.

When he is three feet from me, he brandishes a gleaming knife above my head with a roar.

As for me, I am petrified.

It seems Sylvan was also mistaken on this point.

I will definitely die tonight.

CHAPTER FOUR

THE SMELL OF FIRE AND BLOOD

I am petrified with horror.

Like in a waking nightmare, the Fuegis brings his knife down towards me, aiming to pierce my throat.

With a plaintive cry, I barely evade his strike by diving to the side. The blade grazes my shoulder. I collapse to the ground on my side; my hip cushioning the impact of my fall.

My attacker regains his balance and launches another attack, this time aiming for my exposed chest.

A muscular hand intercepts his wrist, and the knife stops two inches from my left breast.

Daegan!

The giant's elbow crashes into the face of the screaming Fuegis. A spray of hot, sticky blood splatters across my astonished face and chest. With the coldness of a skilled fighter, Daegan grabs the man by the neck, disarms him with a punch in the crook of his arm, and throws him several feet away. My assailant sprawls on his back, three feet away from the royal stage.

At Sylvan's feet.

His eyes bulging with legitimate panic, the Fuegis half-turns toward the predatory shadow looming over him.

The young sovereign lowers a dark gaze toward my assailant, tilting his head to the right, like a curious animal. In his movement, a black lock falls over his left eye.

He looks like a beast lazily sizing up the prey he plans to devour.

"Who sent you?" Sylvan asks.

The man shakes his head and spits blood on my future husband's dusty boot.

Sylvan delivers a lightning-fast kick to his chin. My attacker's head snaps back. His cry of pain echoes throughout the throne room. The nobles delight in this brutal spectacle with undisguised eagerness.

As for me, I'm still in shock. Curled up on the ground, I feel a lead weight in my stomach and an acidic taste on my tongue. My heart races like a wild stallion at full gallop.

"This individual is likely not a Fuegis, Your Majesty," declares Leonal from the stage, stuffing his hands into the pockets of his doublet.

"I had already figured that out, Uncle," retorts Sylvan, looking at the amateur assassin who presses his palm across his bloody face, whimpering. "Show us your true form, Stowne," he adds, walking toward him with a martial stride.

"By all the Renegades fuck you, Mad King!" cries the injured man on the floor, crawling backward as best he can to escape my dark fiancé.

A Stowne. Possessing with the elemental magic of the Earth, he can therefore shapeshift. However, his powers are limited and weakened in this context, since he's not in his kingdom, and his season of influence is spring—not the summer we are currently immersed in. The Fuegis have an undeniable position of strength.

His assassination attempt was suicidal.

The Stowne knew he could not get close to Sylvan, who would have stopped his grim plans from a distance with his Fire magic. In desperation, he chose his backup solution: assassinate *me* to prevent the tyrant from claiming the throne of the Fourth Clan and ruling the entire island of Symbiosis.

But thanks to Daegan—or because of him, depending on your point of view—he failed.

Sylvan draws his century-old sword with a swift motion. Flames flicker on the silver blade engraved with Fuegis runes. This legendary weapon once belonged to his father. It was named Nesayan by one of his ancestors. If I remember my history lessons, its translation into the common language is "Dragon's Breath."

My eyes widen like saucers.

Because Sylvan's sword is turning red and crackles, radiating power.

"The *Mad King* is running out of patience, brainless scum," scolds my future husband, pointing his weapon at the man. "Which High-Stowne sent you to infiltrate my Clan? Speak, it's an order! Otherwise, I'll prolong your agony for days until you beg me to finish you off."

His words give me chills, just as the weapon grows incandescent under its owner's elemental magic. Panting, the Stowne seems as hypnotized as I am by *Nesayan's* glowing blade, from which tiny sparks fly, illustrating Sylvan's fury.

"You're pure evil!" the rebel finally spits out, his features twisted by hatred. "The gods of Symbiosis won't leave your crimes go unpunished, butcher! You and your kind murdered my whole family. My wife! My children! My youngest daughter was only three, you bastard. You enslaved my people! You burned my king alive. You deserve a thousand times worse than death!"

"Your rantings are as monotonous as they are unoriginal, Stowne."

"Your father was a good and just king," the man continues vehemently. "You stain his memory with your despicable acts. If he were alive, Saradin Ren-Fuegis would be ashamed of his only son. You dishonor his legacy! May your father's soul haunt you for eternity and consume yours!"

The expression of bestial fury that paints on Sylvan's face paralyzes me.

His green eyes blaze along with his blade.

A flash of fire and silver whirls through the air.

And half a second later, the Stowne's head separates from his body in a burst of smoking blood.

I press my palm against my mouth, stifling the horrified scream rising from my throat. Several Fuegis women scream in the crowd.

By the gods, some men— courtiers and soldiers— applaud their king's *feat*!

The decapitated corpse of the Stowne convulses one last time as his head continues to roll across the throne room floor, leaving a red trail. His surprised face is no longer the same: his violent death restored his original appearance, that of the young brown-haired man, tanned skin, and hazel eyes that he was before his transformation into a Fuegis.

A characteristic stench of grilled flesh and coppery blood assaults my nostrils.

Of course, this isn't the first time I've seen a dead body, nor witnessed a death of this kind. In my kingdom, I have witnessed similar grim scenes during the war. Citizens and soldiers of Oceanar were mutilated, disemboweled, and slaughtered by Fuegis monsters.

Yet, I feel nauseous and tears well up in my eyes each time.

And I systematically pray that it will be the last.

No matter how much that this man, driven by distress and grief, wanted to kill me, I will never be able to acclimate myself to the death, suffering, and violence in which the Fuegis Clan lives.

The flames that consume Sylvan's sword suddenly extinguish. He sheaths Dragon's Breath with an air of exasperation tinged with boredom, as he looks over the Stowne's corpse.

"Your Majesty, if I may say—" Leonal sighs.

"No need, Uncle. I can easily guess the nature of your reproaches. And I guarantee you that this man would not have confessed the identity of his master, even under torture." He gestures with his chin to the nearest royal guards. "Clean up this mess right away."

As the soldiers promptly carry the Stowne's body and head of out of the room, two servants appear out of nowhere and mop up the blood on the floor with practiced efficiency.

Tomorrow morning it will be my turn.

The guards will take away my body and my head.

The servants will wash my blood off the wooden scaffold.

I closed my eyes my tear-streaked eyes.

When I reopen them a few moments later, I startle.

Sylvan is crouched in front of me.

What about the ten symbolic steps of distance?

He approached me so silently that I didn't hear him. Beneath his furrowed brows, his clear eyes move from my distressed face to my breasts smeared with Stowne blood. I imagine I don't quite fit the image of the radiant bride-to-be he'd like to lead to the temple altar.

Our eyes meet.

His is unreadable.

Mine is filled with weariness.

Without a word, he removes his scarlet cloak from his shoulders and offers it to me.

Without speaking, I take it with a trembling hand and wrap myself in the light fabric imbued with his subtly spicy scent.

I feel a vague relief. At last, I am no longer naked in front of all these Fuegis.

My future husband stands up, surveying me from his full height, his fist resting on the hilt of his sword.

That hand which has just taken a life…

That weapon that just beheaded a man…

Because the man had offended him with a mere reference to his late father, Saradin Ren-Fuegis.

There is no longer any doubt. My future husband is mad.

"Daegan," Sylvan calls, shifting his attention back to my jailer, who takes a step forward. "Take Alena to her quarters and get maids to make her presentable. I want her ready for our wedding ceremony in an hour."

I close my eyes again. A fresh tear slides down my burning cheek.

I am alone in the darkness, surrounded by my enemies.

My death will have a bittersweet taste.

At this precise moment, I almost yearn for the comfort it implies.

CHAPTER FIVE
A MOURNING BRIDE

The suite that the Fuegis King assigned to me is located in the south wing of the palace, directly overlooking the royal gardens.

I have no idea where his quarters are… and I don't want to know.

"Don't try to escape or harm yourself, Glace," Daegan warns me from behind as I cautiously enter my new quarters, pulling Sylvan's cloak tighter around my tense shoulders. "The bay window is locked, all sharp objects have been removed, and two guards will be stationed outside your door, listening for any suspicious sounds. Your maids will be here in a few minutes."

"Did they spend their last night here?" I ask, crumpling a piece of royal cloak between my fingers.

"The maids?"

I briefly roll my eyes, even though he can't see me. Clearly, my bodyguard may be an excellent warrior, but he doesn't stand out for his intelligence.

"The princesses from the Aeria and Stowne Clans, Daegan."

"I'm not allowed to give you any information about them," my jailer replies abruptly before slamming the door behind me—and locking it, of course.

Shaking my head, I survey my vast gilded prison, which has three rooms separated by amber, gold, and crimson curtains hanging from red stone arches: the dining room, the bedroom, and the bathroom.

The luxurious decor and refined furniture are worthy of an empress.

In the dining room, warmly colored tapestries and golden chandeliers adorn the walls. On the floor, colorful silk cushions are scattered around three low ebony tables. here is also an elegant chaise longue in front of the French window, a massive bookcase overflowing with books, and a small desk flanked by a wooden armchair carved with floral motifs. A magnificent marble statue of the Goddess of Light gazes at me. Several potted plants are scattered around the room: palm trees as tall as I am, orange trees, lemon trees, and fire-colored roses bushes.

I test Daegan's words by checking the bay window's handle. Indeed, it's locked. Of course, the three other windows of the suite don't open either: there are no handles.

I move to the entrance to the bathroom. Three tall mirrors are mounted on the walls, whose mosaics display a pretty gradient of blues: sapphire, cyan, cobalt, azure. A square basin about nine feet wide sits in the center of the room. Holes are craved into the walls. Does water come out of these slits? I admit, it intrigues me. We don't have such hydraulic systems in my kingdom: we bathe directly in the ocean, lakes, or rivers. In the few remote villages away from the coast and water sources, collective basins have been created to collect rainwater. Thus, all the villagers bathe together in a joyful and relaxed atmosphere. They enjoy creating waves and whirlpools with their Water elemental magic. Parents create iridescent bubbles with their hands to delight their young children. Teenagers engage in epic water battles.

A small, fleeting smile of nostalgia appears on my lips.

I conclude my tour with the bedroom, where I don't linger. The enormous four-poster bed takes up half the room. A wardrobe, a folding screen, a vanity, an armchair, a dresser, a chest complete the furnishing. Only one painting hangs on the wall: a sumptuous oil on canvas representing the city of Astranis set in the middle of the Red Desert at sunrise. It's strikingly realistic.

Returning to the main room, I ponder. I'm not complaining, but why does Sylvan bother to house a condemned woman in such a luxurious suite when he could lock me in a tiny cell? To make my last night less difficult? I don't believe it: there's no trace of magnanimity in him. There must be other reasons for his strange gesture.

Daegan didn't want to answer my question before leaving, but I suspect that the Fuegis King's two previous wives also stayed in this suite. I anxiously fidget with my slave necklace.

"That is your destiny," Sylvan told me in the throne room before the Stowne attack.

The key turns in the lock.

I pivot on my heels, every muscle tense.

Five women enter my quarters.

Four young maids…

And, leading them…

A stunning woman in her forties.

I've never seen her before, but I know who is she: the royal tattoo on her forehead speaks for itself. A silver feather.

The most famous High-Aeria of the Fuegis Clan.

Nadya Ler-Aeria is none other than the cousin of the late King Cyriel, who was killed by Sylvan.

About fifteen years ago, shortly after the death of Sylvan's mother, Nadya Ler-Aeria was sent by her cousin Cyriel to Sylvan's father, King Saradin Ren-Fuegis, as a token of peace and alliance between their two clans. She was a diplomatic gift. She became Saradin's official mistress, as he didn't wish to remarry. This woman is, in a way, Sylvan's mother-in-law.

Although her lover is no longer alive, Nadya retains significant power at the Fuegis court: she is the most powerful, wealthy, and influential woman in Astranis.

In my kingdom, it's said that she secretly leads the best courtesans to collect the secrets of the High-Fuegis. She's rumored to have had many scandalous affairs, even when Saradin was alive. It's said she even slept with Leonal …

And Sylvan.

If there's any truth to these rumors, this woman is essentially a madam who uses her serpent-like intelligence and charms on men to wield her power.

But she's not a queen and never will be. She's just an ambitious schemer who uses sex as a weapon to achieve her ends.

I must admit that her beauty is simply breathtaking. I understand why she was chosen to be the mistress of a king. Her delicate face and perfect body must captivate every man's gaze, regardless of which Clan he belongs to.

Like all Aerias, Nadya has platinum blonde hair and a complexion as pale as mine. Her full lips are highlighted with a coral balm, and her large smoky gray eyes are accented with a black liner. Her silky curls are held in place by a golden net adorned with crystals. She wears a deep crimson corset and flowing skirts of the same color. Hanging from a gold chain, a ruby the size of a quail's egg accentuates her small breasts. Her confident movements are marked by a graceful, ethereal voluptuousness.

The courtesan assesses my pitiful appearance with a gaze completely devoid of sympathy. Her pleasant smile looks even more false.

I don't forget that she recently left her young cousin, Princess Lia, to die on the scaffold. This woman is no longer an Aeria, despite the silver feather on her forehead. She's now a Fuegis. A traitor.

An enemy of the Glaces, Stownes… and Aerias, the members of her past Clan.

Nadya claps her hands. Immediately, two maids' heads to my bedroom while the other two disappear into my bathroom; a few seconds later, the sound of running water fills my ears. They are preparing a bath for me, clearly.

Sylvan's mother-in-law and I are alone in the dining room.

"Good evening, Your Majesty. I humbly introducing myself: Nadya Ler-Aeria," she greets me with surprising kindness.

I raise a skeptical eyebrow. Since my kidnapping, this is the first time someone has addressed me by my queen's title. Nevertheless, I don't detect the slightest trace of irony in her sentence.

"I've heard about you, Nadya Ler-Aeria," I reply defiantly. "To what do I owe the honor of your unexpected visit?"

"I wanted to meet our future sovereign, of course."

"As long as her head is still attached to her body."

A small, affected laugh shakes Nadya's chest. She smooths a fold of her skirt with calculated slowness.

"Your sense of irony is deliciously entertaining, my child. It's a refreshing change from the women of the Fuegis court. They have no sense of humor, which is a shame."

"Glad to entertain you. Did your cousin Lia also have a sense of irony the night before her execution?"

Nadya's smile suddenly vanishes at my pique. Her gray eyes are filled with coldness.

"You should measure your words more carefully in this palace, Alena Kan-Glace. If you had been married before, King Sylvan would not have been so lenient with you after your bloody outburst in public."

This means that Nadya was there in the throne room among the crowd earlier.

"His point didn't hold water. I wasn't looking to die by his hand. I wasn't manipulating him."

"Oh, I'm aware, Alena. You're an impetuous and impulsive young woman, aren't you? It's understandable. The loss of your kingdom and your people has tested and weakened you. Not to mention the prospect of your imminent end." Her voice softens and lowers to a whisper. "But a curious thing intrigues me. I was assured that the Queen of the Glace Clan was a woman of a thoughtful nature. And I had understood that you were taller and less, how shall I say..." She glances at my ample breasts and my hips wrapped under Sylvan's cape. "Curvy."

My heart races, I bristle like a cat threatened with a stick.

"I hope I haven't offended you?" Nadya asks with a sardonic tone. "King Saradin complained about my lack of tact with other women. I tend to verbalize all my thoughts. That's an interesting thing we have in common, Alena. Our straightforwardness."

This woman is really dangerous, I realize, shivering.

"Rumors distort reality. That's a universal truth," I counter with a hoarse voice.

I shouldn't be justifying myself to her, even vaguely. I'm exposing my weakness.

Nadya's sly smile returns, sending chills down my spine.

"I share your opinion, my child. It's something I tirelessly repeat to those who judge me without knowing me. And you, for instance, how do you perceive me? A mistress burdened and grieving for her love? A skilled and unscrupulous courtesan who leads the Fuegis men of power by their dick? A gold-digger who seduces one royal after another?" I don't answer. She nods with a sigh. "I'm all these things and much more, Alena. But I won't waste your precious time any longer. If you were late to your own wedding because of me, dear Sylvan would hold it against me, and I would blame myself just as much. Ah, what a waste to see you being decapitated tomorrow!" She doesn't mean a word of it, the bitch. "I would have liked us to be friends, Your Majesty. We could have done great things together at the Fuegis court."

With this cynically sentence, Nadya Ler-Aeria exits my quarters, leaving me worried and unsettled after our conversation.

As the four maids begin preparing me for the ceremony, a stream of dark thoughts obsesses me. Could Sylvan's mother-in-law suspect something about me? If so, will she report her suspicions to the king?

The Fuegis women don't speak to me, nor do they look me in the eyes as they prepare me like a ritual—or sacrificial—offering.

One of them slides Sylvan's cape down my arms.

I walk down the steps of the tub, suppressing a sigh of relief as the water closes around my legs. The hot bath soothes and relaxes me—temporarily, at least. Still dressed in their finery, the maids join me in the tub to wash my face with sponges coated with orange-scented soap. My body gradually regains its milky complexion under their expert hands. The water, topped with steam, turns red. They wash my long pearly hair, brush my nails, and clean every inch of my body to remove sand, blood, and sweat. I don't resist their hygienic and cosmetic care; on the contrary, I savor them, trying not to think about what awaits me tonight and tomorrow. The women's gestures are quick and meticulous but still delicate.

Then, I get out of the tub. Fluttering around me in silence, they dry me with cotton towels and apply iridescent scented oil to my skin.

The first maid untangles my mane and styles it with pins. The second maid applies makeup to my face. The third maid dresses me in luxurious fabrics. The fourth adorns me with expensive jewelry.

Half an hour later, I'm ready for my wedding.

On the surface.

I look at myself in the mirror, my heart infinitely heavy. The reflection sends me back to a feeling of powerlessness. I barely recognize the made-up woman with dull eyes, dressed in a flowing gown of burgundy and gold.

To me, this wedding ceremony feels like a funeral.

When one of the maids put a scarlet veil over my sorrowful face, I mentally mourn myself.

For the Fuegis, the color of mourning is white.
For the Glaces, it's red.

CHAPTER SIX
THE CORONATION

The Royal Palace Temple is a solitary and enigmatic gem in the middle of the luxuriant gardens.

Flanked by my imposed escort, consisting of Daegan and five Fuegis guards who might as well be part of a funeral procession, I walk up a cobbled path of white pebbles lined with oleanders. The vibrating chirping of crickets hidden in the underbrush marks my dragging steps.

I've always loved the special atmosphere of the night, its softness, its calm, its mysteries.

Yet, due to the mists of anxiety clouding my troubled mind, this night feels radically different.

The silver crescent moon dominating the sky looks like the malevolent grim of a dark god.

The petty stars seem ready to fall from the vault and crash down on my head like a rain of deadly stones.

The flickering shadows lurking around me seem threatening, like bloodthirsty creatures waiting for me to falter.

Between the elongated silhouettes of the palm trees, columns, galleries, and sculptures are outlined, illuminated by the flickering flames. For the first time in the history of Symbiosis, the sacred Temple of the Fire God in Astranis will host the wedding of a Fuegis King and a Glace Queen.

It could have been a wonderful symbol of the unity between two Clans… in another context. In reality, it's nothing more than an administrative formality that initiates the beginning of my will.

I enter the sanctuary, dotted with candles, where the spectators, the priest, and my fiancé are already present.

Surprisingly, the witnesses are a select committee. Seated on couches, the eight High-Fuegis are all much older than Sylvan. They give me an indifferent glance before resuming their chatter as if I were part of the scenery. Next to Leonal Ren-Fuegis, Nadya Ler-Aeria stands straight, chest out, chin up, and gives me a more persistent stare. A venomous smile is painted on her lips: she openly revels in my misery. I glare at her, but she doesn't look away; on the contrary: her smile widens. *I amuse her.*

I believe I have never hated a woman as much as I do at this moment.

In front of the altar, carved with golden runes, Sylvan speaks quietly with the young priest of the God of Fire, a young man dressed in a red toga and a matching turban.

With one hand behind his back, my royal fiancé doesn't bother to interrupt his conversation upon my arrival; however, his unyielding gaze scrutinizes every inch of me. When he nods almost imperceptibly, I don't know if it's a sign of approval for my dress or if he's simply acknowledging what the priest is whispering to him. He's still wearing his warrior's armor, and a burgundy velvet cloak, the same color as my dress, which brushes against the hem of his boots, but the item resting on his head is not his dragon helmet.

His crown is a thick circle of gold in which is set a sparkling ruby surrounded by two ambers… each containing tiny scorpions. The royal attribute perfectly matches the man who wears it.

Once again, I am struck by the majestic beauty of his face highlighted by the dim light of the candles. How can such an attractive being hide such a dark soul?

Daegan escorts me to his king while the guards close the temple doors behind us. I shudder at the sound of the heavy wooden bar slamming into the brackets, locking the room from the inside. We're now trapped for the duration of the ceremony, as the stupid Fuegis tradition demands.

My breathing quickens. I feel like I'm suffocating. I'm terribly hot under my dress. I'm stifling.

I would rather be quarantined in my quarters.

"Fire consumes air. Fire devours flesh. Fire destroys life," my mother used to tell me when I was younger. *"But remember one thing, darling. water always extinguishes fire."*

No, mother. The water of my tears won't extinguish any fire in this place.

The priest shows me where to stand with a formal gesture of his hand: on the other side of the altar, ten steps in front of my future husband.

I do so without protest. get this charade over with as quickly as possible.

The ceremony begins with a liturgical chant addressed to the God of Fire. All the Fuegis rise, close their eyes, and bow their heads to sing with the priest. Except Sylvan. Over the altar, he watches me with a peculiar intensity. I hold his gaze without blinking behind my blood-colored veil. Even if he intimidates me, I refuse to show it to him.

An alarming thought, which, despite its logic, had never crossed my mind until now, preoccupied as I was with my execution, suddenly takes my breath away.

Does he intend to consummate our marriage tonight before my death?

I shudder violently at the terrible possibility.

How could I have forgotten such a fact?

No matter what it takes, I won't let it happen.

"King Sylvan Ren-Fuegis," the priest proclaims in a solemn voice at the end of the chant, "create the Purifying Wall of Fire that no mortal is permitted to cross."

The young king raises a hand to summon his elemental magic.

Immediately, flames three feet high appear near his feet. Quickly, they trace a large incandescent circle around the altar, enclosing the three of us inside.

Another Fuegis tradition completely opposed to ours. During their marital union, the Glace couple immerses themselves together in an icy lake and share a long kiss underwater to seal their vows.

From what I know, Fuegis marriages involve two elements: blood and fire.

The philosophy of their Elemental Clan reflects these key words.

"The sacred fire of the Fuegis warrior is fueled by the blood of his enemies."

It's both strange and disturbing that this sentence also applies to their marital unions.

Therefore… I dread the rest of the ceremony.

"Now, Your Majesty, with the protection of the flames, you hold the sacred right to approach your bride," the priest declares.

Sylvan walks around the altar and stands directly in front of me. The priest hands him a golden-bladed ritual dagger, which he takes without hesitation.

"Sylvan Ren-Fuegis, Alena Kan-Glace, it's time to mix your blood."

My future husband swiftly cuts his palm with the edge of the blade before doing the same to my hand, which trembles in his. Under my veil, I bite my lip to stifle a cry of pain.

Then, Sylvan's wounded palm rest on mine with disconcerting softness. His skin is hot and rough. He pronounces his vows solemnly, looking at me with, it seems, a touch of ferocity, "I, Sylvan Ren-Fuegis, take you Alena Kan-Glace as my wife and queen. I swear before all the gods of Symbiosis to maintain the sacred flame that binds us alive until death separates us."

I swallow. The end of his oath sounds like a grim threat.

It's my turn, but I don't want to talk. My dry tongue sticks to the roof of my mouth. The priest clears his throat to urge me. Sylvan, his brows furrowed, squeezes my hand painfully to remind me of my duty. There is no more gentleness in his gesture: he crushes my fingers between his. I hold back my tears. Unfortunately, the moment has arrived.

"I, Alena Kan… Kan-Glace… I take you… Sylvan Ren-Fuegis… as… as…"

"As husband and for king," says the ruler in an authoritative tone. "Say it."

"As husband and for king," I repeat in a dull voice, avoiding his steely gaze. "I swear before all the gods of Symbiosis to maintain the sacred flame that binds us alive until… death separates us."

Sylvan relaxes slightly. His hand releases mine and lifts my red veil, exposing my face. I must look pale. I'm in a daze, barely reacting when the king brings the glowing tip of the dagger to my sternum.

"It will be painful," Sylvan warns me in a whisper. "But as you said earlier before the entire court, Alena, suffering doesn't last."

Hilarious.

The priest begins to sing again.

With his ritual weapon heated by his powers, the king himself etches the Fuegis emblem on my skin: the red sun. The sharp point slices through my flesh, making a slow incision. A stream of blood runs between my breasts, staining the collar of my dress.

He brands me like a slave.

The pain is excruciating. With my eyes closed, to keep from screaming at the top of my lungs. A pitiful whimper escapes me. The stench of my own burning flesh makes me gag. Reflexively, I grasp Sylvan's outstretched forearm and dig my nails into his flesh with all my strength. It doesn't stop him from continuing his horrible task: he remains relentless.

I am breathless and drenched in sweat when the burning tip of the dagger finally pulls away from my wounded skin. My legs tremble. I cling to the arm of my tormentor with one hand and to the edge of the altar with the other, unable to do otherwise.

The rest of the ceremony becomes a blur. Sylvan's grows increasingly hazy. Flames swirl around me. I'm on the verge of fainting in the sanctuary; I feel dizzy and nauseous. I vaguely sense that the sovereign is placing a metal object on my head.

A tiara.

For a few hours, I am now a Fuegis queen.

"Sylvan Ren-Fuegis, Alena Ren-Fuegis, by the powers of the God of Fire vested in me, I declare you husband and wife," the priest states solemnly.

The witnesses applaud.

The Wall of Fire dissipates.

A small, malevolent smile forms on Sylvan's lips.

He's now the king of all Symbiosis…

Or at least, that's what he believes.

CHAPTER SEVEN
THE WOLF AND THE LAMB

While I slump on the chaise lounge in my quarters, a maid gently dabs the blood from my skin with a fresh, damp cloth. From time to time, she looks up at me briefly. Jaw clenched, eyes vacant, I allow her to tend to me in silence.

The pain from the Fuegis mark on my chest is painful. I wish I had a knife to scrape off that tainted piece of skin that has become impure.

The young maid who takes care of me brought back a basket of exotic fruits, consisting of mangoes, bananas, and passion fruit, but since the wedding ceremony, I've had no appetite. As soon as I entered my quarters, I took off that damn tiara and hurled it violently against a wall. Daegan, who was behind me at that time, roared in fury, cursed me out, and carefully retrieved the royal ornament, meticulously checking that it was undamaged. To him, this object clearly holds more value than my life.

He then left with the tiara, glaring at me for the umpteenth time before locking the door behind him.

"Queen Lia was as furious as you after her wedding," my healer confesses in a whisper.

I turn my eyes toward her, trying to hide my surprise. This is the first time since my arrival in Astranis that a Fuegis maid has spoken to me.

I realize she's really very young, no more than fourteen. She has a pretty, sun-kissed face with round cheeks, framed by black braids cascading over her slender shoulders. Her amber eyes express a childlike gentleness.

"What's your name?" I ask softly, using my most friendly tone.

She hesitates, glancing nervously at the door of my quarters. I assume she has been forbidden to speak to me and ears that the guards in the hallway might overhear us. After a few seconds, she whispers, "Selaine, Your Majesty. My name is Selaine."

"Selaine, were you the one who treated Lia Ler-Aeria's burn?"

"Lia *Ren-Fuegis*, Your Majesty," she corrects me. "Yes, that was me."

"Did you talk to her before her execution?"

The young girl sighs and makes a sweeping gesture to indicate the room.

"No, Queen Lia broke everything she could get her hands on to vent her frustration. She ravaged these quarters before collapsing on her knees, crying and praying to the God of Wind." I shudder at this revelation. Selaine looks at me sideways, timidly. "You're different, Majesty. I can tell you're angry too, but you manage to keep control and restrain your emotions."

I shrug a skeptical shoulder.

"I wasn't in control of myself in the throne room before the ceremony."

Selaine smiles at me. A sincere and warm smile. I'm pleasantly surprised. Could she be the exception that proves the rule? An altruistic and generous Fuegis? However, I must remain cautious. It could be a role meant to win my trust.

"I'm aware, Your Majesty. The servants are only talking about it… The scandal has already spread throughout the palace and the city." Her lovely smile fades. "Those who dare to speak to our king like that—"

"Don't last long," I finish bitterly. "I know. He decapitated a Stowne right in front of me."

Silent, she lowers her saddened eyes, biting the inside of her cheeks. She sets aside her blood-stained cloth to grab a bottle from the side table. She lightly touches my burn on the sternum with the tip of her index finger, which is coated with soothing, healing balm.

"Why bother treating me, Selaine? I'm doomed," I remind her, disarmed by her kindness.

"I just following the King's orders, Your Majesty."

My eyes widen. *It was Sylvan who gave this order?*

"Our sovereign can sometimes be harsh and severe, Your Majesty, but contrary to what most people believe, he's not entirely devoid of compassion," the Fuegis whispers.

A bitter laugh escapes my throat. She seems much less endearing all of a sudden!"

"You're so young and so naive." So foolish, I want to retort! "Sylvan Ren-Fuegis is a tyrant. A mass murderer."

"With all due respect, I never said he wasn't, Your Majesty," the maid replies, meeting my gaze. "I simply said that the man and the king are two very different beings."

But what does she mean by that?

"Selaine, why—"

Two loud knocks on the door cut me off and makes her jump. The young girl nervously caps her bottle and leaps to her feet like a gazelle fleeing from a cheetah. A guard unlocks my door, opens it wide… and the Fuegis servant darts away at full speed.

I tense up as I see the tall figure standing in the hallway.

My husband's figure.

He's come to claim his due.

He's coming to fulfill his marital duty.

For the first and last time.

If only I had a weapon to defend myself!

If only I weren't what I am…

If only…

The door to my quarters closes.

Sylvan and I are alone in the room. Until now, we had always had people around us. So, it's not impossible that he might decides to make me pay for my act of rebellion in public in the throne room. My terror reaches its peak. My back is soaked with cold sweat under the fabric of my dress.

We size each other up like the adversaries we are. He's only my husband on paper. He remains the enemy of my people. *My* enemy.

He has taken off his armor. He's wearing a black silk shirt decorated with gold buttons that highlights his athletic build, and tight-fitting leather pants. He's not wearing his crown and hasn't brought his sword, but he might have a knife or dagger tucked in his boot or sleeve. Besides, Sylvan is the most powerful High-Fuegis in Symbiosis. His elemental magic is a weapon in itself. Even without his armor and sword, the young Feugis sovereign exudes power and violence.

And he's "*not completely devoid of compassion?*" The brain of that poor Selaine must be as shriveled as a raisin! Sylvan is a monster, period. There's no debate. No argument can justify his vile cruelty.

Sylvan's piercing emerald gaze doesn't leave mine as he walks toward me.

Stiff as a tree trunk, I follow him with my eyes, on high alert.

Accentuated by the silence, the tension that weighs in the room is palpable.

But he stops in front of the coffee table, where the basket of fruit sits, and picks out a ripe green mango. He pulls a knife from his sleeve—I knew it!—and begins peeling it with a nonchalance that puts me even more on edge. Is he doing this on purpose? Is he playing with me to inflict psychological torture?

As he peels his damn mango with a skillful gesture that shows he handles the knife to perfection, Sylvan's gaze roves over my blood-stained wedding dress. His clear eyes linger a bit too long on my neckline. I can't tell if he's watching the symbolic mark he inflicted on me or the curve of my breast. Either way, his brazen scrutiny deepens my discomfort.

"Burgundy suits you much better than it did my mother," he suddenly declares, catching me off guard.

So, this dress belonged to his mother. She must have worn it for her wedding to King Saradin, Sylvan's father.

"You have a gift for telling women what they want to hear, Fuegis King!" I retort in an acid tone. "Is your kingdom's treasury so poorly managed that you can't afford a new dress for your soon-to-be-dead brides?"

"Lia and Belise didn't wear this dress," he denies without answering my question.

He dares to call them by their first names when he ordered their execution!

He disgusts me.

"My uncle was right," he remarks thoughtfully, slicing a slice of mango with his knife before bringing it to his lips.

Sylvan stuffs the glistening orange piece into his mouth, then chews it quietly as he stares at me. The way his powerful jaws and full lips move, the strange voracious glint deep in his darkened eyes.

It's extremely unsettling.

And crude.

And disturbing.

A spasm stirs my stomach as he slowly swallows his bite.

Fear, probably.

"What was he right about?" I ask, frowning.

"Your beauty, Alena," he says in a hoarse whisper.

My breathing quickens as I realize what he's getting at.

Desire.

That strange, voracious gleam in his eyes is raw desire.

I instinctively move back on the chaise, putting several more inches between us. My reaction, however futile, makes him smile. A cold, almost sadistic smile, contrasting with the fiery look in his eyes.

"Why don't you ask me what I'm doing here, my wife?" inquires Sylvan calmly before stuffing another piece of mango in his mouth.

I weakly shake my head, my fists clenched in my knees.

"Some predators play with their prey before tearing them apart with their teeth and claws, my edelweiss," my brother used to tease in the forest to scare me when we were children.

I didn't take him seriously back then.

"I won't make it easy for you," I announce fiercely despite my trembling hands.

"I wouldn't expect anything less from you, Alena."

He leans forward, moistening his lips, and places his barely touched mango back on the coffee table. I watch his every move like a deer locked in a tiger's cage. My heart hammers against my ribs as if trying to escape from my chest and flee.

Without breaking eye contact and without haste, Sylvan sits on the chaise, about a yard away from me.

I am paralyzed. I want to leap to my feet and dart to the other side of the room, but my body refuses to comply.

"Lady Nadya came to my quarters before the ceremony," Sylvan informs me casually. I bite my tongue. He folds his arm over the back of the chaise and strokes his thin, bearded chin, looking pensive. "You made a strong impression on her."

What, did that Aeria bitch say to him, by all the gods? And how close are they?

"Lady Nadya is an incorrigible little curious," he continues with a smirk that sends chill down my spine. "She loves to snoop around, especially when it concerns me."

"Because she's your mistress?"

He raises an eyebrow. I curse inwardly. The question escaped me.

"Rumors, Alena, are tenacious weeds," he finally says, before changing the subject. "Let's take a concrete example: you. Your reputation as a manipulative bitch and man-eater precedes you in this kingdom. Several High-Fuegis warned me about you."

"About *me*? Seriously?"

Why is he telling me this? And why is he wasting his time talking to me?

Is this some kind of twisted test?

"Some of them were taken aback by your boldness in the throne room. They thought you'd try to use your charms on me and curry favor from the start to survive, not that you'd provoke me in public with such fervor. Lady Nadya and my uncle were among them."

I let out a bitter laugh.

"Glaces are as unpredictable as their element."

"But so are the Fuegis, my beautiful wife."

"No. Not you, at least. Given your brutal temperament, it was obvious that you'd slaughter that Stowne without any pity."

He frowns in displeasure.

"He tried to assassinate you, Alena."

"So what? You could have spared him, but you didn't. Therefore, you're predictable."

"If I were predictable, I would have decapitated you myself when you disrespected me in front of my entire court," he says with a tone as icy as it is hostile.

I freeze. My heart skips a beat.

"In that case, you… you would have said goodbye to the Symbiosis throne," I manage to articulate.

"I agree. I might have regretted it afterward. Since my father's death, I've become much more impulsive." His gaze returns to me, harder than ever. "You've met him, I believe?"

feel like I'm walking a tightrope. I need to watch my words.

"Yes. During a Great Symbiosis Council. Back when the four Elemental Clans were still allied," I say, not going into details.

"I was sixteen. I would have liked to have been present at my father's side during that rare event. To meet you under different circumstances," he clarifies, his expression impassive. *What a weird comment!* "But I couldn't attend the Great Council. He had sent me on a trip to Land of Fire as an ambassador for our kingdom."

"Why are you telling me this, Sylvan?"

He flinches at hearing his first name from my mouth but quickly regains his composure.

"I'm not sure, Alena. Maybe, because you intrigue me. I usually can figure people out quickly," he argues with a restraint hat slightly unsettles me.

"But not me?"

"No. Not you."

And he brushes my bare arm with an ambiguous caress.

I tense up, short of breath. My skin burns almost as much where he touched it with his fingertips as where my painful red mark is.

"That's proof of what I'm saying," Sylvan points out mockingly. "You're labeled as a man-eater who collects lovers at the Glace court, but you can't even stand my touch. You could try to seduce me to buy time, but you don't."

"And y-you, will you… try to… consummate our marriage?" I stammer.

"It's my right as your lawful husband, Alena."

Does he want me to beg him not to? I will never lower myself to that!

His words disgust me. I go from terror to anger in a flash. When I was a little girl, my mother used to say that these two emotions were twins.

"Did you also use your *lawful right* over your two previous wives, Sylvan? Did you force them before watching them die on the scaffold?

Did their fear excite you?" I spit out suddenly, seized with a new surge of uncontrollable rage.

His face darkens, and his eyes blaze. His breath becomes shorter. His fury echoes mine.

But there's not just fury in him.

There's also that carnal fever flaring up even stronger.

An imperious, unreasonable, excessive desire.

My provocations *stimulate* him.

I lower my eyes. A strangled gasp shakes me.

Under his leather pants, King Sylvan Ren-Fuegis has an erection.

Goddess, I need to shut my big, stupid mouth!!

But seeing him tense up like a drawn bowstring, I have an unpleasant feeling that it's too late.

The wolf is about to pounce on the lamb's throat.

CHAPTER EIGHT

SURVIVING THE WEDDING NIGHT

Despite my fear, I brace myself for a fight.

I prepare to use the weapons nature has given me: my fists, my nails, and my teeth.

Facing his enemy, a Glace sheds no tears, and never relinquishes his weapons.

I'm aware Sylvan will get what he wants from me. He's a great warrior. He has wielded steel and fire magic since he was a child. He's much stronger and faster than I am.

But I swear to myself that he will leave with a few scars.

Yet…

The wolf's attack doesn't come.

He doesn't move from his place.

"Alena," he says in a guttural voice, "do you think of me as a beast?"

Yes. Because that's exactly what you are.

Wary and tense, I don't answer.

"I never forced Lia and Belise, Alena," Sylvan assures me with a voice vibrating with restrained anger. "And I won't force you either. You can accuse me of being a murderer and a tyrant, but I'm not a rapist."

Is this a deceptive ruse to make me lower my guard?

"Give me your word of honor that you won't abuse me, Sylvan."

Even if I give it only relative credit and a less value…

He grinds his teeth when he hears my demand… but, against all odds, he agrees to comply.

"I give you my word of honor that I won't abuse you, Alena."

I relax slightly, though I continue to watch on him. He leans back against the back of the chaise with an exasperated sigh.

If I irritate him this much, if he doesn't plan to rape me, why does he remain here? I don't understand why he's here. He claimed I intrigued him, but that doesn't change the fact that he's going to execute me. I have as much trouble understanding him as he does with me. Could it be some kind of unhealthy curiosity?

Moreover… he desires me.

While I am his enemy *and* his prisoner.

While he plans to have me killed tomorrow.

Maybe there's a weakness to exploit.

A new weapon to draw.

What he confessed to me a few minutes before resurfaces in my mind.

"They thought you would try to use your charms on me and curry favor from the start to survive."

"You could try to seduce me to buy time, but you don't."

Sylvan expects precisely this kind of trivial manipulation. If I played to my feminine assets to use his carnal desire for me in order to buy time and postpone my execution, he would see through me immediately.

Butter him up isn't an option either. If I suddenly turned into a kind and cordial wife, he would suspect I was plotting something. He's not stupid.

I need to be *much more* subtle and clever if I want to survive my wedding night… and especially the day after.

It's a very risky challenge, of course, but I have to give it a shot.

An idea pops into my head. A crazy idea. One that has so little chance of working!

And if it worked by some miracle, I would still not be saved: I would only buy myself a day.

But it's my only idea.

In my situation, gaining one day would already be a victory.

Those few hours of reprieve would help me better understand my husband's personality, detect his weaknesses, and plan the next step of my strategy.

I have a talent.

I'm a storyteller. I have a gift for inventing stories. My family has always said so. I can adapt to my audience and give them exactly what they're looking for. To touch them. To evoke emotions. To allow them escape into other worlds so they can detach from the difficult reality. I even happened to tell improvised stories to Glace children sitting around me. My words captivated them. Silent, they all listened to me religiously, even the most agitate ones. At the end, they applauded me eagerly demanded new stories, which made me laugh out loud.

But Sylvan isn't a child, far from it.

And I've never told a story where the stakes were my *survival*.

Besides, how do I bring up the subject without him suspecting my intentions?

To hook the audience's attention with a bait.

"Praise be the Goddess of the Ocean," I sigh. "I'd rather die as a virgin."

The king turns his incredulous eyes on me.

"You're joking, Alena."

"No, Sylvan. I'm not joking."

He frowns. He thinks I'm lying.

"Rumors distort reality," I add, trying to keep my calm, repeating word by word what I said to Nadya before the wedding. "Especially when they concern powerful men and women. Just because I'm called… what term did you use? *Man-eater* doesn't mean I really am one. Some of my detractors at the Glace court spread slander about my virtue to discredit me with the people. It's easier to call a queen a whore than a saint."

"Is that what you think you are?" he retorts, his expression neutral. "A saint?"

"No, I don't have that pretension. I'm neither a whore nor a saint. I am what I am."

Sylvan nods, thoughtful. I believe I've given him a wise answer and scored a first good point.

"Rumors distort reality; I agree with you. But it's those who are the subject of them who pay the high price. It's easier to call a king a tyrant than to—"

He stops, shakes his head, closes off, and doesn't finish his sentence. What was he going to say?

He gets up from the chaise. My heart leaped in panic.

He's going to leave.

If he leaves, I'm a dead woman. I must keep him here at all costs.

"What are you doing, Sylvan?"

"I'm leaving. You definitely need to be alone tonight. To reflect, pray to your goddess, rest."

"No, I don't want to be alone. Stay," I plead, a hint of desperation in my voice.

He turns his head toward me, his expression doubtful, his eyes wary.

"Why? You hate me."

Because you're the only man who holds the power to spare me, you fool.

"I judged you too quickly," I claim, even though the lie burns my tongue and irritates my throat. "Please, stay a while. The solitude and silence scare me."

"If you want me to send you a priest to hear your confessions, I can arrange that."

"No priest! I don't want to confess. I just want to talk. With you. Think of it as… my last wish."

He hesitates.

He wavers.

Stay, Sylvan Ren-Fuegis. Don't take away my last hope.

"What do you want to talk about, Alena?" he sighs, sitting back down.

A wave of relief washes over me. I rub my thigh and bite my lip, feigning indecision.

"I… I don't know," I lie again, pretending to stammer. "No politics or war, that's for sure. Maybe… maybe you'd like to hear a story?"

He raises an eyebrow, surprised by my suggestion.

"A story?"

"I really enjoy telling stories to children. It relaxes me and clears my mind. I read a lot of tales when I was little. I had a library three times bigger than this one," I say, pointing to the shelves filled with books.

He gives a brief smile.

"A scholarly queen. Surprising. You don't look like one."

"Appearances can be deceiving, Sylvan."

"Indeed. My mother often told me stories to help me fall asleep when I was a child," he confides with a touch of nostalgia. "All right, Alena. Tell me a story of your choice if it will help you relax."

Another victory. Another step forward.

I adopt a thoughtful look for ten seconds, clearing my throat, then slowly nod.

"Well, would you be interested in a story about deceptive appearances and a young virgin Glace?"

"Start, and I'll tell you if it interests me"

"Fine," I agree, leaning back against the seat and using my storytelling voice, both deep and passionate. "Once upon a time, there was a young Glace named Enola…"

CHAPTER NINE
THE VIRTUE OF ENOLA

"Once upon a time, there was a young Glace named Enola.

She lived in a small fishing village in the north of Oceanar with her mother and brother, Elanos, in a tiny blue stilts house that shook with every ocean breeze. Her father had died in a shipwreck a few days before she was born.

After a violent horseback riding accident, her mother was paralyzed in both legs; she could no longer walk and had to stay in bed. Enola and Elanos took turns taking care of her. While one of them would stay by her side, telling her stories to help her escape from her monotonous daily life, the other would go fishing or collect seashells to sell at the market in Oceanar. But sometimes, their hard work was not enough. The two young people also had to steal to feed themselves.

One day, Elanos was caught red-handed by a Glace royal guard and was taken to the grim dungeons of Oceanar Castle to serve a long prison sentence. In despair, Enola was left alone with her mother. The young woman was then twenty-two years old. And unlike her family, she was still Powerless from birth."

"How could a twenty-two-year-old Powerless girl have escaped the ruthless judgment of the High-Glaces?" Sylvan cuts in, giving me an imperious look.

I hide the exasperation at his rude interruption. Fuegis children born with a silver spoon in their mouths don't learn politeness, apparently.

"Despite their powers, the High-Glaces can't keep an eye on every subject in the kingdom, Sylvan. Sometimes, Powerless who are discreet and cautious manage to slip through the cracks. Enola was one of them."

"A Renegade who wasn't caught by the authorities!" comments the king with open disdain. "This fictional story hardly interests me, after all."

"Give it a chance and set aside your prejudices for a few minutes."

"These are not prejudice, Alena; this is reality." He exudes an arrogance and smugness that make the hairs on my neck stand up. "I'm well aware of this. I've fought against the renegades many times over the years. I assure you that they're all pests to be eradicated."

I frown. My tongue itches to respond. So does my hand, for that matter. He deserves a monumental slap to put him in his place.

"May I continue?" I ask coldly. "If you intend to punctuate my story with a barrage of belligerent and uncompromising remarks, let me know now so I can think about censoring my tale as I go along."

He shrugs, his face closed off.

Capturing his interest, and keeping it, isn't going to be easy, given his preconceived notions on so many topics. Sylvan is neither forgiving nor an easy audience.

"Go on with your tall tale. Don't bother watering it down; I'm not easily impressed," he says in an indifferent, almost bored tone.

I grit my teeth, counting mentally to ten before continuing with my story. It might be wise to include a character he could relate to…

"Money cruelly ran out in the household. Enola no longer dared to steal for fear of being imprisoned like her brother. Their paralyzed mother had no one else but her. Left alone, she would have withered away.

One day while gathering crabs near her village, Enola was forced to jump out of the way of a mysterious hooded rider who was galloping down the beach as if he were fleeing from a demon. The rude rider didn't stop to check if she was hurt; in fact, he didn't even slow down. Furious, the young Glace curses him, shouting, 'May your manhood rot and fall off your body!" The rider suddenly yanked on his reins and came to an abrupt halt. Enola's heart stopped beating."

I gauge Sylvan with a speculative look, deliberately pausing to build suspense. I also adjust the tone of my voice according to the events in the story and a small gesture with my hands to capture my listener's attention. When I mentioned the mysterious horseman, he tilted his head slightly and squinted. I piqued his curiosity, which is relatively encouraging.

"According to everyone in the village, Enola had inherited her mother's beauty. Nature had gifted her with long, pearly hair, large sapphire-colored eyes, and delicate features."

"Just like you," points out Sylvan, casting a bright look at my face.

I sigh, at the height of the irritation.

"Goddess, but you're more unruly than a toddler!"

A look of outrage crosses the young king's face. Under different circumstances, I would laugh.

"Stop interrupting me every thirty seconds, Sylvan; your habit is infuriating."

"Stop verbalizing every thought you have, Alena; your habit is even more infuriating."

We glare at each other like two stubborn teenagers.

After five seconds, I nevertheless agree to continue my story.

"On the beach, the rider turned his horse around with a snap of the reins and trotted over to Enola. Covered in sand with her old, patched dress, the young Glace straightened up, hands on her hips, with a determined and resolute stance. She was afraid of the ominous rider dressed entirely in black, but she refused to show any weakness. The man dismounted and stood right in front of her. He was tall and appeared well-built under his dark velvet clothes. A warrior, no doubt. Without flinching, without backing away, Enola peered into the darkness that hid his face.

"I'd appreciate it if you'd apologize for almost stepping on me!" she exclaimed fiercely.

The hooded man looked at her and burst into a deep, resonant laugh. Offended, Enola crossed her arms over her chest.

"Do I amuse you, sir?"

He removed his hood.

Enola was left speechless.

Because she recognized that handsome face c with laughing topaz eyes and silver hair cut short, bristling in all directions.

In fact, all the Glaces knew him.

King Vidal Ken-Glace, in the flesh, was standing right in front of her.

"Indeed, little girl, you do amuse me. Where did you learn such curses?"

Enola had lost her voice. She attempted a clumsy curtsy, blushing with embarrassment.

"No, stop that," Vidal said gently. "We're not at the Glace court. What's your name?"

"My name is Enola, Your Majesty," she murmured, lowering her eyes.

Vidal placed his hand under her chin and lifted her head delicately to get a better look at her, an indescribable smile on his lips.

"Enola. A beautiful name for a beautiful woman."

Sylvan Ren-Fuegis bursts into a cynical laugh, forcing me to pause again. I frown in offense, my stomach tightening.

"*A beautiful name for a beautiful woman?*" he repeats, shaking his head in disbelief. "How original, this Glace King is! Such admirable words!"

"What compliment would you have made in his place?" I grumble, annoyed by his jab.

"I wouldn't have said anything at all, Alena. My gaze would have spoken for me."

And he gives me a *very* eloquent burning look.

I swallow.

I don't like the sensations that his intense gaze generates in my body. Especially, the wave of heat spreading in my stomach's hollow.

I ignore it by focusing and continue my story.

"Enola was troubled by King Vidal's gesture and charisma. She had many suitors in her village, all of whom she had turned down one after another. But she had never been attracted to a man until that day. And, to her great surprise, the magnetism seemed mutual.

Vidal told her he would escort her back to her village to make up for knocking her to the ground unintentionally. Enola found this embarrassing, but how could she refuse her king? He helped her into the saddle and sat behind her, his strong arms around her waist. Enola felt so comfortable against him that she fell asleep, lulled by the horse's step and the calm breathing of her rider. When her companion woke her up with a gentle touch on the cheek, they had reached the edge of the village, and the sovereign was once again hooded to preserve his anonymity.

"I would love to see you again, Enola," Vidal said softly, looking at her intensely.

Enola bit her lip. Like all Glaces, she knew that Vidal was promised to a Fuegis princess he was to marry in a month. It was a political alliance, not a love marriage, but this union was essential for the people of Symbiosis. Even though she wanted very much to see him again, Enola couldn't imagine becoming the king's mistress. Especially since she was a virgin and was saving her virtue for her future husband."

"Are you trying to sell me a sadly conventional romance between a penniless virgin who has nothing, but her beauty and a brainless king engaged to someone else, Alena?" Sylvan sneers, raising an eyebrow.

"You're really impossible!" I snap, twisting a fold of my dress between my fists. "If you don't like my story, go to hell!"

Despite my offense, a teasing smile spreads across the Fuegis king's lips. Surprising…

"Go on, my dear wife. I never said I disliked it. Besides, you're very pleasant to look at when you're telling a story."

Very pleasant to look at? I brush off his inappropriate remark with a quick wave of my hand.

Something unexpected—that's the essential element to include in my tale if I'm going to capture Sylvan's attention.

"King Vidal began courting Enola in secret. He seemed to have fallen in love with her. He sent her gifts, magnificent jewelry, and expensive dresses. Out of pride and principle, even though she was poor, the young woman refused all his gifts; the messenger always returned with the king's offerings. Vidal was dismayed by her rejections.

The situation was becoming more and more critical for Enola and her mother, who was getting thinner by the minute. With a heavy heart, the young Glace decided to sacrifice the last valuable thing she had: her virginity. Not to the king, whom she loved, but the man willing to spend a fortune to take it. She went to the most famous luxury brothel in Oceanar and presented her proposition to the old madam, who had contacts at the Glace court. Enola promised a whole night to the man who would win the bet, a night where she would give herself to him without any conditions. An auction was organized at the brothel. Many masked nobles attended, drawn by Enola's beauty and purity. Some were known for their depravity and sadism in the establishment, which was not very reassuring… The madam dressed Enola in a sheer black gown trimmed with lace that hinted at her sensual curves. With tears in her eyes, she climbed onto the stage that had been set up in the brothel, and the bidding began."

I clear my throat to give myself time to gauge Sylvan's mood.

He's much more absorbed and attentive than he was a few minutes ago.

If I can captivate him the way I do with children, my plan might just have a chance to work.

"And then, Alena? The bidding?"

I smile inwardly. His impatience is a good sign.

"The madam started the bidding for Enola's virginity at the modest price of fifty crowns. With a blank expression and eyes staring into space, Enola listened to the bids with one ear, not daring to look at the clients who were fiercely competing to buy her virtue and spend a whole night of debauchery with her.

"One hundred crowns on my right!" called out the old woman, pointing a finger at a masked man in the crowd. "Two hundred crowns to my left! Five hundred crowns for that gentleman over there! A thousand crowns in the front row!"

The bids were increasing at a staggering pace, and the nobles were giving up one by one. When the price reached fifty thousand crowns, only two bidders remained. A nervous, chubby man in the front row wearing a lion mask and a calm man in back row wearing a gray wolf mask.

"Sixty thousand crowns for the lion!" boasted the madam, as the bidder raised six chubby fingers in the air. "One hundred thousand for the wolf in the background! One hundred and fifty for the lion! FIVE HUNDRED THOUSAND for the wolf! ONE MILLION for the lion!"

The crowd was stunned, as was Enola. In the entire Glace kingdom, only five men were wealthy enough to bid such exorbitant amounts. Four were famous High-Glaces… and King Vidal himself. Heart racing, gasping for breath, Enola found herself hoping it was the wolf in the back, shrouded in darkness. The lion's chubby figure didn't match the athletic build of the man she'd met on the beach, the man she secretly loved.

"Two million for the wolf! Five million for the lion!"

A deadly silence fell over the crowd. The wolf didn't raise his hand.

Pale as a ghost, Enola was falling apart on stage. Her legs trembled, and her breathing grew short.

"Five million for the lion, going once!" shouted the madam. "Five million for the lion, going twice…"

The wolf raised both hands.

"AND TEN MILLION for the gentleman in the wolf mask!" roared the old woman with a huge smile.

The High-Glace with the lion mask shook his head with frustration, signaling his surrender.

"Sold! The virginity of the beautiful Enola is sold to the gentleman in the wolf mask for the incredible sum of ten million crowns!" declared the madam, clapping her hands with delight."

"Ten million crowns for the virtue of a woman!" Sylvan exclaims in astonishment. "What madness!"

"Yes," I confirm with a small, lazy smile. "Who could be crazy enough to spend such a sum… except a man madly in love?"

Thoughtful, my husband doesn't say a word. Leaning forward with his elbows on his knees, he encourages me to continue my story with a nod of his chin.

I take a deep breath.

I'm approaching the most delicate part.

I lower my voice to a soft whisper, "Enola found herself in the best room of the brothel with the mysterious client who had bought her virginity. He didn't speak; he just watched her from a distance, a glass of red wine in his hand. She struggled to make out the color of his eyes due to the dim lighting in the room and the shadows created by the wolf mask. His eyes were light, but she couldn't tell if they were blue, green, or gray.

The young woman was extremely nervous. In her memory, King Vidal seemed taller than the man she was about to offer herself to tonight. She had doubts about his identity. She shyly asked his name, but he remained silent.

With a commanding gesture of his finger, he signaled for her to undress.

Reluctantly, Enola obeyed.

She slipped off her shoes one by one.

Then, she let down her silver hair, took off her satin gloves and the necklace of precious stones that the madam had lent her. She then began to slowly unlace the front of her dress, watching the client with a timid gaze. His eager eyes followed her every movement. His breathing grew heavier every second. His fingers gripped the stem of his glass tightly.

She wasn't even naked yet, and he was already crazy with desire for her.

With hesitation, Enola slid the straps of her black dress slide down her graceful shoulders. Her gauzy dress fell to her feet, revealing her creamy skin and perfectly curved body. A pure, unblemished femininity with a disarming sensuality that beckoned to the sin of the flesh. Enola was shaken to see something bulge in the man's trousers. A strange heat she had never experienced before flared in her lower abdomen. Her breasts felt much more tense than usual.

She didn't understand her body's reactions.

The man motioned for her to lie down on the bed.

So, Enola lay down on the bed.

He set his wine glass on a table and walked toward her with a feline grace.

The young Glace held her breath, praying with all her soul that he was King Vidal.

He brought his hands to his wolf mask and took it off, revealing his face."

I go silent at the end of this sentence. My heart is racing wildly.

Sylvan frowns, his jaw tight, and hisses through his teeth, "What's next, Alena."

I take a furtive look under his belt.

His erection is back, thanks to the erotic details of the passage I just told.

My *sadly conventional romance* has quite an effect on him…

I look back into his eyes, swallow hard, take a deep breath, and face the anger starting to blaze in his green irises.

The time has come to play my cards.

In a calm and steady voice, I tell him, "I'll tell you the rest of my story tomorrow night, Sylvan Ren-Fuegis."

CHAPTER TEN
CONFRONTATION

Sylvan and I stare at each other.

His furious eyes look like a mountain lake under dark, stormy clouds. He snarls, practically spitting his words, "Alena, stop your childish tantrum. Finish this story. Right now!"

"No, Sylvan," I counter, staring him down with arrogant defiance, even though I am painfully aware that I'm playing an incredibly dangerous game.

It's all or nothing.

The tyrant exhales slowly. A small vein throbs on his temple. He's frustrated beyond measure, just as I'd hoped.

"Then at least tell me if the man who won the auction is King Vidal," he demands in an icy voice.

"No, I won't tell you."

"You are in no position to negotiate!"

"And yet, if you want to hear the rest and the end of this story, you'll have to postpone my execution and wait until tomorrow night, when I'm in better shape, my husband," I state in a calm but firm tone. "I'm exhausted, weakened, and aching all over. All I want is to rest, and I think I've had my fill of emotions for today. Do I need to remind you why, Sylvan? I was ripped away from my kingdom and my people. I spent the entire day in the Red Desert, chained to a horse's saddle under the blazing sun, and as you know, I can't handle heat as well as you can. I haven't had anything substantial to eat all day; in any case, my appetite was completely ruined when you so delicately beheaded the man who tried to assassinate me in your throne room. I was humiliated like a mangy sheep when you decided to display me naked in front of your army, your people, and your court. Tonight, I was married, crowned against my will, and branded with fire, and you Fuegis haven't stopped telling me that I'm going to die at dawn tomorrow. Don't be surprised that I'm tired of all this! Don't I deserve a day of rest to make up for all these… trouble? What difference does it make to you? I'll tell you: none. Give me one more day of life, and in exchange, I'll tell you the rest and the end of this story tomorrow night at the same time. Otherwise, my story dies with me."

Before I can understand what's happening, Sylvan springs like a coiled spring and literally jumps for my throat.

His long fingers wrapped around my neck, he throws me backward under his weight and slams my back against the seat of the chaise lounge in a fit of rage. I try to fight back, but he easily captures both my wrists in his other hand. His thighs on either side of mine pin down my legs. I let out a strangled cry, overwhelmed by fury and terror. He tightens his grip on my wrists and neck; his hateful face moves closer to mine until we're nose to nose. I gasp for air, arching and writhing beneath him. It's all in vain.

I'm trapped, at the mercy of the wolf's jaws.

"It turns out appearances are not deceiving in your case, Alena Kan-Glace!" he rages, tightening his burning fingers around my neck. "You are indeed the manipulative and pretentious bitch that popular rumors portray! Gaining a day of rest in exchange for a pathetic story, has anything so absurd ever been heard of in Symbiosis? Extending your life by trading it for a foolish tale? Do you think I'm fool, Alena?"

Gasping for air, I shake my head weakly, unable to say a word. I must be turning blue by now. My vision blurs, and my ears buzz. I'm about to pass out.

"If you don't tell me who bought Enola's virtue, I'll kill you right here and now, Alena!" he threatens harshly, this demand contradicting his earlier words.

I shake my head again, even more feebly.

I feel myself slipping away. My eyes roll back…

His fingers loosen around my throat just enough for me to breathe.

I take a huge gulp of air and cough in his face. Sylvan's weight is still pressing down on me, crushing me against the chaise. His muscular body is a furnace, heated by the magic coursing through his veins, so much that I'm drenched in sweat under my wedding dress. I feel like I'm buried under a collapsed volcano. His broad, solid chest is pressed against my heaving one. I can feel his heartbeat through the layers of fabric between us; it's racing almost as fast as mine. H His ragged breathing matches mine, and his breath smells like mango. He lowers his head. His lips graze my chin as if he's barely holding back from sinking his teeth into my flesh.

"And your virtue, is this another sly trick to tease me, Glace whore?" he growls, pushing his hard sex roughly against mine.

For the third time, I shake my head to deny it. How I wish I could beat him and tear his flesh with my nails!

"Never forget that you are mine, and your life and body belong to me," Sylvan hisses, his hot, damp mouth against my sweaty cheek. He grabs my hair and yanks my head back roughly. "I decide everything about you. Do you think you know what I'm capable of, Alena? By the God of Fire, you have no idea! I was lenient with you in many ways before our wedding. You don't know the true meaning of suffering, but I can still teach it to you for the next few hours! You're not worthy of the title of Fuegis queen, nor are you worthy of being my wife. Don't delude yourself; you're nothing but slave in this kingdom. *My* slave." His calloused palm flattens between my breasts over my freshly Fuegis burn, which hurts like hell. "You breathe because I allow you to. I'm the master of your life, Alena. And I will choose the moment of your death. Not you."

His possessive, commanding reminder shows he's trying to regain control of the situation. To reassert his dominance over me.

So… this proves his weakness.

It also proves that I got to him.

And he wants me. Judging by the way he forcefully presses his rock-hard erection against my lower belly, it's driving him crazy

"I don't forget it!" I shout fiercely. "How could I, Sylvan? You took everything that mattered to me!"

He leans close to my ear. His rough whisper against my earlobe sends a shiver down my spine, "So did you, Alena. So did you…"

Why is he saying that?

"What are you talking about, Sylvan?"

"Innocence doesn't suit you, witch. As for your precious virtue… Well, I should check for myself if your hymen is intact, as you claim," he snaps, moving from my chest to rest on the top of my thigh.

I twist, completely panicked by his threat. He begins to roll up my dress, keeping me trapped in his grip. A deep, visceral terror sizes me. It feels like barbed wire is crushing my heart.

"No, no! You gave me your word!" I protest, trying to free myself and push him away.

He bursts into a hateful laugh.

"You have no honor, my dear; so why should I?"

"Don't do this, Sylvan!"

"If you don't want me to fuck you like a street whore, tell me the end of your story," he demands, lifting the hem of my dress with a sharp motion. "Right now."

"Please," I beg in a desperate voice, my eyes filling with tears as I tremble uncontrollably. "Sylvan. You told me you weren't a rapist. And I believed you. I believed you, Sylvan. Don't take that away from me. Don't force me. I'm begging you."

His hand stops above my knee. His green eyes, filled with intensity, lock onto mine, as if trying to read my wounded soul.

Then he looks at the Glace emblem tattooed on my forehead.

Next, at my heavy slave necklace.

And finally, at the Fuegis mark on the sternum.

Something indefinable, though fleeting, passes through his clear eyes.

The young ruler pulls his hand away from my thigh.

Freeing me from the weight of his body, he rises from the chaise, his expression hardened.

Then, he turns on his heel and heads toward the door.

"Fine, Alena. Take your history and your secrets to the grave; I don't care! You'll die at dawn as planned. I'll see you tomorrow at first light on the scaffold," Sylvan concludes in a chilling whisper not looking back.

The door to my room slams shut behind him.

I close my eyes and bury my tear-streaked face in my hands, my throat tight with a sob.

My plan failed.

In five hours, I'll be beheaded in public.

CHAPTER ELEVEN
"WHAT IS MY NAME AGAIN?"

How can a night so beautiful and gentle be so nightmarish?

I haven't even tried to sleep in this oversized bed that isn't mine. I already know that as soon as I close my eyes, the image of a gleaming axe falling on my neck will rise in my boiling mind.

After Sylvan left, I cried for an hour until my eyes were dry. Now, I have no tears left to shed. They're useless anyway. They won't save me. Nor will prayers: it's not the Goddess of the Ocean that is haunting my thoughts right now.

With my forehead pressed to the bay window, my hands limply clutching to my gold necklace, I gaze at the moon and stars, thinking of my family, who I miss terribly. My brother's mischievous smile. My mother's loving gaze. Disordered childhood memories flood my mind. Of course, we have had some hard times, but we were quite happy once. Before the war. That time seems so distant now…

I feel terribly alone.

Daegan is wrong. I could hurt myself before the guards in the hallway realized it.

Yes, I could kill myself to rob Sylvan of the satisfaction of executing me. Hanging myself from the frame of the canopy bed with the sheets, for example. Or, with my feet, breaking a mirror wrapped in fabrics to muffle the sound, then open the veins of my wrists with a shard of glass.

But I don't even have the courage.

The hours tick by like the grains of sand in the hourglass of my existence. I almost hear them fall one by one. Plop. Plop. Plop.

What is my name again?

Alena Kan-Glace?

I shake my head to myself. I am no longer that woman.

Alena Ren-Fuegis?

Neither.

I will never be that woman.

"Don't deny your name, my little sapphire," my mother once told to me with a smile, tapping the tip of my nose with her finger. *"Your identity, like your roots, is anchored in your soul for eternity."*

I failed my promise, mother. Please forgive me.

I shouldn't regret my decision. If I am here today, in this hostile palace, it's for her and my brother. At some point in my life, I had to make a choice. My death will ensure their survival and safety in the Glace Kingdom.

"A necessary sacrifice," she *told me.*

I hope she keeps her word.

I scrutinize my reflection in the window. My makeup has run: two black streaks stain my white cheeks.

A stranger.

This face is the source of all my troubles.

My curse. My death sentence.

No. I am not Alena Kan-Glace.

I am just a grain of sand in the middle of the Red Desert.

✷✷✷

"The Fuegis have opened a breach in the southern ramparts!" an urgent voice cries out from the crowded street, wielding a poorly made sword. "Oceanar is lost!"

Beneath my white hood, which conceals my royal mark on my forehead, I exchange a glance with my mother, Bleuène. Her face, expressing fear, sadness, and worry, surely mirrors mine. Her skeletal fingers clutch my hand tightly.

Neither of us knows if my soldier brother is still alive. He was sent by his captain to the southern ramparts. Before entering the building to shelter with other women and their children, I saw flashes of flames and jets of ice above the walls. Glaces and Fuegis warriors are using all their weapons against their enemies: their blades, but also their magical powers.

I saw the blood cascading down the stones and flowing between the cobblestones.

And the charred corpses of Glaces.

"The foghorn hasn't sounded yet," my mother whispers to reassure me without conviction. "As long as the horn hasn't sounded our defeat, Oceanar will hold the siege, and we will be in—"

A long, mournful sound echoes in the distance, cutting off the end of her sentence.

The foghorn.

Everything is over. Oceanar is falling.

With eyes wide in horror, Bleuène looks at me as if she is seeing me for the last time.

"I have to go, Mother," I whisper in a shaky and resigned voice as a young Glace guard signal me to follow him. "The Fuegis King will invade the castle any moment now. He must find me in the throne room."

"Sapphire, no, you don't have to do this! Don't let them capture you!

I embrace my mother, holding her close. She clings to me, shaking. My heart and my soul bleed. I am about to surrender myself willingly to the enemy.

"I can't go back, Mother. I swore an oath—"

"There must be another way!"

"No, there isn't. We both know that," I sigh.

"We have to go now!" the Glace soldier urges, pulling me by the arm, tearing me away from my mother.

"Do everything you can to survive until the rise of the Rose of the Elements! Stay alive and come back to me, my sapphire!" Bleuène screams as I walk away, forcibly led away by the zealous guard.

I don't answer her.

My mother has always believed in the legend of the Rose of the Elements, but it's just a fanciful tale that parents have told children since the dawn of time.

No Symbiosis being will ever develop all the powers of the four Elemental Clans.

As for me… my martyr's fate is already sealed.

I am about to become Sylvan Ren-Fuegis's wife and slave before I die.

✳ ✳ ✳

Dawn lights up the rooftops of Astranis.

A new day begins.

My last day on Shynighgar.

I will not see the twilight.

Sitting cross-legged on a cushion, I wait for the guards to come and get me to the scaffold. The slightest sound in the hallway quickens my heartbeat; yet, I'm surprisingly calm and detached. My mind floats in another world. I have the strange feeling that my soul has already left my body and that I am a spectator of my own end.

She should be in my place.

Because I am not *her*.

I am twenty-six years old.

Alena Kan-Glace is twenty-five.

I am five feet five inches tall.

Alena Kan-Glace is nearly six feet tall.

I have a rather voluptuous body.

Alena Kan-Glace is very slim.

My eyes are the color of sapphires.

Alena Kan-Glace's eyes are sky blue.

My royal emblem was tattooed on my skin recently.

Alena Kan-Glace has had hers on her forehead since she was five years old.

Even though we don't share a drop of blood, our features are similar as if we were twin sisters.

Hence the reason for my presence among my enemies.

A bitter smile forms on my lips as the key turns in the lock.

I will not take the end of Enola's story to my grave, Sylvan… I will take my true secret to my grave.

Sylvan Ren-Fuegis doesn't know this, but he did not marry Queen Alena Kan-Glace.

He married a simple Powerless fisherman's daughter.

My name is not Alena.

My name is Enola.

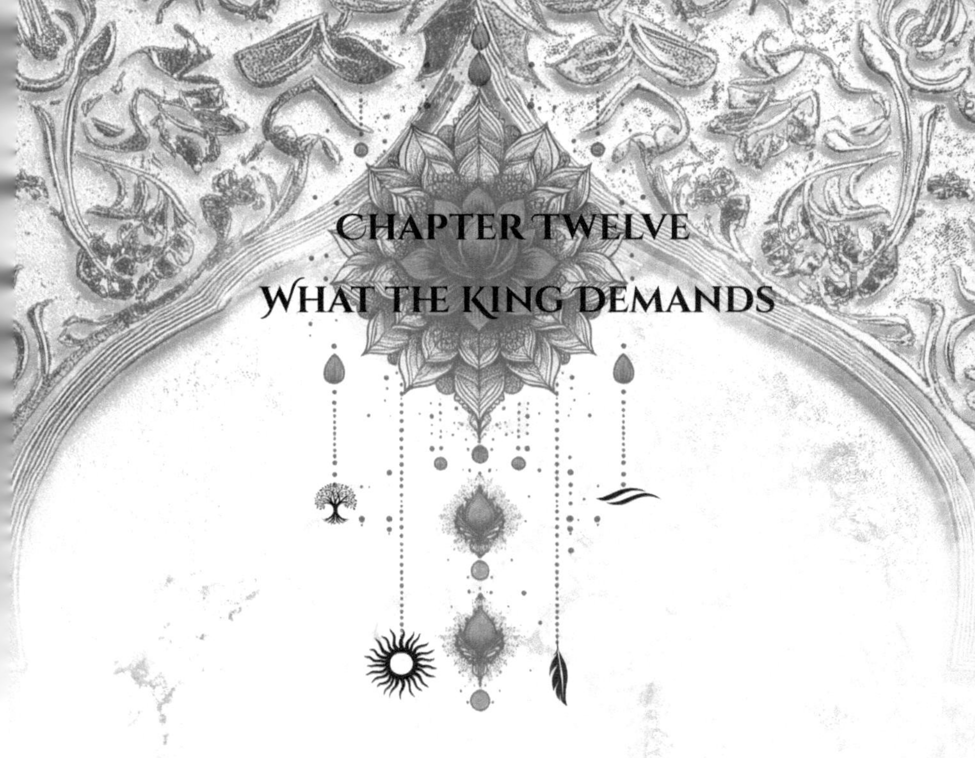

CHAPTER TWELVE
WHAT THE KING DEMANDS

The door to my quarters opens.

To my great surprise, it isn't the guards assigned to my surveillance. It's the young Fuegis servant, Selaine.

I blink three times as I examine the pastries and fruit cluttering the silver tray she holds in her arms.

"What is this?"

"Your breakfast, Majesty," informs the young girl as she sets the tray on the coffee table.

I cast a bewildered glance at the door left wide open and meet the irascible gaze of Daegan, who standing in the doorway, has crossed his arms over his broad chest.

"And how much time do I have to enjoy my last meal, Daegan?" I ask with a hint of arrogance.

He sniffs with a disdain at least similar to mine.

"Your execution has been postponed until tomorrow morning," he informs me, addressing me formally in bad faith. "In his great and *incomprehensible* mercy, King Sylvan has decided to grant you an extra day, *Majesty*."

A stifled gasp escapes from my throat.

I'm stunned by this news.

Goddess, my plan worked! I think feverishly.

I catch Selaine's small smile as she humbly lowers her head, her hands clasped before her. It seems she's secretly pleased with this turn of events.

"May I go for a walk in the palace gardens this morning?" I ask, striving to control the emotions stirring within me.

Daegan laughs.

"And what else? You don't want us to throw a ball in your honor while we're at it? Of course not, you'll remain locked up here. The king will visit you tonight. Selaine, come!"

The young Fuegis trots toward the soldier, who gently places his hand in the small of her back, and whispers something in her ear. His familiarity with her makes me bristle. In fact, seeing them side by side, I admit they do resemble each other. Could Daegan be Selaine's father?

As the door closes, I'm still stunned. I can't hardly believe it!

I, Enola, am not going to die today.

It makes me feel better.

Hope swells in my heart.

Determination replaces fatigue.

Optimism sweeps away fatalism.

Because if I won one more day of life thanks to a story…

It means I can win another day.

"The king will visit you tonight."

Let him come.

This time, I'm ready for him.

As my hand traces the outline of the books in my library.

Like the vast majority of girls from low social backgrounds, and even though I've claimed otherwise to my husband, I can't read. At this moment, faced with all these colorful book covers that could have alleviated my crushing boredom, I deeply regret it.

Alena Kan-Glace had the best tutors in our kingdom since her very young age. She learned to read, write, embroider, sing, dance, and paint. From what I've been told, our queen can play five different musical instruments and speaks all the languages of Symbiosis fluently. She also masters flattery with impressive skill.

I have nothing in common with her, except for our facial features.

To be honest, even though I've only met this woman who looks like me twice in my life, and even though I respect her because of her title, I don't particularly like her.

Alena has never cared about her people. Her only interests are shockingly superficial and selfish. Wealth, fame, men, and herself. Three years ago, she spent so much money on her spectacular court festivities that she raised the monthly tax by ten crowns per household, which is a lot of money for the poorest families, like mine.

If the Fuegis put a useless magical necklace around my neck to neutralize her powers—since I never had any—it's because Alena is known as the most powerful Glace in her generation. Her Water elemental magic may not be as dangerous as Sylvan's Fire magic, but it's still formidable. My mother told me that our queen could create tidal waves, snowstorms, and torrential downpours.

I have always wondered if these words were exaggerated, and more importantly, why Alena didn't use her *formidable* powers to defend our people during the Fuegis invasion.

As soon as she realized that her beautiful city would fall, she abandoned her subjects and fled through the underground tunnels under the castle of Oceanar while I was brought into the throne room to take her place and deceive the tyrant Sylvan Ren-Fuegis.

I don't know where she took refuge. In the kingdom of Aeria or Stowne, I suppose. She assured me that she would find allies, raise troops, and seal pacts to overthrow Sylvan. I'm supposed to buy her time so she can secretly carry out her plans for rebellion.

I don't have much hope in that regards.

I may not be as smart and cultured as she is, but I'm not the stupid little village girl she thinks I am. Alena only cares about saving her own skin; she won't risk losing her head by attacking the Fuegis kingdom. In my opinion, she told me this to clear her name, ease her conscience, or more likely, justify her future escape.

Sylvan is right about one thing: Alena is a manipulative bitch.

Like most powerful men and women, she lies with disturbing ease.

That's why I can't rely on my queen in any way in my situation. She won't come to rescue me. The only person I can count on to get out of this is myself.

Me and my gift as a storyteller—my only talent.

I spend several hours admiring the illustrations of the books in my library, especially those in a history book about the Continent. One of the pictures is so fascinating that I gaze at it for long minutes. It represents a fabulous creature: a gigantic dragon with onyx scales gliding above clouds tinged with gold and red. Did these terrifying monsters really exist in Land of Fire? Ever since I was little, every time I heard someone mention their legend, I asked myself that question. My brother Elanos, being practical, scoffed at me, claiming that creatures of that size couldn't have existed because they would have been far too heavy to fly. One thing is certain: on the island of Symbiosis, no one has ever seen one, not even our ancestors.

In the middle of the afternoon, I receive a rather noisy visit from Nadya.

Followed closely by a bodyguard, she doesn't seem pleased at all.

Her annoyance doesn't bother me, by the way…

"How did you do it?" she exclaims without even greeting me.

Sitting on the velvet chaise lounge, smoking a m blend of tobacco and fruit essences with my large water pipe to relax, I don't bother to get up when she arrives.

So, Sylvan didn't tell his court why he postponed my execution.

On the other hand, what could be more logical? If he announced that he temporarily spared me because of a story, he would lose all credibility and incur everyone's wrath.

I remove the pipe's mouthpiece from my lips and exhale a puff of smoke before responding calmly.

"You forgot to add *Your Majesty*, Lady Nadya."

"Don't look down on me! Don't get any ideas; your execution will happen no matter what. You're a dead woman walking," she says coldly.

Well, the mask of civility falls off…

"In that case, why are you wasting your precious time talking to a dead woman walking? Don't you have some gossip and toxic rumors to spread around the Fuegis court?"

"I know you're hiding something from us, Alena. No secret is safe from me in this palace. I will find yours."

Despite the sharp anxiety her venomous words cause in me, I give her a sly half-smile.

"Please do, my dear. I have nothing to hide, except maybe the feeling of jaded contempt you inspire in me," I reply, bringing the mouthpiece back to my lips to inhale another drag of tobacco.

Nadya shoot me an evil glare and slips away with her guard.

Good riddance.

Excuse my common language, but she can go to hell.

***

The sun disappeared behind the rooftops of Astranis an hour ago when about ten servants enter my quarters to set the table. Without saying a word or even looking at me, they file past, carrying steaming and sophisticated dishes served on fine china.

Seeing the obscene abundance of food that could feed my entire village, I realize my royal husband is going to *honor me* with his presence for dinner.

Partridge, lamb, wild boar seasoned with spices and served with dates, plums, and cooked figs; red wine in a crystal decanter; various types of cheeses; and cream pastries. I've never tasted such rich food. Like most common Glaces, I usually eat fish, shellfish, bread, eggs, and potatoes. Meat, wine, and pastries are reserved for the nobles of Oceanar.

Tonight, like yesterday, I didn't have any say in what I'm wearing. My maids came to do my hair, makeup, and dress me. The dress is, simpler, lighter, and more pleasant to wear than the lavish wedding gown. It's made of black silk, embroidered with red beads around the V-neckline. The asymmetrical skirt reveals my right leg up to mid-thigh; while my left leg is hidden by fabric pleated down to the ankle. My silver hair is pinned up in a bun with gold pins encrusted with tiny rubies. Dressed like this, I look like a Fuegis courtesan. A certain mystery emanates from the woman I saw in the reflection of the mirror, who is neither really Alena Kan-Glace, nor quite Enola.

Sylvan appears about fifteen minutes after the servants leave.

He completely ignores me, and with a determined stride, takes a seat in the chair at one end of the rectangular table. He pulls cut his knife and starts to serve himself by slicing a piece of lamb and placing it on his plate. *How rude!*

"What are you waiting for to sit down, Alena, a sandstorm?" he snaps without even looking up, grabbing the decanter to fill his cup with wine.

"For you to properly invite me to do so, perhaps?"

"Sit, eat, drink!" he exclaims, waving his hand. "I'm hungry and irritated, and don't feel like doing anything proper."

"A rough and tiring day?" I ask, sitting down across from him. "Too many innocents to slaughter?"

"Your humor is unwelcome," he growls before taking three gulps of wine.

"Sadly, it wasn't humor."

"I was wrong to think you'd thank me for granting you the favor you asked me last night."

"Oh, I do thank you for giving me another day, Sylvan. But that doesn't mean I'm going to behave with cutesy kindness toward you. I'm not like all the hypocrites who surround you at the Fuegis court."

"I had noticed. Come on, tell me the rest of your story while I eat."

"No, I don't like talking while I eat; it's not proper. I'll tell you the rest of the story after our dinner."

"God of Fire!" he sighs, giving me a shady look. "You're the most stubborn woman I've ever met."

My mom says exactly the same thing, I think, smiling inwardly.

"I'll take that as a compliment, Sylvan," I murmur with a hint of irony as I start to eat.

CHAPTER THIRTEEN

TAMING THE WOLF

"By the way, I have a question for you," I begin between two succulent bites of lamb.

Sylvan takes a sip of wine, sets his cup down, and briefly wipes his lips with a corner of a cloth napkin.

"I thought you didn't like talking while eating," he remarks cynically.

"Indeed, but it doesn't bother me to listen."

"The stories I know would fuel your nightmares, Alena," he whispers in a gloomy tone that makes me shiver. "Ask your question, if you dare."

"You've traveled to Land of Fire, haven't you?" He nods curtly. "Did you… did you see any dragons there?"

I expect him to laugh. My brother would have responded with a mocking reaction.

However, Sylvan doesn't laugh. With his head tilted to the side, the Fuegis king scrutinizes me with puzzlement, as if thinking about how to answer. His elbows rest on the table on either side of his plate, is long fingers intertwined in front of his mouth.

"Why do you ask, Alena?"

Alena… Goddess, how I hate hearing that name that isn't mine!

I gesture to my library with my chin.

"I was flipping through an illustrated book about Land of Fire this afternoon. I've always wondered if dragons actually existed or if they were just another legend."

"I couldn't say. I didn't see any dragon in Land of Fire. It seems their kind became extinct at the end of the Continental War, a decade before I visited in the capital, Alkanthar."

My disappointment must be obvious on my face because he adds, "However, I did meet someone who claimed to have seen one of those creatures up close."

I raise an eyebrow. A smirk plays on Sylvan's lips.

"Of course, I have no guarantee that what this man said was true. But in Land of Fire, he has a certain… credibility. He took part in the Continental War. One could even say that he was one of the triggers of that war. H He fought alongside two black, fire-breathing dragons against the emperor nicknamed the Bloody One, the tyrant who had enslaved an entire people."

My eyes shine with interest. I hang on his every word.

"Who was that man, Sylvan?"

"I'm too tired from my day to tell you the rest."

His comment, echoing what I said the night before, leaves me speechless.

This time, I least expect it, Sylvan burst out laughing for the first time in front of me. A warm, deep, and captivating laugh that that makes a little sensitive chord vibrate in the pit of my stomach.

"He was an elfid," he finally replies with a smile, which softens the harshness of his eyes incredibly.

"An elfid?"

"A shadow elf, if you prefer. They have gray skin, dark hair, and pointed ears. They have special abilities. They're stronger and faster than humans, have better senses, and live much longer than we do. They're known to be extremely dangerous. They also have what they call the Gift, a different kind of magic than ours. The elfid I'm talking you about is one of the founders of the Guild of Shadows."

"What is the purpose of this guild?"

"Death, Alena… They're assassins who serve the Goddess of Death."

Goosebumps spread across my skin. An evil deity, no doubt.

"Oh," I reply, my enthusiasm suddenly cooled. "Assassins. Now,

I'm hesitant to ask how you met their leader…"

"During a Harvest. The annual celebration during which all the guilds renew their oath of allegiance to the Universal Truce and pay a tax to the ruling brotherhood, the Mercantile League. As an ambassador of Symbiosis, I was introduced by the three Merchants to all the other guild leaders during the Harvest.

"The Merchants?"

"The three leaders of the Mercantile League, Alena. The brotherhood that has governed Land of Fire since the end of the Continental War and the fall of the Bloody One's Empire. These men are almost as powerful as kings and exercise their authority over all the leaders of the other brotherhoods. Didn't you learn this during your history lessons and from personal reading?" he asks, arching a perplexed eyebrow.

"Yes, of course, but I have a short-term memory," I reply nervously.

I can't think of a better excuse at the moment.

Luckily, Sylvan doesn't dwell on my vague excuse. He's lost in the depths of his memories.

He tears a bit of bread from his piece, rolls it into a ball, and swallows it like a child would. As he chews, his slightly pearly scar deforms slightly.

"His name was Jerys Targam[1]," the young ruler continues, his thoughtful gaze lost over my shoulder. "We spoke together in the palace of Alkanthar after the Harvest. I noticed the black dragon tattoo on his arm and asked him what it meant. He explained that it was the emblem of the Guild of Shadows of Clepsydra, also known as the City of Vices. He told me that the two dragons who had fought the emperor alongside the allied brotherhoods were killed in the last battle of the Continental War. From there, I asked him more questions about these amazing creatures, as the subject fascinated me. There were once four

---

1   Jerys Targam is a mysterious key figure in *The Guild of Shadows, the Gift of Death*, and one of the two founding Lords of the Brotherhood of Clepsydra Assassins, elfid warriors endowed with Earthly Gifts. Jerys Targam ended the Continental War by cutting off the head of the tyrant Callistin III, known as the Bloody One, who was oppressing the people. By his gesture, Jerys marked the history of Land of Fire, which went from an imperial dictatorship to an oligarchy.

races connected to the natural elements, like our Elemental Clans. The beings Jerys Targam was acquainted with were pyros, fire dragons. If he wasn't exaggerating his words, they didn't just fly and breathe fire, Alena. They could speak and perform many other wonders. I wanted to continue my unusual conversation with this elfid, but a Merchant interrupted us and pulled me inside the palace to introduce me to another brotherhood leader. I sensed he was upset that the Lord of the Shadow Guild and I had somewhat hit it off."

"Why's that?"

"I don't know, Alena. Political tensions between the brotherhoods of Land of Fire, I imagine. Let's eat now."

I understand without him saying it that the subject is closed.

After dinner, Sylvan gets up from the table and invites me to do the same. Like the previous evening, he sits on the chaise longue. As for me, I hesitate. I finally decide to sit on a thick cushion on the other side of the coffee table, just to be cautious. I haven't forgotten that yesterday he lost all self-control and lunged at my throat—in fact, I still have the mark of his fingers on my skin. I have no desire for that incident to happen again, so I put a physical barrier between us to give myself time to escape if needed.

Sylvan frowns slightly as he sees me keeping my distance, but he doesn't make any unpleasant comment or order me to come closer.

"Continue your story, my wife," he commands in a gruff and curt tone that betrays his impatience.

I clear my throat and place my hands flat on the table. I've spent all day thinking about what tactics should use tonight. It's crucial that I stay natural and seem spontaneous. Time to act!

"So, Enola lay down on the bed. He placed his glass of wine on a table and walked toward her with a feline gait. The young Glace held her breath, praying with all her heart that it was King Vidal. He raises his hands to his wolf mask and remove it, revealing his face.

An overwhelming emotion filled Enola, making her tremble on the bed.

The winner of the auction, who had paid ten million crowns for her virtue... Was indeed King Vidal, the man she loved."

Is that a hint of a smile I see on Sylvan's lips? I'm not quite sure.

I decide not to dwell on this detail and focus on the next part of my story.

The next few minutes will be crucial.

CHAPTER FOURTEEN

MISE EN ABYME

"King Vidal lay down on the bed next to Enola, who was frozen like a porcelain statue. The king's gentle gaze traveled over her naked body, caressing every curve, before looking back onto her eyes.

"Enola, bear the thought of another man touching you. I thank the Goddess that I heard about your reckless plan at court… When I found out, I was filled with rage. But why did you put your virginity up for auction? Why such madness?"

Tears rolled down the young woman's cheeks. She told him the whole truth: her brother's capture, her mother's disability, the depth of her despair.

"Don't cry, my sweet Enola," Vidal sighed, covering her tear-stained face with tender kisses. "You should have told me about all this long ago! I will order your brother's release. I'll send the best doctors from Oceanar to care for your mother."

"But I could never… repay this debt. I can't become your mistress, Your Majesty."

"I never asked you to become my mistress, Enola, and there will never be any talk of debts between us. However, if you would accept becoming my wife, I would be the happiest Glace alive."

The young woman's stunned eyes widened like saucers.

"Your… your wife? But I'm nothing! And you're promised to a Fuegis princess!"

"A woman I barely know and don't love, Enola. She's quite unlikable, anyway… I'll find another husband for her. One of my cousins will be delighted to take on this duty in my place. It's you my heart chose on the beach the day we met. At that moment, I knew that my soul was bound to yours for eternity. You're not *nothing* to me. You are my everything."

Overwhelmed with emotion, Enola tilted her head back to offer him her lips. The king kissed her passionately. They lost themselves in that long, deep kiss, expressing the sincere and unconditional love they felt for each other."

Sylvan's piercing eyes focus on my mouth. His desire is rising. His pupils are dilated, his pupils darkened. With a hint of nonchalance, I push a strand of hair behind my ear in what I hope is a graceful gesture.

"Unbelievable," he mutters, almost as if talking to himself.

"Excuse me?" I ask, trying to contain my frustration.

"A king couldn't break an engagement with a princess on a whim to marry a common woman. It would be both irresponsible and selfish. He could risk starting a war between the two Clans. Even if his cousin, with royal blood, took his place, it would still be an unspeakable affront."

"And what about love?"

"Love has no place among kings and queens, Alena."

"In my story, love plays a central role, quite the opposite of what you think. It doesn't matter if it's unrealistic in your eyes. If that aspect bothers you, I can still stop telling it."

"Don't be sensitive, my wife. Continue; I'm listening."

"Don't interrupt me again, Sylvan. I'll lose my train of thought with your childish comments."

"Vidal's hands began to discover Enola's body, honoring her with slow caresses. With her eyes closed, she surrendered completely to these new voluptuous sensations. His long, strong fingers traced invisible runes of fire over her trembling skin. *Is this what love between a man and a woman feels like? How could I live until now without knowing such bliss?*" she thought sighing with pleasure. When Vidal's hand reached the sensitive area between her thighs, Enola let out a moan, parting her legs to encourage him to deepen his intimate exploration. She could feel herself warm and wet in that secret place she had never dared to touch herself, except while bathing.

The king who had stolen her heart now covered her throat with increasingly heated kisses, whispering how beautiful she was, how much he desired her. Enola bit her lip until it bled when he gently slid the tip of his finger inside her. Overcome with a sudden urge to feel his skin under her hands, the young Glace began to untie his tunic, her breath coming faster and heavier. Vidal shed his garments and was soon as naked as she was on the bed.

"Enola, I love you," the king declared intensely, his translucent eyes locked onto hers as he slowly penetrates his member in her untouched sanctuary.

To her great surprise, the young woman's pain was brief. The sovereign was so careful as he broke her hymen that all she felt was a brief, quite tolerable pinch in her lower abdomen. Waves of pleasure soon followed with Vidal's slow, measured thrusts as he panted above her trembling, perspiring body. She clung to him desperately, letting out a muffled cry as a mysterious ecstasy washed over her. Her lover cried out as well, his body tensing, and she felt his release deep inside her.

"Is this magic?" she asked, in awe a few minutes later.

"No, my love," he replied, laughing, "you simply climaxed."

"How can you call that *simply*? It was extraordinary!"

Vidal gave her a tender smile and kissed her lips softly.

"Not all women speak so highly of their first time, my sweet Enola."

"I imagine that depends on the lover. I suppose you have… some experience?"

"I won't lie to you, I do," he admitted without the slightest hint of arrogance. "I've been with many women, but none of them ever set my hear, my soul, and my body on fire the way you do."

The young woman blushed with a hint of shyness, turning toward him as her hand lightly brushed his strong chest.

"Would you tell me about your first time, Your Majesty?"

"You want to know that kind of detail?" he replied, surprised.

"I want to know everything about you, my love. Everything," she declared passionately.

"Promise me you won't tell anyone, Enola. If this reached the ears of the Glace court, it would cause a scandal."

"I promise, my king."

"I was fourteen. She was an… older woman. My father's wife."

"Your stepmother," Enola whispered, her eyes wide.

"Yes. She was my stepmother."

With my hands clenched on my tight knees, I carefully look toward Sylvan, allowing the silence to hang heavily in the room.

The king closes his eyes for a few seconds, as if trying to force himself to remain calm and patient.

"Alena, Alena… A story within a story?"

I nod slowly, apprehensive of his reaction. The muscles in my back and shoulders are so tense they are painful. I must not falter.

"You don't intend to finish your tale tonight," guesses my husband in a serious tone.

"No, Sylvan, indeed."

"And you're going to ask me for one more day."

"Y–yes," I confirm, swallowing. "One more day."

A cold, bitter smile adorns my husband's lips. Did he expect this?

"Will you do the same trick tomorrow night, Alena?"

I don't answer.

"That's convenient because I have a request of my own. Grant me something, and I'll give you an extra day."

These words are both reassuring and alarming. Sylvan is a master at this.

"What do you want?"

"A kiss, Alena. Just a kiss from my wife," he murmurs in a velvety voice, as he pats his thigh to invite me to sit on it.

I don't blink. My eardrums are ringing. A weight presses in the pit of my stomach and chest.

"A… kiss?"

"Just a simple kiss. I don't ask more, as long as it's consensual," he specifies with an innocent look that doesn't suit him at all.

Consensual? Is this how he sees things? He's trying to extort a kiss from me in exchange for the promise of temporarily sparing my life, and he calls this a *consensual* kiss?

Alas, I have no alternative…

I stand up, gathering my skirts to the side, and with a glaring lack of confidence, I sit on Sylvan's firm lap, which seems quite satisfied with my docility.

His arm immediately tightens around my waist, almost hurting me. He pulls us together with authority, drawing my body against his, hard and hot. Goddess, I can feel his erection against the line of my hip... I knew my story would turn him on—that was the point, but there's an ocean between knowing and feeling!

"Give me a kiss of love as if you were Enola and I were your Vidal, my manipulative little virgin," he whispers with a cynical smile, his full lips an inch from mine. "Play your act brilliantly. Make me believe you love me, my queen. Put in the effort as if your life depended on it..."

My trembling fingers rest on his broad shoulders.

I take a deep breath, then lean toward Sylvan, preparing to give my first *love* kiss to the man I hate the most in the world.

CHAPTER FIFTEEN

JUST A KISS

Sylvan pierces me with his sea-green gaze as I lean my face toward his.

I don't know how to do it. I've never done this before.

I merely brush against the fullness of his lips with excessive caution, as if I were tasting an exotic fruit with a bitter reputation for the first time. His large warrior's hand rest on my waist, and his mouth tightly sealed, my enemy doesn't make no move at all. I notice that his lips are surprisingly soft… warm, of course, but soft and pliable. I pull my head slightly, bewildered by our mock kiss.

Sylvan narrows his eyes slightly, producing a deep, displeased growl from his throat.

"Again," he demands in a hoarse whisper that sends shivers down my spine.

"Play your act brilliantly. Make me believe you love me, my queen. Put in the effort as if your life depended on it," he told me just a moment earlier.

I let out a deep sigh that sweeps across his temple scar and close my eyes to gather a new surge of courage.

I place my lips back on his, pushing aside the identity of the man I'm kissing.

I imagine savoring this strange exotic fruit with its warm, soft texture, convincing myself that its taste is pleasant. I explore the curve of his mouth millimeter by millimeter with my own, tilting my head from side to side.

His lower lip is fuller than his upper lip, and the coarse hair of his beard brush against my skin. He smells of sand, sunshine, and spiced wine. Beneath my finger, the muscles in his shoulders are taut; it feels like I'm touching marble.

Sylvan doesn't return my kiss. He remains stoic.

Yet, his erection hardens against my hip.

In response, my hands tighten on his shoulders. Instinctively, I part my lips. Very briefly, I graze his lower lip with the tip of my tongue.

His taste is *really* delightful. A tiny drop of red wine lingered in the curve of his mouth. Without thinking, I lick it away.

I realize a second pulse is beating between my thighs.

No. No. I don't desire him; it's impossible, I reason to myself, on the edge of panic, abruptly reopening my eyes.

He has closed his.

I pull back, breathless. My mind screams at me to flee while my body cries out with its insatiable thirst. Sylvan opens his fever-bright eyes, and with an agonizingly swift movement, he grabs me by the back of the neck, preventing me from rising from his lap.

My husband turns up the heat and takes control.

Without gentleness, he tilts my head toward his, claiming my lips with a wild fervor. My heart races, mirroring the fire pulsing in my lower belly. The blood seems to thicken in my veins. In a vain attempt at mental protection, I close my eyes again. Instead, my lips part, defeated by the incredible hunger of his kiss. His demanding tongue invades my mouth, seeking mine. Without giving me a moment's respite, he explores, marks, devastates, devours me, asserting himself as master. I feel dizzy, breathless. Yet I am unable to push him away. My fists clench on his shoulders, pulling at the fabric of his tunic.

The fiery power of his magic flows into me through his kiss, a force that could consume me in an instant. My breasts are hot and taut; my being has turned into flammable liquid. Between my legs, a sharp delightful pain awakens. I want… to feel that power deep inside me, that strength, that virility. To let his unleashed energy overwhelm me, coursing through my dried fibers and flooding me again. To feast on it until agony.

The thought that crosses my mind frightens me more than anything.

I want *him* inside me.

Goddess of the Ocean!

How can I crave this infamous man?

Why is my body betraying me at the worst possible moment?

Sylvan kisses my lips as he slides his hand down my hip. With a dark sensuality, his fingers caress the bare skin of my thigh through the slit of my dress.

My ardor intensifies. I trap his face between my hands, and without fully understanding what I'm doing, I drink him in. My aggression matches his. I swallow his tongue, dragging him into a whirlwind of forbidden taste. I impose the rhythm, roughing up his lips. I try to steal control and regain the upper hand. But he doesn't give in; he fights back. Do all warriors kiss like this? All I know is that our teeth clash and our tongues overlap, fierce and eager. As aroused as I am irritated, I bite him fiercely. He doesn't even flinch, as if he doesn't feel the pain.

When I realize that his hand is now between my thighs, it's too late.

Sylvan lets out a triumphant groan against my mouth. He can feel the deceitful wetness soaking my underwear and knows now that the inexplicable desire he feels for me is mutual. I can't fake something like this.

He kisses me even harder. I press against him, digging my nails into the skin of his cheeks.

I hate him. I despise him.

I want him. I desire him.

"Put in the effort as if your life depended on it."

Beneath my dress, I spread my legs, feverish.

As he slips under my lingerie, Sylvan begins to slowly push his thick finger inside me, inflicting a delicious burn on my soaked femininity. I let out a small, muffled moan that gets lost in his mouth.

He meets a resistance of flesh.

Suddenly, everything stops.

He pulls his hand away as if he's just plunged it into and frozen well and moves his head away from mine, looking at me as if he's seeing me for the first time.

We are both breathless. His lips are red and swollen. I suppose mine must look the same. He shakes his head slightly to regain his composure.

"You're really a virgin," he murmurs, an incredulous expression on his face.

"I told you so," I retort coldly, despite my burning body.

"Get up, Alena."

I slide off his lap and take a seat on the chaise. I shiver all over as my skin is coated in sweat. I'm shaken by the bestial intensity of our physical exchange. I can't believe we kissed and… that he penetrated my intimate place with his finger.

How could I let him do such an obscene thing? Am I going crazy?

Or has he somehow influenced me with his damned elemental magic?

Sylvan stands up and takes a step back, his expression dark. Goodness, what is he thinking?

"Did I *play my act brilliantly*, husband?" I ask him in a harsh and provocative tone.

"Have you ever kissed a man, Alena?"

"No, Sylvan. You can be proud to have extorted that kiss from me. You're the first."

"Extorted?" A raspy laugh erupts from his hoarse throat. "I took nothing more than what you gave me!"

"Don't fool yourself; I took no pleasure in that act."

"My wife, my finger is still wet," he reminds me, casting a glance that rekindles the flame scorching my weak flesh.

I turn away, my cheeks flushed with shame.

Goddess, may he leave quickly!

"We'll see each other tomorrow night, and you'll tell me the rest of your story," decrees the sovereign after a sinister silence.

"I'd like to take a walk in the gardens tomorrow morning. Would you grant me this modest request?" I ask casually.

Another silence. I don't dare look at him. I'm too afraid to see the reflection of my desire on his face.

"I grant it. A one-hour walk, not a minute more. Daegan will accompany you, of course."

I focus my eyes on him, pleasantly surprised by his approval. While his voice has been soft and dull, his gaze is hard as stone. A conflict rages within him.

And I am the cause.

One step closer to freedom.

One step closer to survival.

I nod, speechless.

Sylvan studies me, frowning. His expression seems to ask, *"What am I going to do with you?"*

"I'm glad my little stories interest you so much," I add with a hint of sarcasm.

A half-cold smile curls Sylvan's lips.

Those soft, warm lips that were on mine…

"My beautiful wife, Glace… Don't you understand that it's not your stories that excite me?" He runs his gaze over my mouth, then my throat, my breast, and finally my exposed leg. I hold my breath, shaken by the extraordinary intensity emanating from his proud person. "It's the way your lips pronounce the words *kiss* or *caress*. It's the smooth, enchanting intonations of your voice. It's the captivating way your breasts rise with each of your breaths. It's your eyes that sparkle like sapphires when you tell me your little tall tales. While other speakers merely recount a story, you live it moment by moment and make it thrilling, whereas it would be utterly bland coming from the mouth of another woman." I breathe out, viscerally disturbed by his words. "But your petty schemes greatly bore me. I've had enough of this little game. Tomorrow night, you'll finish your stupid tale and confess me the whole truth."

"The… truth?"

Frozen, I can't suppress my trembling.

His stern, haughty gaze lingers on the royal mark tattooed on my forehead.

"You know exactly what I'm talking about," he snaps before leaving.

As soon as the door closes behind him, I run into the bathroom to throw up my dinner.

He knows.

CHAPTER SIXTEEN
THE MARKS OF WAR

"You know exactly what I'm talking about."

Sylvan's last words have lodged in my mind like poisonous roots.

They haunt me. They afflict me. They terrify me.

What is he going to inflict on me once I finish telling my story?

"What do I have to lose? My life? It's already hanging by a thread!" I proclaimed in the throne room the day I arrived in Astranis.

He had then retorted in a wintry tone, *"Don't you fear suffering?"*

Of course, I fear it! You would have to be insane or stupid not to be afraid of pain!

He can't know. It's impossible!

No Fuegis knows my true identity. Nadya harbors vague suspicions that I'm hiding something, but I can't see how she could have figured me out! Despite my extreme caution, have I betrayed myself in front of her or Sylvan without realizing it? Through words, attitudes, or expressions that sounded false?

Could someone have spilled the beans?

If this theory were true… it would have to be a Glace. Those who are included in the confidence, those in Queen Alena's inner circle, can be counted on one hand. A prisoner who might have confessed my secret under torture?

A traitor? A spy?

This dilemma should have prevented me from reaching the treasure of sleep, but I'm so exhausted from my previous sleepless night that I end up falling asleep fully dressed in my bed.

Unfortunately, my sleep is filled with nightmares, each more morbid than the last.

I dream that Sylvan tears my lips away while kissing me.

I dream that Nadya beheads me with a golden axe.

I dream of the corpses of my mother and my brother at Alena's feet, who laughs at my naivety.

I even dream of the character from my story, King Vidal, who tramples me under the hooves of his horse on a red sand beach before violating my dying body.

I wake up after dawn, even more exhausted than before I went to bed. With a terrible migraine.

Daegan picks me up an hour later to escort me to the Palace Gardens. He doesn't put chains on my wrists, but he warns me that at the slightest attempt to escape or rebel, he'll knock me out with the pommel of his sword and drag me back to my quarters, dragging me by my hair.

I can't appreciate the sun caressing my face, the wind blowing through my hair, or the scent of flowers pleasing my senses. I barely notice the cheerful chirping of the birds and the soothing murmur of the small waterfalls flowing over the mossy stones. I can't even savor the beauty of the lush vegetation and the marble statues poignantly realistic that emerge on either side of the path.

I have the taste of ashes and death in my mouth.

"You're unusually quiet and withdrawn this morning," Daegan remarks, following me like my shadow.

Why is this stupid Fuegis guard talking to me?

"Would you prefer that I rave about each grove, sharing my knowledge of gardening?" I snap without turning around.

"You're the one who insisted on this walk," he reminds me in a neutral tone. "I thought you'd be a bit more enthusiastic, that's all."

"No special hostility towards me this morning, Daegan? Be careful, I might think you're softening up!"

"I'm just as surprised as you are, but my daughter likes you," he admits quietly. "She asked me not to be too hard on you."

I stop on the path and turn toward him, the rustle of my skirts echoing in the stillness.

"Selaine?" He nods. "The apple fell far from the tree."

He opens his mouth to say something back, but someone interrupts us.

"Your Majesty. What a happy coincidence to find you here."

Leonal, I realize as I see a shaved head glinting in the morning sun. Coincidence, I think not…

"High-Fuegis," Daegan greets stoically, bowing his head.

"Leave us, Captain," Leonal orders in a contemptuous tone without sparing him a glance.

Captain. So that's the military rank of my bodyguard.

Daegan puffs up his chest. A palpable tension has arisen.

"The king gave me orders, Counselor. I'm not to leave the queen's side."

Leonal's black eyes turn toward him. An expression of unpleasant surprise paints his features. Clearly, he's not used to having his demands contested.

"Your dedication to my nephew is remarkable, Captain, but your zeal could be interpreted as insubordination toward me, and I don't tolerate that kind of attitude. Stay about twenty yards away from us to keep an eye on her if you wish but stay back." Daegan hesitates. "God of Fire, how slow-witted you are! What do you want her to do? She has an enchanted artifact around her neck and knows I would use my powers to neutralize her if she attempted something foolish."

I grit my teeth. I don't like being talked about in front of me as if I don't exist. And oddly enough, I also dislike the condescending way Leonal speaks to Daegan. The man of power belittling the man of the people… It strikes a chord deep in my chest. I, too, have had to endure the open disdain of the High-Glaces and Queen Alena more than once without being able to defend myself.

"Thank your god, Leonal," I comment softly.

The arrogant counselor shifts his attention back to me, taken aback by my interruption.

"Why should I thank my god, Your Majesty?"

"For having this necklace around my neck."

The High-Fuegis darkens at the threatening connotation of my words.

"Let's walk," he says in a sharp tone.

Daegan stays behind as I reluctantly continue my walk alongside the desert jackal, who, hands clasped behind his back, gazes at the flower beds with a bored expression.

"You're a resourceful woman, Alena." *No more* Majesty *in private, of course!* "You should have been executed two days ago, but my nephew seems to think you could still be of use to us."

If I read between the lines correctly, Sylvan didn't tell his uncle why he spared me. He came up with a vague excuse as justification. And if Leonal is here this morning while I'm walking in the gardens, by *coincidence*, it's precisely to try to learn more about the situation.

"An *object* is useful, Leonal."

"Do you consider yourself otherwise?"

Goddess of the Ocean! Between Nadya and Leonal, I can't decide who is the most antipathetic. Even Sylvan is a little less…

No. Sylvan is antipathetic too. Sylvan is the worst of the three.

"I wish I could blindly trust my nephew's judgment of you, Alena," the High-Fuegis continues with fake boredom. "However, I fear it may be clouded by your beauty and your skills in the marital bed. Sylvan is a good leader and an exceptional warrior, but he's still young and sometimes lacks objectivity. His male impulses can sometimes outweigh his reason."

So Leonal thinks I'm sleeping with Sylvan to gain more days of life… Like Nadya, I imagine. Why would I deny it? It's better for him to think I'm a whore than to suspect the truth. By default, I remain silent.

"'Facing his enemy, a Glace sheds no tears, and never relinquishes his weapons,'" quotes the adviser with a caustic smile. "Isn't it that right, Queen Alena?"

I don't answer. I swallow back the seeds of hatred and fury that have taken root in my belly.

"Women are sadly predictable," adds the jackal. "I warned my nephew that you would use your charms to survive. Alas, he willingly fell for it."

I force a similarly sardonic smile as Leonal's.

"And I am still alive; what a *happy coincidence*."

"Until he gets tired of you, Alena…"

But he already is.

"But your petty schemes greatly bore me," he told me last night.

"Don't delude yourself, young lady," the counselor continues in a hardened tone. "My nephew always ends up making the right decisions."

"Thanks to your benevolent influence, I presume?"

"Among other things. Follow me; I'm going to show you something."

I cast a quick glance over my shoulder. With his dark gaze and stern expression, Daegan walks along the path about twenty yards behind us. I'm almost reassured. The thought of being alone with Leonal sends chills down my spine. His mere proximity already makes me very uncomfortable.

After several minutes of walking, we emerge onto a rocky promontory overlooking a vast sandy courtyard lined with olive trees.

A training area.

"You're fighting with your weapons, Alena… But so is my nephew. Never forget that you're not up against an ordinary man," Leonal suggests to me ironically.

Sylvan stands motionless in the center of the courtyard, shirtless. In his fist, his flaming sword, *Dragon's Breath*, brazes and smokes.

He is surrounded by eight soldiers, preparing to attack him.

With his legs spread, he slowly scans his opponents, assessing them, every muscle in his chest tensed in anticipation.

The sight of his long, thick arms covered in delicate thin, purple vein-like lines intertwining like a bloody spiderweb!—paralyzes me. Goddess, there must be hundreds. These tattoos symbolize all the lives he's taken over the years… and he's only twenty years old. His dark hair is tied back, and I notice numerous gold rings in his ears, other morbid trophies. His broad, bronze-skinned chest is crisscrossed with scars. With his formidable sword Nesayan in his hand, he looks like a legendary war god, ready to unleash his majestic fury on the mortals foolish enough to challenge him.

The first attack comes from his right.

A Fuegis soldier raises his hand and launches a fireball, the size of a fist, in Sylvan's direction.

With breathtaking speed, Sylvan lift Nesayan in front of him. The blade absorbs the fireball and sends it back in a powerful, blazing stream. The guard doesn't have time to dodge. He's hurled hundred feet backward, screaming as he crashes into a palm tree, which shudders under the impact.

If he weren't immune to fire, that Fuegis would've been burned alive.

Seven guards remain.

Two men attack Sylvan at once. My husband's magic sword blocks their halberd with ease, one blow after another. The clash of metal and the war cries of the of Fuegis soldiers assault my ears.

The king disarms one of his opponents with a swift spin of his blade, then kicks him hard in the stomach, sending him rolling several feet away. He parries the second halberd strike from the other guard, and with another kick, he swiftly sweeps the man's legs out from under him. The soldier collapses face-first, narrowly avoiding impaling himself on his own weapon.

Five guards left.

A soldier attacks Sylvan from behind. My husband ducks at the last moment—the Fuegis's blade whistles through the air, just inches above his head. The king spins around. His flaming sword slices through his opponent's halberd. The man doesn't lose his nerve, though; he swings both broken pieces of his weapon toward Sylvan—the shattered staff and the sharp blade. My husband grabs the stick with his free hand to intercept it and deflects the axe blade with Nesayan. A moment later, the Fuegis finds himself disarmed and lies on the ground at Sylvan's feet, groaning in pain, a long, bloody gash across his cheek. Sylvan steps over him carelessly, moving toward his remaining opponents.

He has four guards left to neutralize.

Half of them.

Thirty seconds later, two more guards collapse to the ground.

Now, there are only two left.

A morbid fascination grips me as I watch the surreal spectacle unfold before me.

I'm amazed, impressed… and aroused.

I don't understand why all this masculine brutality is having such an effect on me… The idea should disgust me! But the fluid way Sylvan fights and defeats his opponents, one after the other, his movements as graceful as a cat's, his energetic body with powerful muscles, sculpted like a living weapon of war… I can't help but find him mesmerizing to watch.

Suddenly, he bursts into an almost joyous laugh, spreading his arms wide, and throws his magic sword to the ground. Deprived of the human contact that gives it power, the sword extinguishes before touching the sand.

I hold my breath.

What's is he doing? Is he out of his mind?

The two guards must be wondering the same thing, as they exchange nervous glances.

Too calmy, Sylvan signals them to come to him with a wave of his hand.

They charge, roaring, weapons aimed forward, attacking their king simultaneously.

The scene unfolds too quickly for me to catch all the details, but Sylvan moves with unbelievable agility, diving between the two clashing halberds. He slips behind one of the guards, wraps an arm around his neck, and grabs his wrist. Like a puppeteer controlling a wooden doll, he uses the soldier's arm to fight the other man. The second guard's halberd is torn from his hands. Sylvan delivers a precise punch to the temple of his captive, knocking him out cold, steals his weapon just as he falls, and ends the training session by striking the last guard standing with the handle across his face, sending a spray of blood into the sand.

Beside me, Leonal claps slowly.

Breathless and disheveled, surrounded by the eight wounded bodies of his men, Sylvan looks up at us and freezes when he sees me.

He hadn't noticed we were here, I think, swallowing.

Our eyes meet despite the distance between us.

My husband turns away, tossing aside the halberd, and marches toward his palace, leaving the Fuegis soldiers on the ground.

Leonal calls for Daegan to join us, then turns to me, a smile on his lips as satisfied as it is devious. I shiver.

"Have a great day, Your Majesty," he says calmy as he walks away. "See you tomorrow… or never."

"See you tomorrow, Leonal," I whisper, watching him leave. "See you tomorrow…"

✳✳✳

A thousand dark thoughts swirl in my mind as I walk ahead of Daegan down the hallway to return to my quarters. As I move, the suffocating feeling that the stone walls of the palace are closing in on my hunched body becomes more and more intense. The heavy footsteps of my jailer force me into a quick pace, matching the rhythm of my racing heart. The venomous words of Sylvan and Leonal haunt me, intertwining and echoing in my damaged memory, creating a fiery knot of distress that grows deep in my stomach.

"Hurry up, Your Majesty," Daegan growls, impatient to escort me to get rid of the burden I represent in his eyes. "I've got things to do."

"If I rush, I'll break my neck," I snap over my shoulder. "But then again, that would save your king from getting his hands dirty!"

Just as I utter those words, we reach an intersection, and a figure suddenly emerges from a side hallway, grabbing my arms roughly and spinning me a quarter turn. A wave of panic hits me, and a garbled cry escapes my throat. I'm about to call Daegan for help when I realize it's the one man in Symbiosis, he won't protect me from. Confused, I look up into Sylvan's burning gaze.

"What were you talking about with my uncle in the gardens?" he snarls, tightening his painful grip on my arms.

Telling him what I discussed with Leonal would be a huge mistake. Sylvan doesn't trust me; he'd certainly accuse me of lying.

"You can go ask him yourself," I retort, squirming, trying in vain to free myself from his brutal hold. "Let go of me, for god's sake!"

His eyes burning with dangerous fire, Sylvan gives a curt nod to Daegan, who stands behind me. In an instant, Daegan's thick hands close around my wrists, twisting my arms behind my back, trapping me. My eyes widen in horror as the king draws a dagger from his belt, its handle gold, its blade gleaming silver. If his goal is to terrify me, he's succeeded.

"What are you doing? Sylvan!" I shout, struggling.

I freeze as the sharp edge of the dagger rests against my throat, just above the necklace I wear. My erratic breathing echoes in the hallway. If someone—anyone—could just come along, would he stop whatever he's planning? In this heavy moment of uncertainty, a strange desire creeps in, wishing he'd just end it here and now. I'm so tired of living in constant fear and doubt. I'm on the verge of giving up, maybe even begging him to slit my throat. It would be so much easier… The will to live—or rather, to survive—seeps out of me as if I no longer have the strength to fight the inevitable.

"I'm asking *you*, Alena," Sylvan murmurs, colder than ever.

"Your uncle seems a little upset that I'm still alive, that's all," I weakly argue.

"He's not the only one."

I close my eyes as the tip of the dagger scrapes against the metal of my necklace and glides down to my collarbone, pricking my pale skin without cutting it. Slowly, Sylvan traces the edge of my neckline with his weapon, grazing the soft curve of my right breast.

"You're not going to convince me that your conversation was limited to such an obvious observation," he continues, following the tiny, embroidered patterns along the edge of my dress with his blade. "What did you tell him, Alena? Were you trying to seduce him?"

I open my eyes, stunned by his accusation. My gaze instantly collides with his, blazing with heated reproaches.

Could… he be jealous?

No, I quickly reason. That's impossible.

"Of course not, that's absurd! Daegan was there, he can attest to that! Tell him, you oaf!"

"Daegan couldn't have heard the details of your conversation," Sylvan argues "Every Fuegis know that courtesans don't need to touch a man to charm him. All it takes is a lingering look, two or three smiles, and a few well-chosen words, spoken in the most seductive tone they can muster."

"I'm not a courtesan," I remind him, unable to hide my disdain.

Over my head, Sylvan exchanges a caustic glance with Daegan, who continues to hold my arms tightly behind my back, unflinching. Then, the king bends toward me. His scorching breath brushes against my lips as he whispers, "That's true. You're far worse than those little sand vipers."

The dagger slides down the delicate valley between my breasts, making me shudder in discomfort. It moves toward my left, circling around my nipple over the fabric of my dress. My heart jumps, my breathing quickens, and my legs tremble.

I bite my lip, holding back the moan rising from deep in my throat as the flat of the blade grazes the tip of my nipple, which hardens at the touch of the cold metal. My body's disloyal response fills me with shame. A twisted, undeserving flicker of desire mixes with the intense fear I'm feeling.

"I've never tortured a woman before," Sylvan announces, his voice low and insidious. "But I once read in an old book that cutting off a woman's breast can be as painful for her as castration is for a man."

The imagined sensation of the dagger slicing through my tender flesh and the thought of my blood dripping onto the floor banish that sickening desire, leaving me with nothing but a familiar pit of despair.

"Sylvan, please," I whisper, hating myself for begging. "I didn't make advances toward your uncle."

"Do you think she's telling the truth, Daegan?"

With a skeptical air, the king traces tormenting circles around my nipple with the tip of his dagger.

My guard and captor remains silent for a good ten seconds, deep in thought, torn by hesitation. If he answers no, I know I'm in for a very rough time…

"Yes, Majesty, I think she is."

The dagger finally moves away from my trembling breast, and I let out a deep sigh. I hadn't even realized I'd been holding my breath for the past few seconds.

"Very well. You can thank Daegan for giving you the benefit of the doubt," Sylvan declares, sheathing his weapon and turning back. "I'll let your imagination run wild until tonight regarding how we'll resolve our conflicts. It mostly depends on your cooperation, Alena. I trust you'll give me full satisfaction."

The Fuegis captain releases me. But I remain completely still, paralyzed by my husband's cryptic, double-edged words.

CHAPTER SEVENTEEN

ACCUSATION

Escorted by Daegan, I make my way to Sylvan's quarter. I don't know why, but tonight, he insisted that *I* come to him.

Willingly? Of course not.

Anguish pulses through every part of my being. The memory of the dagger on my breast is still fresh.

Fear pulses through every inch of my being. The memory of the dagger on my breast is still fresh. While I was dining in my suite, when Selaine had her back turned, I managed to steal a knife and hide it beneath my dress. A pitiful weapon against a man like Sylvan, I know, but in my extreme despair… I'm willing to try anything. If I must die by his hand tonight, I'll take my last breath fighting.

A few minutes later, I find myself alone with him in his quarters. Sitting behind his desk, shirtless, he's writing a letter using a long red quill. As usual, he doesn't acknowledge me with a word or even a glance. He continues writing with steady concentration. I'm not particularly surprised anymore; I'm getting used to his rude and obnoxious behavior.

What does surprise me, though, is the look of his quarters. Even though I'm just a prisoner, mine are decorated with royal splendor.

His, by contrast, are stark, cold, and impersonal. The colors of the tapestries and curtains are neutral. Even though the furniture appears to be of excellent quality, there are no embellishments. No painting on the walls. No luxurious trinkets. I can guess why: he probably doesn't spend much time here. When he's not on a military campaign, he's busy managing the affairs of his kingdom. His apartments are functional and comfortable but simple. Order is the reigning theme. A bed, a desk, a wardrobe, a bookshelf, three chests, a table, a chaise longue… and that's it. The only personal touch is the black and gold armor displayed on a wooden stand in the corner of the room. The dark slits of the dragon-shaped helmet seem to stare at me menacingly. I imagine that his most prized possessions—his sword, crown, and other weapons—are locked away in those chests.

My gaze returns to Sylvan. He has lifted his eyes from the letter and set down his quill. I realize that while I was inspecting my surroundings, he had been watching me closely.

"What are you thinking, my wife?" he asks in a neutral, distant tone.

He acts as if his intimidation in the hallway never happened.

His behavior lacks consistency or logic. His moods shift in an instant. One moment he's ice, and the next second he's fire. I've rarely met someone so unstable. Did he succumb to a burst of anger and jealousy earlier? Would he really have slashed my breast, or was he just trying to scare me?

Is he playing games with me, too?

Fine, if that's the way it's going to be…

"I was just thinking that your quarters suit your personality perfectly. Or rather, your lack of personality."

He chooses not to respond to my jab.

"Who were you writing to?" I sigh.

"You don't really think I'm going to tell you, do you?"

"My husband, if that letter were some state secrets, you would've hidden it before I arrived."

"Your sharp mind never ceases to amaze me," he says, shaking his head as if it were both a virtue and a flaw. "I was writing to one of my subjects, a scribe who submitted a personal request. Twenty copies of a controversial book were recently destroyed by one of my vassals. The scholar also had to pay a hefty fine to avoid being imprisoned for insulting the Fuegis monarchy. He still has the original. He asked me if he could copy it again and distribute it, this time toning it down a bit more. I granted his request. He'll show this letter, stamped with my seal, to my vassal as proof of my official consent."

"What kind of book?" I ask, noting the red marks on his arms and the scars on his chest.

"A pamphlet."

"What's the subject?"

"Me."

"You?" I mutter, skeptical. "You mean you gave this man permission to mock and criticize you in his writings?"

"Freedom of speech and thought may have its place in your kingdom, my wife, but in mine, I encourage it. At least when it's possible. I happen to have a copy of that book in my library; I read it a few months ago. Its content isn't that insulting toward me—it's more of a parody. I admit that some passages, though not flattering, even made me laugh. The author has a sense of humor, and his writing style is enjoyable. Since I'm already unpopular, a few bold writings won't change my reputation," he concludes with a mix of bitterness and sarcasm.

"But… you execute anyone who… oppose or… defies you… Your subjects, your soldiers… and…" I stammered, losing my words.

"Who told you I executed my subjects and my soldiers, my wife?" he retorts sharply. "The High-Glaces? God of Fire, what a bunch of fools! I execute my *enemies*. Not my allies, and certainly not my subjects."

He's lying. I don't know why, but he's lying. He's a dictator. A murderer. An oppressor. He's violent, cruel, shameless. His own people hate him.

He gets up from his chair and walks over to…

The bed.

"Come, sit by my side, and finish telling me your little bedtime story, my virginal wife. And remember well what I told you last night after our kiss…"

How could I forget? I thought about it every minute of the day!

"I've had enough of this little game. Tomorrow night, you'll finish your stupid tale and confess me the whole truth."

"You know exactly *what I'm talking about."*

With a great effort of will, I tear my eyes away from contemplating the slender muscles rippling under the bronzed skin of his back and chest. I can feel the cold blade of the knife beneath my dress. I have tied it securely to my thigh with a silk ribbon.

I sit on the edge of the bed, a few feet away from Sylvan, my neck stiff with tension, my hands flat on my knees. Goddess of the Ocean, please don't let my voice tremble!

"My stepmother, Celina, was a one-of-a-kind woman," King Vidal said pensively, caressing Enola's bare belly. "My father was thrilled to parade her around on his arm because all the men only had eyes for her. She had an unconventional beauty that stood out compared to the aesthetic standards of the Glace court. Her silver hair had fabulous blue highlights, and her eyes were black as a moonless night. If she captivated men so much back then, it was also because she exuded raw sensuality, had a brilliant mind, and a musical laugh. As a child, I was captivated by her too. I would stammer and blush in her presence."

"You, blush, my king?" Enola teased. "I find that hard to believe."

"It's the truth, my dear. My father was madly in love with his second wife, even more than he had been with my mother when she was alive. Celina exerted a lot of influence over him. The older I got, the more obsessed I became with her. My feelings for her were so strong that I paid no attention to girls my age. By the time I was fourteen, I found myself envious and jealous of my own father. Every time she gave me any affectionate gesture, even something as simple as a touch on the arm, I was over the moon. She even began to appear in my dreams, and I would wake up trembling, sweaty, and physically frustrated. I was ashamed of my secret feelings for her. I felt as if, in some way, I was betraying my father by imagining myself in his place, on Celina's arm."

Enola hung on Vidal's every word. Vidal didn't speak with regret or melancholy, but she could sense that this mature woman, whom she didn't know, had meant a lot to him and that—"

"I've never slept with Lady Nadya," Sylvan abruptly interrupts me.

I look at him wide-eyed.

"Why… why are you telling me this?"

"o set the record straight. You're drawing from real-life events for your story, and King Vidal shares some similarities with me. So, I'm making it clear that I never betrayed my father by sleeping with my stepmother. Just so you don't confuse fiction with reality in that sharp little head of yours."

Despite the unease his strange words stir in me, I clear my throat and resume my story.

"I was fourteen when Célina first started acting ambiguously toward me," Vidal said. "I was tall, well-built, and looked four or five years older than I actually was. She began looking at me differently. She complimented my appearance, telling me I was becoming a man—a very handsome man, too. Her glances and words sent my teenage hormones into a frenzy. I feared and hoped for what finally happened between us. One evening, during a drunken banquet where my father and the other Glaces of the court were all drinking heavily, she pulled me into a secluded side room under the pretense of needing to talk to me. No sooner had the door closed behind us than she took off her dress and offered herself to me, naked, confessing that she's had been wanting me for weeks. I didn't think for a moment. I threw myself on her soft lips and kissed her. She undressed me, caressed me between my legs, and showed me how to take pleasure and how to give it to women. We continued our forbidden meeting for months behind my father's back. Celina would come to my room at night to crawl into my bed, or we would meet up in the woods to make love. She said she loved me and that I was a much better lover than my father... Then, one day, I realized that my feelings for her had gradually faded. Once my passion for her had been fulfilled in every imaginable way, all that was left in me was a vague tenderness for her and overwhelming guilt toward my father. What I had mistaken for love was nothing more than a physiological desire, idealized by the immaturity of adolescence. I ended things with Celina because I couldn't pretend any longer. She cried, screamed, and threatened to expose our scandalous affair to my father. But she never did. I guess she really did love me... In the end, she left my father because she could no longer bear to see me every day with a new woman, and she moved away to start a new life. My father never knew the real reason for their separation. Me."

Enola nodded sadly. Vidal smiled at her.

"That's why I know I love you and want to marry you, my love," he said, brushing her lips with a kiss. "I've never loved anyone before you. I'd be willing to do anything for you, even give up the crown if I had to."

But Vidal didn't have to give up the crown, because, to his great surprise, no one opposed their unusual marriage.

He married his dear Enola a few days later, and they lived happily and had many children."

Sylvan stares at me with such disbelief that I would laugh if the situation weren't so serious.

"What? That's how your story ends? You must be joking?"

"Are you disappointed with the ending of my little fairy tale, husband? After all, everyone loves a happy ending," I remark, my tone sharp.

"*No one opposed their unusual marriage?* How is it possible for a Powerless peasant to become a Glace Queen without anyone raising a fuss? That's completely unrealistic!" he says, supremely annoyed.

"If the ending doesn't satisfy or suit you, I can consider changing it. But for that, I need *time*, Sylvan."

Without warning, my husband bursts out laughing—a cold, cynical laugh that stings my skin like thousands of icy needles. My hand instinctively moves toward the knife hidden beneath my dress.

"God of Fire, I never expected this new trick! The rumors about you don't even come close to the truth, wife!" He claps his hands in ironic applause. "You're the queen of manipulative wenches—you beat them all!"

I frown in confusion.

"The rumors about you?"

If Sylvan knows I'm Enola and not Alena…

Why would he say that?

"If you tell me the *whole* truth about yourself, my wife… I'll spare you. Not for a day. Not for a week. I'll cancel your execution—completely. Tell me the truth, and you'll receive a royal pardon. But lie to me *one* more time, Alena… and I'll strangle you with my own hands tonight in this bed."

I flinch, stunned.

Not because he's offering me a new hope of survival.

Not because he's threatening me with death.

After all, it's not the first time…

But because he called me *Alena.*

Sylvan does *not* know my secret.

He thinks I have another one, or rather… Queen Alena Kan-

Glace has one!

Except I have *no idea* what he's talking about.

"I don't know what you're talking about. I swear to you, Sylvan. You're mistaken," I defend myself, helpless and panicked.

"Alena. Admit what you've done, and I'll spare you. Tell me now! I need to know the truth—I need to hear it from your mouth!" he roars with endless rage, his fists clenched.

In less than two seconds, his hands begin to glow red-hot, bursting into flames like torches. His eyes burn with hatred.

By all the gods! He's so furious at me that he's lost control of his fire elemental magic!

I look at him with terrified confusion, which only fuels his anger.

Looks like a cornered animal.

A wounded beast.

He terrifies me even more.

We've reached the point of no return. It's obvious.

Suddenly, I remember something he hinted at before our wedding.

His steely gaze left a deep mark on me when he said it.

There was an accusing gleam in his eyes....

As if I were a *criminal*.

"Since my father's death, I've become much more impulsive. You met him, didn't you?"

And on our wedding night, I told him:

"You took everything that mattered to me!"

He then replied, *"So did you, Alena. So did you..."*

Goddess! I turn pale.

I just realized something crucial that had escaped me until now.

Sylvan thinks it was me—or rather, the real Alena—who was responsible for his father's death.

CHAPTER EIGHTEEN

A HALF-TRUTH

Sylvan thrusts his fiery fist toward my throat.

I need to decide *quickly*.

He's not doing this to pressure me this time. He's determined to hurt me, driven by a ravenous grudge.

I can either continue to lie about my identity, taking on a crime that isn't mine and hoping he'll keep his word—which I highly doubt, since who would spare their father's killer?

Or I can persist in denying what my husband accuses me of, and he'll either burn me alive or strangle me with his own hands…

Or I can reveal to him that I'm not Alena… with all the dark consequences that implies.

Desperate, I choose what seems to be the least terrible of the three options.

"I'm not Alena Kan-Glace."

The tyrant's fist stops two inches from my neck.

The sparks dance on his clenched fingers. The heat radiating from his skin is unbearable. A trickle of sweat runs down my temple. I brave his gaze, filled with confusion.

"Sylvan, I am *not* Alena," I repeat slowly, my heart heavy with anxiety despite the impassive expression I wear like armor.

Sylvan opens his fist, extinguishes the flames, and lowers his arm.

"What is this latest trick?" he hisses, glaring at me.

"The truth, Sylvan. I don't know what you blame Alena for, but I'm not aware of anything. My name… my name is Enola. I… used my own name in the story I told you."

Frowning, my moody husband stares at me intently as if trying to uncover traces of a lie on my features. His pupils flicker.

He's disoriented.

If I were in his place, I'd be just as confused.

Then, without preamble, he grabs my arm, rises from the bed, and forcefully drags me toward a door, pulling me behind him. I struggle like a wild animal, trying to break free from his iron grip. I scratch him, I hit him, I resist, I scream, but to no avail.

"SYLVAN! What are you doing? Let me go!"

Goddess, where is he taking me?

To the High-Fuegis?

To prison?

To the gallows?

To his… bathroom?

He opens the door and shoves me inside roughly. Thrown against the wall by my momentum, I curl up, watching him with a frightened eye as he closes the door to the small room at the back of his quarters.

"W-why did you—"

"So that no one can overhear our conversation," Sylvan interrupts, both surly and impatient. "Whoever you are, you're going to tell me everything. To start, where is the real Alena?"

"She's dead," I say without flinching.

He frowns, tilting his head to the side as if he misheard me.

"Dead?"

"She committed suicide when Oceanar fell into your hands. She didn't want to be captured by… you. She preferred to die rather than be the slave and wife of her enemy. She plunged a dagger into her heart during the siege. The High-Glaces hastened to throw her body into the ocean to conceal her death, and… and I replaced her. It's not the first time," I add, improvising as I go.

Starting from the truth to make my lies more credible is a delicate task. I must be careful not to get tangled up and pay close attention to the details.

"What do you mean, not the first time?" Sylvan asks, his expression dark, eyes narrowed. "Are you her double?"

"I'm her twin sister."

At these words, my husband straightens his back and squares his shoulders. A silence heavy as lead stretches between us. I seize the opportunity to delve deeper into my thoughts, formulating the next part of my story while trying to anticipate his objections.

"Alena Kan-Glace has no sister. No brother. She's an only child," he says through gritted teeth.

"That's what my family and the High-Glaces managed to make everyone believe. Yet here I am, Sylvan. Alena was born one minute before me, but we both came from the same womb. I have lived in my sister's shadow since our birth. I was her hidden face, as she used to point out to me."

"You're telling me that your family and the High-Glaces kept your existence a secret all these years?"

I nod, praying with all my being that my plan works.

Muttering in the Fuegis language, he begins pacing the bathroom, watching me with a feverish eye as if he has an urgent need to move in order to think. He resembles a leopard in a cage, disturbed by its captivity. *Turnabout is fair play…*

"A twin… A twin. A twin!" he hisses, clenching his fists until his knuckles crack. "Even after her death, that disgraceful woman torments me and mocks me!"

He seems to be talking to himself. I decide it's wiser not to interrupt him, given how on edge he is. Nevertheless, a frail hope has just been born deep within me, as his words confirm that his rage is not directed at me, but solely at Alena.

He suddenly pivots toward me.

"For what purpose?"

It takes me several seconds to grasp his question. Fortunately, the answer seems logical.

"First, so that no one can contest my sister's supremacy regarding the throne. Then, to ensure her protection and security. I took her place at major events at risk."

"Official where an assassination attempt on the queen could occur," Sylvan guesses, grumbling.

"Exactly."

I can't believe it. Goddess, I feel… that he's starting to believe my half-truth.

I invented this story about twin queens for a very good reason: if Sylvan learns that I don't have a drop of royal blood and that I'm just a common Powerless, I will have no value in his eyes. As for the alleged suicide of *my sister*, it gives Alena and me some much-needed time, of course.

"It doesn't make any sense, by all the gods," he growls, rubbing his temple with two fingers. "If Alena killed herself as you claim, and if the High-Glaces disposed her body in order to erase any evidence of your twinship, why did they sacrifice *you*? It would have been much easier for them to do nothing to and let me become king of the entire island of Symbiosis!"

I swallow. I hadn't seen it from that angle, but… he's not wrong. I need to find a relevant argument to counter his, and quickly.

"Because they thought… they thought that if you had known you were going to leave without Queen Alena as a hostage after invading the palace of Oceanar, you would have razed our kingdom to the ground and exterminated our people in your fit of rage."

He shakes his head with irritation.

"No one knows about your ruse except the High-Glaces?"

"That's right."

"And some of them fled during the assault, according to my men. The number of bodies didn't match my information."

"I… suppose."

"Where are they?"

"Do you think they were stupid enough to tell me where they were going, Sylvan Ren-Fuegis? Knowing you were going to take me hostage and… and potentially… make me talk about them using your strength and magic?"

"Indeed. Tell me… Before sending you to the front instead of your twin, the High-Glaces tasked you with seducing me and spying on me while trying to delay your scheduled execution for as long as possible, didn't they, *Enola*?"

My name rolling off his tongue sends a small shiver down my spine. His deduction is all too obvious… Tell him what he wants to hear, my mother's mental voice encourages me.

"Yes, Sylvan. I admit it. That was my mission."

"This means they intended to retrieve you in case you survived."

I nod. The opposite would have been incoherent.

"My uncle Leonal was right! What do you know about the plot hatched by the three kingdoms that led to my father's death?" he barks with a hint of aggression.

A plot hatched by the three kingdoms….?

The wave of astonishment that sweeps over me is entirely sincere and shows on my face.

"I… I know nothing. I swear to you."

"Your sister never confided in you?"

"No. Never. We weren't close at all, Sylvan. She despised me."

"She despised you," he repeats under his breath with a skepticism that suggests I need to elaborate on this point.

The best stories are those where the narrator uses their emotions to build the plot. They must believe it themselves to make it more credible to others and to draw them into their world.

With my eyelids half-closed, I fill my lungs with air as I recall Alena's jabs about my clothing, my low social standing, and my speech, determined to flesh out the raw truth by sprinkling in a few additional lies tailored to my version of events.

"I was useful to her, certainly, but… she didn't love me. She kept me carefully away from the Glace court. I only stayed at the palace during the brief periods when I had to be her, which was rarely. Most of the time, I lived on an isolated farm several miles from Oceanar. I had formal orders to cover my face outside the house and not to speak to anyone about my blood connection to the queen, under penalty of immediate execution. My sister sent me a little money each month to cover my basic needs. I limited my outings and social interactions. When I was a child, a High-Glace was my tutor at home. He educated me as a court lady and taught me some notions of royal etiquette so that I could pass for my sister in public. That's why Alena's death… didn't affect me much. She never considered me a sister. And neither did I."

My husband stares at me in silence as if he's discovering me in a new light. His features have softened slightly as I tell my story. He seems a little less tense and defensive than he did a few moments ago.

Have I been persuasive enough? The sad, bitter tone I employed wasn't feigned. I used Alena's real animosity toward me to coat my story. My emotion was palpable.

Sylvan's sharp gaze roams over me as he hesitates. Nothing escapes his hawk-like eye. My hair. My forehead tattoo. My eyes. My face. My Fuegis mark on my chest.

And even my curves.

A few remnants of doubt still flicker in his speculative gaze. He's trying to untangle the truth from the falsehoods. To decipher my hesitations, my silences, my unspoken words. To determine if he can trust a woman who isn't who she claimed to be. I hang on his lips and the judgment that hovers over my neck like a blade ready to fall on my flesh. My chaotic heartbeat echoes my anticipation.

His inspection is strange. Conflicted. He weighs the pros and cons. But behind the transparent veil of his inner turmoil, I instinctively feel that he sees me… differently.

It seems he's partially reevaluating his judgment of me.

He realizes I am not Queen Alena. He also realizes that I am not responsible for his father's death, as he had believed until now. So… his perception of me is changing.

At least, that's my impression.

"This explains why you don't really resemble the portrait I was shown of Alena and why you don't always act like a queen is supposed to…"

I don't answer.

Sylvan approaches like a predator. Extremely tense, I press my back against the wall of the room, crossing my arms over my chest as if to shield myself. He stands in front of me, his face lowered toward mine. He towers over me.

"How could I ever trust you, my wife? You've been lying to me from the very beginning."

His voice no longer carries hostility. He's just… cautious. And intrigued? Yes, a small flicker of curiosity lights up his eyes.

"I had no choice," I whisper.

"Survival instinct, Enola?"

"Survival instinct, Sylvan."

The Fuegis studies my features with an analytical gaze, trying to read me more deeply. I fight

the urge to look away from his piercing stare, a reflex that might betray my discomfort.

"If I'd known you weren't Alena, I wouldn't have been so harsh with you," he admits in a voice so low I think I've misheard, catching me off guard.

"No, you would have killed me without hesitation."

"You're wrong. I don't harm the innocent. Not personally, at least. The collateral damage of war is, unfortunately, inevitable."

"But Princesses Lia Ler-Aeria and Belise San-Stowne were innocent, Sylvan."

"That's exactly what I'm telling you, Enola," he says, letting his hand slide gently through my silver hair draping over my shoulders. "Read between the lines."

"I can't."

He sighs, leans toward me, and whispers in my ear, "They're still alive, Enola."

"That's… that's impossible. They were publicly beheaded," I protest, incredulous.

I catch a slight mocking smile on the young sovereign's lips.

"Who told you that?"

"My sister."

"Alena knew nothing about what was really happening in my kingdom. She didn't know me. She blindly trusted rumors. Both executions were private. And more importantly, *fake*. No one saw the princesses' bodies for the simple reason that they aren't dead. I spared them because they weren't involved in the plot to kill my father, unlike Kings Cyriel Ler-Aeria and Idric San-Stowne, whom I personally executed."

"You… you've kept them both imprisoned?" I ask, stunned by this revelation.

He nods, his hand brushing through my hair again, surprisingly gentle.

"Until peace and order are restored on Symbiosis, and I've eliminated all my enemies, one by one. Detaining my two former wives was necessary. Just like detaining you is."

Goddess of the Ocean.

I understand everything now.

This is why Sylvan started this terrible war on our island.

To avenge his father's murder.

"No, I don't trust you, my sweet Enola," my husband reaffirms in a hollow whisper. "However, I am certain that you won't repeat a word of what you've just told me to Fuegis. This is *our* secret now. You will continue to play your role as queen until further notice, acting exactly as your twin sister Alena would in your place. You'll follow all my demands to the letter to please me. And, as a sign of good faith, Enola… Tomorrow, I will summon the citizens of Astranis to the palace courtyard. I'll officially announce that your execution is canceled and that I am sparing your life." My eyes widen in disbelief. "And you will stand by my side on the terrace of the Tower of Eternal Flame as I present you to my people as the Fuegis Queen."

With that, he brushes my trembling, closed lips with a fleeting kiss, as if sealing a solemn pact between us.

Chapter Nineteen
Making an Entrance

As it has been every day since my arrival, a blazing sun crowns the dunes of the Red Desert and the crenellated towers of Astranis. to the oppressive heat that rules this place. I barely sweated last night.

"Are you nervous, Your Majesty?" Selaine asks, her small, nimble fingers braiding my light hair along the sides of my head.

I'm always nervous, my dear; I want to tell her.

Today, I will be introduced to the Fuegis people as their rightful queen. Sylvan will officially announce to his subjects that he is sparing me and keeping me by his side.

And yet, paradoxically, I don't have a single drop of royal blood in my veins, nor the slightest trace of elemental magic within me.

Even though Sylvan decided to spare me, I can't really call him an ally. He wants to use me, just as Queen Alena and the High-Glaces did before him. He hasn't even hidden it. By revealing my secret, I've tangled myself even deeper into this web. As for the story about my twin sister… I pray to the Ocean Goddess that he keeps believing it wholeheartedly.

"Before her coronation, while I helped her get ready, Queen Lia asked me to hum a song from my homeland to soothe her anxiety. Would you like me to sing for you too, Your Grace?" Selaine offers.

I look up at my young servant. So much kindness. So much innocence.

"I simply said that the man and the king are two very different beings," she told me about Sylvan after my forced marriage.

Does she know that Lia and Belise are alive?

Who else in the palace knows?

Where are they imprisoned?

To be honest, I feel like I dreamt my conversation with my husband last night. I find it hard to believe he didn't lie to me about the fate of the two former queens. I'm so used to lying myself that I can't tell truth from falsehood where Sylvan is concerned. However, his hatred toward Alena Kan-Glace wasn't faked. He holds her as responsible or his father's assassination as he does Cyriel Ler-Aeria and Idric San-Stowne. Or rather, he *did*, since he now believes her dead. But did he truly spare Lia and Belise? Or is he just trying to manipulate me too, shaping me into the obedient, devoted wife he hopes to mold to his liking? Nothing is certain.

After all, he doesn't fully trust me. If he did, he would've freed me from this cursed bewitched slave necklace still squeezing my neck.

I don't know what to do right now. I'm caught between several fires—more like between fire and ice. My heart longs to return to my homeland, to reunite with my family. If I followed it, I'd be making a plan to escape Astranis at the first opportunity. Yet my mind warns me against it. The risks are too great. It would inevitably backfire on us. Alena would make us pay dearly for it… sooner or later. Her influence and grudge are well-known. Or it could be Sylvan who retaliates. Because now, I've become an unwilling double agent.

I may be alive, but I'm still a captive in more ways than one. Prisoner of my secrets, my feelings, my duties, my desires, and my fears.

I need to wait a little longer. To watch all the key players carefully, to uncover their weaknesses. To understand the stakes, all the ins and outs.

Then, once I have the clarity I need, I will make the right decision at the right time.

"With pleasure, Selaine. Please, sing."

As she continued to braid my hair, the young Fuegis girl began to hum softly and clearly.

"The blood of wars is absorbed by the red sand,
The red sand is covered by the darkness of the night.
The darkness of night bows before the red sun,
The red sun will turn to gold on the day of prophecy.
The prophecy announces the coming of the Rose of the Elements,
The Rose of the Elements will whisper her love to the f—"

Selaine abruptly stops singing when the door to my quarters opens, revealing Sylvan and Daegan. The sovereign's eyes lock on mine.

"Leave us," the king orders to my servant, never breaking eyes contact with me.

The girl bows her head in his direction and quickly leaves with her father.

Once the door closes behind them, I size up my majestic husband from head to toe. He's dressed in a ceremonial outfit, and of course, wearing his golden crown, with its central ruby and amber stones encasing scorpions. A black velvet doublet embroidered with golden arabesques highlights his broad, muscular frame. No cape today; but his sword hangs at his hip. His gloved hand casually rests on its hilt, slightly leaning on it. I noticed that he often adopts this stance when he's armed with *Nesayan*. It must mean he's always on guard.

As for me, I'm wearing a red satin gown adorned with delicate golden flowers. It's so tight, I wouldn't be able to run even if I tried. Another typical Fuegis courtesan's dress! And one my husband doesn't seem to mind, judging by the intensity of his gaze tracing my curves…

"You are breathtakingly beautiful, Enola," he murmurs.

I shiver at hearing my real name on his lips.

"Spare me the remarks that might make me roll my eyes, Sylvan. This dress is so tight, the fabric wouldn't survive a deep breath."

A cynical smile spreads across Sylvan's face. Half-lidded, he steps closer and lightly brushes my bare shoulder with a gloved finger.

"Well, perhaps I should tear it off myself to prevent such a public scandal, my queen."

A fiery tingle flutters in my lower belly at his suggestive comment. I lower my head, so he won't notice the traitorous blush creeping up my cheeks.

"Wasn't it enough to parade me around like a trophy on the day I arrived, humiliating me by forcing me to stand naked in front of all the people of Astranis, Sylvan?" I retort bitterly.

My husband gently takes my chin, lifting my head and tilting it back so his gaze can sink deep into mine. His expression grows more serious.

"I didn't do it to humiliate you. I was simply following an ancient Fuegis tradition," he says, brushing the line of my jaw with his leather-clad thumb, which only intensifies my unease.

"What tradition?"

"Before entering my city, you had to present yourself naked, humble, and vulnerable before my people. Authentic. Honest. The symbolism is clear: you had nothing to hide from your future subjects. You were yourself, pure, without artifice, in tune with your elemental nature. Before marrying my father and being crowned queen, my mother went through the same rite. It's a centuries-old ritual that precedes all royal ceremonies in the Fuegis Kingdom."

"You should have explained that to me before throwing me into such a situation!" I protest, stunned.

His gloved hand rest on my cheek as he leans in and whispers in my ear, "I took you for Alena, remember? I had no need to explain myself to my worst enemy, the one behind my father's murder."

A war slave. A woman he planned to execute the day after their wedding.

"You too?" I murmur, not daring to make any move.

"What do you mean, Enola?" he whispers, his warm mouth hovering just above my neck, as if he's struggling to resist temptation.

"You too… did you have to…" I take shallow breaths; his scent is intoxicating. "…undress before your coronation?"

Sylvan pulls back his head, his predatory eyes shifting to my parted lips. I sense his hesitation, as if he's considering kissing me. If he did… Goddess, I don't think I'd stop him. I might as well admit it, I want it too.

But my suzerain husband… does nothing.

His gaze, clouded with desire, returns to mine. Slowly, his fingers release my face, and my skin suddenly feels cold, as though deprived of a crucial source of warmth.

"Yes, on the day of my coronation, I was naked before entering the temple of the God of Fire."

He turns and retrieves my gold diadem, inlaid with rubies and garnets, which Selaine had brought earlier. The regal object sits on a cushion atop a dresser.

"I walked through the palace gardens like that, in front of all the members of the Fuegis court," he continues as he returns to me. "I didn't dress until I had passed through the temple gates. There's nothing shocking or surprising about this for us. The Fuegis aren't as prudish or modest as the Glaces. And we don't question our traditions and customs every month, unlike the Aeria Clan, who change their rites on a whim, depending on the fickle moods of the High-Aerias," he adds, placing the diadem gently on my forehead, then stepping back to admire me with an appreciative look. "You have the bearing and grace of a queen, Enola. Even if you weren't raised as one, you are far more deserving of this diadem than your sister. Now, follow me, my beautiful wife. Our people await," he finishes, extending his hand to me.

I slip my fingers into his and rise from the chaise, fighting against the gnawing anxiety that threatens to unravel me completely.

Like an actress who stayed behind the scenes until now, I am about to step onto the stage…

And to play my part before thousands of spectators.

Chapter Twenty
An Unexpected Proof of Trust

Everyone in Symbiosis knows the legend of the Tower of Eternal Flame. The flames are said to have been ignited by the God of Fire himself the day after the construction of Astranis Palace was completed. The first Fuegis king, Sylvan's ancestor, was said to have witnessed this event. In the form of an old man with a silver beard, the god placed his golden staff into the vast brazier at the top of the tower, sparking the Eternal Flame.

It's said that no mortal can extinguish these flames… not even torrential rain or a powerful wind. There is also a belief that only two mortals can pass through the Eternal Flame without being burned—the rightful ruler of the Fuegis Kingdom and the Rose of the Elements. Long ago, a pretender to the throne ventured into the divine flames, convinced it was a myth and that *all* Fuegis were naturally immune to fire. The man was reduced to ashes within seconds, consumed by his arrogance. Since his spectacular death, no Fuegis has dared to repeat his mistake.

My heart pounds in my chest as I gently pull back the heavy velvet curtain separating the terrace from the circular room where Sylvan has brought me, to get a glimpse of the palace courtyard below the Tower of Eternal Flame. A wave of dizziness washes over me at the sight of the human sea gathered under the sun.

Thousands of Fuegis citizens await our appearance.

I let the curtain fall back, taking a deep breath.

"Do I… have to say something?" I ask, nervous, without turning to face my husband, who stands a few steps behind me.

"If you want to."

"No, I don't want to."

What could I possibly say to all these strangers?

"Then I'll speak," Sylvan reassures me, his tone indifferent. "You'll stay by my side during my speech. Don't lower your head. Stand tall. Don't fidget, don't smile, don't flinch. Keep your hand in mine. We must show our people we are united."

"A perfect illusion."

"Illusions rule Symbiosis, my wife. You'd better get used to maintaining them."

"Like you do."

"Yes. Like me."

At that moment, the door to the room swings open suddenly. Sylvan and I turn to see Leonal. The High-Fuegis looks furious.

"What madness is this, my nephew?" he exclaims aggressively. "Why didn't you consult me before summoning your subjects?"

"Because I am the king," my husband snaps, with such authority that his uncle freezes in the middle of the room as if struck by lightning.

Leonal's expression changes instantly. His anger vanishes, his face relaxing as he regains the cool composure of a seasoned politician. Only his dark eyes betray him, still burning with fury and confusion. He bows his head slightly to Sylvan, apologizing for his disrespect.

Illusions truly reign on Symbiosis, indeed… especially within this palace.

"May I speak with you privately, Your Majesty?" Leonal asks, his voice calmer, though still tinged with tension.

"No. My decision is final, uncle. I won't change my mind," Sylvan declares firmly, removing his gloves and tossing them onto a nearby console.

Leonal shoots me a cold, reproachful look. I meet his gaze without flinching. If I aim to *maintain the illusions* as well, I cannot allow this man—or any other, for that matter—to intimidate me.

"As you so kindly reminded me during my walk yesterday, my husband always makes the right decisions in the end, High-Fuegis," I add with a biting sharpness though my tone remains artificially sweet. "Even with his youth, lack of objectivity, and… his impulses as a man."

The counselor stiffens at my words. Out of the corner of my eye, I see Sylvan looking at me, his brow furrowed in confusion. I doubt his uncle has mentioned our little conversation in the palace gardens while Sylvan was busy training with his soldiers. I don't forget that Leonal's words were wrapped in with implicit threats against me. He insulted me by comparing me to an object… and a whore.

So, if the chance to sow discord between Sylvan and Leonal presents itself, I won't hesitate to take it.

That way, the bald-headed desert jackal will better understand that I am not the *predictably pathetic* woman he believes I am. And most importantly, that I am far from stupid.

"You've undoubtedly misinterpreted my words," Leonal defends, shoulders tense, his gaze lingering on my crown with open disdain.

"And you've undoubtedly forgotten to add Your Majesty," I reply sharply.

The High-Fuegis shoots a nervous glance at his nephew, clearly hoping for his support. But Sylvan remains silent and stoic, assessing the situation.

"You twisted my words, Your Majesty," the advisor insists coldly.

I allow a mocking smile to spread across my face.

"I don't believe I twisted or misunderstood your words, Leonal. Quite the contrary. I was listening very closely."

"Your Majesty," Leonal says evasively, his tone measured as he turns to Sylvan, trying to reason with him, "I truly believe that a decision of this magnitude should be presented to the Council of High-Fuegis for approval. Acting behind their backs will only earn you their disapproval. We are here to help you govern this kingdom in the best possible way. Your father often said that we formed a united body, meant to unite our people, my nephew," he reminds him, his voice dripping with false affection, playing on familial sentiment.

Sylvan blinks twice, doubt creeping into his expression.

A weight settles in my stomach.

Goddess of the Ocean, Leonal is undoubtedly a masterful politician. His influence over his nephew is significant. If I want to counter it, I must intervene carefully and choose my words wisely.

I too, can play on the emotional aspect.

"But precisely, Leonal," I murmur, stepping closer to Sylvan and gently resting my hand on his bicep. "What greater symbol of unity could there be than a king who chooses to spare his enemy and make her his queen? It shows the mercy, clemency, and moral strength he possesses. The ability to forgive is a rare virtue. The Fuegis people need hope, Leonal. They need to believe in their sovereign. Your nephew understands this well. He made this thoughtful decision with the goal of strengthening the unity of his kingdom."

Both my husband and his uncle stare at me. Leonal grits his teeth in frustration. To my surprise, Sylvan covers my fingers with his own. Our eyes meet. I see surprise and admiration in his gaze. It reassures me that I chose the right words and behaved as… a true queen. The weight in my stomach lightens slightly.

"I agree with my wife, uncle. There's no need for further debate," my husband declares, his determined green eyes now fixed on Leonal.

"As Your Majesty wishes… But there may be consequences. I hope we will be able to handle them," the High-Fuegis whispers, watching us both with bitter resentment.

"Don't worry, we'll handle them," I assure him, lifting my chin proudly. "You may take your leave."

A shadow of hatred darkens Leonal's eyes before he exits.

It seems I'll need to keep an even closer watch on my back from now on.

"His Majesty King Sylvan Ren-Fuegis and Her Majesty Queen Alena Ren-Fuegis!" the herald announces in a booming voice as two servants pull back the velvet curtains.

Hand in hand, my husband and I step onto the terrace of the Tower of the Eternal Flame. with solemn steps. We stand side by side before the balustrade. The scorching wind from the Red Desert makes the hem of my scarlet gown flutter around my ankles. I'm grateful to Selaine for braiding my hair, keeping it off my face, so I don't have to worry about it whipping around in the wind.

I don't know if Sylvan has prepared a speech or if plans to improvise. A few years ago, I attended a public announcement by

Alena Kan-Glace at Oceanar with my mother and brother. We sat in the third row. A servant held a parchment in front of her, and Alena read it aloud in a lifeless tone to the crowd. I don't even remember what her speech was about.

But I do remember finding our queen ridiculous that day, to the point that I had to stifle an inappropriate burst of laughter, covering it with a forced cough. My mother shot me a scandalized look. My brother smiled discreetly and pinched my waist playfully.

Goddess, I miss them.

I let my awestruck gaze wander over the crowd below us. All these Fuegis, raising their heads toward the royal platform, heighten my sense of vertigo. Men, women, and children from Astranis fix their eyes on Sylvan and me. More than half the city must be here. Hundreds of armored guards are stationed around the crowd, forming a massive security perimeter. As soon as we stepped onto the terrace, all the murmurs I heard behind the curtains ceased. Once again, my husband's tyrannical aura commands both respect and fear.

However, although I still don't fully trust Sylvan, I'm starting to seriously wonder if his reputation as a bloodthirsty, merciless tyrant is truly deserved.

Instinctively, I squeeze his burning hand in mine. In response, he grips my cool hand more tightly.

He clears his throat slightly and begins speaking in a strong, clear, and composed voice to his people. I hold my breath, waiting for the crowd's reactions.

"Citizens of Astranis! I've gathered you here today at the foot of the Tower of Eternal Flame to share important news that marks a new era for our kingdom. As you know, I married Queen Alena Kan-Glace after winning the battle against our enemies from Oceanar. She entered our grand city as a war slave, naked and in chains. But today, she stands before you as a crowned Fuegis queen, dressed in our colors.

"You are also aware that I intended to have Alena executed after our marriage. The reasons for this: I believed she was responsible for the plot that led to the death of my father, your former king." I fix my wide eyes on him, stunned that he's addressing this in public, and with such bluntness. "It turns out that Alena did not personally take part in this assassination. She was manipulated by the High-Glaces, who advised her to take full responsibility for this disgraceful act. She has proven herself to me, and therefore, to all of you. She earned her place in our kingdom by humbly confessing the full truth and seeking my mercy. After careful consideration, I decided to grant her my forgiveness and spare her life." A collective gasp of surprise sweeps through the crowd. "Because Alena is no longer our enemy. She is our ally.

"And now, I will prove to you that she is as worthy of your trust as she is of mine, citizens of Astranis!" he declares with a powerful tone that reverberates in my chest.

He slowly turns to me, pulling me by the hand, guiding me to face him. We are now standing eye to eye. I blink, my throat tight with apprehension. I have no idea what he's about to do. A buzzing noise ripples through the crowd below.

Sylvan gives me a fleeting, unreadable smile before gently placing his palm on my cheek. His other hand releases mine. He leans down toward me with calculated slowness.

And kisses me on the mouth in front of thousands of people.

I'm frozen. The courtyard falls into total silence.

His free fingers rise, slipping around my neck. They slide under the thick slave necklace I wear.

I hear a faint metallic click.

And, while pressing his lips to mine with strange restraint …

Sylvan Ren-Fuegis removes the enchanted artifact —the collar that only he, in the entire world, can take off.

Shaken to my core, I exhale deeply when he pulls away, the golden necklace now in his hand.

This can't be real. It's just for show. He'll put the necklace back on me as soon as we're inside the tower.

Sylvan turns to face the crowd again. I'm not the only one in shock.

I have no elemental powers. But no one else knows that. To everyone but me, Sylvan is taking an enormous risk by freeing me from this necklace.

"Citizens of Astranis, I present to you your new queen, Alena Ren-Fuegis!" the king roars, gripping my hand and raising the necklace— the gleaming symbol of my captivity—high into the air.

Everyone watches me, waiting. They fear I might unleash my Water magic on my enemies, or even strike at Sylvan directly.

But I don't move a muscle. My insides churn painfully, and

my breath comes in short, strained gasps. My hand trembles in my husband's grip.

A few seconds later, from somewhere in the crowd, a Fuegis shouts, "LONG LIVE OUR QUEEN!"

Then another voice echoes it.

And another.

Dozens of voices pick up the chant with growing excitement. Men, women, children.

And then, like a sandstorm breaking loose, a thunderous wave of cheers erupts in the courtyard, shaking the ground beneath our feet.

And rattling all my organs.

A shiver runs through my entire body as I exchange an incredulous look with Sylvan. He gives me a small, satisfied smile—relieved, if I'm not mistaken—as he lowers his arm. What he had hoped for has come to pass. His bold move has paid off.

I glance out at the thousands of people chanting their approval… for me.

Even though the collar is no longer around my neck, I can't say I'm truly free.

But at this moment, that doesn't matter.

Because it seems that, thanks to Sylvan's speech and act of trust, the Fuegis people have accepted me today as their rightful queen.

CHAPTER TWENTY-ONE
IMMERSION IN THE FUEGIS COURT

I've spent the entire day mentally preparing myself for the ordeal of attending my first banquet at the Fuegis court, set for tonight. After our public appearance, Sylvan sent Daegan to escort me back to my chambers, as he had several private meetings with dignitaries. He didn't return for me until the evening, just as the sun was setting. After giving me a few instructions on Fuegis etiquette, my husband took my hand and led me to the reception hall on the ground floor of the Tower of Eternal Flame, where we were to dine with the members of the court.

My initial encounters with the courtiers were somewhat disorienting. Sylvan introduced me to each High-Fuegis. I couldn't remember half of their names. Some of the older men offered me obsequious smiles and asked ridiculous questions like, *are you adjusting to the heat of Astranis, Your Majesty?* or *What do you think of our kingdom, Your Grace?* I answered vaguely, unable to return their smiles. I was on guard, though I tried my best to hide it.

To my dismay, at the table, I was seated between Sylvan and Nadya. While my husband recounted his latest desert hunting trip to Leonal, seated to his right, I did my best to ignore the inquisitive stares from Nadya, who sipped her wine and silently scrutinized me as if trying to dissect every detail of my appearance to uncover the truth.

Annoyed by her relentless attention, I finally locked eyes with her.

"If you'd like a portrait of me to hang in your bedroom, Lady Nadya, I can summon a painter for you tomorrow," I say.

"That's a splendid idea, Your Majesty," she replies with a sly smile. "But that portrait would be more fitting in my latrines."

The wretch whispered it low enough so no one else could hear, of course.

Looking down in irritation at her dress, I waited until she took another sip of her wine before replying, "Your dress is beautiful, Lady Nadya. Is it silk? Such a soft and well-chosen fabric. If you don't mind, I'd love to borrow it to wipe my ass after a trip to my own latrines."

Just as I hoped, she choked on her wine and started coughing. Several Fuegis courtiers turned toward her, perplexed. I greeted them with a nod and a mocking smile. Nadya had to excuse herself to the hallway to avoid further embarrassing herself in public with her fit of coughing. Under the table, I take the opportunity during her absence to discreetly spill a few drops of red wine onto her chair. I'm aware of how childish and petty my act was, but it gave me a small sense of satisfaction that I badly needed in this situation. If Nadya accuses me of wetting her chair when she returns, I'll simply claim clumsiness.

"I saw you, petty Glace," a deep voice whispered in my ear.

I turn my head toward Sylvan, swallowing nervously. However, I don't find a look of disapproval. In fact, his eyes are sparkling with amusement and a hint of complicity.

"Will you keep my secret, Your Majesty?" I ask in an ambiguous whisper, my gaze locked into his.

"I'll be as silent as the grave, my dear wife," he promises, placing his warm palm on the lower part of my thigh, under the table.

He resumes his conversation with his uncle as if nothing had happened, but his hand remains where it is. In fact, it makes itself more comfortable. Sylvan starts drawing lazy circles above my knee with his fingertips. It doesn't take much for my body to respond to the intimacy of his touch. A rapid, strong pulse throbs between my legs in rhythm with my heartbeat. My face heats up. My cheeks must be red, but the courtiers will likely think it's from too much wine, even though I haven't had any yet. I easily recognize the signs of desire he stirs in me now… and I don't quite know what to make of it. It would be so much simpler if the Fuegis sovereign, left me indifferent, but… that's not the case. My body is fixated on his. Every time he touches me, my thoughts become muddled.

"Tell us about the Glace Court, Your Majesty," says the young wife of a High-Fuegis seated nearby asks me. Keen eyes lock onto me, eager to hear what I'll say. "I'm dying of curiosity. I've heard the children of the High-Glaces play a game called *Neigelune*. What's it like?"

Sylvan's hand tightens on my thigh in a warning. Clearly, my husband can follow two conversations at once, which is impressive given the noise in the hall. I place my hand over his under the table and tap the back of it, signaling that I can handle the question.

"This is an outdoor game, Lady Basla." Goddess be praised, I remembered her name. "Our servants use their elemental magic to create six small columns of ice. They place the frozen pillars about ten feet away from the children and hand them six snowballs each. One by one, the players throw their snowballs at the translucent columns. Without using their powers, of course. The one who knocks down the most pillars with the fewest snowballs wins the game."

"Oh, that sounds like a wonderful game!" she exclaims innocently. "I'd love to see a demonstration of *Neigelune* here, my queen. Could you show us how it's played after dinner?"

I freeze, my breath caught at her suggestion and what it implies. A cold ball of anxiety settles in my stomach like steel. I'm no longer wearing the collar, and I have no idea how I'll escape this request! Should I claim fatigue to avoid using my *powers*? Or—

"Lady Basla, I'm sorry to temper your childlike enthusiasm, but I remind you that the climate of our kingdom is not suited for such a demonstration," Sylvan says harshly. "With the heat in these parts, the ice and snow would melt in seconds."

"You're right, Your Majesty," the young courtier concedes, slightly disappointed.

I swallow a sigh of relief, but my husband, whose jaw is now tense, seems suddenly preoccupied. His intervention came at just the right time. I wonder if he felt my leg stiffen under his hand and my fingers tremble on his when Lady Basla cornered me, and if that's why he deemed it necessary to pull me out of the situation. He must not understand why I panicked like that. Goddess, I hope he doesn't question me about my elemental magic! I'm not sure I'd be able to fool him on that.

Especially if he were to demand a private demonstration of my powers…

Moreover, I notice Leonal watching us both closely. Clearly, he didn't miss a single moment of the scene.

But right now, it's not the Fuegis advisor who's the source of my concern. It's my husband, who has suddenly withdrawn into himself like a clam.

I gently slide my palm along his veiny hand and firm arm over the sleeve of his doublet, silently praying that my touch might ease his tension and soften his mood. Sylvan doesn't look at me, but his muscles tense under my fingers. Beneath the table, his large hand grips my thigh tighter, pressing it painfully.

With my fingers wrapped around his wrist, I pull his arm slightly toward me, encouraging him to move his palm across my leg. He resists for a brief moment… then gives in to my unspoken invitation. Guided by mine, his hand travels up the curve of my thigh, veering toward the inside. This change in position sends a shiver of both pleasure and frustration through me. His fingers, now tracing mysterious patterns on the red satin, are dangerously close to my burning center. If my dress weren't so fitted, he would easily reach it.

It reminds me of our first passionate kiss and the gentle way he began to slide the tip of his finger into my core… before suddenly pulling back when he realized I hadn't lied about my virginity. I wish he would touch me again as he did then. I want him to push his finger deep inside me so I can feel it fully. His finger and perhaps… more.

Goddess, I'm losing my mind. And I haven't even had any wine yet.

Nonetheless, I place my hand on his thigh in return. Without hesitation. My gaze instinctively drops to his trousers. A noticeable bulge distorts them.

We exchange a glance. His eyes are so fiery that my whole body ignites. My inner thighs, my stomach, my breasts, my face. If we were alone in this room, I'm certain he would pounce on me like a beast and lay me down on the table. In his eyes, I see every erotic thought crossing his mind… and they're nothing like the romantic sensibility in my gentle tale about King Vidal and his mistress Enola. The thoughts occupying my husband's mind are raw, commanding, primal, wild. But they don't scare me. On the contrary, I welcome them with a strange pride, surprised to find that I can have such an effect on such a powerful man. There's something intoxicating and satisfying about being the object of King Sylvan Ren-Fuegis's fierce desire. It proves that, in some way, I hold a form of power over him. I almost want to provoke him, to push him to the edge, to make him lose control. I want him to burn for me like a living torch.

Do I dare touch the bulge that's pulling my hand toward it like a magnet?

With deliberate slowness, I stroke his long thigh up and down. His leg quivers under my palm. Sylvan's breathing has quickened, and the thin scar on his temple is now creased. I imagine the rough texture of his scar under my tongue. As my fingers inch ever closer to their destination, I let myself imagine his commanding tongue on my skin, my curves, between my thighs—

"How do you like the snake, Your Majesty?" a voice hisses from my left.

I immediately pull my hand away from Sylvan's thigh. He leaves his in place.

Nadya has returned to the table, though she's still standing. A servant is wiping down her chair with a cloth. My husband's stepmother has noticed the spilled wine—and likely more than that. A cold fury burns in her eyes. Whether it's jealousy or not, it certainly seems like it.

"The snake?" I repeat, not understanding.

She nods toward my plate before sitting down, dismissing the servant curtly.

"Is it cooked enough for you?"

I glance down at the meat swimming in sauce on my plate. So, it's snake.

Perhaps Nadya is hoping I'll refuse to eat it, repulsed by the exotic dish.

There's no way that's happening.

Just as I'm about to take a bite, Sylvan catches my wrist. I give him a puzzled look. He raises a hand and gestures to someone behind us. A tousled-haired young man steps forward between our seats.

"Alena, this is Jall, our official taster," my husband introduces in a detached tone.

Jall gives me a polite smile and bows.

"He'll taste every drink and every dish before we do," Sylvan explains. "He already does this in the kitchen under my supervision before any meal is sent to your chambers."

My eyebrows rise at this revelation, though I hold back the questions bubbling up inside me.

Jall dips a wooden spoon into my plate, scooping up a piece of the snake drenched in sauce, and brings it to his mouth. He chews slowly, a look of concentration on his face, then swallows. A few seconds later, he repeats the process with Sylvan's plate. He also takes a small sip of wine from both our glasses before nodding and stepping back. I watch as he leans against the wall behind us, stifling a yawn.

Despite my nerves, I start eating. After chewing and swallowing my first bite, I turn a cynical, challenging gaze toward Nadya.

"I find the snake delicious."

CHAPTER TWENTY-TWO

INTIMACY

"Congratulations. You've survived your first day at the Fuegis court," Sylvan says with irony, closing the door to my quarters.

After the banquet, he insisted on escorting me himself. Two guards are stationed outside in the hallway, as always.

decide to be completely honest with him, even if it might upset him.

"I don't know how you tolerate all of that," I murmur, rubbing my bare arms in the dim light.

"I've been immersed in court intrigue since childhood. I suppose that gives me the right to be jaded," he says, lighting all the candles in my room with a lazy circular gesture of his hand.

What a useful power, I think, glancing at a four-branched golden candelabra. It would have taken me at least fifteen minutes to light everything by myself.

I've always envied other Glaces, mesmerized by the incredible things they could do with their elemental magic. When I was little, my brother Elanos would create life-sized ice statues of animals to amaze me. I waited for years for my powers to awaken. Alas, it never happened. I had to accept my abnormality. Everyone in my village could control water. I, on the other hand, had to be careful not to reveal my secret, lest I be declared a Renegade, separated from my family by the authorities, and sent to the Forest of Exile.

"You don't really seem to belong among them, Sylvan."

"Because I'm a warrior at heart. I belong on the battlefield. My weapons are fire and steel. The courtiers' weapons are lies and flattery. That applies to the other three courts as well."

He's probably right. From what I've seen, the Glace Court is also full of vultures circling for scraps of royal power.

"Do you trust them?"

My husband gives me a sidelong glance as he unbuckles his sword belt and sets his blade on the table. Then he removes his crown.

"Some are worthy of my trust. Not all," he replies evasively.

"Hence the need for a taster."

"My father was poisoned, Enola. I have no intention of following his example."

I flinch at his revelation.

"Poisoned?"

He simply nods stiffly. I wait, hoping he'll elaborate, but he doesn't. He's clearly not inclined to share more about his father's murder.

"You handled yourself well today, for a novice queen," he finally says, closing the distance between us. "You found the right balance to be believable. Keep doing it."

I glance up at him absently.

Just two days ago, being this close to him would have filled me with anxiety. Yet now, I feel calm. It seems I no longer fear my husband the way I did before last night. I'm not sure if that's a good thing or not. I still know that Sylvan is a wolf and I'm just a lamb caught in his paws. But now, I also know deep down… he won't bite.

Am I worthy of his trust as well? And is he worthy of mine? Either way, our relationship has changed in unexpected ways in a short time, and he hasn't put the slave necklace back on me after presenting me to his people this morning. Maybe he sees me as far less dangerous than Alena, and thus… almost harmless?

"Why did you panic earlier when Lady Basla mentioned the Glaces children's game, Enola?"

That's the question I was dreading. Fortunately, I prepared my answer during dinner.

"I'm not as skilled with my powers as my twin was when she was alive, Sylvan," I sigh. "I don't have a fraction of her strength. If I had to demonstrate my elemental Water magic in front of your court, I might not have been able to create ice columns and snowballs on the first try, especially with the anxiety clouding my mind. My clumsiness could have given me away."

"That's not surprising," he replies, nodding as if my explanation make sense. "No one taught you how to control your powers, unlike her. But you share blood with Alena Kan-Glace. You could be much more powerful with the right training." *How wrong he is!* "I can't be your teacher, of course. I have no affinity with Water magic."

"I'm not interested in developing my powers anyway. Power tends to corrupt weak souls."

My bitter comment pulls a skeptical smile from the young king.

"Is that how you see yourself, my wife? A weak soul?"

I purse my lips and shrug one shoulder.

"That's not how I see you. You're the strongest woman I've ever met, in any Clan."

I can't meet his gaze. I feel unworthy of his compliment. Sylvan doesn't know the real Enola. He only knows the persona I've created to survive, a fragile, unstable mix of lies and truths.

"Enola," my husband continues with a blend of gentleness and firmness, misinterpreting my downcast eyes. "When I was a child, every time I failed to summon flames, my father would reassure me, telling me that elemental powers don't define a person's strength. It's the strength of the soul within that matters. And you have plenty of that."

"Your father was a wise man."

A shadow crosses his face.

"He was, yes. A better man than me, without question," he murmurs, sadness flooding his voice like an icy stream into my heart.

I can sense the depth of the love he had for his father. A love so strong that his father's brutal death changed him, turning him into a bloodthirsty king willing to start a war for vengeance. I'm certain now: my husband wasn't always this way. Sometimes, like now, I catch a glimpse of the other Sylvan—a once-idealistic prince with moral principles, likely shaped by the revered model of his father.

It seems that, like me, Sylvan Ren-Fuegis wear two faces.

I raise a hand and trace his scar at the temple with my fingertips, following it from one end to the other. He closes his eyes. Whether from pain or pleasure, I can't tell. Perhaps both.

"Tomorrow, I have to travel to the northeast of the Red Desert to appoint a new village leader," Sylvan announces in a husky voice, slowly reopening his eyes. "I'll be presiding over a ritual ceremony. You'll accompany me."

He reaches for the branches of my diadem and gently removes it from my head before stepping away.

A thought crosses my mind as I watch him place my diadem next to his crown on the table. Without these symbols, we are no longer king and queen. We're just a man and a woman, almost like any other.

"Why do I have to come with you?" I ask.

"First, because you're my queen. And second…," he hesitates briefly as he walks back toward me. "Because I don't want to leave you here while I'm gone."

"Are you I might run away?" I tease, a note of provocation in my voice.

His expression darkens instantly.

"No, Enola, it's not that. As I mentioned earlier, not all of the Fuegis courtiers are worthy of my trust."

A shiver runs down my spine. In other words, he believes I'm not safe within the walls of his own palace when he's not around. How comforting.

Sensing my unease, Sylvan moves closer, placing his hands on the small of my waist. As usual, his touch burns through the satin of my gown.

"You're under my protection now. I give you my word that I won't let anyone harm you," he vows, locking his intense gaze with mine.

"Not even you?" I stammer uncertainly.

The amused smile that crosses his face softens the severity of his features.

"I won't hurt you, my sweet Enola…" His fingers drift lower, drawing circles on my hips. "In fact, I'll only make you feel good."

Before I can even grasp the meaning of his words, his mouth is on mine in a passionate kiss. A tremor runs through me from head to toe as his tongue slips between my lips and caresses mine. His hands tighten around my hips, pulling me firmly against his body. I cling desperately to the fabric of his doublet, my mind incapable of coherent thought. His arousal presses insistently against my stomach. His hands slide behind me, grabbing my backside through my dress. I pull on his collar, accidentally biting his tongue. But he doesn't stop the kiss. In a swift motion, he dips me in his arm and lifts me off the ground while still kissing me.

He carries me to the bed.

It's only when I feel the mattress beneath my back and Sylvan's body pressing down on mine that I begin to fully realize what's happening… My hands grasp his stubbled cheeks, forcing him to pull his mouth away from mine. I take a deep breath, the air burning my throat like I'm inhaling sulfur.

"Sylvan, I… I don't…"

I don't know what to say to him, honestly. Because I don't know what I want. I think my body has been ready to take that step since our first kiss.

But my mind? Not yet.

Still, in the conflicted look in my eyes, my husband seems to decipher the words I can't manage to form.

"I'm not going to take your virginity tonight, Enola," he assures gently brushing the sensitive skin of my neck with the pad of his thumb. "We'll take things step by step. But let me give your body the release its craving. I've spent hours just thinking about hearing you."

"Hearing me? You mean hearing… the alternative ending to my story?"

"No. No stories tonight. I want to hear your *moans*, my queen." he clarifies in a deep growl, nestling his face into my neck, letting his eager lips trail over my skin

I arch against him, my breathing erratic. I shouldn't have had so much wine at dinner; my thoughts are too muddled. Each of Sylvan's demanding kisses on my throat ignites me, sweeping me away like a sandstorm battering a lonely dune. My hands tangle in his dark hair, discovering its silky texture. His hands travel up my body, cupping my breasts, their hardened peaks straining against the red satin of my gown. He kneads the tender globes slowly, biting gently at the base of my neck, where it meets my shoulder. Despite the pleasure these new sensations bring, something holds me back from letting out a sound.

Is it modesty? Decency? Fear? Distrust? Inexperience?

But I believe Sylvan Ren-Fuegis has the power to break down that mental barrier.

As if sensing my hesitation, he stops kissing me. With my breasts still trapped in his hands, he pushes up on his elbows above me, locking his fevered—but questioning—gaze with mine.

He won't go any further unless I say yes.

With my heart pounding out of my chest, I nod, giving him my consent.

Chapter Twenty-Three
The Intoxication of the Senses

Kneeling above me on the bed, Sylvan quietly unties the ribbons that crisscross the front of my gown. I remain still, barely daring to breathe as he loosens the ties with surprising skill. I've heard that members of the royal families of Symbiosis never undress themselves, always entrusting the task to their servants. Apparently, this is not the case with my husband. Or, another equally plausible explanation, he's used to undressing women.

Once the laces are undone, he tugs simultaneously at the two satin straps. I lift myself slightly off the mattress to assist him. Focused solely on his task, he pulls my gown down in small, steady movements along my chest, my stomach, my hips, my legs, my ankles… before tossing it to the floor at the foot of the bed. His darkened green eyes travel back up in the opposite direction, from my feet to my head. They linger especially on the thin cotton undergarment hiding my most intimate parts and my bare breasts, covered in goosebumps. I fight the instinct to cover my chest.

He's already seen me completely naked the day I arrived in Astranis with his army, but those circumstances were completely different. We were enemies then. Now, what have we become? Temporary allies by default? Actors in a false marriage?

Potential future lovers?

"Enola, stop thinking," he growls, putting his fingers on my hips to rid me of the last layer of fabric preserving my modesty. "This isn't the time for introspection."

"Every moment is right for introspection, Sylvan. Especially this one," I weakly protest as my undergarment joins my gown on the floor.

"You always have a retort for everything."

No, not for everything, Sylvan. Not when it comes to you.

With an infuriating calmness, he continues to visually explore my pale body lying beneath him. I'm certainly fuller than the Fuegis women he's normally with. The only clue that he's enjoying what he sees is the obvious outline of his erection straining against his trousers. It's even more unsettling to be completely naked in front of a fully clothed man hovering over me, subject to his silent examination. I feel even more vulnerable.

"Could you just… take off your doublet?" I venture to ask, my throat dry.

A soft, mocking laugh shakes my husband's chest. He shakes his head.

"Sylvan!" I scold him, blushing.

"Do it yourself, Enola."

I rise to my knees as well to face him. Gathering my courage, I carefully undo the laces of his collar. Sylvan's hands mold themselves to the curve of my shoulders and slide down my arms, providing a delicious distraction.

"I would've paid far more than ten million coins," he admits thoughtfully. "My entire fortune, if necessary."

At first, I don't understand what he means.

"What are you talking about?"

Without answering immediately, he raises his arms. I lift his doublet and pull it over his head. My hazy eyes drift over the red tattoos that adorn the bronze muscles of his chest.

"I'm talking about the fictional auction in your story, Enola. I would have given my entire fortune. Not to buy your virtue… but to have you."

I look up at him, shaken by the tenderness in his whispered words. His behavior toward me tonight is different. Maybe it's the wine. He must be a little drunk too. Could the sweet taste of the drink mixed with alcohol have softened this man's usual harshness?

"But you have me, Sylvan. I'm your wife."

With a somber expression, he lightly touches my barely healed Fuegis mark on my sternum.

"I married you by force. It wasn't your choice."

"That's true, it wasn't my choice," I whisper, placing my palm on his warm chest as he takes a deep breath. "But I chose to be in this bed with you tonight. Isn't that all that matters right now?"

His hand spreads over my left breast, over my heart. He presses his fingers hard against my skin, as if to feel every one of my erratic heartbeats.

I don't belong to him, and he knows it. Even when I was his slave, I was never entirely his. I haven't given him my heart or my soul in this marriage. Desire is one thing, love is another. But his reaction is absurd, if not irrational. Why does he care so much about my opinion? And more importantly, why would he wait for me to feel something stronger for him? Does he want total control over me, to claim mastery over every fragment of my being? Is his instinct for domination and possessiveness at its peak with me? Or is it simply the wine making him say strange things?

I can't think of another explanation. After all, Sylvan himself told me while I was recounting my *sadly conventional* romance between Vidal and Enola: *"Love has no place among kings and queens."*

But his confession disturbs me more than I care to admit…

With my nails, I trace the winding lines of the scarlet vein-like marks that streak his powerful chest, drawing a small shiver from my husband.

"Do you really count them?" I murmur, frowning in confusion. "Every time you take a life on the battlefield, do you add one to the number already in your memory?"

"Yes, Enola. Like all Fuegis warriors, that's what I do."

"It's a barbaric tradition."

"It's ours, whether you like it or not. As queen, you must accept our customs and culture as if they were your own. Every Clan has its traditions. Only the gods have the right to question them."

"But you take pride in being killers, Sylvan."

"Your Glace prejudices astonish me," he retorts with obvious exasperation, a tone that feels more like him. "You still have much to learn about your new people. We don't take pride in being killers; we honor the bravery and strength of our enemies who fall under our blades and flames. These are commemorative symbols to glorify their souls, Enola. Not macabre trophies to flatter our pride as warriors."

"You're full of prejudices too," I shoot back through gritted teeth, stung. "About the Glaces, the Renegades and—"

Grabbing my arms with authority, Sylvan suddenly forces me back down onto the bed.

"This is neither the time nor the place for such debates, my defiant wife," he growls, taking my wrist and pressing my hand between his legs, shocking me. "*This* makes the point quite clear."

I can't help it—I burst out laughing, clearly catching him off guard.

"You think *this* will shut me up?" I tease, raising an eyebrow.

My husband's green eyes blaze with a devastating fire.

"No. But *this* will," he says a second before capturing my lips with his.

Without delay, his aggressive tongue plunges into my mouth. My fingers instinctively tighten around the growing hardness in his pants. His full weight presses down on me, trapping my arm between our bodies, which are both buzzing with desire. The tips of my breasts rub against his bare chest, making my whole-body burn. I awkwardly knead the hard bulge that fills my palm, drawing another groan from him—muffled by our heated kiss. So, this is the mysterious organ that has driven men's primal instincts since the dawn of time… I want to see it from every angle, touch it along its length, and explore every detail.

Frantically, I fumble with Sylvan's belt buckle, but he suddenly pulls away from my lips and body, pushing my eager hand aside, breathless.

"I said not tonight, Enola. Don't put on the war chariot before harnessing the horses."

I glare at him, annoyed by his resistance. A smug smile spreads across his lips as he shakes his head, sizing me up.

"God of Fire, to think Feugis men say Glace women are frigid—this really shows just how foolish ethnic prejudices can be."

"Goddess of the Ocean! And for your information, Your Arrogant Majesty, those *frigid* Glace women claim that the Fuegis men don't know how to wield their swords of flesh because they're too small for their clumsy, oversized hands," I snap back coldly.

This time, it's his turn to laugh.

"You are far from frigid, and I'm certainly not clumsy… and I'll prove it to you," he declares with arrogant confidence as he leans in toward me. "I know a thousand other ways to silence you, my queen. And a thousand ways to make you moan," he adds, kissing my Fuegis mark softly.

"You're presumptuous, Sylvan," I murmur, watching him plant wet kisses on my left breast, quickening my heartbeat. "This is completely ridic—"

He cuts me off, covering my mouth with his hand while capturing my erect nipple between his lips, sucking hard.

My eyes fly open as I arch my back, breathless from this new kind of kiss that sends a jolt through every nerve in my body, like a spark igniting a whole pile of dry branches.

I think I'm starting to understand why he's so confident when it comes to women…

But as he said himself, this isn't the time for introspection.

With his hands on my trembling thighs, Sylvan slowly spreads my legs before shifting lower. I force myself not to close them as he inspects the most intimate part of my body, his face impassive, hovering just above my sex. I've never felt this vulnerable in my life. His thumb grazes through my soft curls, and his breath teases my pubic area. Every muscle in my body tightens. As I stare up at the ceiling, I wonder if I've made a mistake letting things go this far tonight. Maybe there's still time to stop and…

"Enola. Stop thinking and look at me," my husband commands in a firm tone.

Reluctantly, I obey. I lift my head and meet his gaze, uncertain.

"Don't be afraid," Sylvan advises, his voice gravelly as he caresses the inside of my thigh with the back of his hand. "Surrender to me, and it will be all the more pleasurable."

"I'm not afraid."

I'm terrified.

His rough thumb brushes a small, sensitive spot, and I jerk, exhaling sharply. I was right—the fabled *bud of pleasure* I've mentioned in my stories is indeed highly sensitive. Without breaking eye contact, Sylvan leans down and places a chaste kiss on it, making the heat there intensify. His finger roams between my legs, lingering on the edge of my entrance. I'm already wet, naturally. It makes his entry easier despite my body's tightness. His finger slides inside so gently, there's no pain at all. As I arch my back to feel more of him, Sylvan takes the opportunity to give a quick flick of his tongue between my thighs.

I can't hold back a soft moan, which earns a pleased smile against my skin.

He wanted to hear me moan. Well, now he has.

Then he licks me again, slower this time. I bite my lip to keep from crying out.

But Sylvan doesn't plan on stopping there. His finger begins to move inside me, a slow, sensual rhythm. His lips press against my pleasure point, all while his free hand travels up my body, squeezing my breasts with fervor. I feel like I'm melting under his touch, drowning in this ocean of pleasure. A muffled cry escapes my throat, followed by a sharp gasp. I place my hand on the top of his head.

"Sylvan… Sylvan, it's too much…"

Instead of easing off, my plea spurs him on, and he intensifies his erotic attention. I'm lost in a mix of desperate moans, ragged breaths, and gasps, my hips undulating beneath his mouth as he sucks my most sensitive spot with fierce determination. My fingers grip his dark hair in a trembling fist. The sensation of falling into a burning cloud consumes me, pulling me into its fiery depths.

Then something inside me shatters, an invisible wave crashing through me, igniting every nerve. I arch my back, letting out a long, unending moan that echoes in the room. I convulse beneath my husband's bearded face, as if overcome by a sudden fever. My vision blurs for a moment. I collapse back onto the bed, utterly ravaged.

I realize I've just climaxed for the first time in my life.

My own words swirl through my mind…

After their lovemaking, the other Enola, the one from my story, had asked Vidal innocently, *"Is it magic?"*

"No, my love, you simply climaxed."

"How can you call that simply? It was extraordinary!"

Goddess, I had been so close to the truth without realizing it…

Sylvan presses a kiss to the top of my thigh, closes my legs swiftly, and covers my nakedness with the silk sheet. He stands up, moving quickly to pick up his doublet, while I watch in disappointment. He doesn't seem to want to linger by my side for even a minute longer. My throat tightens as I see him hastily put on his clothes and reach for his crown.

I thought he would stay longer… and try to… to…

"What are you doing?"

"I'm going back to my quarters," he replies, his voice tense and distant.

To find another woman?

"So, I guess you won't be sleeping with me tonight," I say, unable to hide the bitterness in my tone.

I'm surprised at my own words. My conflicting emotions, reflecting his, hit me all at once. I had assumed he would force himself into my bed without asking for my consent, though deep down, I hoped he would. Still, I hadn't expected him to leave like a thief after making me climax, leaving me alone again after our… agreement.

"No. Another time."

He moves toward the door without another word.

"Don't you want to, *husband?*" I cry out, struggling to contain my anger and hurt.

Sylvan freezes at the door, his fingers gripping the handle. He turns his head slightly, but without looking at me, he mutters under his breath, "Yes, Enola. Of course I want to. That's exactly the problem. But I told you, we're taking this in steps, and I won't take your virginity tonight. If I stay one minute longer in your bed, I'll break that promise, and we'll both regret it. So, no, I can't stay with you tonight. In the state I'm in, I wouldn't be able to stop myself from taking you roughly. I might hurt you, in one way or another. That's not what you want, and it's not what I want. Good night, love."

The young king gently closes the door behind him, leaving me frozen in my bed, stunned by his words.

No, he said he could take me brutally.

But because he just called me *love*.

CHAPTER TWENTY-FOUR
THE NICKNAME OF DISHONOR

I had the most unbelievable dream last night.

I was wandering naked in the Red Desert under a scorching sun. Lost, thirsty, starving. My skin was raw, burned crimson by the unbearable heat. I kept shouting four names.

Bleuène, my mother. Elanos, my brother. Alena, my queen. Sylvan, my husband.

But none of them answered my desperate call. I was alone in the middle of nowhere. I wanted, at all costs, to return to Astranis, but I had no idea which direction to take.

Then, a supernatural wind rose across the desert. A burning wind, whispering a lament in a language I did not understand.

The voice was melodic, transcendent. The voice of a deity.

The red sun turned to gold in the azure sky.

A whirlwind of sand began to lash my raw skin. I froze at the top of a massive dune, my eyes stinging with tears as I felt a sharp pain stir between my thighs. Tiny drops of blood fell into the red sand between my legs, igniting as they touched the ground and turning into embers. It filled me with unspeakable dread.

Suddenly, the sand beneath my feet caught fire.

But I didn't feel the merciless sting of the flames licking at my ankles.

And then, I saw a figure at the base of the sandy hill.

Sylvan.

He wore his gleaming black and gold armor, along with his dragon-shaped helm. He was climbing the slope to reach me, his gloved hand stretched out toward me, calling my name. "Enola!" I was paralyzed, trapped by these flames that didn't burn my skin, by this strange pyre that caused me no pain. The only thing I could do, with a great physical effort, was to extend my hand toward him as he climbed, step by step.

He was halfway to me when the sand beneath my feet trembled violently. Several gaping chasms opened up in the Red Desert behind Sylvan.

I raised my horrified eyes to the horizon.

A massive wave of boiling blood surged into view, like a monstrous mass of molten lava.

All the elements are my enemies.

The wind. The fire. The earth. The water.

"Sylvaaaan!"

As I sank into the darkness of unspeakable terror, trembling in the grip of the flames, my husband continued to walk toward me calmly, unconcerned by the tidal wave racing toward us, blotting out the golden sun and plunging us into shadow.

"Don't be afraid, Enola. Fear is your greatest enemy," he reassured me in a deep, hollow voice from beneath his helm.

I curled up in the fire.

"I'm not afraid. I'm not afraid," I repeated in a feeble whimper.

"In your hands lies the secret of peace and the key to truth, my love. Have faith in yourself and in us. You are not *nothing*, Enola. You are my everything," he said now just a few steps away from me—just like King Vidal in my story.

At the moment our fingers were about to touch…

The wave of blood engulfed us both, and I woke up with a start in my bed, my heart pounding in my chest. The madness of that dream shook me so deeply that it took me a full ten minutes to regain my senses.

As I wiped myself after my morning ablutions, Selaine entered my chambers. As she did every morning, she brought me my breakfast. I slipped into a loose cotton tunic.

"Is everything all right, Your Majesty?" she asks, studying my face, marked by fatigue and distress.

"Yes," I reply curtly as I sat down in front of my tray. "Selaine, have you had your breakfast yet?"

After a brief hesitation, the young girl shook her head, her eyes lingering longingly on the food. She's so thin, I assumed she doesn't get much to eat.

"I'll never finish all this. Help me do justice to these Fuegis fruits and pastries," I say.

"My queen, thank you for your kindness, but I'm not allowed to—"

"Who decided you're not allowed to have breakfast with me, anyway?" I mutter irritably.

"But… the protocol, Your Majesty. Tradition," she says, as if it were obvious.

"Fuck protocol and tradition, Selaine."

My young servant burst into laughter, then quickly slapped a hand over her mouth, shocked and frightened by her own reaction.

"My dear child, you haven't committed a crime against Fuegis royalty by laughing, as far as I know. Come sit with me," I sigh, patting the back of a chair.

She bit her lip as she eyes the tray, then cautiously sit beside me, her back tense with anxiety, her hands resting on her knees. I hand her a sugar-covered pastry he had been eyeing. She takes it cautiously before bringing it to her lips. A look of pure delight crossed her face, which makes me smile warmly. I imagine this this kind of food is reserved for the Fuegis elite, and the servants rarely, if ever, got the luxury of tasting it. Yet another absurdity imposed by the upper class.

"Do you live in the palace with your father?" I ask in a soft voice.

She shakes her head after swallowing her bite.

"No, Majesty, we live in the military barracks built at the foot of Astranis's walls. Usually, we come to the palace together at dawn and return home well after dusk."

"Don't call me *Majesty* when it's just the two of us, Selaine. Back in Oceanar, all my ladies-in-waiting called me by my name in private without exception."

"Okay. I… I'll try, Maj… Alena," she corrects herself, whispering shyly.

"That's better. Is it just the two of you, you and Daegan?"

She nods weakly, her gaze distant.

"I'm an only child. I was two years old when my mother joined our ancestors, taken by the desert fever. I don't remember her."

"I'm really sorry, Selaine."

The young girl looks up at me, surprised by my condolences. She whispered a timid thank you.

"Do you have any hobbies outside of work?" I ask, trying to lift her spirits.

"At home, I take care of the cleaning, cooking, laundry, and—"

"No, Selaine. I wasn't talking about chores, I meant passions." She stares at me as if she doesn't know the meaning of the word. "Is there something you enjoy in particular? A game or an activity?"

She thinks for a moment, placing a finger on her chin. I find her endearing. She is a breath of fresh air, a genuine soul among the predators and vultures of Fuegis.

"Well, I like… singing. And dancing. And reading stories about Symbiosis" What a happy coincidence. I don't know how to read myself, but I tell them… "Your husband often lets my father borrow books from his personal library."

"Those are wonderful passions. Who taught you to read?"

"King Sylvan, Alena. Before… before his father's death. He was close to our family before grief struck him. You could even say he was friends with my father. Their bond didn't sit well with the courtiers and the High-Fuegis, though. But King Saradin didn't mind."

"My husband explained the circumstances of the poisoning," I say, hoping to gain more information. "He's still struggling to recover from the trauma." She nods sadly, confirming my words. "Were you there that day?"

"No, but my father was on duty at the banquet. He didn't want to tell me, but I eventually got him to. Even he was shocked by the violence of the scene, and he's not easily shaken. King Saradin suffered terribly before he died in your husband's arms. Vomiting torrents of blood and watching his limbs blacken and decay before his eyes for several minutes… it's a cruel end that no one deserves."

I shiver all over. My appetite vanished.

"Goddess of the Ocean! What kind of toxin could cause such horrific symptoms?"

"Didn't your husband tell you that the poison was never identified?"

How clumsy of me...

"No, Selaine, he left out that detail in his story."

"After the tragedy, His Majesty hired a team of experts, including herbalists and doctors, to perform an autopsy on his father's body. They analyzed the contents of his stomach and his blood using a combination of science and magic to find the substance responsible for his death. They found nothing. They were completely stumped. Only a prominent Stowne alchemist suggested the poison might have come from outside our lands. No known poisonous plant or venomous animal on Symbiosis causes such grotesque symptoms."

"What did the alchemist mean by that?"

"According to my father, the Stowne said it might have been a poison made from several toxic ingredients and plants, carefully combined. A blend likely crafted by a master poisoner from a foreign land."

An assassin's Guild likely has master poisoners among its ranks....

"A poison from Land of Fire, perhaps?"

"It's possible," she admits with a shrug. While I'm thinking, she peels a small banana, watching me closely. "I believe you're a good person, Alena. Since we met, I've felt that your soul is as pure as your heart is strong. Would you allow a simple servant like me to offer some humble advice to the great queen that you are?"

I smile at the unintentional irony of her words. *A great impostor, more like it.*

"Of course, Selaine. Speak your mind freely."

"Don't trust the members of the Fuegis court. Those who smile the most and show concern for your well-being are often the vilest. Don't form bonds with the High-Fuegis, especially not with the wives and concubines who rule in their shadows. But most importantly, don't provoke them. The most malevolent among them have already started spreading harmful rumors about you since yesterday, trying to discredit you. They don't like the idea that a former Glace of war is now their queen. Servants hear a lot in the corridors, and what's being said about you isn't flattering, I'm afraid."

My jaws clench. Nadya Ler-Aeria. I'm not surprised by this, but it still shakes me.

"What's the nature of those petty rumors?"

"The Fuegis women are saying that you bought your survival with your husband by submitting to all his intimate desires—no matter how violent, degrading, or humiliating. That you abandoned all dignity to become his flesh slave, and paradoxically, that you now hold him by the—" She turns red.

So, I'm officially branded as the king's whore.

"They've also given you a nickname with satirical overtones. It spread like wildfire throughout the palace… and beyond, Alena. By now, all of Astranis likely knows about this degrading label."

"What is it, Selaine?" I whisper, clenching my fists in anger under the table.

She locks her large amber eyes with mine.

"*The Courtesan Queen*, Your Majesty."

CHAPTER TWENTY-FIVE
RIDE IN THE RED DESERT

"What's her name?" I ask as I gaze at the massive horse with sleek muscles and a fiery coat, pawing the ground with her hoof.

Fifty royal guards are preparing their mounts around us with strict discipline. The journey to the village, where we'll attend the ceremony, will take about half a day. We'll sleep there tonight before heading back to Astranis around noon tomorrow.

"Her name is Jada," Daegan informs me, arms crossed over his chest. "She's His Majesty's favorite mare. She was a gift from Saradin to celebrate his son's tenth birthday. Our late king tamed her himself before giving her to your husband."

"She seems a bit nervous, doesn't she?"

"That's because she's eager to gallop through the desert like a flaming arrow," explains a voice behind me. "Good morning, Alena."

I turn to see my husband, who just joined us in front of the royal stables, dressed in a loss black tunic and pants. He gently places his hands on my shoulders and brushes my lips with a fleeting kiss that sends a shiver through me, before moving around me to stroke his mare's neck. At his touch, Jada immediately calms down and presses her head affectionately against his arm. Sylvan checks that the saddle strap is properly fastened and motions for me to come closer.

I cautiously obey, watching the mare, who's eyeing me just as warily.

"She's looking at me in a funny way," I mutter to the king as his horse snorts in displeasure. "I think she doesn't like me."

"I've got just the thing to win her over," my husband replies, placing an exotic red fruit the size of a fig in my palm. "Hold out your hand."

"She's going to bite my hand off and spit it out on the ground. I can see the murderous intent in her eyes!"

Sylvan and Daegan laugh together. I glare at both of them, irritated by their treacherous alliance.

"As fierce as she is, this beast doesn't eat Glace flesh," my bodyguard teases. "Only Stowne flesh, and only if she has nothing else to chew on."

"You should've been a court jester instead of a soldier, Daegan. You've got the talent," I grumble as he mockingly bows before me.

"She won't bite you if I'm here. Give her the treat," my husband encourages, taking my arm and raising it horizontally.

Reluctantly, I watch Jada move her head toward my hand, sniff the fruit, and devour it in one bite, drenching my fingers in sticky saliva. After chewing and swallowing my sweet offering, she thanks me with a lick on my palm, which tickles. I laugh and pat her warm muzzle. The *fierce beast* isn't so bad after all.

"There you go, you've won her over," Sylvan remarks with a broad smile before swiftly mounting his mare's back. "That wasn't so hard, was it, my wife?"

It was definitely easier than it was with you, my husband.

"And where's my mount?" I ask Daegan while wiping my horse-saliva-covered hand on my cotton cape.

I get my answer when the Fuegis King extend extends his hand to me. Apparently, I don't have a choice: I'll be riding with him. Sighing, I grasp his forearm. He lifts me off the ground effortlessly and places me in front of him on the saddle. His arm wraps around my waist, pulling my back against his chest. His jaw rests against my temple over the hood of my cape, which shields my pale skin from the harsh sun. His arms form a solid, protective cocoon around me, and honestly, I feel perfectly safe there.

His closeness, his scent, his body… I remember the overwhelming pleasure from last night when he licked between my thighs, and the pulsing source of my desire awakens instantly.

This journey is going to be challenging in more ways than one, and I'm not just talking about the scorching heat that will soon overwhelm me in the Red Desert.

✳✳✳

"Do you often remember your dreams when you wake up, Sylvan?"

"I don't dream," my husband states as Jada steps energetically through the desert sand, rocking us both on her back.

"Everyone dreams."

"Not me, my sweet. I never dream. But sometimes, I have nightmares," he confesses in a low, somber voice.

There's no need to ask him what kind of nightmares. The gruesome details Selaine revealed this morning about his father's poisoning still haunt me.

"Why do you ask, Enola?" he says with a hint of curiosity, his hand slipping through the folds of my cape.

He speaks softly. Even though his soldiers ride too far behind to hear us, he's careful. He would never call me by my true name in front of others, of course.

He begins stroking my stomach through my shirt. Now I understand why he gave me control of the reins… I thought it was a gesture of trust, but it was mainly so he could free his hands to place them on my body.

"I had a strange dream last night."

"Was I the subject?" He teases, tracing circles around my navel with his thumb.

"You weren't the subject, but you were a part of it."

"You've piqued my interest. Come on, tell me what's troubling you."

I don't know why I feel torn between wanting to share my entire dream with him and the instinctive urge to keep this new secret to myself… Maybe it's too soon? Or maybe I fear he'll dismiss it all as part of my growing madness…

So, I decide to filter my story, leaving out certain events. I tell him about the singing wind, the red sun turning gold, the earthquake, the giant wave of blood, and our hands reaching out for one another. I don't tell him, however, that I was bleeding between my thighs, that the flames held me captive without burning my legs, and I don't mention the enigmatic words he spoke in my vision.

"That probably reflects your sense of insecurity," Sylvan supposes. "The natural elements attacking you with all their majestic violence symbolize your inner fears. Air, earth, water… But wasn't there fire in your dream? You only mentioned three elements."

"No, no fire," I lie reluctantly. "This element was probably represented by the sun."

"It reminds me of something… *When the red sun becomes a golden orb,*'" he quotes thoughtfully. "Where did I read or hear those words?" He lets out a frustrated sigh, his hand frozen on my abdomen. "God of Fire, I've been devouring so many books lately that my memory is starting to fail me. I've got it on the tip of my tongue, it's so annoying. I'll remember later, I'm sure."

"You know the Aeria adage… *Don't dwell on the memories that slip away like feathers in the wind because they hold little importance.*" Then, suddenly struck by an idea, I turn my head toward him, "Sylvan, are you aware of the scandalous nickname they've given me at court?"

"Daegan told me this morning. Considering the diabolical imagination of the Astranis courtesans, I'm surprised it's so mild and conventional," he remarks with an infuriating air of indifference.

I had expected him to get angry and promise to scold the culprits. How wrong I was.

"*Mild and conventional?*" I snap coldly. "You can't be serious."

"It could have been much worse, Enola," he responds, unfazed.

I shake my head, outraged.

"Take a step back," he urges with a light tone. "I've accumulated a fair share of unflattering nicknames myself. I don't pay them any attention anymore. It's kind of ironic when you think about it. These Fuegis hyenas are calling you a depraved whore, yet you're a virgin."

His bluntness makes the hair on the back of my neck stand up.

"You're officially the most boorish man in all Symbiosis."

"You're right. As a devoted husband, I should defend your wounded honor. When we return, I'll have all the courtesans beheaded and present you their heads on silver platters. I do have a reputation as a tyrant to maintain."

"You're an idiot," I mutter, trying to suppress a smile.

"Do you know why they started that rumor about you, Enola?"

"Because I'm a former Glace slave."

"No. Even if you had been from the Fuegis court, it would've been the same. They simply can't stand that they've been replaced. More than half of those women have been eyeing your crown since I was of marriageable age"

"And they paraded through your bed, hoping to achieve that goal, I suppose," I retort dryly.

He doesn't deny my accusation. Instead, he resumes caressing my stomach, either to soothe me…

Or to torment me…

"What man in his right mind would have been foolish enough not to take advantage of such opportunities?"

"An honorable and upright man, perhaps."

"I never claimed to be made of such stuff."

Did Nadya Ler-Aeria also aspire to the throne? After all, she wasn't married to King Saradin Ren-Fuegis. She was merely his concubine. So maybe she tried to seduce the son after the father's death, which could explain her bitterness toward me and the rumors about her. But Sylvan swore he never slept with his stepmother, and… I really believe he's telling the truth.

Another question has been itching at my tongue since I woke up.

"Did you have a courtesan come to your quarters last night to relieve your tension after you left my bed, Sylvan?"

"What do you think, Enola?" He teases me with maddening nonchalance. II grip the reins tightly in my fingers, irritated by the subject of our conversation. "Since you're so keen to know, I drastically relieved my tension through the sharp pain of an ice bath."

"You're joking."

"God of Fire, if only."

A loud laugh escapes my lips. As rare as they are, his moments of humor are quite effective.

"You won't turn me into an adulterous queen, Sylvan Ren-Fuegis?" I ask in a playfully casual tone, though I dread his answer.

Paradoxically, I remain lucid. Polygamy is a common among the Fuegis. My husband's ancestors had many wives and concubines. And I haven't forgotten that unofficially, Sylvan is still married to Lia and Belise, wherever they are…

Under my cloak, his hand slides down to my hip and slips beneath my shirt. His palm rests on my bare, sweat-dampened stomach. He begins to massage it in slow, circular motions, sparking tiny butterflies deep within my heated core. My cheeks flush as his languid fingers graze the waistband of my cotton pants. My breath becomes uneven when his other hand moves along my side and closes around my stiffened breast in an even more intimate caress.

"Never, my little *Courtesan Queen*," he whispers in my ear, pinching my hardened nipple slightly beneath my shirt.

"Sylvan, you… that's enough; we're not alone," I murmur, squirming in the saddle, trying in vain to escape his sensual teasing.

"My men can't see anything, Enola. They're far behind us, and I really want to touch my wife after this little bout of jealousy that makes her even more desirable to me," he confides in a warm voice that sets me ablaze inside.

While kneading my breast, he slides his other hand into my pants and brushes against the crease of my thigh, forcing an odd sound from me—somewhere between a moan and a growl.

"Your wife has no desire to be touched on a horse in the middle of the desert, Sylvan," I counter in a husky voice, clinging to his arm.

Even if my drenched privacy betrays my words.

"You love it when I touch you here, Enola," he whispers against the curve of my cheek as he gently strokes my sensitive bud, sending a shiver through me. "Say it."

"No."

He pulls me tightly against him, pressing the top of my backside against his rock-hard erection. Goddess of the Ocean, he's impossible!

"Enola, say it to me right now, or I'll make you scream so loud that my soldiers will have no doubt about what I'm doing to you."

"Fine, you asked for it," I snap, exasperated by his indecent stubbornness.

With that, I give a hard kick to Jada's flanks and snap the reins.

The fiery mare bolts forward like lightning, galloping up the side of a dune, nearly unseating my husband. Cursing in Fuegis he's forced to pull his hand out of my pants to grab hold of my waist.

In the heart of the hostile, arid Red Desert, far from my homeland, I laugh like I haven't laughed in months.

Three hours after leaving Astranis, we stop at an oasis to hydrate both beasts and men. The place is enchanting: the spring, surrounded by palm trees, rocky outcrops, and bushes, is partially shielded from the wind and sun by a massive wall of dunes. Kneeling by the turquoise water, which reflects the sun's crimson rays, I see my face on the surface. The two bluish waves of the royal Glace Clan tattoo on my forehead blend with the ripples of the water, the element they represent. My eyes appear lighter than usual in the bright light. From this angle, my features resemble Alena's so closely that a sudden, unpleasant feeling grips my stomach, as if seeing her in the reflection. I quickly dip my hands into the warm water to distort the image, then drink a few clear sips from my cupped palms and splash my arms and neck to cool off.

While Sylvan talks with his men and the horses drink, Daegan brings me a pastry filled with candied fruit, similar to the ones I had for breakfast. I shake my head, claiming a lack of appetite, but the captain waves the sweet treat under my nose, grumbling, "King's order, no arguing!" Rolling my eyes, I take the pastry. Standing in front of me, my bodyguard inspects me with a squint, his expression almost paternal in its suspicion. He's clearly waiting to see me eat. Tired of resisting him, I take a bite just to get rid of him. His eyes light up with approval, and his lips twitch as I swallow the bite. Then, he walks off in the other direction.

"By the way, Daegan, there's something on your face," I call out after him.

He stops dead in his tracks and glances over his shoulder, raising a hand to his chin reflexively.

"What is it, Your Majesty?"

"A smile," I say teasingly.

He gives me a murderous look and marches off in military fashion.

After eating, I carefully make my way toward a rocky outcrop, sore from the ride, my legs and backside aching.

My husband stops brushing the sand off Jada's coat and watches me intently from a distance, over his mare's neck. He doesn't call out, but his clenched jaw and stiffened shoulders irritate me. I'm not about to ask his permission for my natural needs! Does he really think I'm foolish enough to try running off alone, on foot, in the middle of the desert? I turn my back on him and decide to ignore him.

Circling the rocky mound, I find a secluded spot in a crevice where my modesty won't be threatened by the watchful eyes of the Fuegis. Just as I begin to untie the lace of my pants, a shadow blocks the sun. I look up angrily at my husband. He's followed me and is staring at me with a look I don't like one bit.

"Sylvan! A little privacy is it too much to—"

He swallows the rest of my complaint by crashing his lips onto mine, like a man dying of thirst who finds an oasis after crossing the desert. His passionate onslaught takes my breath away, like smoke from a fire suffocating my lungs, preventing me from breathing. His eager tongue tangles with mine, overwhelming me with a rush of erotic sensations, while his fingers tangle in my messy hair. Without breaking the kiss, he pushes me back until I'm pressed against the rock. His entire body, tense with urgency, screams his desire for me, and I suddenly connect the dots with the look he gave me as I walked away earlier. The lingering tension from last night and the annoyances of this morning have stoked his desire to the point that he's now giving in to his impulse, forgetting all restraint despite the proximity of his soldiers.

Without warning, he pulls away from my mouth and stares intently at me, letting his hands glide down my face, neck, and arms, causing my body temperature to spike. In the midst of these desert dunes, he resembles a lone predator who has just cornered his prey after an intense pursuit. His alluring face holds me captive, and his lust-filled gaze takes me hostage.

"You're torturing me without even realizing it, Enola. If you weren't a virgin, I would have taken you already," he murmurs in a low, velvety voice, wrapping his arm around my waist. "I'm dying to touch you. Do you trust me?"

Yes. No. I don't know…

Unsure, I don't answer.

"I'm giving you five seconds to push me away, not a second more," he warns, a predatory glint in his eyes.

He's giving me the chance to refuse. But like last night, I have no intention of doing so. Today, I don't have the excuse of wine. I'm sober and clear-headed. Maybe this is what trust feels like? Half-closing my eyes, I lock my gaze with his.

"The five seconds are already up, Sylvan," I murmur, eager to see what he'll do.

No sooner have I finished speaking than he spins me around and pins me against the rock face. I gasp, my mind reeling. With practiced ease, he lifts my cape over my right shoulder, unbuttons the top of my shirt, and pulls it down, exposing part of my neck and my left breast. Then, he slips his hand in front of me. I expect him to slide his hand into my pants, but instead, he quickly unties the lace and… pulls them down to my thighs, along with my underwear.

Now my backside is bare, much to my surprise.

"Sylvan, what are you—"

"Be quiet," he commands, his voice firm as his lips tease my earlobe. "We're not alone."

I hear the sound of him unbuckling his belt and feel him moving behind me, brushing against me now and then. When he slides his hand between my legs and grips my bare breast, I inhale sharply… and exhale when he presses his hot, hard sex against my rear, forcing me to flatten against the rock, arching my back. A wave of heat floods my cheeks as I realize the raw, animalistic nature of our position. I've become a willing prisoner… and a bare bottomed one, at that.

"I didn't imagine things would take this… turn," I confess, panting as he nuzzles the sensitive skin behind my ear.

He inhales deeply, breathing in my scent. I must reek of sweat from the desert heat, but it doesn't seem to bother him… On the contrary, judging by the way his hardness stiffens even more against my backside.

"You never stop talking," he growls, teasing both my nipple and my sensitive bud, which harden under his skilled fingers.

It's not the heat of this kingdom that will be the death of me— it's its king. The intensity radiating from this man is as untamable as fire. He stirs up extreme emotions in me that I struggle to understand, thrilling yet terrifying, unlike anything I've felt before. I realize how much things have changed since we met. I resisted submitting to him, thinking that submission was akin to enslavement. But now, submission no longer holds the same meaning. Whether physical or emotional, it's a shared understanding. It's not about surrender—it's about mutual will.

The tip of his tongue traces a hot, wet path along the curve of my neck, between my shoulder and jaw. With my palms flat against the rock, I wince as the Fuegis prince begins to rock behind me, matching the frantic rhythm of his hand between my thighs. The friction of our bodies is uncomfortable, thanks to my aching muscles.

"Slower… You're too rough," I manage to say over my shoulder.

He slides half of his finger inside me, twists my nipple, and presses his body harder against mine, as if punishing me for speaking and criticizing him. I bite my lip to stifle a cry of pain. He eases the sensation by caressing my sensitive bud with his thumb. The mix of pleasure and pain he inflicts on me is bewildering.

"Don't make a sound, Enola. You don't want us to get caught," he whispers, kneading my **breast**.

Truthfully, after a moment's thought, I don't care at all. All I want is to be freed from my desire and to release his by surrendering to the overwhelming passion that pulses between us. I want to feel the incredible ecstasy I experienced last night. The setting and propriety are irrelevant. As for the discomfort, I'm sure I can ignore it.

I tilt my head to the side, giving him access to devour my neck with soft kisses and eager bites. Every ounce of blood in my body rushes to my lower abdomen, burning hotter with each press of Sylvan's calloused fingers on my erogenous zones.

He lets go of my breast and withdraws his finger. I feel his hand brush my butt before wrapping around his sex, which he positions lower, between my thighs. I freeze, a surge of fear hitting my stomach. Has he changed his mind? Is he about to… Goddess, I don't want him to take me hastily against a rock for my first time! Though… I can't deny how much I want him, just not like this!

To my immense relief, Sylvan doesn't try to enter me. He rubs his sex against mine, sliding it between my wet folds, teasing my entrance. I arch my back even more. My hips start moving instinctively, grinding against his, amplifying the intoxicating pleasure consuming us both. My husband buries his face in my neck to muffle his primal groan. He grips my hip tightly, all while continuing to stimulate my sensitive spot with his finger. He intensifies his thrusts, his burning hardness rubbing against my slick skin. He's so close to my entrance; all it would take is a slight shift of his hips for him to claim me completely.

My surrender is so complete that my last reservations begin to crumble, and in my heightened state, I even consider begging him to take my virginity like this, standing up, while his soldiers are just on the other side of the rock... I'm certain he wouldn't hesitate for a second and would drive himself into me with a fierce thrust.

But a new wave of pleasure sweeps away my unreasonable idea. A moan of delight escapes from parted lips, growing louder as the first contractions of the long-awaited orgasm tighten within me. Anticipating what's to come, Sylvan clamps his hand over my mouth to muffle the guttural cry that accompanies my release. Without meaning to, I bite the fleshy part of his palm. Three heartbeats later, he pulls back with a long, ragged sigh. I feel his sex pulse against the curve of my backside, spilling several streams of warm, thick liquid onto my lower back.

I suppose I should feel dirty, but I don't. Instead, I see his seed as... an offering. Yes, that's the word that comes to mind.

We catch our breath in silence. Dazed by the intensity of my climax, I peel myself off the rock, swaying on shaky legs, forcing the young man to step back. After a few seconds, he adjusts his clothes, wipes my soiled skin with his hand, and crouches down to clean it off in the sand. I turn toward him as I pull up my pants and watch him dust his palms, erasing all evidence of our pleasant crime. He gives me a languid smile as he slowly rises. It's strange how different he seems after release—softer, more relaxed. His eyes are as bright as emeralds, as if all his fierceness was drawn out with his release. It's an enchanting sight.

"What is it, my queen?" Sylvan asks calmly, moving closer to me.

"Nothing," I reply, feeling a bit unsettled.

He places a gentle kiss on my bare shoulder and covers my breast with my shirt, buttoning it up himself, like the caring lover I imagine in my stories.

"Let's join the others, Enola," he says, taking my hand.

"I... I need to do something first," I stammer, feeling embarrassed.

"What's that?"

"I need to... relieve myself, Sylvan. That's what I came here to do in the first place."

A chuckle rises from his throat. He nods knowingly and leaves me alone, still dazed by the stolen moments we've shared, moments that only deepen the powerful pull he has on me.

CHAPTER TWENTY-SIX
THE WEIGHT OF TRADITIONS

The village of Raockar is located in the northern part of the Red Desert, just a few miles from the southern border of the Kingdom of the Stowne. From the rocky hill where Raockar perches, you can see the high jagged peaks of the Ancestor Mountains, beneath which lies Stalagmis, the city of the Elemental Clan associated with Earth. The vast underground city was conquered by Sylvan troops months ago, along with Oceanar and Eolan—the stronghold of the Aeria Clan. Without me even asking, my husband explained many interesting things along the way. He's stationed thousands of Fuegis soldiers in the three other cities of Symbiosis to oversee their governance. The dignitaries and nobles of Stowne, Aeria, and Glace are closely monitored by his Fuegis officers. Some have attempted to rise against the new political regime, but their conspiracies were foiled one by one, and the troublemakers were sent to prison without trial.

This information surprised me at first, as Sylvan could have easily ordered their execution. He admitted that he had hesitated, then added that enough blood had already been shed during the war. He would have ordered public beheadings if the conspirators had resorted to physical violence, but since they were only in the planning stages, he chose to spare them. In his eyes, words and ideas do not warrant a punishment as extreme as death—actions, however, do.

I'm beginning to see new sides of my husband, and it's clear that I've misjudged him. I'm starting to understand him better, to grasp more of who he is. The thick veil of mystery that surrounds him is slowly lifting. In some ways, I even find myself feeling a sense of admiration toward him. Of course, he has his faults—he remains an assassin—but I realize he also has principles and qualities that I never would have suspected just days ago. His worldview seems a little broader than that of other High-Fuegis. The more I get to know him, the more I want to explore his mind. He's not the brainless brute or the heartless dictator most people think he is—I'm certain of that now. There's something fascinating about him, and it's not just his physical appearance. His mind draws me in just as much as his body.

I also want to know the whole truth about the vast conspiracy that led to his father's horrific death, but I feel that if I press Sylvan for details, he'll retreat into silence. I think it's best to wait until he's ready to tell me on his own—if he ever is.

We dismount at the entrance of the picturesque village, made up of small red stone houses built near a large oasis. Sylvan empties the stirrups and helps me down from the saddle, his hands casually resting on my backside. A few villagers gather in front of our military escort. Even some children wave at us. I sense no hostility from the adults either, only curiosity. It's nothing like the cold reception we received in the city of Astranis. I soon realize why, when I see an old Fuegis with a strong build, dressed in dusty rags, walking toward us with a huge smile on his face. My husband turns toward him, his arm still around my waist.

"Sylvan Ren-Fuegis!" the old man exclaims warmly, completely ignoring royal protocol.

"Talbêk-Elir," the king replies with an affectionate smile.

Sylvan steps away from me to embrace the newcomer, as if greeting an old friend he hasn't seen in years.

This unexpected scene leaves me speechless.

"Beard suits you well," Talbêk-Elir comments, giving a familiar pat on my husband's arm. "You've become quite a man, by the God of Fire! Last time you came to Raockar, you barely reached my shoulder, you rascal. You look a lot like your father now."

Rascal? He calls his king rascal?

"My father didn't have a scar on his face, Talbêk." Sylvan replies, casually gesturing toward me. "My friend, this is my wife, Alena Ren-Fuegis. Alena, meet Talbêk-Elir, the chief of Raockar."

Talbêk bows his head in my direction, and I return his respectful greeting.

"Your Majesty, welcome to Raockar," he says with formality.

The old Fuegis examines me with a hint of caution and restraint—not aggression, but the wariness one shows to strangers before knowing them.

"Thank you, sir." An awkward silence hangs between us, so I break it. "This village is very charming."

Talbêk's broad shoulders relax slightly at my compliment.

"My great-grandfather founded it," he tells me, swelling with pride under Sylvan's amused gaze. "He laid the first stone with his own hands and carved the first steps into the rock. Then other Fuegis came to build their homes around his. A few years later, the population of Raockar reached around fifty people.

"And now?" I ask, smiling at his pride.

"Three hundred and eighty-seven Fuegis live here, Your Majesty. When I was a child, there were more than five hundred of us, but for the past decade, the death rate has been higher than the birth rate, and several families left the village for Astranis. Departures are inevitable, especially since we only have one doctor for all of us. And as you can see, we're isolated from any real civilization. If Sylvan didn't regularly send us supplies and raw materials, like his father did when he was alive, many villagers would leave to settle elsewhere." I glance thoughtfully at my husband, who nods while listening to Talbêk. "The dessert's natural resources wouldn't be enough to feed us all."

I now understand why the people here seem simpler and less rigid than the citizens of Astranis. They see my husband differently. To them, he isn't a conquering tyrant. He's first and foremost the son of his father, the friend of their leader… and personally brings them help.

I already like this place. It reminds me of my small home village in the kingdom of Glace.

A handsome young man, about fifteen or sixteen years old, with long dark hair cascading over his shoulders, appears beside Talbêk. He gives an awkward bow to Sylvan, who bursts into a deep, hearty laugh—a sound I've never heard from him before.

"Metân-Elir, don't act formal with me. I've known you since you came wailing out of your mother's womb with those tiny lungs of yours! True, I was your age the last time we saw each other, but we used to wrestle in the sand every time my father visited when we were kids."

"You forgot to mention that I always won, Sylvan," Metân retorts, visibly relaxing at my husband's friendly tone.

"And you forgot to mention that you won because you never fought fair. How are you, my friend?"

"I'm doing well, Sylvan. I can't wait for tonight, when I'll get to give orders to my father and reverse our roles."

Talbêk grumbles something under his breath, making his son chuckle. So, this is why we're here: Metân is going to take up the mantle and become the new chief of Raockar. The young Fuegis turns to me, his coal-black eyes filled with a warmth I'm not used to.

"And you must be Alena Ren-Fuegis, the lovely queen who somehow managed to tame the wild heart of our king… It's a pleasure to meet you, Your Majesty. I hope your journey across the Red Desert went smoothly?"

I exchange a glance with Sylvan, who raises a sarcastic eyebrow, his lips curving into a suggestive smile.

"The heat was stifling, but I think I'm starting to get used to it," I murmur, pulling back my hood.

As night falls, we leave the village and head to the oasis, where the villagers are making the final preparations for the ritual.

Unexpectedly, I've made a whole group of new friends today—thanks to my storytelling skills.

They range from three to twelve years old.

It all started at midday when we were eating on the ground in the center of Raockar with Talbêk, Metân, and their family. An adorable little girl with dark skin, barely taller than my knee, shyly approached me to touch my tangled hair. She was fascinated by its white color. The little Fuegis innocently asked if the color of my hair and skin was because I ate snow, which made me burst out laughing. I explained to her that all the girls in my kingdom are born with pearl-white hair and fair skin. Other children came over when they saw I wasn't going to bite their friend and bombarded me with questions about the Glace people. I was happy to answer them. By the end of the meal, I offered to tell them a story. They sat in a circle around me, just like the children in my own village used to, as I told them a popular folktale from my kingdom about a greedy giant ice creature sleeping in a cave.

Here's a brief summary: A careless young Glace wakes the fearsome creature from its centuries-long slumber by stealing the diamonds embedded in its icy body. The terrified thief flees with his loot, while the enraged creature attacks his village and kidnaps his two younger sisters. But in the end, everything turns out fine: the hero returns the stolen gems, the two Glace girls are saved, the creature, now appeased, goes back to sleep in its cave.

The Fuegis children loved my story. They cheered enthusiastically and immediately begged me for another one.

While talking with Talbêk, Metân, and Daegan on his side, Sylvan was watching me as I tried my best to meet the demands of my lively young audience. Every time I caught my husband's sea-green eyes, I'd lose track of my words, stammer, and feel a strange warmth bloom in my chest. At one point, I even thought the four Fuegis were talking about me because all their gazes turned to me at the same time. The dazzling smile Sylvan flashed at me in that moment set my heart racing.

Now, we're all gathered at the oasis, just steps away from the central water spring. A long path of embers has been laid out on the sand between the village and the lush green space. The moonlight casts a silver glow on the palm leaves, and the stars twinkle by the thousands above our heads. I sit on the grass next to Daegan and the little Fuegis girl who's been glued to my side ever since this afternoon when she touched my hair. Her name is Kara-Elir, the youngest daughter of Talbêk and Metân's sister. She's braiding my hair while humming a Fuegis lullaby. She's the one who led me to the oasis, pulling me by the hand. On the way, Kara made me blush with joy when she said I was the most beautiful woman she'd ever seen—after her mother—and that King Sylvan and I made a magnificent couple.

"Aren't we eating tonight?" I ask Daegan, surprised, as my stomach rumbles loudly in protest.

"After the ritual ceremony and the Fire Dance that follows. The villagers will celebrate the rise of their new chief with food and song."

"The Fire Dance?"

"After the ritual, Metân-Elir will dance with the nine unmarried women who've already expressed their interest in him. He'll choose one to spend the night within the new house he built with his father and brothers. If their… encounter meets his expectations, he'll marry her."

"And if not?" I ask coldly.

"Then he'll sleep with another of his suitors tomorrow night," Daegan says with a casual shrug.

I'm outraged by his nonchalant explanation.

"Daegan, are you saying that this girl could be dishonored, cast aside? And then eight other village girls after her, as well? No man would marry them afterward if that happened."

"No, Your Majesty, that's not how we see things in our kingdom," he corrects, briefly rolling his eyes. "First, know that this kind of situation rarely occurs. Most young Fuegis chiefs choose to marry the first woman they sleep with because it's usually their first sexual experience, and they have no basis for comparison. Second, polygamy has been part of our traditions for as long as we can remember, and virginity only holds symbolic value for the royal family. If Metân's first lover were dismissed tomorrow morning, she'd have no trouble finding a husband in the village. In fact, she'd have her pick. The chief's desire is considered a great honor among the Fuegis people. Knowing that this woman had been Metân's lover, even if he didn't keep her as his wife, would flatter the pride and vanity of other men. She could choose several husbands if she wanted. And even if the young chief does choose her, he could still decide to marry the other eight women after sleeping with them too. Take his father, Talbêk-Elir, as an example. He has seven wives, Your Majesty—one for each day of the week. A third of the village's children are his."

I turn my stunned gaze to Kara. The little girl nods vigorously to confirm Daegan's words.

"I have thirty-two brothers and sisters," she reveals in her sweet, high-pitched voice as she braids one of my white strands. "Father couldn't choose between his seven mistresses; he loved them all the same. So, he married all seven."

"Isn't your brother Metân the eldest son of Talbêk?" I ask.

"No, my queen, the oldest of my half-brothers is forty. He's already a father himself," she explains, gesturing vaguely toward a man in the crowd. "The God of Fire chose Metân to become chief of Raockar because he's the best warrior in the village, the strongest and fastest in our family. All my brothers over fifteen fought in the flames last month, and Metân defeated them one by one."

"And your father's wives? Do they have other husbands?"

"Some of them, yes. My mother married two other men after my father, with his consent," she adds, beaming at me with a radiant smile.

blink, fully realizing the stark difference between Glaces and Fuegis customs. In other words, adultery doesn't exist among the Fuegis. The freedom of choice they show in their romantic relationships is incredible to me, someone raised in the strictly monogamous culture of Glaces.

"And you, Daegan? Do you have other wives?"

The Fuegis army captain shakes his head, his gaze fixed on the line of dunes on the horizon. His tough warrior's mask cracks for a moment.

"No, Your Majesty," he grumbles with palpable sadness. "I've only loved one woman in my life, Selaine's mother. There was no room for another Fuegis in my heart, even after her death."

His emotion moves me. I'm at a loss for words to comfort him, so I awkwardly pat his large, scarred hand. He looks down at me, surprised, but says nothing.

There's nothing more to add, I think…

"The ritual is about to start," little Kara announces, abandoning my hair to climb onto my lap.

The sounds gradually fade, carried away by the warm night breeze blowing over the Red Desert, until a reverent silence settles over the oasis.

CHAPTER TWENTY-SEVEN

THE FIRE DANCE

Three men begin to beat their drums slowly with their palms, setting the pace for the traditional march. In unison, the nine women vying to be the future chief's wife begin a mystical chant that rises into the night. I mimic the villagers, whose eyes drift to my left. The silhouette of Metân-Elir appears under the torchlight, standing out against the sand.

I barely recognize him. From head to toe, the Fuegis man is covered in countless red tribal paintings that blend with his warrior tattoos. He is as naked as the day he was born, symbolizing the purity of both his body and soul. His head is shaved, his once long hair cut before the ceremony—a sacrificial offering to his god, no doubt.

His father and his king flank him during his march, matching his steps. My husband wears his armor for the occasion, though not his helmet. His onyx-colored breastplate reflects the two-meter-high fire burning near the oasis's water source, a blaze lit by the elemental magic of Metân's older brother.

With his eyes fixed straight ahead, his walk solemn, Metân advances to the rhythm of the chant, walking over the glowing embers. The crackling coals crunch beneath his feet, but they do not harm him.

Like all members of his people, he is immune to fire and heat.

At the end of the ember path, Talbêk-Elir takes his son's face in his hands and whispers something to him. Metân nods silently, staring at his father with deep gravity. With a proud smile, Talbêk kisses his son's forehead, bestowing his blessing and sealing the transfer of power. The former chief's eyes shine, unashamed of his tears. I see an intense expression cross Sylvan's face at that moment—pain, regret, sorrow.

His clear eyes are locked on Talbêk and Metân, but his mind is elsewhere, in a place no one else can access. His memories.

I'm sure he's thinking about his own father.

His emotional vulnerability moves me so deeply that it tightens my throat and makes my fingers tremble on Kara's arms. She leans in and asks quietly if I'm cold.

With his hands behind his back, the old man steps aside, standing beneath a palm tree as a benevolent witness to the powerful, unspoken legacy he is passing on to his young successor.

As if sensing my attention on him, Sylvan lifts his head toward me. Our gazes clash over the small girl sitting on my lap. His face hardens again, becoming impenetrable and unreadable, just as it was when he believed I was Alena Kan-Glace. I find myself staring at that marble wall once more. There are still parts of him he doesn't want me to see. He refuses to show me any vulnerability, any crack in his armor.

These are his last defenses—the strongest, the tallest, the thickest. The ones no one has ever crossed.

I will be the first to cross them.

I can feel it, I know it. My instinct is certain.

At that moment, a fleeting, elusive word passes through me, like a breeze that makes me shiver all over.

Fate.

But the word whispered by the desert wind doesn't linger in my mind.

It vanishes abruptly… because it has no solid foundation to rest upon.

Not yet, Enola. Not yet.

With a metallic scrape, Sylvan draws his majestic sword, the blade reflecting the flickering flames. Metân kneels humbly before his king, shoulders hunched, arms extended, palms open.

The nine women stop singing, but the drums quicken. So does my heartbeat.

"Metân-Elir, son of Talbêk-Elir! I, Sylvan Ren-Fuegis, son of Saradin Ren-Fuegis and king of Symbiosis, grant you the title of Chief of Raockar from this day forward," my husband declares in a strong, regal voice, placing the tip of his sword in the crook of the young man's elbow.

Sylvan traces two bloody scratches along Metân's forearms, and the young man winces in pain, his breath coming in ragged gasps.

Once the ritual wounds are inflicted, Metân rises, clenching his fists. Thin streams of red drip into the sand as he marches toward the fire with determined steps. The musicians now beat their instruments with furious intensity.

Fire and blood. Just like at my wedding ceremony.

I touch my Fuegis sun on my chest, then the small scar across my palm. Sylvan had marked my skin with fire after cutting my hand to mix our blood.

Talbêk's son steps into the flames, arms spread wide. He spins in place, head thrown back, reciting a solemn oath to the God of Fire.

The flames extinguish abruptly just as the drumming stops.

All the villagers rise as one, surrounding Metân and erupting into joyful shouts to celebrate the rise of their new chief.

And I raise my voice with theirs.

"What did you think of the ceremony, my wife?" Sylvan asks, slipping behind me as the nine women lead Metân to the edge of the water. "Do you find this tradition barbaric as well?"

He's referring to our conversation last night about the commemorative tattoos that adorn the sun-bronzed skin of the Fuegis warriors.

Kara had left to join her mother at the end of the ritual, and Daegan yawns beside us, not bothering to hide his boredom.

"The blood didn't seem necessary to me," I remark, watching the women wrap linen strips around Metân's wounded arms.

My husband spreads his legs as he sits on the ground, pulling me back into him with his arms around me. It seems as though it's become second nature for him to touch me, regardless of the situation. I lean my back against his breastplate.

"Since the Dawn of Time in Shynighgar, blood has symbolized awakening, Alena. It accompanies birth, death, and rebirth. It marks the change. It's the messenger of fate," Sylvan says, intertwining our fingers over my stomach.

Blood is awakening. It accompanies birth, death, and rebirth. He marks the change. It's the messenger of fate.

Why do these simple words unsettle me so much?

I frown as I watch the new chief's suitors undress amidst the applause of the villagers. With carefree laughter, the nine young women remove their robes and veils for all to see. Metân, grinning blissfully, devours the sight of their exposed, youthful curves with his gaze. He doesn't know where to look first. He even starts… to get aroused. I quickly avert my eyes. I'm not as comfortable with nudity as the Fuegis.

"Please tell me they're not about to have an orgy in front of us?" I whisper nervously into Sylvan's ear.

"No, Alena. The act of intimacy remains private. The Fire Dance is a display of feminine seduction, its essence rooted in desire," he explains in a deep voice. "Watch, the show is worth it."

The soft sound of a pan flute drifts through the night, accompanied by the measured beat of drums. The traditional instruments create a mesmerizing, sensual tribal melody. I focus on the scene, squeezing Sylvan's hands in mine.

Metân stands still in the center of a circle formed by the nine women, who slowly twirl around him, their bodies undulating with feline grace in time with the music. Their hands trace elegant patterns in the air, and they move their hips seductively while keeping their eyes locked on the young village chief. Their long black hair swirls around their heads as they sway, moving their heads, shoulders, arms, chests, bellies, hips, legs, and feet, all in perfect synchrony. The way they move their bare bodies with such sensuality and eroticism is hypnotic. They resemble mysterious flames trembling in the warm desert breeze. I've never seen anything like it… and this is just the beginning.

The undulating circle tightens around the young man, and he reaches out his hands. They brush against him fleetingly with their fingers as they dance faster, their coordination astonishing. Little sparks crackle at each touch of their skin, which begins to redden visibly.

Suddenly, the fire joins the dance.

Stunned, I widen my eyes, gripping my husband's fingers tightly.

Eighteen long, fiery ribbons shoot from the hands of the nine women, like flaming serpents. These blazing tendrils wrap around Metân-Elir, grazing his head and torso, coiling around his arms and legs in a swirling mass of golden light that forms wide, mysterious patterns in the air. The flute's melody grows stronger, the drums beat faster. The fiery snakes fly higher, suddenly spreading out behind Metân, intertwining around the dancers and clashing with each other in almost martial violence. My breath quickens, my heart pounds in my chest. I am utterly captivated by this spectacular display.

The lines of fire change color, multiplying. Red. Blue. Green. White. Pink. Purple. There are so many now that I can no longer make out Metân's silhouette amidst the whirlwind of crackling, multicolored flames. Tears prick my eyes as I watch this enchanting blaze.

Suddenly, the music stops, the nine women collapse into the sand, and all the luminous serpents disappear at once. They lie around Metân, their bodies trembling from the energy they've spent during the Fire Dance. He lowers his head, casting an uncertain gaze over their outstretched forms.

"How will he choose his mate?" I whisper to Sylvan.

"The elemental magic of one of them connected with his during the Fire Dance," my husband calmly reveals, tightening his arms around my waist. "I felt the wave of their connection. Metân will find her, and their souls will bond. It seems fate is on their side tonight. I have no doubt he will make her his wife and never take another after her," he concludes confidently.

Fate. That word again.

A single ribbon of fire emerges from Metân's palm and caresses the faces of his suitors one by one. On the fifth woman… the flame stops. It lingers on her trembling skin, as if savoring her. It's her… Another serpent of fire springs from the Fuegis woman's hand and moves to meet the chief's. They caress each other gently, intertwining with sensuality, and unite with passion until they become one. Then, they extinguish.

They recognized each other. Their souls destined to be together from the start.

Metân approaches the woman and offers his hand. Their eyes meet, and they share a tender smile that stirs something deep inside me. She intertwines her fingers with his, and he helps her to her feet. The two future lovers slip away, hand in hand, under the joyous cheers of the crowd, ready to consummate their love in private.

I feel Sylvan's fingers on my cheek. Without a word, he gently wipes away the tear at the corner of my eye with his thumb. I cover his large hand with mine and press it against my face, closing my eyes. With a sigh, I surrender to my overwhelming emotions and to my husband's embrace.

He says nothing. Neither do I.

We don't need to.

In this moment, our silence speaks louder than all the music and all the dances of Symbiosis.

CHAPTER TWENTY-EIGHT

EMERGENCE

Tonight, as a gesture of gratitude, Talbêk-Elir gave us his stone house and went to sleep in one of his wives' homes. It's the largest and most comfortable house in Raockar. Perched on top of the rocky hill, it overlooks the entire village. When the old man passes away, Metân will move in here with his wife and their future children.

"Were you here often in the past?" I ask Sylvan as we enter the room.

"Several times a year. My father was a close friend of Talbêk. I consider him an uncle."

"You're closer to him than you are to Leonal."

"In some ways, yes." He hesitates. "My relationship with Leonal has been strained for a while. We often disagree on how to manage the kingdom. We're forced to compromise with each other for the common good."

I approach him as he begins to remove the straps of his armor. He's just opened the door to his thoughts, and I have no intention of letting it close.

"Let me help. Was it the same during your father's reign?" I softly ask while undoing the buckle on his chest plate, just as I used to help my brother at the end of the day.

A faint, bitter smile tugs at Sylvan's lips.

"My father rarely made political concessions. He took a clear stand for the people and imposed his decisions on the High-Fuegis Council, ignoring their opinions. In a way, you could say I'm more diplomatic than he was. But that's also why my subjects loved him so much, and why I'm far less popular. I try to balance the interests of the people with those of the High-Fuegis. It's not an easy task."

"Leonal and Saradin often disagreed."

"Hm," he confirms, rubbing the royal tattoo on his forehead absentmindedly.

"Is it through him that you learned the three kingdoms allied against yours to poison your father, by any chance?"

Sylvan doesn't answer my question. He stiffens, as if I'd just personally threatened him.

"What are you implying?" he snaps, his tone suddenly so cold and severe that it sends a chill down my spine.

"I'm not implying anything," I stammer, shaking my head, stunned by his aggression.

"Be careful with your words and rash judgments, Enola. Just because we're not at the palace tonight doesn't mean I'll tolerate your disrespect toward Fuegis authority any better. I forbid you to question the loyalty of a man you don't know, who shares my blood."

"You've told me yourself that you encourage freedom of speech and thought within your kingdom."

"I also told you that my patience has its limits. Don't push them," he snaps, turning away to continue unstrapping his armor alone in the corner of the room.

I study the lines of his broad back, searching for what I might be missing. His visceral reaction could mean something.

Could my words reflect his own doubts?

"Some are worthy of my trust. Not at all," he admitted to me yesterday about the members of the Fuegis court.

I thought I had made progress with Sylvan, but by speaking without thinking, I seem to have taken two steps back. My husband was beginning to open up to me. Now, I'm unsure if he'll risk being vulnerable again, knowing how much I despise Leonal.

But I'm not one to give up easily. It's not in my nature.

As Sylvan removes his breastplate and sets it on a wooden bench with tense movements, I approach him cautiously, as if trying to soothe a wild stallion. He scowls and glances at me out of the corner of his eye while undoing the clasps of his chainmail at the collar.

"Forgive me, Sylvan. I shouldn't have said that. I didn't mean to offend you."

A flicker of surprise crosses his gaze. It's true, this is the first time I've apologized to him. He shrugs before stripping off his chainmail, revealing his war-scarred, chiseled chest. I step closer, placing my hands on his pecs, which tense under my palms. Slowly, I trace my gaze up to the scar cutting across his brow and into his temple. I venture to ask, "Who gave you this scar?"

His expression darkens.

"A Renegade warrior on a battlefield at the edge of the Forest of Exile. I was reckless, overestimated my strength. If my father hadn't saved me, I might've lost my eye… or my life. But that's how you gain experience, Enola. Through pain and fear. Every time I look in the mirror, I remember that lesson."

His father saved his life… and he couldn't save his father's.

One of the roots of his inner torment becomes clear. Guilt. I should have guessed it sooner.

"Do you hate them, Sylvan? The Renegades?"

He takes a few moments to think before answering.

"No. Not in the literal sense. They are Symbiosis's enemies, not mine. The only ones I truly hate with all my soul are my father's assassins and everyone involved in the conspiracy."

"Then that means you hated me too," I murmur, disheartened.

My husband refutes this with a half-smile. His features soften, his body relaxes—he's no longer defensive. His fingers slide into my silver hair, massaging my scalp at the base of my skull. An exquisite sensation.

"I was never able to truly hate you, my exquisite Enola. Even when I thought you were your sister. I tried with all my might to despise you, but …"

My heart skips a beat. A fiery jolt ignites in my stomach. I hang on his every word, losing myself in the iridescent green of his eyes.

The calm after the storm.

The stillness before the hurricane.

"But?"

"There was something about you… the way you looked at me, the way you carried yourself. How you defied me even though you were terrified, how you fought to survive, how you told me your stories. Your courage impressed me, despite myself. Your intelligence, too. Your persistence. Your sharp wit. Your beauty. Your inner fire. Everything about you as a woman, really. I despised your name, I hated the thought that you were one of those responsible for my father's death, but I couldn't stop admiring you, against all lo—"

I don't let him finish. I grab the back of his neck, pulling his head down to mine, and kiss him passionately. I slip my tongue between his lips with a boldness I didn't know I had. After his initial surprise, Sylvan cups my face in his hands and returns my wild kiss, slamming me roughly against the stone wall. My hands travel along his shoulders, down his chest and sides, tracing the sculpted contours of his muscles, the jagged terrain of his scars, and the winding designs of his tattoos. Our kiss deepens, and I bite his full lips with pleasure. But as my fingers grasp his belt, he pulls his mouth away, his gaze falling to my hands as I unbuckle it.

"Enola," he growls in a warning tone, his chest heaving with ragged breaths.

"I want you, Sylvan," I murmur, my voice filled with unwavering determination.

His forehead rests against mine as his fingers wrap gently around my throat. His skin trembles against mine. He struggles to control himself.

"You're not ready," he declares in a voice thick with desire.

But he doesn't stop my fingers from swiftly undoing the laces of his pants, nor does he resist my eager lips that trail along his stubbled jawline.

"I am ready. I want to feel you inside me, Sylvan Ren-Fuegis, and I know you want me too. So, take me, my king. Make love to me as you would your wife or take me as if I were a mere courtesan—I don't care, but let's see this through tonight," I exclaim into his ear as my hand wraps around his heated sex inside his pants.

Sylvan's powerful hands leave my neck and slam against the wall on either side of my head, forming fists. He takes a long, shuddering breath as I stroke his erect length with awkward tenderness. It's longer and smoother than I imagined, and at the tip, I feel… something metallic.

Stunned, I open my fingers to examine what I've found. His swollen head is pierced with a gold ornament that glitters, adorned with two small side balls.

"Goddess of the Ocean! Y-you… you have…" I stammer, blinking rapidly, flushed all the way to my hairline. In the heat of passion, I hadn't noticed this when he rubbed himself between my thighs in the desert.

A rough laugh rumbles from my husband's chest as he pulls his fists away from the wall.

"Does that detail bother you, Enola?"

"I… I don't really know. Does it… hurt?"

"No, quite the opposite. It will increase the pleasure. For both of us," he assures me in a velvety voice, tightening my fingers around his hardened length, guiding my hand in a steady rhythm.

His other hand slips confidently into my cotton pants, molding to the curve of my pelvis. I part my legs slightly, my breath faltering. He teases my sensitive bud for a moment before slipping a finger inside me. I grip his shaft tighter, moaning into his shoulder with excitement.

"God of Fire, you're so tight," he growls, his head leaning heavily against mine. "I can't wait to be inside you, my queen. It's all I've thought about since the night of our wedding. I dream every night of hearing your divine moans, of watching your beautiful sapphire eyes roll back in ecstasy, of feeling your tight sheath clench around my cock while I come deep inside you," he whispers heatedly into my ear.

I turn my chin, unable to resist the urge to trace the tip of my tongue along his thin scar, as if the gesture could heal his old wound. Sylvan exhales a muffled groan, his hips giving a slight thrust as his heated member swells in my hand. He releases my hand, allowing me to explore him freely, and moves to knead my breasts urgently beneath my shirt. My palm brushes the gold ornament at the tip of his shaft, causing him to twitch under my touch. His gaze, both fiery and magnetic, locks onto mine, and I lose myself in it without hesitation.

I crave this man—once my enemy—with every fiber of my being. I want him to make me a woman in the most primal, physical sense. My body arches toward his, yearning with a desperate hunger. This intoxicating pull between us feels almost animalistic.

I didn't realize I'd been waiting for him all these years. Now, I know I have been. Him and no one else. I feel it in my core.

At this moment, I'm finally at peace with myself. There is no doubt clouding my mind. Fear is a thing of the past.

My soul is calm.

My mind is clear.

My body is ready.

As we kiss and touch each other, we quickly strip one another's clothes, driven by the same uncontrollable need. His pants and my garments fall to the floor. Like last night, he lifts me in his arms and lays me on the bed. But this time, he is as bare as I am. His fingers circle my throat as he fiercely claims my lips, rubbing his knee between my thighs. I shift my hips, intensifying the sensual friction that ignites the wet heat at my core. His shaft moves against my belly in time with the delicious pressure of his thigh between my legs, while my hardened nipples graze his abdomen. I'm already breathless, slick with sweat, burning with desire for him.

"Sylvan…" I plead against his mouth, clinging to his waist.

He peppers my face with small kisses, ignoring my desperate plea. My hands slide down to grip his firm buttocks, urging him to understand that I can't wait any longer.

His fingers slip between us, closing around the base of his cock. He positions his hips between my thighs, hovering above me. The gold ornament at the tip of his head presses against my swollen, throbbing bud. Struck by the sensation of that tiny piece of metal teasing my sensitive flesh, I moan even louder, writhing beneath Sylvan.

"I'm going to enter inside you, Enola," he warns, positioning himself between my slick folds. "Just a little, at first. If it hurts too much, I'll stop. We don't have to go all the way tonight."

I nod, biting my lip. He leans down to lick it before beginning to push inside me, so slowly that it feels like time itself has slowed. I let out a long, trembling sigh as his hardness spreads and fills me.

It's an indescribable experience, beyond anything stories can convey. But just as the tip of him slips inside, he stops, locking eyes with me, searching for any trace of pain or discomfort on my face.

"More," I breathe, spreading my legs wider, my hands pushing at his hips.

His burning gaze stays locked with mine as he moves forward cautiously, inching in a little further before stopping again, his face set in concentration. Only the tip of him is inside me, and it's nowhere near enough.

"More, Sylvan!" I command in a voice thick with desire, pulling a shadow of a smile from him.

"And they call me the tyrant…" he quips, his tone dry, as he resumes his careful advance.

A faint sting awakens deep in my lower belly—more like a pinch or a bite, but nothing unbearable. A strangled groan escapes Sylvan's lips, and his chest muscles tense against mine. I can tell his primal instinct is urging him to take me harder, faster, but he reins it in, holding back to protect my body. Instead, his fingers grip my thighs, digging into my skin so hard they're sure to leave red marks.

I wrap my legs around his hips, holding him captive in my embrace, inviting him to go deeper into my sanctuary. He's about halfway in now.

Heat unfurls in my belly, my breasts, my throat, and my head, as if a kind of lethargy is spreading through me. Strange shivers run down my arms and legs, and tingling spreads at the base of my scalp. Sweat coats my back. My vision blurs. My heart pounds furiously in my chest, and my lungs fill with icy air.

None of these sensations feel normal. I've never been with a man, but I'm not ignorant or naive. My mother had explained what my first time would feel like. But something unusual is happening inside me as Sylvan claims me in the most intimate way, and I can't pinpoint what it is. It's not pain, exactly—it's powerful and indescribable. All I know is that this emergence… was inevitable.

Like fate.

Sylvan frowns his eyebrows slightly, his gaze probing me as if he too has sensed something strange.

"Enola, if you want me to stop, just say the word."

No, more! Something inside me roars, like a caged beast yearning to be set free.

"Sylvan, I'm fine. I swear, it doesn't hurt. I want you with everything I have. Please, do it," I say, my trembling fingers tracing the scar on his face.

With heart-wrenching tenderness, he kissed me as he thrust fully into me.

I gasped, feeling an invisible arrow pierce through me… but the sharpness lasted only a moment. Sylvan pulled back to let me catch my breath, concern etched into his features. I inhaled, tasting something indescribable in the air. *How could air have a flavor?*

Suddenly, I was neither hot nor cold. I wasn't sweating anymore. My heartbeat had calmed. All that remained within me was a deep physical satisfaction and a sense of peace unlike anything I'd ever felt before. *The calm after the storm. The stillness before the hurricane.*

But another kind of storm hit when my husband began to move inside me, stealing my breath away. A whirlwind of pleasure swept through my soul. My heart trembled in its quake. My body burned everywhere. My mind drowned in a sea of bliss, far more intense than my first climax.

"Harder, Sylvan!" I demand, arching into him.

He let out a primal growl at my command, my passion feeding his.

Our hands entwined on the bed. Our breaths mingled. His hips met mine in perfect rhythm. I moaned without restraint, needing to give voice to the wild storm of sensations and emotions swirling within me. I surrendered completely to the hold this man had over me. His body surged into mine again and again, faster, harder, without ever hurting me. My body, fully sated, welcomed his with endless joy. I wished this union would never end. Gasping, Sylvan leaned down to lap at my neck as our bodies collided in a savage frenzy. His pelvis struck my sensitive spot with every forceful thrust. The gold piercing grazed a mysterious place deep inside me, heightening my pleasure. I was so close to breaking.

"My sweet, warm, tight wife," he murmurs hoarsely in my ear, squeezing my hands in his.

His mouth crashed down on mine as he drove between my thighs with one final thrust, sealing both my undoing and my rebirth. A thunderous roar echoed in my belly, a bolt of fire tore through my heart, and an exquisite flood of sensation melted my mind. Sylvan swallowed my cry as I whispered his name, finding his release moments after mine. His beastly roar resonated in my mouth. I felt him pulse deep inside me, my core throbbing in sync with his, in perfect harmony. A shared sigh of ecstasy shuddered through our bodies as our kiss became more serene.

Our lips parted, our hands loosened, and Sylvan withdrew from me slowly, reverently. His absence left me feeling empty, uncomfortable, and cool inside. He looked at me intensely, his hand flat on my chest—on my Fuegis mark—while I caught my breath. He said nothing, only watched me, as if committing every detail of my face to memory. His eyes were bright, alive with something indescribable. Feeling a sweet drowsiness and pleasant exhaustion wash over me, I closed my eyes. Sylvan brushed a hand tenderly across my cheek before pulling the blanket over our bare bodies. I relaxed into him as he wrapped me in his arms, his lips pressing softly against the royal Glace emblem on my forehead.

For the first time in ages, I feel wonderfully good. Peaceful. Confident. Safe.

And it doesn't take long before I slip into a dreamless sleep in the arms of the man to whom I just gave my virginity.

CHAPTER TWENTY-NINE
THE WHISPERING OF THE WIND

I open my eyes in the dim light, barely disturbed by the faint glow of the embers.

I feel the peaceful, steady breathing of Sylvan against my neck, the weight of his arm draped around my waist, his muscular body pressed against mine. Gently, so as not to disturb his deep sleep, I lift his arm, pull back the blanket, and slip out of bed. He stirs slightly, letting out a soft groan, and rolls onto his stomach, his face buried in the mattress. My gaze drifts over his tousled dark hair splayed across his shoulders, the curve of his bare back traced with scars, and the beginning of his round hips. A tender smile plays on my lips.

The king of beasts asleep. It's not a sight you see every day, certainly… I have the urge to stroke his bronzed skin, but I don't want to wake him.

I turn my thoughtful gaze towards the slightly open window. The moon and stars still reign as sole mistresses in the deep blue night sky. Dawn is far off yet.

A warm breeze has slipped into the room. As it brushed my face, the breath of the desert pulled me from my restful sleep.

A dull cramp tugs at my lower abdomen. Sitting on the edge of the bed, I place a hand between my damp thighs. My eyes are drawn to the tips of my fingers, now slightly stained red. I furrow my brow, hypnotized by the vivid color of the liquid contrasting against my pale skin.

Blood is the awakening.
It accompanies birth, death, and rebirth.
It's the signs of the change.
It's the messenger of fate.

Shaking my head to dispel these strange and fleeting thoughts, I wipe my hand on the sheets and rise from the bed to close the window.

My mother was right about one thing. She had warned me that after losing my virginity, I would feel different, deep inside, without being able to explain it. It isn't about the symbolic significance of the powerful act that transitions one from childhood to womanhood; at twenty-six, I've felt like a woman for years.

No, this is something else.

As I approach, the wind changes.

It becomes… audible.

Alive.

I listen, intrigued. Sounds no earthly instrument could produce. Esoteric chords. Disembodied voices. It sings a strange melody, sending dozens of tiny shivers across my skin and stirring the depths of my body. Its music wraps around me like a ghostly ribbon, enveloping my organs, pulling me towards the Red Desert with an irresistible urge.

The wind is *speaking* to me.

But just like in my last dream, I don't understand what it's saying.

An irrational sense of dread swells within me.

With my hands resting on the windowsill, my white hair tousled by the breeze that sings louder and louder in my ears, I peer into the darkness that surrounds the village of Fuegis. The line of dunes, crowned by the pale glow of the moon, seems to ripple in the distance. Beneath my bare feet, the stone floor vibrates ever so slightly.

Then this sensation begins to intensify, like the early rumblings of an earthquake. The embers in the brazier crackle and glow more fiercely. I focus on the darkness of the desert, but I see and hear nothing out of the ordinary. No movement. No sound.

Yet, I *feel* something.

A knot forms deep in my gut. My blood boils in my veins. My breath quickens. The fine hairs on my arms stand on end. My fingers tremble against the windowsill.

Fear.

Threat. Blood. Danger. Death, the wind whispers to me.

"Sylvan," I murmur without turning around.

A rustle of the blanket. My husband stirs in his sleep.

"Sylvan!" I repeat more urgently, glancing over my shoulder.

"Enola, what is it?" he grumbles in a sleepy voice.

"Wake up."

"Why, by the God of Fire?" he asks, sounding clearly puzzled.

Shivering, I swivel towards the bed, locking my alarmed gaze with his.

"Something is coming."

PART TWO

CHAPTER ONE
PREMONITION

SYLVAN

"Something is coming."

Enola's voice echoed through the room, a foreboding whisper.

Instinctively, driven by my military reflexes, I leap to my feet in an instant and join her at the window. Following her gaze, I scan the dunes stretching beyond the walls of Raockar. The villagers are all fast asleep in their tightly clustered stone homes.

"I see nothing but the shadows of the night, Enola."

She shakes her head slowly, her brow furrowed with worry. Her cold hand grips my wrist, her nails digging into my flesh hard enough to hurt.

"I sense we're all in great danger, Sylvan," she declares, her voice heavy with an unsettling gravity.

Jaw clenched, I scan the landscape again, finding no sign of any disturbance. The night remains silent, broken only by the desert wind's whistle and our breathing. I turn my skeptical gaze to my queen.

Those same shadows seem to cloud her eyes, so much that their usual deep-blue hue now appears almost black. Her pale, ivory face reflects the onset of a panic she's barely containing. I can't grasp what has her in such a state. Perhaps it's related to the intimate moment we shared just hours ago. Maybe she wasn't truly ready to take that step after all… I should have shown more restraint. I gave in far too quickly to the unnamed desire that's been gnawing at my gut and setting my bones on fire since we first met. I should have been more disciplined.

"If it will ease your mind, I'll send a sentry to patrol the dunes."

"It'll be too late. We need to leave. All of us. Right now. We must evacuate the village," she insists, her trembling fingers digging into my arm.

"Enola, I'm not evacuating hundreds of Fuegis in the middle of the night over a mere premonition," I reply as gently as possible, placing my hand on her neck, tense with fear, and massaging it softly with my thumb. "You must have had a bad dream, my wife. Your fear lingered after waking, and you believed that—"

"I'm not imagining anything, Sylvan!" she snaps, jerking her head away from my touch. "Doesn't your warrior's instinct warn you of danger? Don't you hear the sinister wail of the wind? Don't you see the sky darkening before our eyes and the moon stained with blood? Don't you feel death creeping into the sand? The entire Red Desert is screaming it—how can you not sense it? I beg you, Majesty, sound the alarm!"

Her request isn't just unreasonable—it's irrational. Yet, there's no madness in her gaze, only raw terror, which is far more disturbing. Still, I can't wake an entire village on a whim. That wouldn't be—

At that moment, a sudden movement at the top of a dune in the night catches my attention.

Beside me, Enola's breathing grows quicker. I narrow my eyes, peering into the distant darkness, my body tensing like a drawn bow. There *is* something out there… an animal, perhaps?

"Sylvan," my wife pleads, her voice desperate. "Sound the alarm, I beg you. Think of the women and children."

"Stay here," I order, slipping into pants and a tunic, opting not to waste time donning my armor. "I'll take a few men and check it out, secure the perimeter."

"No, no, don't go!" she protests.

"I won't be long, and you're not alone, Enola. Don't forget, Daegan and two other soldiers are stationed outside. You have nothing to fear," I reassure her as I pull on my boots.

"It's not for me I fear, Sylvan," she retorts sharply, dressing quickly as well.

Fastening my belt around my waist, I glance at her in disbelief. It's been a long time since anyone's truly worried about me. The last was my father, if I remember correctly.

"Since you won't listen, I'm coming with you," she declares, her nervous determination both irritating and alarming.

"Absolutely not!" I snap, my voice sharp, echoing through the room with authority.

"While we argue, we're wasting precious time," he points out, her gaze full of reproach.

If she keeps defying me, I'll tie her to the bed.

"God of Fire, you're impo—"

A knock at the door interrupts our marital spat. I exchange a dark look with Enola. She blinks, biting her lip, her arms wrapping around her body in a subconscious gesture of self-protection.

"Majesty, it's me," Daegan's deep voice calls out. He must have overheard our raised voices and realized we were awake. "We have an urgent problem."

"Come in!" I call.

The captain carefully opens the door. Over his shoulder, I see the two other guards assigned to watch Talbêk-Elir's house. Daegan casts a brief, tense glance at my wife standing to my right, then turns his full attention to me.

"I need to speak with you alone, Your Majesty. Can you step into the hall?"

I nod, preparing to follow him, but Enola grips my arm tightly again, holding me back.

"No," she whispers, her voice barely audible, unsettling me. Her breathing is uneven, and she's staring at Daegan in a strange way, as if she doesn't recognize him. Has she lost her mind?

A sliver of doubt begins to creep into my gut.

I lock eyes with my captain. His face is tense with worry. Then I notice his hand resting on the hilt of his sword, the other twitching slightly near his thigh.

Daegan is known for his unshakable composure in the face of danger. He never shows anxiety, not even before a battle. My sharp gaze moves up to his scarred face.

A single bead of sweat rolls slowly down the scar across his cheek.

But the Fuegis are immune to heat.

They don't sweat.

In other words…

The man standing before us is not who he claims to be.

"Enough of your nonsense, Alena!" I exclaim coldly, pulling free from my wife's grasp as she whimpers my name in protest. "Let's go, Daegan, I'm right behind you," I add, striding towards him with military confidence.

He nods flashing a dark, twisted grin, and starts to turn.

In a flash, I draw my sword from its sheath and, with all my strength, plunge the blade into the back of the man impersonating "Daegan," just as Enola screams.

At that exact moment, as I skewer the assassin—Stowne sent to kill us—the eerie toll of the village alarm bell echoes loudly through the central square, signaling the start of the night attack… and my harsh realization.

My wife had been right all along.

I should have evacuated Raockar.

CHAPTER TWO
BLOOD AND SAND

My own scream shreds through my ears as Sylvan's sword plunges violently into the back of the man who had stolen Daegan's appearance, with such force that the bloodied tip bursts through his abdomen.

The other two impostors charge at my husband, drawing their weapons.

With his left hand still gripping the hilt of his sword, Sylvan raises his right hand. Immediately, a fiery ribbon, like those wielded by the nine women in the Fire Dance, bursts from his palm.

But his is nothing like a graceful serpent.

It's a deadly whip, slicing through the air with blistering speed.

His spell strikes one of the attackers across the neck, severing his head from his body in one powerful, precise blow. The decapitated man falls to his knees, then collapses face-first, while his head rolls into the wall of the room.

The second soldier, taking advantage of the brief moment, lunges at Sylvan with a lateral thrust. My husband pulls his blade from the corpse of "Daegan" and easily deflects the sloppy strike. The fiery ribbon retracts into his hand and condenses into a flaming orb, about the size of a fist, which he hurls directly into the face of his assailant, less than a meter away.

Before my horrified eyes, the man's skull explodes in a spray of bone, brain, and blood, scattering across the floor.

With unimaginable brutality, Sylvan has slaughtered three warriors in less than a minute, using both his sword and his powers.

The savage expression on his face, and the searing hatred blazing in his eyes, terrify me almost as much as the sheer brutality of his actions. At this moment, he's not the man I made love to just hours ago, but a ruthless, desperate fighter. I'm frozen near the window, paralyzed by the scene I've just witnessed.

Stepping over the body of the Stowne assassin he stabbed from behind, Sylvan checks the hallway for more enemies, then gestures for me to follow.

"Enola, we need to get the hell out of here *now!*" he growls, his tone sharp and filled with anger as he sees me standing motionless, like a statue of ice.

My dazed eyes drift back to the window.

The alarm bell has stopped ringing, but other sounds fill the village.

Screams of terror. Cries of pain. Groans of the dying. Roars of battle. The clash of metal blades. The frantic neighing of horses. The pounding of hurried footsteps. The smashing of wooden doors.

I can also make out several figures moving between the houses. The men are fiercely fighting off the invaders, while the women and children run to escape. Flames intermittently light up the dark, narrow streets.

It all reminds me of the nightmare siege of Oceanar.

I don't know how the Stowne soldiers learned of Sylvan's arrival in Raockar, or how many there are, but one thing is certain: they chose to attack the Fuegis village in the dead of night to catch us off guard. And I highly doubt they plan on taking prisoners.

A hand grabs my arm like a claw, jerking me from my grim thoughts. As Sylvan pulls me toward him, sheathing his sword, a vibration spreads through the ground beneath us. My husband stands firm, legs wide apart to keep his balance, letting out an angry growl that echoes the low rumble of the earth as his eyes drop to our boots.

"Fucking Stowne magic!" he hisses between his teeth as a crack splits dangerously along a wall. "Run, Enola!" he shouts, dragging me toward the door.

We stumble through the hallway as the tremor grows in intensity, creating new cracks that spread across the walls, floor, and ceiling. Debris, haloed in dust, rains down around us, grazing us dangerously. My breathing is erratic, my heart feels like it's about to burst—I am utterly panicked.

Collapse.

The moment this thought tears through my mind, a massive block of stone breaks loose from the ceiling and crashes down right in front of us, blocking the door and crushing one of the corpses with a deafening thud. Sylvan and I freeze, eyes wide in shock. The seismic tremors continue to shake the Talbêk-Elir home as more rubble collapses around us. My husband strains to push the boulder, his arm muscles bulging… but it won't budge. The obstacle is too heavy, unmoving. I join him, trying to help shift it, but we accomplish nothing.

We're trapped in this room as the house crumbles down around us.

But my warrior husband isn't ready to give up.

Without explaining his plan, he abruptly grabs my hand and rushes toward the only window. We zigzag through the falling stones and leap over the rapidly widening cracks in the floor. Sylvan flings open the window, stepping onto the ledge, and orders me to do the same. This time, I obey quickly. We have no other choice. I glance nervously at the drop below. If we survive the fall, we'll probably break several bones.

"Climb onto my back and hold onto my neck," Sylvan urges, turning halfway toward me.

"What?" I gasp.

"Don't argue! Hurry up and do what I say!"

I wrap my arms around his shoulders, pressing myself tightly against his rigid body.

Sylvan raises one hand, lifting his head. The fiery whip bursts from his palm and, like a grappling hook, latches onto the stone ledge of the roof. With a flick of his wrist, he coils the flaming ribbon around his fingers, and without any warning… he leaps into the void. I scream again, shocked by his reckless action, clinging to him with all my strength—nearly choking him. The hot wind bites at our faces as we swing down the side of the building, the blazing rope extending, as if by Sylvan's will, to lower us toward the ground. And just a few seconds later, I feel the solid earth beneath my feet.

Goddess of the Ocean, I'm on the verge of a heart attack!

We run away from the collapsing house. The earthquake was indeed the work of Earth elemental magic, as it only affected the building we were in seconds ago.

"Don't *ever* do that again, you asshole!" I shout, slapping my husband's shoulder as he dismisses the flaming whip with a clenched fist.

"It was fun, though," he replies with a slight smile, rubbing his still-hot palm against the back of his other hand.

I nearly choke at his nonchalant words.

"Fun? Really?"

"Maybe not the best choice of words, I admit." He surveys the village with a darkened gaze, his hand gripping the hilt of his sword. "Daegan's alive, we need to find him fast, Enola. He can make sure you're safe while I go fight the Stownes. I have to defend my people against our enemies."

I purse my lips. I don't like that, but he's right on all counts.

"I can't protect you and fight them at the same time—it's too dangerous for both of us. If not Daegan, I'll entrust you to a few of my men and—"

"Daegan is alive, Sylvan," I cut him off, my eyes fixed on a distant point.

"How do you know?"

"I… I just feel it."

I don't know how else to explain it. I can sense the familiar presence of Captain Fuegis's somewhere in the village, like a distinct warmth radiating from a hidden source. Sylvan studies me in silence. I don't see any skepticism in his eyes, unlike earlier when I warned him of the looming threat just before Raockar's bells rang. He doesn't understand how I know this… but he believes me.

"Where is he, Enola?"

I point in the direction I sense him.

"The stables," Sylvan murmurs. "When the alarm sounded, he must've gone to get our horses so we could escape, leaving the other guards at the house." His eyes dart toward the entrance. We can now make out two still figures lying on the ground, confirming his theory. "The three Stowne assassins must've arrived just after Daegan left. They might have seen him on the way, which explains how one of them mimicked his appearance. Sylvan's face hardens as he continues,

"We're heading down into the village, Enola. Stay behind me at all times and stay alert. If I give you an order, follow it immediately. It's our only way to survive."

I nod weakly, summoning what little courage I have left. In my mind, I'm no longer a queen; I'm just a simple village girl, unsure if she'll live to see the sunrise. My hands tremble uncontrollably at my sides. Sylvan gently grasps the back of my neck and presses a brief but intense kiss to my lips, trying to reassure me.

As we make our way toward the heart of the battle raging below, I swallow my nausea, but I can't shake the insidious terror gripping my insides.

✳✳✳

SYLVAN

As discreetly as possible, we move through the narrow streets of Raockar, sticking close to the walls, alert for any danger. I'm fortunate to know the village inside out, having visited it many times with my father during my childhood and adolescence. Enola follows closely behind, her hand on my waist, not uttering a word.

We hear the echoes of battle around us, beyond the stone houses. For me, the terrified cries of children are harder to bear than the agonized screams of the men dying in combat. There will be many casualties tonight—a grim reality I accepted the moment the alarm bell rang. My priority is getting Enola to safety, then gathering all the Fuegis villagers capable of fighting to minimize our losses and defeat our enemies. However, if there are too many of them, we won't be able to turn the tide. We'll be forced to retreat into the Red Desert.

At least the survivors will.

A powerful animal growl pierces the night, followed by a long, human death rattle. My jaw clenches. Some High-Stownes have the power to command predators. That means there's at least one High-Stowne in the village likely the one responsible for destroying Talbêk-Elir's house with the earthquake that almost killed Enola and me.

"What was... what *was* that?" Enola whispers behind me.

I don't answer. I don't want to alarm her any more than she already is.

"Sylvan, tell me what kind of beast that was!" she insists, pinching my side firmly.

"You don't want to know, Enola. Stay quiet—we're almost at the stables."

Sticking to the shadows, we stealthily approach the end of the alley.

The sight of the battlefield that has taken over the village's central square sends a chill down my spine. Enola lets out a small, horrified whimper behind me.

Dozens of mutilated bodies—Stownes and Fuegis—lie scattered across the blood-soaked red sand. Men, women, and children alike. Warriors are fiercely engaged in combat amidst the corpses, some on horseback, others on foot. I spot a High-Stowne on a white stallion, standing apart from the fight. This man is royalty: a green oak tattoo marks his forehead, likely a cousin of King Idric—the man I killed.

Chaotic bursts of fire from my Fuegis warriors flicker through the air. Roots, like twisting plant prisons, coil around my soldiers, trapping them and allowing their enemies to pick them off one by one. Daegan is among them. Roaring at the top of his lungs, my captain uses his sword to hack away at the cursed plants winding around his ankles, animated by the Earth magic of the High-Stowne. A few paces away, Metân is locked in a fight against three enemies who surround him like vultures.

His father Talbêk-Elir is there too.

But the old man has already joined his ancestors.

My father's friend lies on his back, arms outstretched in a cross. His lifeless eyes stare at me from across the square. Thick red blood pours from his slashed throat.

An indescribable pain and fury explode within my chest. My elemental magic causes the blood in my veins to boil. My skin heats up suddenly, and a red haze clouds my vision.

"Sylvan, no," Enola pleads, grabbing my arm.

I pull free from her grasp and push her against the wall. My decision is already made.

"Stay hidden here. They won't see you," I order, more harshly than I intend.

"Don't leave me. Don't go—be reasonable. There are too many of them, Sylvan. Even for you."

She's wrong. If I can take down the High-Stowne, who's immobilizing my soldiers with those damned roots, we can turn the tide and push back our enemies. But I don't have the time or the desire to explain that to her right now. The battlefield calls to me. I won't run away like some miserable coward. I will fight alongside my people, even if it costs me my life. Daegan, Metân, and the others are in a dire situation—they need reinforcements, and fast.

"Enola, if things go south, leave without looking back. Don't return to Astranis—it's too dangerous for you there. Go back to your own kingdom," I say firmly, meeting her tearful sapphire gaze that's fraying my nerves.

"Sylvan, please, this is suicide!" she whispers desperately.

"Have faith in me, my love. Don't be afraid. My father always told me that fear is our greatest enemy."

She stares at me, her expression strange, my words clearly troubling her more. I steal a quick kiss from her lips, draw my sword, and charge headlong into the battle, leaving Enola behind.

The High-Stowne on horseback immediately locks eyes on me, pointing an accusatory finger in my direction, shouting to his men in a booming voice, "DOWN WITH THE REN-FUEGIS TYRANT! BRING ME HIS HEAD!"

Chapter Three
Instincts

Enola

"Have faith in me, my love. Don't be afraid. My father always told me that fear is our greatest enemy," Sylvan just said before kissing me.

His words echo those from my recent dream, where I wandered through the Red Desert, threatened by the four elements, *"Don't be afraid, Enola. Fear is your greatest enemy."*

Then, in the vision, he added, *"Have faith in yourself and in us."*

Pure coincidence… or a premonition?

There's no time for such questions in this critical moment. With labored breaths, I press myself against the wall, watching my husband charge the High-Stowne on horseback, his flaming sword raised before him. His boldness borders on reckless madness! The rider bellows, *"DOWN WITH THE REN-FUEGIS TYRANT! BRING ME HIS HEAD!"* which multiplies my anxiety thousandfold. Several Stownes rush at him at once, but the young king doesn't slow his pace. Trapped by the enchanted roots, Daegan shouts a furious "Majesty!" as he struggles to free himself, fending off vicious attacks from a Stowne soldier with his blade. Goddess of the Ocean, how I wish I could help my husband and his men! But I am no warrior. I would probably impale myself trying to wield a sword—if by some miracle I could even lift it off the ground!

Four men attack Sylvan at the same time, and he directs his sword toward the closest one.

A streak of fire shoots from Nesayan slamming into the chest of his opponent, who bursts into flames with horrific screams of pain. Sylvan turns his stream of fire toward a second Stowne, with the same result. But he doesn't have time to use the same attack on the other two, as they are already too close, ready to skewer him with their weapons. Sylvan leaps forward in a fluid motion, dodging the sharp blades that graze his head and shoulder. Rolling across the ground, my husband swings his sword violently at the boot of one of his adversaries, slicing the man's leg clean off at the ankle. The man collapses, screaming in a torrent of blood. Lying on his back, Sylvan swiftly blocks the other Stowne's blade by bringing his sword up in front of his face, and with a war cry, kicks the man hard in the throat, sending him stumbling away.

Seizing his advantage, Sylvan extends his lethal ribbon of fire from his outstretched hand. The burning serpent wraps tightly around the neck of his opponent, searing the man's flesh as smoke rises from the wound. The Stowne drops his weapon, struggling to free himself, convulsing in agony. Sylvan jerks his arm back with a sharp pull, and the flaming whip decapitates the Stowne without hesitation.

But more are coming. Half a dozen Stownes rush toward him. Sylvan may be the best warrior of his Clan and the most powerful of the High-Fuegis, but he is not invincible, and his stamina has limits. Using his Fire magic repeatedly while fighting drains him of energy. His face, pale beneath his tanned skin, shows his fatigue as he struggles for breath. It won't be long before he's overwhelmed.

Metân-Elir tries to fight his way toward Sylvan to assist his king and friend, but he is locked in battle with several Stownes of his own, unable to break free and reach him. The Fuegis soldiers are scattered across the village square, clearly at a disadvantage.

Watching from his horse, the High-Stowne rider grins with a satisfied smile that makes my blood boil.

As for me, I've never felt more helpless and useless in my life.

"M-mama, wake up; you're hurting me," sobs a familiar, small voice amidst the chaos of battle.

My neck stiffens, and my heart skips a beat. My eyes dart to the right.

I spot *her* quickly near a house, pinned to the ground by the bloodied body of a villager. A Stowne arrow juts out from between the woman's lifeless shoulders.

Her mother.

She must have thrown herself in front of her child to protect her, sacrificing herself.

I don't think twice. I slip out of my hiding place and rush to Kara. Her little hand is weakly shaking her mother's lifeless arm.

"Kara, I'm here, sweetheart," I whisper, kneeling beside her.

I fight to keep myself from completely losing it. The sight is horrifying.

"Majesty, Mama won't move," whimpers the little girl.

I roll the woman's body to the side to free Kara, who lets out a troubling gurgle. My gaze drops instantly to the growing red stain on her stomach. The arrowhead pierced her mother's body and struck the child. Tears fill my eyes as I press my hands against the wound to try to stop the bleeding. Kara's pale body shivers uncontrollably as she mutters incoherently in her language.

But what I'm doing… it's useless.

The wound is too deep, her stomach has been hit. It's too late.

She's going to die.

I gently cradle her in my arms. One hand pressed to her belly, the other stroking her face, I begin telling a story in a choked voice. It's about a brave little Fuegis girl named Kira, who one day finds a dragon egg in the Red Desert. Trembling in my arms, her head nestled against my chest, Kara listens in silence, her gaze lost in the starry sky. I continue the story, hastening my words. I tell her that the little girl places her hands on the orphaned egg, and it hatches thanks to the warmth of her Fire magic. A baby dragon, with beautiful ruby-colored scales, as big as a wolf, breaks free from the thick shell and starts sneezing flames, making the fictional girl laugh. The little dragon approaches, sniffs the child, and licks her cheek with its hot, forked tongue.

A faint smile spreads across Kara's pale lips.

"H-how… does she name the little dragon?" she asks weakly.

"Rascal." It's the first name that comes to mind. "She names him Rascal."

"I like that," Kara murmurs dreamily, her eyes growing cloudy.

"Kira and Rascal became the best of friends. She couldn't bring the dragon back to her village—the adults would have been afraid of him and might have wanted to end his life. So, she made him comfortable in a cave. She brought him pieces of raw meat whenever her family wasn't looking. She encouraged him as he tried to take off, though he could only manage small hops, growling with frustration and anger because he couldn't fly yet. Over the weeks, Rascal grew, and grew, until he was the size of a house! But the small chunks of meat Kira brought him every day were no longer enough to fill him; he had to learn to hunt on his own."

Kara writhes in my arms, her breathing ragged, as though she's struggling for air. I hold her gently, painfully aware that her time is running out.

"And then… then one morning, Kira found the cave empty. Rascal had left during the night. The little girl was sad because she would miss her scaly friend terribly, but she was also happy that he had finally learned to fly, maybe even to reunite with his dragon family. As she walked back to her village, a giant shadow covered the sun. She looked up and shouted with joy when she saw her beloved Rascal swooping down, his enormous wings beating the air. He landed in front of her in the Red Desert and extended his wing to Kira, inviting her to climb onto his back. She climbed onto her dragon friend, and for the first time in her life, the little girl flew across the skies of Symbiosis, soaring among the birds and the clouds. They glided over the red dunes of the Fuegis desert, flew past the majestic Ancient Mountains of the Stownes, marveled at the lush valley of the Aerias, swept over the treetops of the Exile Forest, and their journey continued over the pristine snowfields of the Glaces. Then they flew above the Endless Ocean to explore the vast world together and visit the other lands of Shynighgar."

I lower my tear-filled eyes to Kara, who no longer shivers.

And, most painfully, no longer breathes.

Her large, dark eyes are fixed forever on the stars, but her face is strangely serene, and a shadow of a smile lingers on her lips. The little Fuegis has flown away on the back of an invisible, mysterious dragon called Rascal.

I lean down to kiss her forehead, praying to the four gods of Symbiosis to watch over her innocent soul. Warm tears stream down my cheeks and fall onto hers, making it seem as though she is crying too. Kara was only seven years old.

War is an incomprehensible curse. An injustice. A madness. A horror.

When I raise my eyes back to the battlefield, I meet the cold gaze of the High-Stowne on the other side of the square.

He has noticed me.

And at that moment, a low, threatening animal growl rises right behind me.

****

I feel the hot breath of a massive beast on the back of my neck.

The stench of flesh and blood lingers unpleasantly in the air. I can tell it has been tearing apart Fuegis on the orders of the High-Stowne.

I, however, am paralyzed with fear.

Sylvan is busy by the battle, fighting fiercely for his life and the lives of his men. He hasn't even noticed that I've left my hiding spot. None of the warriors in the village square are paying attention to me... except for the High-Stowne on horseback, who commands the carnivorous creature.

If I scream for my husband's help or try to run, I am certain the predator will close its jaws around my head in an instant.

Something heavy presses on my head. The creature's jaws. It's sniffing my hair. A strange little growl vibrates in its throat. A growl... a growl...

That isn't aggressive.

I'm absolutely certain of it.

Sylvan's voice whispers in my mind.

"Don't be afraid, Enola. Fear is your greatest enemy."

I exhale slowly, releasing the breath trapped in my lungs.

With sheer willpower, I calm my erratic heartbeat. I begin to sense the rhythm of the animal behind me. Steady. Strong. The predator continues to sniff me carefully. Its razor-sharp teeth graze my scalp, but they don't cut. I let it continue.

I see High-Stowne frown. He hisses between his teeth as if issuing an order to the beast.

To kill me.

But the animal doesn't obey him.

It keeps sniffing me, emitting strange, guttural growls as though it's trying to communicate with me.

Breathing in deeply, I slowly turn my head toward the creature.

A desert tiger.

Its magnificent red-and-black striped fur gleams in the firelight.

Two hundred pounds of powerful muscle.

Two teeth as long and sharp as knives… stained with Fuegis blood.

Glimmering, hypnotic golden eyes.

A rare and extremely dangerous species, if the rumors are to be believed.

But not dangerous to *me*.

I'm not afraid anymore.

Very slowly, I raise my hand. The tiger sniffs my skin for a moment, then lowers its head, watching me. It rubs its snout against Kara's bloodied stomach, letting out a plaintive whine, as if mourning her loss too. I gently stroke between its eyes, allowing my mind to connect with its own.

I sense no hunger… no malice… no rage.

Only clarity… intelligence… and a deep well of suffering.

The unspeakable agony of being enslaved and forced to slaughter defenseless women and children by Earth magic.

The pain of having to go against its natural instincts to submit to the cruel demands of its master.

A slave.

Like I once was.

With absolute trust rooted deep within me, I enter the prison of its mind. Gradually, I free it from its mental chains. One by one. When the last invisible chain falls, I feel a primal sense of relief—its relief. Animal empathy.

I also feel its overwhelming desire for *revenge*.

After one final caress beneath its jaw, I point toward the High-Stowne, whose expression has turned to one of pure dread.

And the desert tiger sprints toward its new prey with a feral roar.

✳✳✳

SYLVAN

What in the world…

As I parry an enemy's sword, I hear a fierce growl reverberating through the night. I turn just in time to see a massive red tiger chasing down the galloping horse of the High-Stowne. Suddenly, the predator crouches, gathering momentum, and leaps high into the air. It lunges at the rider's throat, knocking him from his horse. Its sharp claws dig into the man's chest as he screams in terror. The tiger pins its prey to the ground, violently shaking him between its jaws like a ragdoll, tearing into his flesh with ravenous hunger. I stare in stunned disbelief. Against all odds, the desert tiger has turned on its master.

As the High-Stowne dies, he loses control over his magic. The roots that had trapped more than half of my men sink back into the sand. Led by Daegan, the Fuegis warriors rejoin the battle, more enraged than ever. Our enemies fall one by one, overwhelmed by our powers, crushed by our weapons, and defeated by our thirst for revenge.

Disorganized by the death of their leader and panicked by the sudden shift in battle, the surviving Stownes retreat. We catch up to some and finish them off. A few manage to escape into the Red Desert. But it doesn't matter. Let them slink back to their underground city with their tails between their legs! Let them tell the other High-Stownes what they witnessed here! It will make them think twice before attacking my people again.

Maybe.

The desert tiger slips away during the chaos of the fight. The High-Stowne's corpse is left in pieces.

After issuing a few final orders to my men, I rush back to the alley where I left Enola…

But she's not there.

A cold steel grip clenches around my heart.

My frantic gaze finally lands on a small figure with silver hair streaked with red near a house.

My wife is curled up on the ground, cradling a small Fuegis girl in her arms. It's Kara, Talbêk-Elir's youngest. Enola rocks the frail, lifeless body against her chest, tears streaming down her face. She's covered in blood, but it's the child's, not hers.

Sheathing my sword, I kneel beside Enola, gently placing a hand on her arm and murmuring her name. She looks up at me with tearful eyes full of pain. Without a word, I pull her softly into my embrace. Resting my chin on her forehead, I let her sob against my chest as I gaze up at the pale moon, its crimson tint eerily matching the color of my wife's hair.

CHAPTER FOUR

SINISTER NEWS

ENOLA

After the battle, there was no way I could sit idly by—nor could Sylvan. While my husband and the other men gathered the bodies scattered throughout the village, I joined the women who had escaped injury to tend to the wounded. The injured were taken to a house on the orders of young Metân-Elir.

I disinfected and bandaged wounds, helped elderly women brew healing balms, brought water and blankets to the patients, and comforted children who had been orphaned. I fought to hold back my tears in front of them. I also assisted Sylvan when he came into the house to amputate the leg of one of his unconscious soldiers. I applied a tourniquet to the man's thigh before Sylvan's sword carried out the grim task. I could see how much this bloody chore repulsed him, but for some reason that escapes me, he refused to let Daegan or anyone else take over. The Fuegis's leg was too mangled; without the amputation, he would have died. He's not out of danger yet, but now he has a chance of survival.

Despite keeping busy with the villagers, I couldn't stop replaying the horrific events of the night in my mind. The ominous warning carried by the desert wind. The ringing of the alarm bells. The foiled attack by the three Stownes in our room. The earthquake that shook Talbêk-Elir's home. The fight in the village square. The bodies, the violence, the blood-soaked sand. The agony of little Kara, whose dying gaze will haunt me for the rest of my life. And finally, the terrifying red tiger that leaped at the throat of the High-Stowne.

The tiger I mentally freed from its master's magical control.

I have no idea how I managed to pull off such a feat.

Between tasks, Sylvan pulled me aside to talk again about my premonition. Thank the Goddess, neither my husband nor the other Fuegis saw what happened between me and the tiger before it launched its dramatic attack on the High-Stowne. The ruler hasn't mentioned it, either. Earlier, I overheard him telling Metân-Elir that, without the unexpected intervention of the desert beast, they might not have been able to regain the upper hand and win the battle.

"How did you know the Stownes were coming, Enola? And how did you know that it wasn't the real Daegan in our room, and that he was alive near the stables?" he asked, his eyes locked onto mine.

"I told you, Sylvan. I just felt it."

"Have you ever had this kind of premonition before?"

"No, this was the first time."

Well, aside from the maybe *prophetic dream.*

"And in your family? Your sister Alena? Your ancestors? Any other High-Glaces, perhaps?"

"No… none of them either."

"You seem to have some kind of clairvoyant power… I've never heard of such a thing on Symbiosis. The gift of foresight has appeared on the Continent before, but to my knowledge, never on our lands."

"You're exaggerating, Sylvan. It was just… just instinct," I weakly objected, holding his gaze, which was shadowed with perplexed gravity.

"No, Enola. It was more than instinct. It was something else."

Our conversation ended there, interrupted by Metân calling for my husband.

Right after Sylvan left, I lower my troubled eyes to my hands, sticky with blood—the same red as the blood from my broken hymen.

Blood is the awakening.

A small shiver ran through me as I thought about the strange mental connection I had formed with the powerful desert tiger.

Sylvan

The flames of the funeral pyres consume the bodies of the Fuegis, villagers, and soldiers in the village square. All equal in the unyielding grasp of death.

We spent over two hours gathering all the bodies across Raockar and building the three pyres. We suffered heavy losses. We counted them as we went: two hundred and four Fuegis were killed last night, without distinction of age or gender. In the enemy camp, one hundred and thirty-three Stowne warriors perished. We tossed the bodies of our foes into a mass grave dug near the village. Immolation is reserved for members of my people, burial for theirs. However, no prayers will be said for them. Our commemorative chants will be for the Fuegis only.

I had to amputate one of my gravely injured soldiers, using Nesayan. Though I detest doing such things, I insisted on doing it myself. Often, I have to make difficult decisions, whether during or after battles. I was raised this way. My father told me more than once that a true king must never shy away from getting his hands dirty for the good of his people when circumstances demand it. Sometimes, he must act like any other man to share in the suffering of his people. A ruler's honor is reflected in his deeds, more so than in his words.

Personal belongings and offerings were placed on the three great pyres before Metân-Elir lit them simultaneously with his powers. Desert flowers. Weapons and clothing for the men. Jewelry and trinkets for the women. Toys and dolls for the children.

Orphans and widows, dressed in white—the color of mourning in our clan—weep as they sing a mournful lament in unison. Each has lost one or more loved ones in the village.

A father. A mother. A child. A brother. A sister. A cousin. A friend. A neighbor.

Metân is grieving the loss of his father, his youngest sister, and twelve other members of his family. His fiancée survived, but a Stowne blade wounded her face. A scar now mars her, and her right eye may never be saved. Her beauty will be forever altered. But this changes nothing for my friend. I already know that the new chief of Raockar will marry her as promised, for she is his beloved.

In the same night, at just sixteen years old, Metân became chief, found his soul mate, fought for his village, and lost dozens of people he cherished. His face, blackened by soot and dried blood, is a mask of stone. He has yet to shed a tear, but I can sense he's on the verge, ready to break down the moment he's alone. My childhood friend is showing remarkable courage and dignity. He will live up to his new role and the legacy left by Talbêk-Elir.

I admire his strength of character. When my father succumbed to poison in my arms, I gave in to an unprecedented fit of rage in front of the entire Fuegis court—a rage born of my endless pain. I was later told that my deafening roar of fury was heard all the way across the palace.

Death is the logical and inevitable extension of life, that's true. We all must accept it. But not in such a violent way. Not when it takes those we love in excruciating suffering. Natural death is one thing; death caused by human hands is another. In starting this seemingly endless war to unleash my anger and pain upon my father's murderers, I lost sight of this distinction. Many innocent lives on Symbiosis have paid the price for my mistakes. Tonight is no exception. If all these Fuegis corpses burn on pyres, it's because I couldn't control my overwhelming emotions after my father's death. I am largely responsible for the tragedy that has befallen Raockar. I have no illusions about this: I am its primary cause.

But I have no choice. If I can't live with the daily guilt that gnaws at me, I will never be able to rule justly or honor my father's memory. I would descend into ruin, or even madness. This tragedy is yet another burden on my shoulders. I will carry this added weight without faltering, for I am king. Despite my weariness, fatigue, and doubts, I cannot shed my torments at will. I must integrate them to improve myself as a man and embrace them to rule better as a sovereign. I long to approach a subtle balance that some people seek all their lives without ever finding.

I have a visceral sense that only one person could help me come close to this balance.

The woman standing to my right before the funeral pyres, her hand in mine.

Enola Ren-Fuegis.

***

"No, Sylvan. We won't return with you to Astranis."

Without flinching, I meet the unyielding gaze of the young chief of Raockar, who has just openly defied my order.

"Our kingdom is at war, Metân. Your village is too close to the border. The Stownes could return in a few days to burn it down and slaughter all the survivors. You must come with us to the capital and take refuge within its walls until peace returns on Symbiosis. You can return to Raockar afterward."

I speak deliberately, with firm words. It's crucial he understands that I will not compromise on this point.

"Even if the scenario you're describing happens, my father would never have abandoned the village our ancestors built, Sylvan. Most of the people here have never left the walls of Raockar, and you want to uproot them after everything they've been through?" He shakes his head stubbornly, which only amplifies my irritation. "If those Stowne bastards attack again, we'll fight back!"

"But you're not your father, Metân. Just as I'm not mine. We have to make our own decisions, taking into account all the external factors. Every house can be rebuilt after the war. But the dead won't come back," I state firmly.

"Yes, think of the living," Enola gently, placing a hand on the young man's shoulder to help reason with him. "Take them to safety, Metân. Don't risk their lives out of pride. Values only have meaning if people are still here to believe in them. People are so much more than stones, and as my husband said, your refuge in the capital is only temporary. Besides, the wounded need proper care. Your fiancée, for example. The only doctor in Raockar was killed tonight, Metân… There are skilled doctors in Astranis, aren't there, Sylvan?"

I nod in agreement.

Metân-Elir's eyes flicker with uncertainty. He looks around at the demoralized and devastated villagers surrounding us, lost in thought.

Then, with a stiff nod, he returns to his fiancée inside his house.

My wife has made the perfect argument to tip the scales in our favor. I couldn't ask for a better queen by my side. She always knows the right words.

"When do we leave, Your Majesty?" asks Daegan, who had been silent until now.

"At dawn, Captain. We have two more hours before sunrise to finalize preparations for the convoy. We'll prioritize transporting the wounded, the elderly, and the children in the wagons. We'll strap the villagers' belongings to the horses."

"Hmm, but where will we house the refugees in Astranis?"

"We'll distribute them among the wealthiest citizens in the capital, those who have room to take them in."

"I don't think the High-Fuegis Council will like that—"

"Honestly, Daegan, who cares?" I growl spontaneously, which earns a nod of approval from him—and a smile from my wife.

The High-Fuegis are the least of my concerns. Especially since it's highly likely that a damned spy is working among my courtiers. A traitor revealed our presence in Raockar to the Stownes, prompting their attack tonight. But the attempt failed. I'm still alive, and I plan to hunt down this traitor and personally see to his punishment. It's quite possible he was also involved in the plot that led to my father's assassination. By the God of Fire, he'll regret ever being born when I force him to confess!

As for the High-Stownes who orchestrated the village attack from the shadows, they will be identified, tracked down, and executed as soon as I return to Astranis.

***

ENOLA

Frozen by the edge of the icy lake, I lower my gaze to my boots, wrapped in a layer of soft snow.

"Enola," calls a mischievous voice. "Come on, it's fun!"

The young man glides easily across the glistening surface, a radiant smile on his lips, arms outstretched, his curly hair floating around his face like a soft, silver cloud. *He is completely absorbed in the moment, relishing his connection with the shimmering ice. His movements are smooth, his balance impeccable, and his body sways with grace and fluidity. In this moment, he embodies freedom and the sheer joy of life. A pang of jealousy stabs at my gut.*

Seeing that I hesitate to join him, he gives me a wide, inviting wave. I shake my head, biting my tongue. My older brother slows his pace, veers in my direction, and stops in front of me, extending his hand. I step back.

"There's nothing to be afraid of, little sister. Nothing will happen to you."

"It's not solid, Elanos," *I object, my voice full of worry.* "What if the ice cracks under our weight and we fall through? You've got your magic to help you breathe underwater and come back to the surface effortlessly. But I'm still Powerless—at least for now. I'm not eager to die at fifteen because of your love for danger."

"Oh, come on, you little scaredy-cat! Even if that did happen, I'd save you. A life without risks isn't worth living. It would be dull, sad, and bitter. Sometimes, to taste the best flavors, you've got to be bold. Even if it means facing death and danger from time to time," *he says, shrugging a shoulder.*

"That's not what Mom says at all!"

"Enola, Mom coddles you. You spend way too much time cooped up at home with her, listening to all those silly stories she fills your head with. You barely know anything about the world outside our village. Trust me, you're missing out on a million incredible things! Enjoy your youth, have your own experiences, and live your own stories. When you're old and frail, you'll regret not listening to the wise advice of your favorite brother."

"For you to be my favorite, I'd need to have others," *I snap, my tone biting.*

Throwing his head back, the young Glace bursts into a mocking laugh that annoys me to no end.

"Goddess of the Ocean, Enola! I pity the man who marries you. He's going to have his hands full taming your polar bear temper!"

"I have no intention of getting married, Elanos."

I've told him this many times, but he loves teasing me about it. For one thing, I believe a woman doesn't need a man to provide for her. Sure, living with so little isn't easy, but we manage. Our mother didn't remarry after our father died. She could've taken the easy way out—two men have asked for her hand in marriage over the years. But she refused to submit to the social codes of our Clan, earning the confusion—and sometimes the gossip—of other Glaces. She stood tall, managing on her own without ever holding back. Even now, she doesn't hesitate to reduce her own portion of food so that my brother and I always have full bellies. I admire her deeply.

And besides, if I married someone I didn't love, I'd be miserable. And if I married someone I did love, I'd be miserable if they died. That's what happened to her. Bleuène never truly recovered from losing my father before I was born. One night, when she had drunk more than usual, I overheard her whisper to Elanos that she would have ended her life if my brother and I hadn't been there. Those words marked me as much as they hurt me.

I want to live my life the way I see fit. In every aspect. If I decide to glide across the ice, it won't be to please my brother. It'll be because I chose to. And that principle applies to my future too.

"Come on, Enola," he insists, raising his eyebrows over his blue crystal eyes. "Everything will be fine, my little edelweiss."

The use of the affectionate nickname he's called me since I was a child pulls a soft growl from my throat. I eye his outstretched hand, reassuring… and in its palm, a translucent ice flower begins to form. A delighted smile spreads across my lips as the delicate petals unfold into a blossom. With his Water magic, Elanos has created an edelweiss, a flower of the mountains. His fleeting creation is beautiful. I wish I could do what he does!

I take the edelweiss, nodding my thanks, then place my free hand in his and step forward onto the frozen lake.

Because I chose to.

That was a juvenile, simplistic, narrow, and naïve judgment on my part. Since then, I've come to understand reality. I believe I've grown a lot, especially since I took on the role of Alena. I still feel like a Glace, but part of me has become Fuegis out of necessity. In a way, I've acquired a dual identity. My perspective is now broader, shaped by two cultures that are very different from each other. To my surprise, immersing myself in the Clan of Fire has taught me nuances I never grasped when I lived in my homeland, isolated from my peers and steeped in prejudice against other peoples. One thing I've come to realize is that we can't control everything. Control is just one of many illusions. Life, death, and love follow their own paths. None of us have the power to anticipate them or bend them entirely to our will.

Take these poor people, for example—they've been dealt a cruel and unjust fate.

As for me, I have no control over the mysteries awakening inside me. I try in vain to understand something that is beyond me. And as for my heart, which pounds faster when a pair of green eyes pierces through me… I have no control over that either.

While the refugees of Raockar prepare to depart, the childhood memory with my brother flashes through my mind. My memory must've made some foggy connection. My thoughts are adrift, like a raft lost in the middle of the Endless Ocean.

"If you could have refused the crown without facing any consequences, would you have become king?" I ask, stroking Jada's flank.

The repetitive motion soothes my nerves. The mare's calm brings me a sense of comfort.

Beside me, Sylvan shifts his gaze from the half-destroyed village to meet mine. He wears a curious expression.

"Of course. Why?"

"It's a heavy burden, that's all. When your father died, you didn't have a choice."

"Every kingdom needs a king," he replies succinct and pragmatic.

"But the people of the kingdom don't choose their king. And the king doesn't decide to be king either. Don't you ever feel like a slave to your circumstances?"

Perhaps I shouldn't have used the word *slave*. It seems to offend his pride. His mouth tightens with displeasure, and his back stiffens.

"No. I'm honored. I'm the legitimate heir to the throne. I was prepared to wear the Fuegis crown from a very young age. I knew exactly what it would entail, including both the positive and negative aspects of the role."

His arrogance draws a sigh from me.

"That's not the point, Sylvan. Set aside your upbringing and beliefs for a moment. Duty and free will are concepts that contradict each other. We both understand those nuances well."

He locks eyes with me, weighing my words for a moment, trying to grasp my particular mindset.

"Very well, I'll give you my perspective. I've never questioned it because I find it pointless. I don't see myself as anyone else. I can't imagine living a different life, no matter how complicated mine is. And I can't see anyone else but you as my wife."

I give him a faint smile, rubbing my tense neck with a weary gesture.

"All of this makes sense. It's logical, obvious. Difficult, yes… but natural. I don't feel chained to my throne. Or to anything else, for that matter," he adds, taking my hand and pressing a kiss to my knuckles.

A fragile silence settles between us. Called away by Daegan regarding some logistical detail, Sylvan reluctantly lets go of my hand. He puts back on his mask of an unyielding ruler and walks away under my veiled gaze.

His confidence leaves me pensive, unsatisfied. Our conversation feels incomplete. He doesn't question things the way I do.

Do I feel chained?

Yes.

But not to my husband.

And not to my throne either.

I'm certain there are still chains left to break, but I have yet to define what they are.

At the head of the refugee convoy, we've been traveling through the Red Desert all day. The return journey has taken twice as long as it did on the way out because the cart wheels don't move quickly in the sand. Moreover, we've had to take many breaks to distribute water to the villagers and check on the injured, especially the soldier who lost his leg and is battling an infection, alternating between consciousness and unconsciousness.

We reach Astranis just before dusk. The townspeople gather in the streets or lean out of their windows to watch us pass; their faces drawn with sorrow at the sight of our somber convoy.

Leonal greets us personally at the open gates of the palace. A scout sent by Sylvan had warned him of our imminent arrival. The High-Fuegis sweeps his gaze over the column of refugees with a dark expression before turning his attention to his nephew, blatantly ignoring Metân-Elir, Daegan, and me.

"You're not injured, my nephew?"

"No, Uncle."

"Thank the Fire God… Unfortunately, we received more bad news this afternoon. Come, I'll give you the message to read immediately."

"Tell me now."

Leonal's coal-black eyes land on me, dripping with disdain. *He doesn't want to discuss it in front of me.*

"It would be better if we discussed this in private, Your Majesty," he says in a low voice. "The information hasn't been made public yet and—"

"Leonal," my husband growls, his fiery glare bearing down on him. "After what we've all just been through, I'm in no mood to be patient. I gave you an order. Now, follow it!"

The High-Fuegis scowls in frustration but finally complies, though with evident bitterness.

"We received a letter by messenger falcon from one of our officers stationed at Stalagmis. There's been an uprising in the Stowne capital. Our entire military garrison has been wiped out, apparently. Sergeant Fuegis sent his letter just as battering rams were breaking down the door of the barracks where he and the last surviving soldiers had barricaded themselves. According to his report, the Stownes have retaken their underground city by force. But what's even more troubling, my nephew, is that they seem to have allied themselves with Glaces and Aerias to carry out this mutiny. And with Renegades, Sylvan."

Behind us, Daegan curses under his breath, and Metân-Elir lets out a muffled exclamation.

"In other words, Your Majesty, all our enemies are mobilizing against us. I fear that war is once again on the horizon in Symbiosis."

I tighten my grip on Sylvan's hand, already guessing what all this means—and who is most likely behind this civil insurrection.

No one else here suspects it yet, but contrary to what I once believed, Queen Alena Kan-Glace is more determined than ever to raise a rebellion against the Fuegis kingdom to reclaim her throne.

CHAPTER FIVE

UNCONSCIOUS CONFESSIONS

SYLVAN

Without making a sound, I push open the door to Enola's bathroom. With her back to me, lost in her dark thoughts, she doesn't hear me come in. Wrapped in a towel that barely reaches mid-thigh, her white hair loosely gathered in a messy bun, she stands motionless in front of the glass bottles lined up on a wall shelf. She's probably waiting for a servant to come warm her bath with magic. Her skin is streaked with dried blood and red dust, just like mine.

Her arms hang limp, shoulders slumped, and she holds an uncorked vial of scented oil in her hand, unaware that the amber liquid has spilled onto the floor near her bare foot. She likely hasn't noticed. Her mind is still trapped in the horrors of the village attack, the death of little Kara, and the grim news we received tonight.

Seeing her so vulnerable tightens my throat. Like all Fuegis warriors, I've lived alongside death and violence since childhood. I've hardened over the years, through countless battles. At one point, the sight of corpses used to churn my insides, but that's no longer the case. Enola, though, is different. We've lived different lives, we have different natures, and our beliefs often stand in stark contrast to one another.

I don't want to startle her or add to her distress, so I softly announce my presence.

"I'm here, my wife."

She gives a small nod.

I step closer, gently taking the empty bottle from her hand and placing it back on the shelf, my chest brushing against her back. With a sigh of surrender, she leans into me, resting the back of her head on my collarbone. My arms wrap around her, pulling her closer, and her fingers intertwine with mine over her chest. Her skin is nearly as warm as mine. I bury my face in the crook of her soft neck, inhaling her feminine scent. She shivers slightly in my arms.

A chilling thought crosses my mind. If I had lost her in the battle at Raockar, I wouldn't be here, holding her like this. I doubt I could have ever forgiven myself for her death. Engaged in the village square's fight, I wouldn't have been able to save her if a Stowne soldier or the red tiger had attacked her. I tighten my hold on her, trying to banish that awful possibility from my thoughts.

Right now, I don't want to delve into the many difficult issues hanging between us, and I'm certain that, for once, she feels the same.

"Will you stay and sleep with me, Sylvan?" she asks, her voice heavy with gloom.

What seems obvious to me is apparently not so clear to her.

"Every night, my queen. In fact, I'd like you to move into my quarters."

She frowns, shaking her head.

"No, your apartments are too depressing. You can come to mine instead," she replies with her usual insolence.

I'm not one to give in to such demands, but I understand why she might find my quarters oppressive and impersonal. I've never cared much for decoration or furniture. When my mother was alive, she lived with Saradin Ren-Fuegis in what are now Enola's chambers. After her death, my father moved out, finding the memories too painful to bear. I had never considered occupying them before now. Had I been alone, the idea would've repelled me, but living there with my wife doesn't bother me. Her gentle presence softens the dark past, replacing it with a brighter future—or so I like to think.

"If I agree to move into your quarters, what will you give me as a reward for my cooperation?" I murmur in her ear, teasing her.

One corner of her lips lifts in a smile. Victory—I've managed to make her smile.

"I'll give you a third of the bed. If you behave," she replies.

A laugh shakes my chest against her back.

"Only a third, Enola? You drive a harder bargain than a Fuegis rug merchant."

"If I start letting you have the royal privilege of stepping on my toes as you please, you'll shamelessly abuse it, don't deny it."

"Will you at least lend me a small pillow and a scrap of blanket, my selfish queen?"

She shrugs lazily, playing with my fingers entwined with hers.

"It all depends on how you behave."

"I'll be on my best behavior," I promise in a suggestive tone, brushing my lips against her earlobe.

"We don't share the same definition of *best behavior*, Sylvan," she replies, her voice turning much huskier.

"In that case, we'll need to find some middle ground to reconcile our differences. Let's start the negotiations in the bath," I suggest, untying her towel with a quick flick, letting it fall to the floor and revealing her tempting curves.

Enola looks down at the towel pooled at her feet. She shivers as my hands trace circles around her creamy breasts, deliberately avoiding their peaks. My body responds, growing hard against my pants. I press my hips into the curve of her back, making sure she feels the heat of the desire she stirs in me.

In other circumstances, I would take her right now—standing, from behind, against the mosaic wall to release the tension simmering between us. But I remember that I only deflowered my wife yesterday. If I were as rough with her as I've been with more experienced lovers in the past, I might hurt her. I can't allow myself to give in to that kind of primal urge with Enola.

Not yet, anyway.

But soon, I hope.

"The water's cold, Sylvan," she objects, as I leave a trail of kisses along her neck, stopping at the curve of her shoulder.

I step back to unlace my tunic, an ironic smile playing on my lips. "Not for long, my little Glace."

***

Holding Enola's hand in mine, I step down the stairs leading into the bath. The water closes in around our feet. I focus on channeling my elemental magic through my legs. In less than a minute, the heat from my power spreads through the water, warming it until steam rises from the surface. A delighted smile stretches across my wife's lips. I tug her gently behind me, the water rippling around our legs.

"I'm going to wash you," I say, picking up the bottle of cleansing lotion I had placed on the edge of the bath before finishing undressing.

"I'm so honored, Your Majesty," she comments sarcastically.

I shoot her a mock-threatening look as I pour a small amount of translucent lotion into my palm.

"Indeed, it is a great honor. You should consider yourself lucky—I wouldn't do this for anyone else."

"Not even a former lover?"

"No," I confirm, pressing my oily hand to the Fuegis mark on her sternum as I begin to massage her dusty skin. "Now, raise your arms."

She complies. When my fingers brush the hollow of her armpits, she lets out a small, musical laugh. I seem to have tickled her. I can't help but smile.

"Will I have the privilege of washing your royal body as well?"

"We'll see, Enola."

I let my hands glide over every inch of her pale skin, alternating between rubbing, kneading, and gentle caresses, adjusting to the sensitivity of each area I touch. Enola watches the movement of my fingers with growing impatience, surrendering to my care with a trust that delights me. She tilts her head, giving me access to her delicate neck, arches her chest as I massage her soft, round breasts, turns so I can wash her back and buttocks, and obediently parts her thighs when my hand rests on her pubis. Her breathing quickens as my fingertips linger over her pink slit, moving languidly. It's hard for me to keep my composure as I linger in this enticing spot, coating it generously with the fragrant lotion. Seeing her bite her full lower lip and noticing the flush of arousal coloring her cheeks, I have to fight the urge to slide my finger inside her. I want to stretch this moment of intimacy, of shared relaxation, as long as possible. After everything we've been through in the last night and day, we both need this.

Enola truly has a magnificent body, and she's completely unaware of it. That's what makes her so graceful and sensual. None of the women I've been with in my life come close to her beauty.

The first time I saw her naked, on the day she arrived in Astranis, I was stunned by the purity and voluptuousness of her figure. I silently thanked the Fire God for my helm, which hid my fevered expression as I took her by the waist to help her down from the saddle. I was even seized by an unprecedented silent fury toward my own soldiers, imagining myself scorching their lecherous eyes with my Fire magic… just to stop them from gawking at her like a tavern wench they wanted to ravage. If I hadn't been able to suppress my power, the consequences could have been disastrous. The intensity of that possessive impulse toward my enemy had troubled me at the time. I couldn't understand how I could desire the woman who killed my father… especially with such force. I realized why when she confessed the truth about herself. My subconscious had known all along that she wasn't Alena Kan-Glace.

When she revealed her true identity to me, something inside me was freed. I allowed myself to desire her. And soon after, that mental release led to the deeper feelings I had also been suppressing.

I don't know what the future holds or where this war will lead us, but I won't let her slip away from me. Enola is mine.

She raises her hands, placing them on my chest, tracing the many scars with her wet fingertips, her gaze distant as if she's trying to read me through the marks of my past.

"There's goodness in you, Sylvan," her voice tinged with sadness, verbalizing her most intimate thoughts. "You care for your people. I regret not seeing it sooner. I used to think you were a soulless, bloodthirsty monster. I didn't see…"

She hesitates. I slide my hands up her narrow waist, brushing her belly with my thumbs.

"What didn't you see?"

"That you were deeply wounded," she says softly, placing her hand over my heart, which races beneath her touch. "I wish I had the power to heal your pain."

But you already do.

My lips claim hers, savoring the taste. My wife welcomes my eager tongue into her mouth with a small, strangled moan. Consumed by desire, I can think of nothing but burying myself inside her. Every fiber of my being is pulled toward that singular goal. This woman is the remedy for my pain, the source of my well-being, the flame that lights my darkness, the breath that revives me, the root of my hope. She is all of this… and so much more.

Without breaking the kiss, I step backward in the bath, pulling her with me until my heels hit a submerged step. I sit down, eagerly pulling Enola onto my lap. She clings to my shoulders, straddling me, her legs wrapped around mine. I devour her neck with passionate kisses. Her pulse races beneath my lips, matching the relentless throbbing of my blood-filled cock. Panting, she presses down on my shoulders, rising to her knees to offer me her tantalizing breasts. I purr with satisfaction at her initiative, capturing one of her pale pink nipples in my mouth and rolling it under my tongue. Enola arches against me, mewling in pleasure, her hands tangled in my hair, her nails scratching my head. Her body writhes under my touch. But she won't escape me. I suckle her delicious breast with tender delight until her hoarse moans turn into desperate cries.

One of her hands reaches underwater, firmly grasping the base of my shaft. Before I can react, my wife begins to impale herself on me, drawing a growl of surprise from my throat. I bury my head between her breasts, overwhelmed by the incredible sensation of her body stretching to accommodate mine. God of Fire, she's so tight that her walls squeeze my cock like a vice, and I'm already teetering on the edge of release. I grab Enola's hips, slowing her descent along my length. She nips at my lips as she gradually lowers herself onto me. She doesn't seem to be in much pain from our union, which is a relief. Once I'm fully seated inside her, I let her move her hips at her own pace, allowing her to take the reins of our ride.

Her hesitant, awkward movements don't last long. After a few tries, she finds the right angle, the right pressure, the right rhythm… and grows more confident and skilled. Her fierce thrusts send me into a trance. Her nails scratch my cheeks. Her sultry cries invigorate me. The wild, defiant look in her eyes holds me captive, just as surely as her body draws me in. With an uncontrollable groan, I place my hands on her hips. To see and feel her better, I lean back on the steps, tightening my abs as I shift my position. The heat of her walls gripping my rock-hard shaft is divine. Her body begins to undulate against mine beneath the water with a perfect, fluid grace, transporting us to the edge of an ocean of shared bliss, where we drown our mutual pain—perhaps even begin to heal it.

✱✱✱

An hour later, in bed, Enola sleeps nestled in my arms, her head resting on my chest, her messy silver hair sprawled across me. Exhausted as I am, I can't sleep. Hundreds of dark, troubling thoughts swirl in my restless mind. Death. Blood. Fear. War. Destruction. Betrayal. Rebellion.

"Sylvan… Sylvan…," my wife murmurs, shifting in her sleep, her features tense, her breathing uneven. I turn my head toward her, frowning. She's having a nightmare.

"It was… the only… way. F-forgive me."

Forgive her?

"Don't… don't leave me, Sylvan," she moans in a terrified voice, her voice terrified, her frail hand clenched on my chest. "Don't abandon me…"

"I'm not leaving, Enola," I whisper, stroking her face, heartbroken by her distress. "I won't abandon you."

A crystalline tear escapes from her closed eyelid.

"She…she abandoned me, too. I can't remember her face… I can't remember her name…"

"Who abandoned you?" I whisper, wiping away the tear with my finger.

"She'll never come back… Never… She's so far away, so far, so far… Come back to me, Sylvan, I beg you… Forgive me for lying to you… Without you, I'll never find the truth… never find peace… I'll be lost in the Red Desert… I'll drown in the Endless Ocean…"

"Enola, my queen," I say solemnly, my lips close to hers. "Listen to me. I swear on my life, I will never let anyone tear us apart. If I must, I'll kill anyone who tries. We are bound like the sun and the moon, day and night, fire and water. You have become my everything. Let all the gods of Symbiosis bear witness, Enola Ren-Fuegis: I love you with all my heart."

As I speak these words, I realize the full weight of them, words I've never said to anyone—not even my parents when I was a child.

I love Enola.

That she is Glace, Alena's sister, changes nothing about my feelings. My heart will be hers until death.

With a gentle kiss, I capture the long, peaceful sigh that escapes her lips. Her face gradually relaxes, and her hand loosens its grip on my chest.

My beautiful wife drifts back into a more peaceful sleep.

But as for me, I don't close my eyes all night, haunted by her cryptic words… especially one in particular.

"Forgive me for lying to you."

CHAPTER SIX
WAR COUNCIL

ENOLA

I dreamed of the Red Desert and Sylvan again last night.

The scorching sand beneath me swallowed me into its depths. Underground flames scorched my legs. An acidic wind flayed the skin on my face. Tears streaked my cheeks as I reached out to my husband, begging him to save me, but he stood still and silent. His features were cold, his expression vacant, and he watched as I sank inch by inch into the sand, never lifting a finger to help me. I was terrified. The more I struggled, the more I screamed, the worse it became. When I was buried up to my neck, Sylvan turned away and began to walk off. He was leaving me to my fate after discovering the truth about me. He was leaving me to die.

"Don't go, Sylvan. Don't leave me…"

But he never came back.

The sand infiltrated my throat, turning not into water but into blood. I was drowning in the darkness of an Endless Ocean, blood-red and sinister. An invisible force pulled me down to the depths. I couldn't swim toward the surface. I opened my mouth to breathe, to cry for help, to survive. Every fiber of my being was screaming, *"Come back to me, Sylvan, I beg you… Forgive me for lying to you…"*

Just as hope slipped away, I heard his voice in my mind.

"Enola Ren-Fuegis, I love you with all my heart."

I gasped for air… and my nightmare ended.

Thankfully, the rest of the night was much calmer.

Yet, this morning, I wake with a lump in my throat when I realize the space next to me in bed is empty. I clutch the sheets between my fingers. They're cold. Sylvan has been gone for a while, attending to his duties. An inexplicable sadness settles over me. I had hoped to wake up wrapped in his protective arms, his long, bare body pressed against mine, so I could kiss him and lose myself in the comfort of his embrace. But my husband is the king, and I have no choice but to accept it. The call of royal duty comes before all else.

It's only a matter of time before Sylvan discovers that Alena Kan-Glace is alive and that I am not her sister. If my former sovereign is indeed leading the rebellion, as I suspect, she will soon make herself known. Then, all the people of Symbiosis will learn that I am merely her lookalike, and that a Powerless woman, with not a drop of royal blood, was crowned as the new queen of the Fuegis.

If Sylvan doesn't have me executed for this massive public deception, the courtiers will tear me apart.

I don't have many options. I can either confess everything to my husband before external events—over which I have no control—bring the truth to light, or I can escape Astranis Palace and join Alena in Stalagmis, hoping to persuade her not to attack the Fuegis kingdom— even though I don't hold out much hope. Either way, I'm risking my life.

I have no desire to choose between the two sides. Sure, I was born in another kingdom, my skin and hair are white, but ever since I was freed from slavery, I've felt more connected to the Fuegis than to the Glaces. I wish Sylvan and his enemies could sign a peace treaty, but I'm not so naive—I don't see how such a favorable outcome could happen.

At the same time, I can't bring myself to leave my husband or give up the precious bond that's growing between us.

I'm unable to make a decision one way or the other. I'm torn.

I feel so alone and helpless in the middle of all this chaos.

Suddenly, a sensation of heat and itching hits me in four distinct spots.

My forehead.

My sternum.

The inside of my wrists.

Did I bump into the nightstand during the night? I flip my arms over to check for bruises. No, two irritated marks have appeared on my skin. Maybe I've developed a food allergy.

Scratching my wrists raw, I head to the bathroom to confront my reflection in the mirror.

My Glace tattoo on my forehead and my Fuegis sun between my breasts… have turned as red as my two new marks. It's like four wounds are becoming infected at the same time.

A violent migraine pounds my temples. A painful spasm roils my stomach.

Feeling nauseous, dizzy, and trembling, I stagger toward the latrine to vomit up all the bile in my stomach.

But I'm not fooling myself… I'm not sick.

That's what frightens me the most.

Something is changing inside me.

Something incredibly powerful.

And I'm not sure I'm strong enough to handle all this raw power.

SYLVAN

At first light, I summoned an emergency council in the meeting room on the fifth floor of the Tower of Eternal Flame. All the High-Fuegis are present, along with Captain Daegan. Sitting in my chair, I reread the letter sent by Fuegis sergeant who led the garrison in Stalagmis. The writing is rushed, the sentences collide on the lines, some letters are twisted and hard to decipher. The officer was panicked when he wrote this message. He's likely dead by now. I hope his death was swift and noble, and that he didn't suffer too much.

"Just before your return to Astranis, I took the initiative to send messenger birds to the officers of our garrisons in Oceanar and Eolan to request updates," my uncle says with a calmness I envy. I nod rigidly, refolding the letter. "I also asked them to alert our spies about the need to gather more information regarding this underground opposition formed by the Stownes, Aerias, Glaces, and Renegades."

"I still can't believe they managed to convince those savage Renegates to ally with them," remarks an old High-Fuegis named Andreas, stroking his braided beard. "They must have promised to reintegrate them into the other kingdoms and grant them equal rights with ours."

"We don't care about the degrading and sacrilegious pacts they've made!" snaps another advisor with a mix of disdain and tension. "What I see is that our enemies are willing to stoop to any level to overthrow us, and they could attack at any moment! Do we have any estimates of their military numbers, Captain?"

"Not yet, High-Fuegis," Daegan mutters, exchanging a serious glance with me. "We're actively working on it. We dispatched scouts across Symbiosis last night. Including one of my best men into the Exile Forest, the stealthiest in the guard. His mission is to check whether all the Renegades who once lived there have left."

"We don't yet know what they're planning," Andreas cautions.

"It seems obvious to me that they'll reclaim Oceanar and Eolan before laying siege to Astranis! Majesty, Lord Leonal, we're wasting time. We should anticipate the danger by mobilizing our entire army to retake Stalagmis."

"Charging headlong into the wolf's den without knowing exactly how many enemies we face or what they're plotting?" Daegan burst out, leaning forward with a clenched fist on the table. "Stripping the capital's defenses by sending all our troops to Stalagmis would be madness. That crude strategy would weaken us and leave us vulnerable. Another army could seize the opportunity to attack Astranis while our soldiers are engaged at Stalagmis."

"Our city is invisible," another old man argues with infuriating confidence. "Even if only a few hundred Fuegis defended it, Astranis would hold. Its fortifications have withstood all the sandstorms over the centuries and—"

"*Sandstorms*, High-Fuegis! But would they withstand earthquakes that would shatter the foundations of the walls? Tornadoes that would rip off rooftops? Rains that would trigger landslides and floods in our streets? Some High-Stownes, High-Aerias, and High-Glaces can unleash these disasters!" the captain reminded him sharply. "Not to mention a prolonged siege, one that could last for months until we either surrendered or famine wiped out our people."

"Perhaps it would be wise to negotiate with them before we face such a catastrophic scenario," Leonal suggests, casting me a meaningful look.

All the advisors turn their attention to my uncle.

He has an idea.

And I already know that I'm not going to like it.

"Negotiate with that pack of dogs?" Daegan growls, skeptical.

"Are you suggesting we bribe them to quell the conflict, Lord Leonal?" adds Andreas before taking a sip of wine.

"Oh, he's not talking about money," I answer coldly, cutting in for my father's brother. "And it's out of the question, Leonal."

"Your Majesty, let's not dismiss this option just yet." My uncle let his gleaming eyes wander over the other High-Fuegis. Frustrated, I leaned back into my throne. "If we showed generosity and diplomacy by returning to the three other Element-Clans what they believe they've lost, we could potentially avoid more needless battles. It all boils down to three names. Lia Ler-Aeria. Belise San-Stowne. Alena Kan-Gla—"

"No. I won't return my three wives to my enemies."

Leonal opens his mouth, but I cut him off, anticipating his objections with my most unyielding tone.

"The discussion is over, uncle! I will not support negotiations of this kind. We will partially reinforce our garrisons in Oceanar and Eolan. Two thousand Fuegis will move there, and we'll have three thousand soldiers left to ensure our defense in Astranis in case of a siege. We will store provisions in our warehouses as a precaution and alert all the villages of the Red Deserts to be ready for mass evacuation if the enemy troops storm our kingdom. Captain, you'll station patrols near all our borders. And with the scouts' reports, we'll gather as much intelligence as possible to better counter the military threats we face."

None of the advisors challenge my decisions, but I detect a shadow of disapproval in the eyes of some, including my uncle. Daegan, however, seems to side with me, as he often does.

The other members of the court are unaware that my two former wives are still alive; this secret has been strictly kept within the small circle of my inner command. Most of the High-Fuegis wanted me to carry out the executions. A few were undecided. I made the final decision, refusing to kill the two innocent women.

I might have considered letting go of my wives as a last resort if it were *only* Lia and Belise. I don't see much point in keeping them hostage in this new precarious situation. The Aerias and the Stownes might have agreed to negotiate with us had we revealed that their two princesses were spared and that I had killed their kings to avenge my father's death—and not to conquer the other kingdoms due to my so-called madness and thirst for power. Especially since Lia and Belise were never mistreated during their captivity. To pacify everyone, I might even have made the enormous concession of annulling my two marriages, emphasizing that they were never consummated. That way, I would officially renounce the Aeria and Stowne crowns and, therefore, the throne of Symbiosis. I would have done it for my people above all.

But let's be realistic before idealistic: this gesture of goodwill would have changed nothing if the enmity between the four Clans was too deeply rooted.

In any case, I will *never* hand Enola over to those High-Glaces scum who didn't hesitate to put her in her twin's place with the intent to sacrifice her. Since I pardoned and freed her, and she didn't attempt to harm me afterward, they probably see her as a traitor now. If they got their hands on her, only the gods know what they'd do. Death, imprisonment, torture, manipulation…

My thoughts are in disarray, except for one thing: my true wife will stay by my side… no matter what happens.

I can't admit it to anyone, but I am overwhelmed. I am not my father. He would have known how to handle such a situation. I am a warrior, not a diplomat. Saradin balanced both roles with ease.

Moreover, I can't trust anyone in my court. There's a traitor among them.

I'm beginning to suspect my uncle… who, on his side, accuses Enola of being the spy who informed our enemies of our arrival in Raockar. He hinted at this before the council when it was just the two of us. I didn't bother responding, too obsessed with my wife's cryptic words in her sleep, *"Forgive me for lying to you."* This morning, as I left her chambers, I thought she might be referring to her past lies, back when she pretended to be Alena.

But I'm not really convinced.

I pray that's all it is—or just some trivial detail that has nothing to do with it.

That would be the least bad explanation.

In fact, I mostly pray that the woman I've fallen in love with isn't *truly* Queen Alena Kan-Glace, who might have taken on the role of a fictional Enola, made me believe in her own death, and concocted some twisted twin story to exploit my weak human emotions against me.

That would be the worst-case scenario. I don't know how I would react. I don't even want to think about it.

In short, until we uncover the traitor in the enemy's camp, I have to carefully watch everything I say in front of the other Fuegis… and even around my wife—at least until I know what she lied to me about.

I feel utterly alone and helpless in the midst of this chaos.

CHAPTER SEVEN

THE KING'S TEAR

ENOLA

I may not be at my best, but I desperately need to keep my hands busy and clear my mind.

After chewing on some medicinal herbs to calm my nausea and dizziness, I head down to the palace kitchens to offer my help.

As I enter, all the Fuegis servants, busy preparing the midday meal, suddenly turn their bewildered gazes toward me and break into awkward bows, completely caught off guard by my presence. With a laugh, I shake my head, motioning for them to continue their tasks. Suspicious of me, they hesitate, exchanging tense glances. I walk over to young Jall, my food taster, who greets me with a warm, genuine smile. He explains that he is the son of the head cook, Amelia, and introduces me to her. The plump, sauce-stained older Fuegis blushes with pleasure when I compliment her on both the quality of her cooking and the cleanliness of her domain. I ask if I can be of any help. She looks at me as if I've just grown a pair of wings.

"But… you're the queen. Queens don't do this kind of work," she protests, eyes wide with disbelief.

"Maybe other queens don't. I love cooking—it relaxes me."

I take the knife from Jall's hand, who had been peeling vegetables and potatoes before I arrived, move to the table, and begin peeling a carrot under the stunned eyes of the servants. With an amused chuckle, Jall grabs another knife and joins me in the task.

This is how I get to know several of the palace kitchen staff—by pitching in. Once the ice is broken, we chat about simple, everyday things: food, market goods, and living conditions in the poorer parts of the city. As they relax, some of the Fuegis even share their names and tell me about their families. I feel much more at ease here with them than at court among the sweet-talking vultures dressed in fine clothes. Unlike the courtiers, these people have no ulterior motives. They're sincere and down-to-earth. They work tirelessly to meet the nobles' demands while earning a pittance.

Two hours later, when I leave the kitchens after wishing them a good day, I notice their view of me has changed. Their eyes are filled with respect and admiration, which warms my heart and lightens my spirit… for a little while, at least.

However, just before midday, I realize I haven't seen Sylvan all morning. I scour the palace from top to bottom, with Anetos, my new guard, following close behind. Eventually, Daegan informs me that my husband has withdrawn to pray and meditate in the palace crypt.

I find the young king kneeling before an imposing sarcophagus, sculpted in the likeness of a noble figure lying on his back, hands crossed over a familiar stone sword.

Sylvan kneels in silence before the majestic tomb of his father, Saradin Ren-Fuegis. Candles burn in each corner of the cold, musty chamber, filling the air with the scent of dust and dampness. Blood-red columns etched with numerous commemorative runes intensify the mystical atmosphere of the room.

The sarcophagus doesn't hold the former king's body but instead his ashes, clothes, and jewels. The Fuegis always cremate their dead.

In a posture of humility, Sylvan sits with his head bowed, hands flat on his thighs, his crown placed on the ground in front of him. At my request, the soldier escorting me closes the doors behind us and stands guard in the hallway, ensuring we won't be disturbed.

I kneel beside Sylvan and place my tiara inside his crown. He turns his head to study me for a long moment, a furrow on his brow.

"You look even paler than usual… Are you running a fever?" he murmurs, brushing aside a lock of hair hanging in front of my face.

His concern should warm my heart, yet it tightens my stomach instead.

Since we made love, we've grown much closer. I hadn't fully realized it until today, as the shift felt so natural.

Before what we experienced in the Desert of Fire, we were playing roles with each other. Now, that's no longer the case.

We are now *truly* husband and wife.

Which brings responsibilities I can no longer avoid.

With my heart pounding, I dodge his comment.

"I have another story to tell you today."

"I'm not in the mood for one of your alternate endings. Maybe tomorrow," he replies, his voice heavy with exhaustion.

I place my trembling hand on his.

"No, Sylvan. Now. It's not an alternate ending. It's… an alternate story. I'm going to ask you not to interrupt. Not to ask any questions. To stay calm. And to listen until the very end."

He pierces me with his green gaze, sensing the gravity of my request. His fingers wrap around mine. He gives a slight nod.

I take a long breath.

Fear is my biggest enemy.

I must have faith in him—and in myself.

In *us*.

It's time to tell him my full story.

"Once upon a time, there was a young Glace girl named Enola.

She lived in a small fishing village in the north of Oceanar with her mother and brother, Elanos, in a tiny blue stilted cabin that shook with every gust of sea wind. Her father had died in a shipwreck a few days before her birth.

Enola had silver hair and deep blue eyes, so her mother, Bleuène, would call her *my sapphire*.

Elanos dreamed of becoming a soldier. On his eighteenth birthday, he enlisted in the royal army of Oceanar, leaving his mother and sister behind in the village. He sent a portion of his pay back to support them.

But Enola felt invisible. Powerless. Incapable. She hadn't developed any powers like the rest of her family. She watched with envy as other Glaces wielded their Water magic. Her mother would often joke that she must have been born on the moon because she was always daydreaming. One day, realizing that she was constantly lost in her own imaginative worlds, Enola began creating stories to enchant the children in her village. She needed to tell these little tales to feel alive. Sharing her dreams by bringing them to life through her characters had become her reason for being. In her eyes, it was another form of magic, one that allowed her young friends to escape their often difficult lives, travel to fantastic lands filled with unknown creatures, and live out improbable adventures.

By the time she was twenty-six, Enola was still Powerless. She left her house less and less, afraid that her secret would be discovered and she would be branded a Renegade, destined for exile in the Forest of Exile. She no longer told stories to the children. She avoided human contact like the plague, dodging the gazes of men for fear her secret would be uncovered. Fear and sadness constantly weighed on her. Anger, too. She found it absurd and unjust to be considered a pariah just because she was different from the other Glaces. All because of ancient traditions that no king or queen had ever thought to challenge over the generations. Enola longed to shout to the world that she didn't have a trace of magic in her, and it didn't matter. Magic doesn't define a person's worth—it's the will that resides in their heart.

Her mother fell seriously ill at the start of the war. Enola and Elanos didn't have enough money to afford the treatment she needed. Elanos took on a debt from a wealthy High-Glace to pay for the care. But Bleuène's condition didn't improve, and the High-Glace refused to lend them more money. He desired Enola's virtue. He promised the young woman that he would send the best doctors in Oceanar if she offered him her virginity. She was willing to do anything to save her mother, so she agreed to the deal, despite the revulsion she felt toward the man.

This High-Glace was named Vidal. Rumor had it that he was the lover of Queen Alena Kan-Glace.

With a heavy heart, her face veiled as her future lover had demanded, Enola went to the castle of Oceanar to carry out the deed behind her brother's back, knowing he would have forbidden her from degrading herself in such a way. But when she entered Vidal's chambers, she was met with the shock of her life. He wasn't alone.

Queen Alena Kan-Glace was there too.

It was the first time Enola had seen the queen up close, and it was a true shock. The woman looked exactly like her. She was slightly thinner, a bit taller, and her eyes were lighter, but their faces were almost identical.

Vidal had lured her into a trap. After meeting Enola, he had reported to his royal mistress that there was a fisherman's daughter who was her spitting image. Alena had instructed Vidal to manipulate Enola with the story about her virginity to test how far she would go for her family. He had acted on the queen's orders.

After the fall of the city of Eolan and the murder of King Cyriel, Princess Lia Ler-Aeria was enslaved by Sylvan Ren-Fuegis and executed the day after their wedding. Alena feared the same fate awaited her if he attacked the Glace Kingdom. She wanted to be prepared, to take precautions.

So, she offered Enola a new deal. If things went wrong during the war, if Oceanar fell into enemy hands, Enola would take her place as the captive queen alongside King Sylvan Ren-Fuegis. In exchange for this sacrifice, Alena guaranteed that Bleuène would receive the care she needed and that her family would be protected.

Enola wore to take on the role of Alena Kan-Glace if the worst happened and the Fuegis won the war. In absolute secrecy, Vidal tattooed the symbol of Glace royalty on Enola's forehead, instructing her to keep it hidden. He taught her basic etiquette, details about the four royal dynasties of Symbiosis, and how to mimic Alena's behavior, all while the royal court's doctors worked to heal her mother.

In the meantime, Belise San-Stowne was also captured by Sylvan and executed the day after her wedding.

Three weeks later, the event Queen Alena feared most came to pass—Oceanar was besieged and quickly fell to the Fuegis invasion.

Alena, her lover Vidal, and a few Glaces escaped through underground tunnels.

Despite her terror, Enola was brought to the castle to cover for the real queen. She was torn from her homeland by Sylvan Ren-Fuegis, who forced her into marriage at Astranis. She prepared herself for death, perhaps even for being violated the night before her execution.

She hated him. She believed he was a soulless monster.

On their wedding night, driven by survival instincts, she made a desperate move to stay alive. She began telling him a story—about the virtue of another Enola, a fictitious alter ego. It was a tale she didn't plan to finish, promising instead to conclude it the following evening. She had nothing left to lose.

Against all odds, Sylvan gave her one more day.

Then another.

Slowly, she became trapped in a web of lies and half-truths. Cornered, she revealed her real name, but not her true identity. She feared that he would kill her if he found out she was a Powerless. She told him that Alena was dead and that she was her twin sister, even though it was a lie. She spun a tale from nothing.

And Sylvan believed her.

She started to see that he wasn't the bloodthirsty tyrant the rumors made him out to be. She saw the light within him, that he cared for his people, that he was deeply hurt by the death of his father, and that this war was driven purely by his desire for vengeance. She realized that he was as lonely and wounded as she was, in his own way, and that they had much in common despite their differences.

She began to desire not the king, but the man he became with her—the man who revealed the hidden side of himself. Gentle. Tender. Sincere. He didn't see Alena when he looked at her; he only saw Enola. And when he looked at her, for the first time in her life, she felt truly seen. She wasn't nothing—she was everything to him.

He gave her his trust by freeing her from her slave collar. He made her his rightful queen. He gave her everything she had never dared hope for, even in her wildest dreams.

The more she came to know him, the more guilt she felt. But she feared losing him even more—being rejected and abandoned.

Far from Astranis, in the north of the Red Desert, she gave him her virginity. Because deep down, she felt she had always been meant for him, and no one else. And that night, as she fell asleep in his arms, trusting him completely after surrendering to the pleasure of their bodies intertwined, she realized that she loved Sylvan Ren-Fuegis with all her being.

Not long after, she decided she would rather die than continue lying to the king—the man who had become her everything.

So, with fear in her heart and her soul breaking, she told him the whole truth."

✳✳✳

"I don't know how this story ends, Sylvan. It's up to you to continue it and finish it," I whisper painfully, concluding my confession.

My husband doesn't answer.

I didn't look away from him as I was telling him everything. He remained as still as a mountain, his eyes fixed on his father's sarcophagus, his face devoid of any expression. It's as if he hadn't heard a single word of what I just revealed.

But I know he has absorbed every syllable that left my lips.

I can feel that every word I spoke hit him like an icy dagger plunging into his back, piercing his heart.

Sometimes, emotional pain is so intense that one would prefer to endure unbearable physical agony. That's what I feel now. Because that's exactly what Sylvan is feeling in this moment.

I wish I had the power to go back and do things differently, but that's impossible. My breathing is ragged from fear as I brace myself for the aftermath of my revelation. His raw anger. His verbal onslaught. Perhaps even his brutal hatred.

But none of that comes.

Instead, something worse happens.

A tear.

Like a glistening drop of dew clinging to a broken reed, it falls from the corner of his eye, tracing the jagged path of his scar.

The king of Symbiosis is crying.

The sight of his lone tear shreds my chest from the inside. My own eyes burn with grief, my breath catches, and my heart breaks.

"Forgive me," I manage to say, my voice breaking under the weight of my despair.

His tear slips from his jaw and lands in the center of our intertwined fingers. It's warm.

He pulls his hand away from mine. I withdraw my palm from his thigh, crushed by his gesture of rejection.

"Leave," he orders, his voice hoarse and cold, still not taking his eyes off the sarcophagus.

"Sylvan, I'm so sorry. I… I love you. I never wanted to hurt you. I never meant to—"

"*Leave, in the name of the gods, go!*" he suddenly yells, his voice unrecognizable, booming like thunder through the crypt.

Suddenly, the flames of the candles stretch and rise like enraged golden ribbons, nearly brushing the stone ceiling.

With a strangled sob caught in my throat, I stand up, nearly tripping over my skirts, and run from him at full speed, devastated. I crack open one of the doors to the hall and flee, shoving past the guard in the corridor.

As I reach the first step of the staircase, I hear a deafening roar—a wounded beast's howl—that reverberates through the palace's underground, shattering every part of me as if my insides had turned to glass.

I was everything to him.

Now, I am nothing.

Chapter Eight
Unanswered Questions

Enola

I race through the palace corridors toward my quarters.

I stop abruptly at the slightly open door. Every hair on my body stands on end.

Someone is inside.

Faint, choked whimpers mix with the venomous hiss of a woman's voice, dripping with hatred—one I recognize.

"Use your Fire magic to defend yourself, girl. Go on, use it!"

I quickly push the door open.

The scene before me chills me to my core.

Nadya Ler-Aeria is in my quarters.

Facing her is Selaine, my young Fuegis servant.

Pinned against the wall by Nadya's Air magic, Selaine is suffocating. Her head is thrown back, her skin turning blue, and her eyes bulge with terror. Her feet hover above the floor, her legs kicking frantically in the air. With her powers, the High-Aeria is cutting off Selaine's oxygen while making her levitate. She can't breathe.

By all the gods of Symbiosis, Nadya is going to kill her!

An unspeakable fury erupts inside me.

Something surges out of my body—a force I cannot control.

With a startled scream, Nadya is flung backward like a wooden puppet, slamming into the wall so hard that the impact knocks her unconscious. She collapses to the ground, limp. Freed from the magical grip, Selaine falls to the floor, gasping for air in a huge, desperate gulp.

Did… did I do that?

Not stopping to dwell on it, I rush to my servant, who lifts tear-filled eyes to me, her hands clutching her throat. I drop to my knees beside her.

"My queen, you are there! By the God of Fire, I thought I was going to die!" she rasps, her voice raw, as she buries herself in my arms.

I hold her tightly against me, my gaze filled with confusion as I look at the wretched woman lying unconscious at the foot of the wall, a thin trail of blood on her temple. Her chest rises and falls, a sign that she's still alive. I could have killed her by accident…

What in the world was she thinking? Has she gone mad?

"What happened, Selaine?" I whisper, gently stroking the girl's hair in a calming gesture.

"She… she was taking advantage of your absence to search through your chambers, Alena." My angry eyes dart toward the scattered books from my library, now strewn across the floor in complete disarray. "I… I caught her when I came to change your sheets, and she attacked me before I could report it to you or my father," Selaine sobs against my chest. "I was so scared!"

"It's okay, Selaine. Everything's okay now. She won't hurt you anymore."

Nadya is a spy.

Could she have been the one who alerted the Stownes to our presence in Raockar? If that's true… hundreds of people died because of her that night. Including little Kara and her parents.

Just then, my new bodyguard bursts into my chambers, looking completely stunned. I lift my head toward him and give him an order, "Go get the captain immediately."

***

Daegan handled the situation with unmatched composure.

Nadya has been locked in her quarters, awaiting interrogation by

Sylvan. A magical collar, the same one I used to wear, now neutralizes her powers, and two guards stand watch outside her door. Before taking his traumatized daughter away, the captain informed me that the courtier was still unconscious and wouldn't wake up for several hours. He asked me how I managed to subdue her. I told him I did nothing, and that I believed Nadya's Air magic had backfired on her. Surprised by my sudden arrival, she likely lost her concentration and control over her powers.

Daegan didn't seem convinced by my explanation, but he didn't insist. His priority was to comfort his daughter, who was still shaken.

Still, something troubles me.

"Use your Fire magic to defend yourself," Nadya yelled at Selaine before I intervened.

That sticks with me. In the Red Desert, on our way to Raockar, Daegan had mentioned that his daughter's elemental magic had manifested about a year ago.

So why didn't my servant at least *try* to use her powers?

Sitting on the bed, my eyes locked on the closed door. I waited for Sylvan in my quarters until late. y already faint hope eroded with each passing minute. By around three in the morning, I had to accept the truth. *He will not come.*

I curled up under the sheets, my soul as battered as my wrists, which I had been incessantly scratching since that morning.

I didn't lie to him at all when I told him my story in the crypt. I love him. I love the hardened ruler. I love the tortured young man. Both have taken hold of my unbearably heavy heart. I burn for him with a fire that nothing could extinguish.

Goddess of the Ocean, it hurts so much.

I was more lost than ever. I didn't know what to do. Leave? Stay? Go to my queen and pray to fix things? Return to my family and unburden myself of responsibility? Hide away in some cave like a coward? Beg my husband on my knees not to turn his back on me?

Not to execute me?

And what did he think of Nadya Ler-Aeria's betrayal? I hadn't heard any news, directly or indirectly, all day. I didn't know if she was still unconscious or if she had woken up… or how Selaine was doing. In truth, I felt like no one in the palace cared about me anymore.

All these questions swirled in my mind as the dark fog of sleep finally overwhelmed me, like a temporary balm on my open wounds.

I dreamed that he slipped quietly into bed beside me. I could feel his warm breath on my cheek, his fingers running through my hair. He whispered my name, his voice cracked in my ear. He smelled of wine. His naked body curled against my back under the covers. His hand rested on the curve of my hip, gripping my flesh as if to claim it. I wanted him to continue. I wanted him never to stop touching me. I wanted to hear him say he loved me and forgave me.

In my dream, I rolled onto my back. I reached out blindly, feeling the taut muscles of his chest. My fingers traveled upward, caressing his throat and tracing the familiar line of the scar on his face, a mark I now knew so well. His lips brushed against mine, as light as a feather. Overwhelmed by the contact, I refused to let his mouth leave mine. I grabbed the back of his neck with my cold hands, pulling him closer. I nipped and sucked on his lips without mercy until he surrendered to my unspoken demand. I slipped my tongue between his parted lips. I trapped his hips between my legs, holding him captive. I ground my hips feverishly against his, showing him what I wanted, what I so desperately needed.

A salty taste on my tongue… our tears, his or mine, running into my throat. He panted against my mouth, trembling against me, burning like a furnace, but he didn't respond to my physical pleas.

At first.

Because I was determined to break through all his barriers, one by one, until he gave in.

Until he pushed his tongue into my mouth.

Until he cupped my face firmly in his hands.

Until he moved his rock-hard erection against my burning core.

Until he said my name, his voice thick with desire.

And he did.

But in my dream, things spiraled out of control for both of us.

At some point, Sylvan tore himself away from my lips and suddenly flipped me onto the bed. Without ceremony, he yanked my nightgown up to my waist and pressed his hand between my thighs to check if I was wet. And I was.

He lifted my hips and pulled me toward him roughly. Three seconds later, he thrust into me with such force that a broken cry escaped my lips. A guttural groan of relief tore from his throat as he buried himself deep inside me, filling me with every inch of him, stretching me, crucifying me. Then his heavy, muscular body began to pound against mine… violently. There was no gentleness in his movements, not a trace of tenderness. His hips slammed against the flesh of my thighs with a relentless rhythm. The walls of my body crackled with both pain and pleasure at every brutal thrust of his cock. Each drive felt like a scorching knife plunging into me. His fist twisted in my hair, yanking my head back with force.

I realized he was punishing me. He wasn't making love to me as his wife; he was ravaging me like a courtesan. But a part of me, the part that fed off our shared suffering, relished this raw, primal act. I submitted willingly to his will. We had to go through this. I could feel his Fire magic surging into me like an aggressive wave of lava, intertwining with the deep mysteries buried inside me. I was sweating, breathless, aroused, outraged, shaken, deliciously bruised.

I moaned uncontrollably, drunk on him. But Sylvan's hand clamped down over my open mouth, his fingers cruelly digging into my jaw. He silenced me, muffling the sounds that poured from my throat. This time, he didn't want to hear me. He wouldn't allow it. It was too painful for him. He was consumed by one singular desire: to fuck me like an animal. The pursuit of pleasure was secondary in this act. He needed to unload his rage and grief into me, to possess me in the most primitive way, to tear me apart, body and soul, to ravage me as he was ravaged.

And yet, I was already broken.

Yet, I came.

And with one final, ferocious thrust, so did he.

As the orgasm slammed into both of us, he bent down and bit into the juncture of my shoulder and neck, releasing a muffled roar. The pain and pleasure were so intense… they woke me up.

I'm not dreaming.

He's really behind me, his pulsing cock still nestled between my thighs.

Breathing heavily, Sylvan gently licks the bite on my neck, as if to soothe it. Then he whispers coldly into my ear, "I love you too, Enola. But I will never forgive you."

This simple sentence triggers a whirlwind of conflicting emotions in me. A burst of joy mixed with an abyss of pain.

Without saying another word, my husband withdrew from my body and leaves my bed hastily. Moments later, I hear the door to my quarters close behind him.

And I was alone again.

***

Dawn is near. I can see its soft pastel glow through the gap in the brocade curtains. I couldn't fall back asleep after Sylvan left. Like a little girl, I cried silently under the covers until my eyes were completely dry.

Exhausted because from my night, I slip out of bed with no energy at all. In the mirror, I examine the bite mark my husband left on my neck. No, it wasn't a dream. He was really here. I brush my thumb over the mark with a sad sigh.

Then I notice something strange—my Glace tattoo and my Fuegis mark are no longer infected. The colors are… different. The blue waves on my forehead and the red sun on my chest are more vibrant than ever. They even have a slight iridescence, as if threaded with silk. I glance down at my forearms, which aren't itching this morning.

What I see stuns me.

And terrifies me.

Both marks have changed. Their outlines have sharpened.

On my right wrist, the green oak tree of the Stownes.

On my left wrist, the silver feather of the Aerias.

I now bear the symbols of all four Elemental Clans on my skin.

CHAPTER NINE
THE THREE PRISONERS

SYLVAN

"How could you let them put that nasty necklace on me and confine me to my own quarters, Sylvan?" Nadya screeches, rising from her seat like a fury as I closed the door behind me. "It's an outrage. Your father would never have treated me this way!"

Her fingers gripped the openwork gold collar fastened around her neck, trembling with rage. My eyes fall on the bandage wrapped around her head. *Don't lose your temper, son*, murmurs Saradin's voice win my mind. *Keep your thoughts clear and be as just as possible.*

"But you never tried to kill a young girl while my father was alive, Lady Nadya." I reply. "Captain Daegan followed standard security protocol, nothing more. I would have done the same in his position until this situation was clarified."

"My status doesn't—"

"Your status doesn't entitle you to treat the palace servants however you please," I cut her off, my tone biting. "Selaine isn't some household pet to be mistreated at will. I demand an explanation, Lady Nadya."

She exhales loudly, lifting her chin defiantly.

"As I was passing through the corridor, I caught that simpering little wretch rummaging through your wife's quarters, Sylvan. She was rifling through her things. When she saw me, she tried to flee, so I subdued her with my powers. I didn't intend to kill her. I'm not a murderer, by the gods! I only meant to intimidate her into confessing. Queen Alena believed that little tramp without question."

The former concubine of my father didn't flinch as she delivered her version of events. Either she's an exceptional liar—which I've never doubted, since I know she can be truly vindictive when she takes a dislike to someone—or she's telling the truth.

I can't tell anymore. Ever since Enola confessed to deceiving me all along, I've questioned everything. I don't trust anyone—not Nadya, not even Selaine.

I was never particularly close to my stepmother. Since I was six years old, I've always kept my distance from her. When I was a child, I resented my father for *replacing* my mother, whom I loved with all my heart. He explained at the time that he wouldn't marry Nadya out of respect for his soulmate, taken too soon, and that her presence in Astranis was primarily a political gesture meant to strengthen relations between the Fuegis Clan and the Aeria Clan.

Over the years, I noticed that Saradin began to develop feelings for her.

But my mother had taken his heart with her when she died. My parents' love was so deep that my father could never feel more than affection and desire for Nadya. It hurt her more than once. Even though she never spoke of it, I could see her face crumble whenever he made a fond reference to my mother in conversation with someone else. I believe Nadya loved Saradin in her own way, and his death affected her far more than the other Fuegis realize.

She also tried multiple times to get closer to me when I was younger, hoping to become my substitute mother. But being naturally solitary and reserved, I never let her. I barely spoke to her until I was fourteen, and eventually, she gave up. I respect her because she was my father's companion, but it goes no further than that.

There are rumors at court that she's sleeping with both my uncle and me. In my case, I obviously know the truth—it's just another baseless rumor. As for Leonal, I'm not so sure. I've seen my uncle gently stroke her arm like a lover might when they thought they were alone. But this was right after my father's death. At the time, I interpreted it as a comforting gesture and didn't dwell on it.

I play along with Lady Nadya to gather more information.

"Why would she be searching through my wife's quarters?" I ask, locking eyes with her.

Regaining her composure, she sits back down, smoothing a part of her fitted gown before crossing her legs elegantly.

"I don't think it was her."

"I don't follow, Lady Nadya."

Her expression falters. She fidgets with the thin gold and silver bracelets on her wrist, something she only does when she's deeply troubled.

"It's not Selaine, Sylvan. I suspect she's a Stowne spy who's stolen her appearance. For weeks now, she's been snooping around the palace, listening in where she shouldn't."

"If we entertain that wild idea, Lady Nadya, then you could also be a Stowne spy."

Her gray eyes flash with anger.

"Take this collar off me, and I'll show you my Air magic! Or ask me about any past event that only your father and you would know—I'll answer without hesitation. But ask that servant to use her Fire magic, and you'll see for yourself that she can't because she's *not* a Fuegis! Her father might also be a spy infiltrating Astranis. The real Selaine and Daegan are probably both dead, Sylvan!"

No, that's not possible. If Selaine and Daegan were Stownes disguised as Fuegis, Enola would have known. She recognized the false Daegan at Raockar the night of the attack.

Unless my wife is also spy, as my uncle claims, I think, my stomach twisting in knots.

I can't rule out any possibility at this point.

"Who knocked you out yesterday, Lady Nadya?"

"It could only have been your wife, Sylvan! She must have Air magic in her—I was thrown several meters. I've always sensed something was off with her, that she wasn't who she claimed to be. Alena, or… whatever creature has replaced her, must have Aeria blood; I can't see any other explanation. We're surrounded by traitors, can't you see? And you accuse *me* of being a spy, after I've been nothing but loyal to your family. You're fighting the wrong enemy, Your Majesty."

I frown, deep in thought. Enola had told me in the crypt that she was born without powers, but several things contradict that claim. On the other hand, if she possessed strong magic and was truly working for Alena Kan-Glace or another Clan, she would have likely tried to kill me the moment the slave collar was removed. And she could have escaped into the desert when the Fuegis were fighting the Stownes in Raockar. She didn't.

God of Fire, this is so infuriating! The more I learn, the more confused I become!

"Sylvan, please, open your eyes," Nadya whispers, leaning forward. "Take the collar off me and put it on your wife. She's dangerous, Sylvan. She always has been. I'm worried about you. Since your father's death, you haven't been yourself and you—"

A sudden knock pounds on the door.

"What now?" I bark over my shoulder.

"Your Majesty, I need to speak with you," Daegan calls from the other side of the door.

"I'm coming," I mutter, turning back to Nadya. "I'll come see you later."

She opens her mouth to object, but at the sight of my unwavering expression, she bites back her words, her jaw tightening with frustration.

I step into the hallway to meet my captain.

"What is it, Daegan?"

"One of our patrols just returned from the Red Desert, my king. Our men captured three Renegade scouts."

ENOLA

Driven by a dark premonition of looming violence, I rush to the palace gardens, my bodyguard following closely behind, grumbling under his breath.

I've wrapped my wrists with silk ribbons to hide my two new marks. If anyone discovers my secret, I'm dead.

Nothing's changed.

I freeze when I reach the training grounds, seeing Sylvan, Daegan, and about twenty guards surrounding three prisoners kneeling in a row, bound like condemned men, their hands tied with rope. Their bare chests show the scars of brutal beatings—bloody slashes, countless bruises, and multiple burns. Goddess, they've already been tortured by the Fuegis soldiers…

Renegades, I guess, observing their patched-up trousers, tangled hair, and starved bodies.

"I'm giving you one last chance," my husband declares coldly, pacing in front of them, sword in hand. "Either you tell me everything you know about the instigators of the uprising in Stalagmis, or I'll execute each of you at random."

The three prisoners remain silent, heads bowed. Sylvan exchanges a grim look with Daegan.

Slowly, he uses the tip of his sword to lift the chin of the Renegade in the middle. Fear is etched on the man's sharp features, though he stands firm. Sylvan gazes down at him with haughty indifference.

"The first one who cooperates, I'll spare him," my husband promises, his tone strict. "The other two won't be so lucky."

The Renegades on the right and left exchange nervous glances. The one in the center, despite his fear, clenches his fists and boldly holds Sylvan's authoritative gaze. A sardonic smile forms on my husband's lips. He lowers his sword and taps the bony shoulder of the prisoner on the right with its flat side.

"A woman. It's a woman!" the Renegade on the left blurts out suddenly.

The man in the center spits in the traitor's face, showing his utter contempt.

"Shut your filthy mouth, you bastard, don't tell this tyrant anything!" shouts the Renegade on the right.

With a small nod from Sylvan, Daegan steps behind the man, grabs his hair, yanks his head back, and slits his throat without hesitation. The Renegade collapses face-first into a pool of blood, convulsing under the horrified stares of the remaining two.

At the sight of the brutal execution, a wave of dizziness overcomes me. I clutch my bodyguard's arm for support, a low whimper escaping my lips. Will this never end?

"Speak," Sylvan hisses, turning toward the Renegade on the left.

"I don't know her name! The High-Stownes never told us, and we never deal with her directly! I've never seen her face—she always wears a cloak and hood in public. Some say she's a High-Glace because there's always a High-Glace with her. It was those two who convinced the High-Stownes and the others to rebel against the Fuegis Kingdom."

My whole body tenses.

Alena and Vidal. Of course.

"How many men in this army?" Daegan asks.

Before the Renegade can answer, his companion lunges toward Sylvan, arms still bound, in a desperate attempt to grab the hilt of his sword… but he isn't fast enough.

With a swift motion, Sylvan drives his sword through the man's throat, then pulls the blood-soaked blade from his flesh.

The second Renegade crumples beside the first.

With an irritated click of his tongue, my husband wipes his sword clean on the dead man's battered back. The third prisoner, tears of regret filling his eyes, lowers his gaze to the corpses of his comrades.

"My captain asked you a question, scout," Sylvan growls. "Answer if you want to live! How many soldiers?"

"With us, the Powerless… about six thousand."

Six thousand men.

A violent shudder runs through me as I hear the number. Sylvan and Daegan's expressions darken.

"Where are they?"

"At… at Oceanar. They're preparing to siege the city to take it back."

"And then what will they do?" insists my husband, unfazed.

"No idea. The officers never tell the Renegades their strategies. Even in the army, they treat us all like dog crap."

"Because that's what you are," Sylvan sneers, glaring at him. "What did you expect? Once they've used you, they'll throw you into a mass grave! They only recruited you to sacrifice you on the front lines. Did they make you believe they'd let you join them and give you my kingdom as loot at the end of the war? BULLSHITS!" he roars, so loud it makes me jump.

"The Renegade is lying, Your Majesty," Daegan interjects. "If they sent these three as scouts, it's because they're planning to siege Astranis soon. Oceanar may already have fallen. Eolan too. They probably attacked all three cities at once to wipe out our garrisons. We need to recall the Fuegis soldiers who went to reinforce Oceanar and

Eolan, or they'll be slaughtered as well."

"I'm not lying! I'm not lying!" the man protests. "You said you'd spare me if I talked. I talked!"

"Yes, that's true, I did promise to spare you," my husband admits softly, sheathing his sword. "But Daegan didn't promise anything."

"No! Please! Mercy!"

"*Silvan stop!*" I shout in a trembling voice, unable to stay silent any longer.

turn toward me, surprised. A flash of anger cuts through my husband's green eyes when our gazes meet. Daegan hesitates, dagger in hand. I shake my head, pleading with my husband through my eyes. *Don't do this, Sylvan. Please. You're better than this.*

Without breaking eye contact, Sylvan says in a harsh tone, "Daegan. Kill the Renegade."

Crushed by grief, I close my eyes just as the captain's dagger slashes the throat of the third prisoner.

***

"You killed them!" I scream, hitting Sylvan with my fists once we're back in our quarters.

He doesn't blink. His winter-cold eyes stay fixed on me, his face unmoving, like a stone pillar. Eventually, he grabs my wrists, pushing me back with such force that I fall hard onto the chaise, shocked by his roughness.

"We are at war, my wife. You'll have to get used to it," he declares coldly, his commanding gaze pressing down on me.

"Those men were unarmed and tied up! They had no power. They couldn't defend themselves! It was vile."

"They chose their side. My enemies deserve neither my pity nor my mercy. And one of them attacked me, in case you forgot."

"It wouldn't have made any difference if he hadn't attacked you; you wouldn't have let him live either! Is that what your father would've done in your place, Sylvan? Or would he have spared all three of them?"

I get my answer when I see his eyes ignite with fury, like emeralds engulfed in flames.

"The King of Symbiosis takes no lessons from a worthless Glace fisherman's daughter."

His vile insult leaves me breathless and cuts straight through my heart.

"You're not a king today," I spit, rising from the chaise. "You're just a tyrant, blinded by your own hatred and rage. I'm not the one who's worthless between us."

"I should execute you right now for your betrayal *and* disrespect," he growls in a dangerous voice.

"Then do it! Execute me like those three Renegades. *Do it now, Sylvan Ren-Fuegis!*" I shout at the top of my lungs, spreading my arms to expose my heaving chest to him.

Enraged, he strides toward me in three swift steps and grabs me by the throat.

But he doesn't squeeze.

He just holds me firmly, his eyes blazing, his breath ragged. His muscular body is tense, his fiery fingers trembling around my neck.

I meet his gaze, unflinching, a deep-rooted confidence filling me. *He can't do it.*

In this moment, he wants to hate me. To curse me. To despise me. But he can't.

Because he loves me. Truly loves me.

Me—*worthless Glace fisherman's daughter* born without Water magic.

And he hates himself for loving me.

He lets go, stepping back.

"You once told me it's not elemental powers that define a person's strength, Sylvan! It's the strength of their soul. You have that strength too, but unfortunately, you're letting your pain and anger corrupt it. You're blinded by all of this."

"You're still trying to manipulate me with your grand, flowery speeches, Enola! Stories. Myths. Fairy tales. Smoke and mirrors. A web of lies!"

"No! I swear on my family's lives; I won't lie to you anymore. I mean every word I say. I am not your enemy, Sylvan. I play no part in Alena Kan-Glace's rebellion or in the schemes of the other kingdoms. I'm your wife, whether you like it or not, and I truly want to help you fix this before this war ravages all of Symbiosis and wipes out half of its people in a bloody massacre. So, either you kill me… or you accept that."

"I could also divorce you and throw you in chains like the Renegade whore and worthless nobody you are."

I flinch.

He's hurt. He doesn't mean what he's saying.

"But you won't," I state, barely managing to contain the pain his words stir in me.

"What makes you so sure?"

"Because I'm your everything. And you're mine."

He stares at me, his expression stoic, as if my words mean nothing to him.

But I know that's not true.

"Have faith in us, Sylvan. Have faith in yourself, in me, in our love. Listen to your heart."

Suddenly, he slams his fist onto the nearest table with a resounding thud. The wooden surface cracks under the force of his blow. His outburst of anger sends my heart and breath into a frenzy. He's spiraling, losing control. He can't manage the inferno raging inside him.

"My heart is as deceitful as you are. It is *not reliable!*"

"It is. It's always been reliable, actually," I counter, forcing myself to stay calm, standing my ground. "But your negative emotions are drowning out its whispers. Fear is my greatest enemy, Sylvan. Yours are pain and anger. To find the secret of peace and the key to truth, we have to help each other overcome them. Together."

His fists are still pressed into the fractured table, his body bent forward, but then he suddenly straightens up. His mouth tightens, his nostrils flare, and his eyes darken.

"What did you say?" he asks in a low voice.

"I said we need to help each other—"

"No. Before that. The secret of peace and the key to truth. Where did you hear that?"

"From you, Sylvan. In my first dream before... the night at Raockar."

"You're lying. You're trying to deceive my heart, to corrupt my soul, to cloud my mind. Again."

I shake my head, trying to dispel his doubt, but he steps back, glaring at me with hostile suspicion. My shoulders sag. Goddess, I'm so exhausted from constantly crashing into the wall of his stubbornness. I don't know how to regain his trust or convince him that I'm on his side, even if I disapprove of some of his decisions.

He lets out a bitter laugh.

"Are you that desperate, resorting to such a crude trick? An old, forgotten legend sung to children at bedtime? I'm not a child, Enola. My gullibility has limits."

"What on earth are you talking about?"

"'*In its wake, war and chaos will admit defeat. In its hands lies the secret of peace and the key to truth*' it's from an old Fuegis song, part of a universal prophecy in Symbiosis. You know this song—don't deny it. You described something similar in your dream. '*When the red sun becomes a golden orb.*' After we returned from Raockar, I found those words in an old book of tales my mother used to read to me as a child."

"What song? What prophecy, Sylvan?"

At that moment, an unfamiliar male voice echoes through the room.

"'*When the red sun becomes a golden orb,*
The Rose of the Elements will unite all the peoples of Symbiosis,
So that they may once again be in perfect harmony.'"

As we turn, Sylvan instantly draws his sword, and I gasp in shock. He pulls me behind him, using his body as a shield.

There are two intruders in our quarters.

Their appearance is so unusual that I recognize them immediately, recalling my husband's tales.

They are elfid men.

Assassins from the Shadow Guild of Land of Fire.

CHAPTER TEN
SIZING UP THE SHADOWS

ENOLA

"By Death, I didn't expect such an unwelcoming reception from a Fuegis king," sighs one of the two elfid men, eyeing Sylvan's sword raised in their direction

"It's not like we aren't used to such greetings," the second assassin remarks casually. "Maybe we should think about making our entrances a little less theatrical in the future. Oh, and by the way, I was right—you lost the bet. You owe me a hundred scepters."

The other mumbles something under his breath and pulls a pouch of silver from his belt to hand to his companion.

These strangers speak the universal language of Symbiosis fluently, without the slightest accent.

They look almost identical, though the first one appears a bit older, with faint lines on his forehead. They're as tall as my husband but have an athletic slenderness where Sylvan is all muscle. Their eyes and hair are as black as raw obsidian. Their delicate features carry a mysterious, exotic beauty—both captivating and unsettling. I've never seen skin like theirs: a charcoal-gray shade. I also notice the pointed ears of the older one, whose hair is tied back in a ponytail, unlike the other assassin, who lets his hair fall freely over his shoulders. They wear red leather armor with a black dragon spewing fire emblazoned on their chest plates. If I remember correctly, Sylvan once told me that this is the emblem of the Shadow Guild. Dark cloaks with hoods hang from their shoulders. The younger one carries two swords, while the older one appears unarmed. *For now.*

They don't seem hostile toward us… at least not yet. But extreme caution is necessary.

Something unspoken inside me thrums like a warning bell. It feels as though they radiate an aura of heat as suffocating as the Red Desert's sun, and a tremendous, unfamiliar energy is coiled within their bodies. Their eyes, gleaming like dark gemstones, have a depth and sharpness I've never encountered. I can't explain it, but I sense that these two beings possess power far greater than any High-Fuegis, High-Glaces, High-Aerias, and High-Stownes I've ever met.

Sylvan and Alena included.

In other words, if these two elfid men decide to attack us for any reason…

We won't stand a chance.

I also have no idea how they entered our quarters without making a sound. The window is closed, and my husband locked the door from the inside when we arrived. Not to mention my bodyguard, who is stationed just outside in the hallway…

"Jerys Targam," Sylvan says in a stunned voice, eyeing the older elfid over his sword.

The Lord of the Guild of Shadows himself, then. What is he doing in Astranis?

"Are you here as friends or enemies?" my husband asks.

"Sylvan Ren-Fuegis, if we were enemies, you'd already be dead at our feet," the younger one replies, flashing a slight, mocking smile.

"I doubt that," my husband snaps back, on the defensive.

A caustic laugh shakes the second elfid's chest. His casual demeanor is startling.

"He's full of arrogance, this little one. I like him," he mutters to Jerys Targam.

This little one?

I don't think anyone on Symbiosis has dared to call Sylvan *little* since he ascended to the throne of the Fuegis kingdom.

Besides, the elfid with the two swords doesn't look any older than my husband.

"And you are…?" Sylvan asks, irritated and disdainful.

"Beladyn Targam," Jerys answers for him. "My youngest son and my second-in-command, the High Master of the Shadow Guild. Unfortunately. Don't take his insolence personally, Sylvan." He shoots a reproachful glance at the other elfid. "Beladyn has a habit of being blunt and has a questionable sense of humor that often gets us into trouble back in Land of Fire."

"I have no doubt about the subtle brilliance of my humor, Father. It's the others who fail to appreciate it," Beladyn quips.

"You're exhausting, kid. I should've left you behind."

"I've never set foot on this island before. This was my chance."

"I told you to behave," he growls softly. "We're not here on a social visit."

"Let's save the family squabbles for later, old man," Beladyn singsongs, nodding toward Sylvan and me. "If I'm not mistaken, our hosts seem a bit on edge."

"Sheathe your sword, Sylvan," Jerys calmly advises, locking his penetrating gaze onto my husband's. "We won't harm you."

"Unless, of course, you try to harm us first," his son adds nonchalantly. "That's an implicit clause."

"Whether you like it or not, I'm keeping my sword drawn to be prepared for any situation, Jerys," my husband insists. "And know that there's a Fuegis warrior in the hallway ready to—"

"Anetos?" Beladyn interrupts, clearing his throat.

But how does he know my bodyguard's name?

"Oh, the little guy went for a nice stroll in the gardens to clear his head. We didn't want to be disturbed during our meeting."

"How did you even get into the palace without being noticed, by the Fire God?"

"We have our ways," Jerys replies vaguely.

Clearly, we won't be getting a straight answer.

"You didn't kill any guards on your way in, I hope?" Sylvan grits out.

"Of course not!" Beladyn exclaims, rolling his eyes toward the ceiling. "Our profession doesn't exempt us from having a code of ethics. We're well-mannered and disciplined, especially when we're guests."

"I don't recall inviting you here!" Sylvan snaps back.

"I don't think he likes me," the young assassin mocks, addressing his father.

"Hard to blame him…"

"But that's hurtful, Father. Usually, anyone I'm *not* trying to kill absolutely adores me."

Jerys shakes his head, visibly annoyed, and snaps something in a foreign language, scolding his unruly son, who merely shrugs and chuckles under his breath.

Cautiously, I step to the side to join the conversation. Both elfids' gazes immediately fix on me, making me swallow hard.

Jerys smile widens, and Beladyn performs a graceful bow.

"Charming Lady Glace, if I had a heart, I'd rip it from my chest with my bare hands and offer the bloody organ to be yours for all eternity."

It's the most bizarre and morbid compliment I've ever received. Yet, in some strange way… I'm flattered. I can't help but smile in amusement. *Beladyn Targam is quite the character.*

"Your behavior toward my wife is completely inappropriate!" exclaims Sylvan, outraged.

And a little jealous, if you ask me…

"Relax, scarface. I'm not going to abduct your beloved queen and force her into marriage and slavery. I can charm women with my *natural* charisma."

How does he know that?

His taunt hits its mark, and a vengeful fire lights in my husband's eyes.

"Beladyn, by all the gods of Shynighgar, hold your tongue!" Jerys grinds out.

"It was just a harmless joke. He's clearly not used to being teased. What a heavy atmosphere here; feels like an official negotiation with the Merchants! Despite everything, I appreciate the atmosphere and the decoration of your palace, I must say it. Still, I do appreciate the ambiance and décor of your palace. The colors, the materials, the incense… it reminds me of my favorite brothel in the west quarter of Clepsydra. Oh, by the way, do you have anything edible in your kingdom? Preferably not cooked snakes or grilled scorpions. Those don't sit well with me. I'm starving, the trip has left my stomach— *oh no, I wouldn't do that, Sylvan Ren-Fuegis!*" he suddenly bellows pointing an accusatory finger at my husband, who… hasn't moved an inch.

My husband pales under his tan, a look of shock washing over his features.

Something's not adding up.

"How… but… how did you…?" Sylvan stammers, completely thrown off.

"A well-honed instinct from years of sensing danger," Jerys Targam interjects calmly. "Your Majesty, let me say this kindly once more… either you sheathe your sword, or I'll take it from you. We won't be able to communicate if you don't make an effort. We understand your stance, but my son and I do *not* tolerate threats well."

"Confiscate Nesayan?" Sylvan chokes out in indignation, his fingers gripping the sword hilt so tightly his knuckles turn white.

"Put your weapon away, Sylvan," I murmur, gently caressing his arm, hoping to soothe him.

My hesitates, his predatory eyes darting back and forth between the two assassins facing us. He's on edge, torn. His warrior instinct is battling his emotions. Trust is already scarce within the palace walls, and now, two Shadows Elfid…

"No. I'm not going to sheathe my sword, Jerys. And you're going to tell me right now what you're doing in my kingdom," Sylvan says, his tone cold and commanding.

Beladyn and his father exchange a knowing look.

Then, the Lord of the Guild of Shadows shifts his gaze to *Nesayan*.

With a force that seems to come from nowhere, the sword is ripped from Sylvan's grip, swiftly spinning through the air before landing smoothly in Beladyn's outstretched hand.

Sylvan lets out a strangled gasp and lunges angrily at the assassin before I can stop him… but he freezes in place, just steps away from me, as if turned to stone, his hand suspended mid-air.

Psychic powers, I realize with a shudder, noticing Jerys Targam narrowing his eyes at my husband.

"Goddess of the Ocean! Please, let him go!" I moan, terrified for my Fuegis.

"What do you say, Your Majesty?" the Elfid Lord inquires calmly, tilting his head. "Will you now follow your beloved's example and finally act reasonably?"

Sylvan can't respond. He's completely paralyzed.

But after a few tense seconds, he begins to move again. He backs away toward me, breathing heavily. I slip my arm under his, deeply relieved.

"Don't ever do that again," he growls, glaring at the two assassins.

Beladyn, paying no attention to Sylvan, is busy examining his sword with great interest, his admiring eyes taking in every detail.

"Look at this noble wonder, Father. Forged with pyro's breath. An alloy of rare metals." He performs a series of quick, agile spins with it, smiling in appreciation. "Exceptional balance, a deadly edge. The fact that it has no nicks after centuries proves it's unbreakable. What a blade! The sword of a great king… You're very lucky, Sylvan. I hope you know that. A wife as selfless as she is beautiful, an enchanted sword, a crown, wealth, and power…"

"Not all of that is as advantageous as it seems," Sylvan mutters, casting a pointed glance at me.

"Depends on how you look at it," I snap back, irritated by his remark.

"Queen Enola Ren-Fuegis… may I call you by your true name?" Jerys Targam addresses me, catching me off guard again. "You are part of the reason we've come to Astranis, my dear. I think we've arrived just in time to help shed light on certain things."

As if to underscore his point, his gaze drops, tinged with a hint of mischief, to the ribbons on my wrists, which conceal my two new marks.

Goddess of the Ocean.

"We don't have time for this nonsense. War is at our doorstep," Sylvan declares abruptly.

"We are aware. It seems that we have… how to put this delicately… Beladyn?"

"That we may have played a small role in these conflicts," his son finishes, pressing the tip of my husband's sword into the floor. "Unknowingly, so to speak. Through a series of unfortunate and unforeseen circumstances, of which we've only recently become aware. In short, we've come to warn you and offer our humble assistance to make amends. As I mentioned before, we do have a code of ethics. Well, some of us do. Sylvan, the threat isn't just external—it's internal. Someone in your inner circle wants you dead badly enough to hire Shadows to make it happen. Rest assured, we will not honor that contract."

The king's eyes widen.

"A contract?"

"Indeed, Sylvan," Jerys confirms, unfazed, as he pulls a folded parchment from inside his cloak. "This is an assassination request that one of our own received in Clepsydra last night, delivered by a messenger pigeon. Two names are listed at the bottom of this document as targets, Your Majesty. Yours and that of your wife. Or rather, that of Alena Kan-Glace. Two hundred thousand crowns are at stake." My fingers dig into Sylvan's arm at this revelation. "I regret to be the bearer of bad news, but the one who resides in your palace and commissioned this is also the one culprit behind your father's poisoning. You may want to inspect their signature and handwriting."

He holds out the assassination contract in our direction.

Sylvan stares at the incriminating document, his face drained of color, as if he can't even see it.

He's frozen on Jerys Targam's last words.

The one culprit behind his father's death.

So, it wasn't Alena Kan-Glace.

Nor Cyriel Ler-Aeria.

Nor Idric San-Stowne.

This person is the mastermind behind the war that's ravaged Symbiosis for months.

If the Shadows are telling the truth, it means Sylvan has killed two kings who were not guilty of Saradin's death.

With my heart racing and my breath heavy, I step toward the Lord of the Guild and snatch the parchment before bringing it to my husband.

"Read it," I command firmly, unfolding the document. He looks more lost and confused than ever. I place my hand on his cheek.

"Sylvan, listen to me. Read the name of the one who ordered this. You must. We need to know. The time has come," I add.

My husband closes his eyes for a moment, then reluctantly lowers them to the contract I hold in my unsteady hand.

The flash of pain in his light eyes tells me who the traitor is before he even says it.

In a broken voice, Sylvan whispers the name already on the tip of my tongue, "Leonal."

CHAPTER ELEVEN

A SON'S PAIN

SYLVAN

The familiar letters of the signature blur on the parchment. They waver, merge, and uncross. My eyes stay fixed on them.

Leonal Ren-Fuegis.

My uncle. My father's brother.

My advisor.

Enola's fingers gently stroke my face over and over. I finally lift my eyes to her. Worry and pain cloud her delicate, graceful features. I must look as lost and disbelieving as I feel. I exhale. Inhale. Exhale again, brushing a stray silver lock from her forehead.

An icy chasm opens in my chest as I pull away from her embrace. I don't want her tenderness, much less her pity. I need to be alone. I need distance.

My father, killed by my uncle?

Fratricide?

The memory that's haunted me for over a year crashes into my mind like a punch to the face.

***

The banquet is as dull and pompous as ever. I've been drinking since the evening began, exchanging heated glances with a young Fuegis courtesan named Nora. She keeps teasing me with sly smiles, licking her lips. I can't wait to slip away with her after dinner, but as the crown prince, I'm stuck here, forced to stay by my father's side.

As always, Saradin commands the room's attention at the banquet. For the umpteenth time, he's regaling the court with one of his amusing stories about his travels to other kingdoms of Symbiose, making grand, exaggerated gestures. I'm not listening. I've heard all his tales a thousand times. His deep, booming laughter echoes through the reception hall. Three-quarters of the guests are laughing along. Some are genuine, others are not. Frankly, I don't care. My interests are simple: women and war. I'm often described as a reserved prince, but really, I'm just bored. I have no desire to partake in this farce.

My father, ever the affable one, thrives in these settings. Me, I do the bare minimum to avoid seeming rude or disdainful. I'm aware that I'm not as popular as Saradin with the court or the people. I'll never have his charisma. It doesn't bother me.

When he finishes his story, the courtiers applaud. With a broad smile lost in his black beard, my father raises his wine goblet and nods his head in acknowledgment.

"My friends, tonight let's raise our glasses to my son and get him to loosen up a bit!"

I let out an irritated grunt. Several guests laugh as they lift their drinks.

"Syl, I know you're eager to be alone with a certain young lady…" he winks at Nora, who blushes, "but enjoy your old father's thrilling tales while you can. One day, you'll miss my ramblings."

"Of course, Father. The day it snows in the Red Desert."

My father bursts into laughter, and his most sycophantic courtiers follow suit.

"Why not, after all? All it would take is a few High-Glaces visiting Astranis, and we might just see that miracle!" He calls out to Leonal, who shakes his head. "Take note, dear brother! We'll invite young Queen Alena Kan-Glace and her whole retinue so they can turn the Red Desert into a White Desert for an hour or two! The children of our kingdom will be thrilled to play in the snow."

What an absurd idea. Where does he come up with this?

"I highly doubt Queen Alena would travel all the way from Oceanar just for your amusement, Your Majesty," my uncle replies with formal austerity.

"It's a diplomatic gesture," Nadya giggles, siding with my father. She's obviously drunk already. "She can't turn down such an opportunity."

"We'll see."

"Is bad temper contagious?" Saradin jokes, his playful gaze flicking between Leonal and me, both of us equally exasperated by his antics. "God of Fire, my family is full of killjoys; I'll have to get drunk just to counter their sour moods."

He downs his entire goblet in one go, wiping his mouth with the back of his hand. The courtiers drink as well, following his lead.

"What's she like?" I ask quietly as the conversation picks back up around us.

"Alena Kan-Glace?" My father mumbles distractedly, tearing off a piece of bread—a habit I've shared since childhood. "Oh, she's a beauty."

He met her at the Grand Council of Symbiosis while I was in the capital of Land of Fire, attending the Harvest organized by the Merchants three years ago.

"Father, a woman's worth isn't limited to her looks."

"Well, Syl, if Queen Alena has any qualities beyond her beauty, they're well hidden," e comments with a roguish grin. "She's as sweet as a viper in public and as cold as an ice statue in private. She's so vain and proud that she'd never marry a man, because that would mean giving up even a fraction of her power. Your mother would have hated her."

"Didn't stop you from sleeping with her," I mutter, fixing him with an accusatory glare.

"I can't resist a pretty face and a nice chest, and Alena's got both," Saradin whispers, making sure his concubine can't hear. "Don't look at me like that, little prince. You're just like me in that regard," he adds with a hint of pride.

"Except I don't sleep with vipers like her."

"Well, she didn't bite me," laughs Saradin. "There's no harm in a little fun between consenting kings and queens, is th—"

A violent coughing fit cuts off his sentence.

An abnormal cough.

His large hand clamps down on my arm as he struggles to catch his breath. The courtiers turn their heads toward him. An unnamed fear grips me. I slap him hard on the back, but it does nothing.

"Father? FATHER!"

He suddenly vomits an alarming amount of blood into his plate, eliciting horrified screams from Nadya and several other women. Someone in the room shouts, "Go get a healer; the king is choking!" and two guards rush outside. I think the voice belongs to Leonal, but I can't be sure.

My father is not choking.

I know this already. I can see it in his bulging, terrified eyes.

His fingers gripping my arm… are blackening. As if they're rotting. His veins darken. His skin has turned a sickly green.

The wine was poisoned.

I grab my father around the waist and lift him from his chair, laying him on the ground. His body convulses, and he continues to vomit blood, splattering my tunic. In my panic, I spout incoherent words, barking out conflicting orders to those around us. Daegan kneels beside me, loosening the collar of my father's doublet.

Saradin clutches me, writhing in agony. My heart races—I don't know what to do. I'm just as terrified as he is. I feel utterly helpless, like a child witnessing a tragedy with an inevitable fatal end. My father, usually so strong, so proud, is dying, convulsing and choking in my trembling arms. The cruel reality hits me in full force. Less than a minute ago, he was laughing heartily… and now, he's suffering a thousand deaths. I babble at him, though I don't even understand the words tumbling from my mouth. I think I'm begging him to fight, to hold on. I'm pleading with him to survive.

His once-bright green eyes, clouded now, lock with mine, then go blank, sinking into a dark void.

The hand gripping my arm loosens and falls limply to the floor.

A second later, Saradin Ren-Fuegis exhales his final breath, taking a part of me with him.

I let out a howl of rage and grief that echoes through the now-silent hall, shaking every fragment of my shattered soul.

"One day you will miss my ramblings."

Not a day goes by since that tragedy that I don't think of those words. I would give anything to have the power to bring him back. I started a war to avenge his death.

And I may have accused the wrong person??

Could I have been such a fool, blind to the evil lurking close to me all this time?

This contract might be fake…

That signature, a forgery…

But my uncle… told me that his spies had reported the rulers of the other three kingdoms were conspiring to assassinate my father just days after his funeral.

Leonal, the man who had always lived in the shadow of his older brother.

Leonal, the man who gained significant influence and power when I inherited the throne because, due to my inexperience, I delegated many of the duties once handled by Saradin to him.

Who is lying?

Who is telling the truth?

I'm going to lose my mind!

"Leonal accompanied me to Alkanthar on that diplomatic trip," I say aloud, shifting my attention back to Jerys and Beladyn Targam. "You said you had some responsibility. You said you bear some responsibility. Are you involved with the mysterious poison that killed my father?"

"Yes, Sylvan," the Guild Lord admits softly, his piercing gaze locking onto mine. "Our poisoner, Belladonna, created several vials of this poison for professional use. The substance is called *The Kiss of Death*. It contains a powerful toxin extracted from a rare black rose that only grows in our lands. Four years ago, during your stay in Land of Fire for the Harvest, one of our young, unscrupulous assassins stole a vial from Bella's lab and sold it to your uncle for a hefty sum… behind our backs. We were unaware of this theft. We would never have agreed to sell poison to anyone without knowing the target, Sylvan. After intercepting the contract you now hold, I investigated with my Shadows and obtained a confession from the guilty party. We then punished the assassin for disobeying the rules of our brotherhood."

"Punished?" repeats Enola weakly. "So, you—"

"Executed him," Jerys confirms without flinching. "His crime and negligence were unforgivable, Your Majesty. All our who remains silent. His jaw is clenched, and his eyes are fixed on the window. He's holding back something. He disapproves of his father's decision. An assassin with a conscience… I've seen everything now.

They claim they received the contract last night via a messenger bird. That would mean Leonal sent it from Astranis the day before yesterday.

But how did they travel from Land of Fire so quickly, by the God of Fire? I spent several weeks at sea before landing on the Continent. The distance between my kingdom and the Land of Fires region is vast…

"Why did Leonal wait three years to act against Saradin?" Enola murmurs, her eyes distant. "He kept the poison all this time. There must be a reason for his actions."

"It is not for us to determine," Jerys Targam replies in a neutral tone. "We are simply reporting the facts; we do not know what motivated this fratricide. Sylvan, we are not trying to deceive you; we are trying to help you. I advise the utmost caution in this delicate matter. Don't rush headlong into it. We will give you some time to process this news before addressing the other reason we've come to Astranis—your wife. We'll return in an hour. Think carefully about what you will do concerning your uncle. If you wish, I can extract the whole truth from him in seconds, without the need for physical torture." *I don't doubt that. These two elfids possess psychic powers.* "Then, it will be up to you to decide whether to condemn him or spare him."

"If it turns out he's truly the culprit, Jerys… Would you accept executing him for the same amount he offered in exchange for Enola's and my heads?" I ask, my voice a mix of coldness and uncertainty.

My uncle is a High-Fuegis. He's dangerous; his powers nearly rival mine due to his royal blood. On the other hand… the thought of killing him myself sickens me. I'm not like him—I don't kill family members. But if he poisoned my father, lied to me, and manipulated me into starting a war… he deserves no mercy. Only death.

"Aside from defending myself when attacked, I haven't killed anyone since the Continental War, Sylvan. You should direct your request to Beladyn," suggests Jerys.

I look to his son. A cynical, predatory smile forms on the lips of the young elfid assassin.

"A contract on the head of a bastard like that, my friend? I'd do it for free."

Without warning, with incredible speed and strength, Beladyn raises his arm and hurls my sword toward the wall to my right.

It whistles through the air, tracing a horizontal line, and embeds itself almost to the hilt… in the stone.

Stunned, Enola and I stare at the glowing sliver of blade, now lodged deep in the stone wall, before exchanging wide-eyed glances.

The powers of *Nesayan* awakened at the touch of the Shadow.

That's never happened before. Only members of the Fuegis royal family can activate the sword's magic.

Mouths slightly open, a thousand questions on the tips of our tongues, my wife and I turn toward the two assassins.

But their exit had been just as spectacular as their entrance—they had disappeared in the brief seconds we looked away.

They literally vanished.

CHAPTER TWELVE

THE PROPHECY

ENOLA

"But… how did they…"

"Don't bother trying to figure it out, you're wasting your time," growls Sylvan, gripping the hilt of *Nesayan* with both hands. "Clepsydra's assassins won't tell you anything about themselves unless they want to. What a pompous, fool elfid," he exclaims yanking furiously at the sword, which refuses to budge.

He presses his foot against the wall, doubling his efforts. If the situation weren't so serious, I'd probably laugh. Maybe I could help by—

Widen the crack, whispers a small voice in my head.

I focus on the point where the sword meets the wall. I can sense the faint vibrations rippling through the stone each time Sylvan applies pressure to his weapon, but… nothing happens. Ever since I flung Nadya through the air and the two other marks appeared on my wrists, I've come to terms with the fact that I possess powers. Every time, these events have occurred in specific circumstances—when danger loomed over me or someone I love was threatened. It's always been survival instincts, defense, or protection.

I've also wondered whether it was me, in my terrified state, who caused the earthquake that destroyed Talbêk-Elir's house in Raockar. The High-Stowne commanding the tiger and the roots was in the village square, far from us, during the battle. This magic, which had barely begun to awaken in me after my deflowering, could have completely slipped from my control.

After a few moments, my husband finally manages to retrieve his sword. Panting and cursing, he stumbles backward, thrown off balance by the force. I rush over, wrapping my arms around his waist to keep him from falling. I expect him to push me away, but instead, he lets me hold him close, though he doesn't return my embrace. I rest my head against his back with a sigh.

"I'm so sorry about your father, Sylvan."

"So am I," he replies in a flat tone, glancing down at the contract I'm still holding. "If they're right, I've made an unimaginable mistake."

"You trusted the wrong person. Someone your own family. It could have happened to anyone."

"Except I'm not just anyone, Enola," he retorts, his voice hoarse. "I'm the king. My decisions affect tens of thousands of people. I don't have the luxury of making mistakes like this, for God's sake. I've killed two potentially innocent kings. I might have ravaged three kingdoms for *nothing*."

"No. Leonal used you—your rage, your grief, your trust in him. He's the one to blame. You were his instrument. *He's* the tyrant."

"Don't soften the truth just to spare me. I'm just as responsible as he is, if not more."

"Then it's up to you to fix what can still be mended, Sylvan. Do what's right. Free Lia and Belise and send them back to their kingdoms. Organize talks with Alena Kan-Glace and the other rebel leaders. Show humility, repentance, and goodwill by telling the full truth to our enemies. Show them that you're committed to peace, that you are your father's son. And… I'll stay by your side. No matter what," I add, stroking his tense abdomen.

Sylvan pushes my arm away and takes a step forward, distancing his body from mine. He sheaths his sword and turns to face me, his eyes clouded with the intense emotions tormenting him.

"You'll stay by my side no matter what, Enola?" he asks, his voice deep. "But who are you?"

"I'm your wife."

"Stop it, you know exactly what I mean. You're the one who knocked Nadya out."

"Yes. It was me."

"The red tiger that lunged at its master's throat; that was you too, wasn't it," he deduces, a flash of clarity in his eyes. "And… the earthquake at Raockar? The ceiling that collapsed in front of the bedroom door?"

I nod, pressing my lips together. My husband starts looking at my wrists. He reaches out, pushing aside one ribbon, then the other, revealing the Aeria feather and the Stowne oak.

"You're definitely not a Powerless," he mutters under his breath, inspecting the marks one by one.

"I was before. Until… until we made love," I whisper, blushing.

"No one on Symbiosis has ever combined multiple elemental magics," he counters, shaking his head as if talking to himself.

"That's what I thought too, Sylvan. Until recently."

"I don't sense any Fire magic in you."

For my part, I can feel the heat of his magic, like a powerful light inside him. It burns through my veins in a pleasant way, magnetizing me like a crackling energy field.

"I haven't used Fire magic yet, nor Water magic. That prophetic song… did you memorize it when you read it again?"

"Yes. But the *Rose of the Elements* is a tale invented by the bards, Enola. You shouldn't put stock in it."

"Recite the whole song to me."

A chill runs down my spine as he begins with the first words, "*The blood of wars is absorbed by the red sand,*

The red sand is covered by the darkness of the night.

The darkness of night bows down to the red sun,

The red sun will turn gold on the day of prophecy.

The prophecy announces the coming of the Rose of the Elements,

The Rose of the Elements will whisper its love to the flames,

It will sing its loyalty to the waves,

It will breathe its sorrow to the winds,

It will roar its anger to the earth,

And it will speak for the outcasts whose voices are silenced.

Its rise will be marked by the first blood it chooses to spill,

And it will bathe in eternal flames to reveal itself.
In its wake, war and chaos will admit defeat.
In its hands rest the secret of peace and the key to truth.
When the red sun becomes a golden orb,
The Rose of the Elements will unite all the peoples of Symbiosis,
So that they may once again be in perfect harmony."

As he spoke the words, *"Its rise will be marked by the first blood it chooses to spill,"* the expression on his face changed.

He's beginning to realize, just as I am, that there's an impressive build-up of coincidences.

"Jerys Targam claims they're here for you, too," my husband points out, studying me with boundless bewilderment. "He knows your true identity."

"I'm as lost as you are, Sylvan. I… I was sick when the other two marks appeared on my skin. I feel strange things within me and around me, but I can't explain or control them."

"Enola, who are your parents?"

"I told you, simple fishermen. My mother's name is Bleuène. My father died in a shipwreck just before I was born. His fishing boat got caught in a storm. There were no survivors."

"What do you know about him?"

"Not much. My mother almost never spoke of him; the subject made her sad and uncomfortable."

"Perhaps your father wasn't a fisherman," he suggests, searching my eyes deeply as if he could pull out the truth I don't have.

"Why would you say that?"

"Because powers as strong as yours, Enola, don't manifest by accident. They're passed down—through blood, through lineage."

"My mom would never lie to me."

"Even to protect you?"

The question renders me speechless and plants a seed of doubt in my mind. My mother has often told me that parents would go to any lengths out of love for their children.

My contemplative gaze shifts to the window. The sun, bathed in blood-red hues, reigns as the sole emperor in the sky.

"Sylvan…"

"Enola?"

"Come with me to the top of the Tower of Eternal Flame, please."

"Why?"

"Because we need to."

In tense silence, Sylvan and I climb the hundreds of narrow, spiraling steps leading to the top floor of Astranis's tallest tower. Unlike my husband, whose physical stamina far exceeds mine, I'm soon struggling, panting harder with each step. I gather my skirts in one hand and cling to the railing with the other, forced to pause several times to catch my breath and calm my racing heart. Sylvan waits on the steps ahead, watching me carefully with an impassive face.

"We're almost there, Enola. Just a little further."

"Goddess of the Ocean, I curse the sadistic architects who designed this tower," I grumble between breath.

A faint smile crosses Sylvan's lips. That small, fleeting smile, not without a touch of warmth and tenderness, gives me the strength to keep going.

Climbing for the sake of reaching peace and truth… through struggle.

This endless, winding staircase is a metaphor for my life.

After several more minutes, we finally reach the top. A gust of hot wind greets us. I glance down into the void, and a wave of vertigo sweeps over me. I grab Sylvan's arm for reassurance. He doesn't pull away. His eyes are fixed, captivated by the ethereal flames illuminating the fluted columns around us.

"The God of Fire lit it hundreds of years ago," he murmurs, almost to himself. "It's burned ever since, without ever fading."

"That's just a myth your people created," says a voice behind us. "The being who created these flames, whom you call the God of Fire is no god."

We turn at the same time toward Jerys and Beladyn Targam.

I'm certain they weren't here when we arrived.

How did they know we'd be here?

"Enough. You're blaspheming, Jerys," Sylvan snaps, frowning.

"Perhaps you're unfamiliar with the first rule the Guild of Shadows," Beladyn intervenes, leaning casually against a column with his arms crossed. "It's the one we teach all our apprentice assassins from day one. *Never trust appearances*. This legend you've believed in since childhood, handed down from generation to generation, is a perfect example. The old man with the silver beard and golden cane who lit the Eternal Fire took on the appearance of a man, but he was not one. Encouraged by your ancestor, Astranis's first monarch, who thought it was better this way, your people have revered this being as the God of Fire. And yet, he never claimed to be. Nor did your three other gods, the Goddess of the Ocean, the God of the Earth, and the Goddess of the Air. These four beings have unwittingly become false idols, and no one on Symbiosis has ever known… except your ancestor. And now, you two."

A cold laugh escapes my husband's throat.

"And you, Shadows, you hold the key to the Truth, with a capital T."

"Naturally. Because we met your *God of Fire*, Sylvan. Even though he's no longer in this world," says Jerys, sharing a tacit glance with his son.

"Oh really? This just keeps getting better," Sylvan mutters, skeptical.

"You, of all people, know that things are not always as they seem," the Lord declares, casting me a knowing smile. "You know it already, Enola… Born Powerless. Raised as a fisherman's daughter. The unofficial double of Queen Alena Kan-Glace. Made a war captive. Became the wife of a king. Crowned queen of the Fuegis Kingdom. And finally… become what you were always meant to be. You fought for it, Enola. With your own weapons. Your love for Sylvan. Your determination. Your will. Your quick mind. Your survival instinct. Your stories." Tears prick my eyes. I tighten my grip on my husband's arm, feeling him stiffen. "And if you'll allow it, I have a story of my own to tell you—about the origins of Symbiosis and the Rose of the Elements."

CHAPTER THIRTEEN
THE ROSE OF THE ELEMENTS

JERYS TARGAM

"At the Dawn of Time, the Goddess of Life and the Goddess of Death created to the five worlds of Creation: Shynighgar, Songegar, the Celestial Kingdom, the sun, and the moon.

Centuries later, the Goddess of Nature gave birth to the four Dryadenes, each associated with one of the natural elements. The Goddess of Fire and Autumn. The Goddess of Water and Winter. The goddess of Earth and Spring, and the Goddess of Air and Summer.

Under their influence, animals and plants began to flourish on Shynighgar.

Then Life and Death created the four pairs of Elemental dragons, the first intelligent and mortal beings who would serve as guardians of the natural Balance and the worlds. The Pyros were fire dragons. The hydros, the water dragons. The Tellurians, earth dragons. The Aeolians, air dragons.

Dragons were the most powerful beings in Creation after the gods themselves. They served as both messengers and trusted agents of Life and Death.

Over centuries, other living species began to inhabit Shynighgar. Elves, dwarves, humans, and many other races. The dragons watched over them from the shadows, intervening only when needed to restore the unstable Balance of the natural order of Creation.

At the beginning of human emergence, Life and Death separated humans into two groups. The first, larger group would remain on the Continent and be deprived of natural magic. The second, smaller group was taken by the dragons to an island off the Continent. This island, raised from the Endless Ocean by the Goddess of Nature, was named Symbiosis. The Elemental dragons erased the memories of the new arrivals so they would forget they were born on the Continent and had been isolated from their fellow humans.

This was an immense experiment, testing humanity's capacity to wield elemental magic wisely. The gods wanted to observe how mortals would react to such power: whether they could live in harmony or if they would succumb to war and the thirst for power. These humans, though unaware of it, were an elite group, carefully selected by the dragons for their virtues of heart and mind.

Following the directives of the Divine Mothers, Life and Death, the Goddess of Nature granted several types of elemental powers to these gifted young humans, just as she had once given to her daughters, the Dryadenes.

She divided the people into four Element Clans—the Fuegis, the Glaces, the Stownes, and the Aerias—and settled them into different realms across the island based on their category of elemental magic.

A few days later, appearing in human form, four of the eight Elemental dragons helped the people of Symbiosis establish their civilizations and their societal rules.

They also crowned the original four kings of Symbiosis.

The matriarch of the Hydro clan founded Oceanar, the city of the Glace.

The patriarch of the Tellurian clan built Stalagmis, the city of the Stowne.

The matriarch of the Aeolian clan builds Eolan, the city of the Aeria.

The patriarch of the Pyro clan created Astranis, the city of the Fuegis.

One night, this Pyro patriarch returned to his natural form, to his natural form, flew to the highest tower of Astranis, and ignited the Eternal Flame with his dragon's breath. Then, assuming the guise of an old man with a white beard, he forged *Nesayan* in the flames, the legendary sword that he gifted to the first ruler of Fuegis ruler, instructing him to pass it down to his descendants.

The people of the four kingdoms revered these dragons, transformed into human form, as deities of Symbiosis.

Unfortunately, as the human population on the island grew over the centuries, things took a turn for the worse, proving to both gods and dragons that utopia was a far-off ideal. The inhabitants of Symbiosis began to be corrupted by their powers, which also gradually weakened, except within the royal families. The elemental magic genes were no longer always awakened, as though misused powers from earlier generations had become a burden that the new hosts' bodies suppressed. Those affected by this phenomenon were cast out of society. The Powerless became Renegades, exiled to the Forest of Exile, and unjustly treated as enemies by the elite of the four kingdoms. Ironically, they were much closer to what the ancestors of the Symbiotes—the original humans of the Continent—had been: mere mortals, free from magic.

Whenever the Renegades rose in rebellion against the political system, Symbiosis's warriors, the Fuegis, were sent to kill them.

Distressed and disappointed by these events yet unable to intervene directly without risking the Balance, the Goddess of Nature consulted her sister, Destiny, asking how to address these deviations on Symbiosis.

Destiny told her that she could choose to bear a mortal child with one of the four kings. A child of royal and divine blood, wise and powerful enough, could work to restore peace and equality on Symbiosis. This child would unite all the island's people and bring a new prosperity through their truth alone.

This child would be the Rose of the Elements.

But for this to happen, Nature would have to abandon her child at birth and accept that she would never see them again. She would have to let them endure hunger, poverty, and hardship… and refrain from intervening when they faced war, fear, and death. She would have to keep both the child's existence and their powers hidden until the time of their rise. Such is the law of Balance, and it is unyielding: no good comes without great sacrifice. Good cannot exist without evil, and vice versa.

Nearly twenty-seven years ago, Nature took the appearance of a Glace queen, the only one of the four rulers who had yet to bear a child. She slept with the King of Oceanar and, as Destiny foretold, conceived a child.

In the Celestial kingdom, Nature secretly gave birth to a girl with sapphire eyes and silver hair. The mother sealed away the child's hereditary powers until the day she would become a woman by giving her virginity to the man she loved. On that day, the four elemental magics would awaken within her, allowing her to begin fulfilling her grand destiny.

With a heavy heart, Nature entrusted her baby to Cristal, the matriarch of the Water element. In the guise of an old woman, the female dragon brought the child to a woman named Bleuène, whom she had observed and found trustworthy. Bleuène, a kind-hearted Glace peasant, already had a young son named Elanos, and her fisherman husband had recently perished in a shipwreck. Despite her poverty, the widow would raise her adopted daughter far better than any queen of Symbiosis could, teaching her to spread goodness to those around her.

She named the precious little girl Enola, meaning *Sapphire* in the Glace language.

Enola was the hidden daughter of the Goddess of Nature and the Glace King, and she was also the half-sister of the future Queen Alena Kan-Glace, who would be born a year later.

No one on Symbiosis knew this except Bleuène, but that little girl with sapphire eyes was, in fact, the true sovereign of the Glace Kingdom… and the Rose of the Elements."

CHAPTER FOURTEEN
THE ETERNAL FLAME

ENOLA

The gazes of the three men surrounding me are fixed on my face, watching for my reaction. Jerys and Beladyn's expressions are unreadable and mysterious, while Sylvan's is as confused and shaken as I probably should be.

But I am neither confused nor shaken.

For as staggering and unexpected as this revelation may be, I feel deep within my tightly wound gut, my pounding heart, and my restless soul that it is true.

Everything aligns. Everything is clear.

Bleuène is not my biological mother, and Elanos is not my biological brother.

My father truly has been dead for years, but he was a king, not a fisherman.

My sister is Alena Kan-Glace.

My mother is…

A *goddess*.

"Do everything you can to survive until the coming of the Rose of the Elements! Stay alive and return to me, my sapphire!" Bleuène yelled at me during the siege of Oceanar as a Glace guard escorted me toward the castle.

She knew *everything*.

And she told me *nothing*.

To protect me.

She filled my childhood with tales and legends about the Rose of the Elements, though she never recited the prophecy outright. Like my husband, I never really believed in it.

Until now.

I recall my own stories, the ones I told Sylvan to delay my execution. I told him I was Alena's secret twin, with royal blood. Before that, I invented an Enola Powerless who became the rightful queen after she lost her virginity to her beloved. I hadn't realized how close I was to the truth—or perhaps my unconscious intuition led me to those words? Or maybe it was just instinct? Yes, I lied… But not as much as I thought.

Still, I don't feel remotely ready for such an extraordinary role. I can't control my powers. How am I supposed to unite all the people of Symbiosis? I barely manage to *pretend* to be a queen.

"Who told you this story?" asks my husband, his tone hard.

"The God of Fire who lit the Eternal Flame and forged your sword is none other than the pyro Elemental dragon who fought alongside us during the Continental War a few years ago," replies Jerys Targam. "He had been struck by a vision of his end linked to his gift of foresight: he saw his own death in the final battle. Before leaving to fight the Imperial forces of Land of Fire, he revealed to my son and me the secret of Symbiosis's origins and the Rose of the Elements. He also asked us to assist Enola when her powers manifested. He was our friend, and we swore a blood oath to journey to Symbiosis when the time came. When we received your uncle Leonal's assassination contract last night, Beladyn and I realized it couldn't be a coincidence—that the time had come."

I feel like Lord of the Guild of Shadows is leaving out some essential details, but I also feel that pressing him further would be useless.

"How could you possibly assist me?" I ask in a small voice.

"By giving you a few useful tricks to master your charming powers, my little Glace rose," Beladyn says with a confident smile. "I'm one of the most talented instructors in our guild." At this boast, Jerys sighs in exasperation, and Sylvan's face clouds with irritation. "In Clepsydra, I teach our young elfids assassins to control their varied Gifts. True, we don't have much time, but you have a significant advantage in learning—your divine blood. I'll give you the keys to unlock your incredible power, and the rest, well, you'll handle that on your own like the great *Derdanoma* you are."

"*Der… danoma?*"

"An elvish term that could be translated in your language as *demigoddess.*"

"Because there are others?"

"Alive? Hell, no. They've all been dead for ages." I feel my face go pale. Beladyn gives his father a nudge on the arm to get his attention. "Symbiosis's chosen one here is looking a bit pale. You were right; I should've kept my mouth shut about that."

"Kid, I should always have a gag handy whenever I bring you along somewhere," mutters Jerys, shooting him a stormy sidelong glance.

"Pest, the only person I ever let put a gag in my mouth was that exquisite lady of the night from High Tower who had an astounding versatility that—"

"Show some decorum," Sylvan cuts in, his voice sharp with annoyance. "Details like that are vulgar and neither the place nor the time for them."

"Nor the audience, apparently. I've rarely met a human of your age who's as serious and dull. Don't deny it; even your father agreed with me."

"You… knew my father?" my husband asks, surprised.

"I didn't have the pleasure of meeting him, but I'm convinced he would have appreciated me for who I am, unlike some. Anyway, moving on. Do you have any more questions on the matter at hand before I fall asleep standing up?"

The unfiltered honesty of this elf is baffling. He says… *everything* he thinks. I'm not used to this—and neither is Sylvan.

"What concrete proof do you have about my wife?" my husband finally asks.

"Are the marks of the four Element Clans on her skin not significant enough for you, Scarface?" Beladyn taunts.

"No, gray moron."

I bite my lip to keep from smiling at Sylvan's retort.

"Just because she has multiple elemental powers doesn't necessarily mean she's the Rose of the Elements… or the daughter of your so-called goddess of Nature and a dead Glace king."

"Sylvan recited the prophecy to you after we left, Enola," Jerys points out insightfully. "That's precisely why the two of you came up to the top of the Tower of the Eternal Flame. One line must've caught your mind. '*And she will bathe in the eternal flames in order to reveal herself.*' So… go on, dear," he encourages, gesturing toward the formidable dragon fire blazing in the basin.

"You've lost your mind!" my husband cries, wrapping his arm around my waist and pulling me against him with a frantic, fearful grip. "This is absolute madness. I won't let her do this, by all the gods!"

"Well then, do it with her. There's a legend about these flames that's true: the only two beings who can withstand the Eternal Flame are the rightful king of the Fuegis kingdom and the Rose of the Elements. Just dip your hands in the flames for a few seconds; it will be enough."

"No. Absolutely not."

I place a gentle hand on his chest, drawing his attention.

"Sylvan, we should—"

"This entire thing is utterly insane, Enola," he whispers, lowering his head toward mine. "If they're not lying, then they're mistaken. Our gods aren't dragons. Our founding fathers weren't born on the Continent but here on Symbiosis. And you—you're not Alena's real sister, you're not the daughter of one of their goddesses, and you're certainly not the Rose of the Elements. It's too much… it's all just too much."

I I've more or less already processed and accepted this truth because I've crossed each threshold gradually, prepared to embrace this revelation. I've felt the changes happening within me, step by step, ever since that night in Raockar. But he hasn't. I understand; everything that's happened has turned our lives upside down these past weeks. I think he'll need to see it to believe it.

"Do you remember the dream I had about the Red Desert, Sylvan? The voice singing in the wind, the red sun turning gold, the cracks in the trembling earth, the wave of blood surging on the horizon," I list softly, wrapping my right hand around his.

"I remember."

"I didn't tell you everything because I didn't understand it myself. Blood was dripping down my thighs, igniting the sand beneath my feet until flames engulfed my legs without harming me." I slide my left hand to the back of his neck, drawing his head toward me. His forehead presses against mine, our breaths mingling, and I shift slightly to the side, gently guiding him with me. "And you told me... you told me not to be afraid that *fear is my greatest enemy*. You told me to believe in myself and in us. You told me that in my hands rests the secret to peace and the key to truth, like in the prophecy. I woke up just before our hands could touch. It was a premonition, Sylvan, a symbolic vision. The voice singing in the wind was a divine voice, maybe my mother's. The blood that ignited the sand was that of my virginity. The fire in my dream didn't burn my skin. I... I think that to fulfill my destiny, I must let go of fear, and we must face the elements and the trials *together*. I believe that's precisely it—the secret of peace and the key to truth: trust and love. Sylvan Ren-Fuegis, my beloved, my king... Now, see and believe," I whisper, pulling back slightly to give him a clear view.

His green eyes drift to our hands, then widen.

Because while I was speaking, his forehead pressed to mine, I called upon my Fire magic for the very first time.

A long strand of flame unfurls from the Eternal Fire, wrapping itself around our intertwined fingers like a ribbon of molten silk. Like a tamed serpent, it caresses our skin without leaving a mark. Without hesitation, I lift our joined hands between us and press my lips to Sylvan's fingers. The flames do not burn my lips; instead, they gather around our hands in a delicate aura, their golden light illuminating my husband's enraptured face.

With a soft sigh, I allow the fiery serpent to retract, slithering back into the Eternal Fire under the young king's awestruck gaze. He looks at me with such deep emotion and reverence that tears well in my eyes, and a shiver runs through me.

On the day I arrived in Astranis, condemned as a slave, I had refused to kneel before him in the throne room. I had declared that a queen does not kneel before any man, king or tyrant. At his command, Daegan had forced me to my knees.

Today, to my utter amazement, no one compelled Sylvan Ren-Fuegis, King of Symbiosis, as he slowly kneels before me, hands resting on my hips, his eyes closed, his head against my stomach.

Yet, that's what he did.

And in that quiet act of devotion and solemn silence, I knew two undeniable truths that struck my heart like twin earthquakes.

First, he forgiven my lies, and he is silently asking me to forgive him in return.

Second, that both the man *and* the king would love me always.

Me, Enola Ren-Fuegis.

His rightful queen.

CHAPTER FIFTEEN

A FAMILY AFFAIR

SYLVAN

"Don't be nervous, my love," Enola teases softly in my ear as she nestles closer. "I'll protect you."

Her improbable promise makes me chuckle. I pull her closer, savoring the warmth of her body, the smoothness of her skin, and the sweet scent of her hair.

We're alone in the meeting room, waiting for our guest to finally appear after my uncompromising summons. My extraordinary wife sits on my lap, and we're indulging in each other's affection like any ordinary couple—even though we are far from ordinary—stealing a quiet moment before the storm to come. When I think about who she truly is, I'm still in awe. I can't stop tracing the four marks on her skin with a nearly childlike fascination. Whenever I brush my fingers over the silver feather of the Aerias and the holm oak of the Stownes, she laughs, pulling her wrists away. My wife, a ticklish demi-goddess—I'd never have imagined such a thought crossing my mind.

How I wish my father were still alive. I'm certain he would've adored Enola.

"I'm deeply honored, my queen. How I managed to survive all those fierce battles without your protection for twenty years is a mystery?"

"Luck, more than skill. You're not that great a warrior."

"I'm not a *great warrior*, my love. I'm the best in Symbiosis."

"Humility is your finest quality. I thought you'd say, I'm the best in Shynighgar."

"Well, I will be in a few years, surely."

"Better than those two elfids?"

"Without their powers? No doubt."

"You've never even seen them fight, my arrogant husband."

"That Beladyn is a show-off; I can smell that type from ten leagues away. Warriors who brag the most are usually the weakest. Except me, naturally."

She laughs heartily, making me smile. Her beauty radiates even more, piercing into me and wrapping my heart in a warm, glowing cocoon.

I'll cherish this woman until my dying breath, and I want to shout to the world that I love her more than life itself.

"So, what about the sword in the wall, Sylvan? Just for show-off?" she teases.

"Some kind of magic, I suppose. There's no way he could've embedded a sword into a stone wall to the hilt with pure strength alone."

"Well, he is quite handsome, in his own way," she says, mocking me—and it works, unfortunately.

"You're seriously in need of an eye exam," I mutter, narrowing my eyes at her.

"Hmm, jealous?"

"Very annoyed."

"Did you notice how he moves? Like a tiger from the Red Desert."

"More like a three-legged old coyote, if you ask me."

"Unlike you, he has a sense of humor," she insists, amused by my sarcastic replies.

"Enola."

"Which is why it's all the more baffling that I fell for your barbaric charm and feel absolutely nothing for him," she says, catching herself as she kisses the lower part of my scarred cheek.

"That's better."

I haven't told her yet, but I plan to attend Beladyn Targam's training session, just to make sure he behaves himself with her. It's not jealousy or possessiveness—it's caution. I trust my wife; him, not in the slightest. He strikes me as a womanizer, possibly worse than I was before I got married. Shadow or no shadow, if he even hints at crossing the line with her, I'll castrate him with the heated blade of *Nesayan* and feed his parts to my hunting dogs.

Speaking of which, what are those two elfids up to? They were supposed to meet us here several minutes ago. They didn't reveal where they planned to go after our discussion at the top of the Tower of Eternal Flame. I can only hope they're not causing trouble in Astranis and are keeping a low profile. Justifying the presence of assassins from Land of Fire in my kingdom would be a tall order.

"Have you seen Selaine?" Enola asks, growing more serious.

I nod, running my hand through the opalescent strands cascading over her shoulder.

"How is she?"

"She's better. Mostly scared but unharmed."

"And Nadya? What did she tell you?"

"She accused your servant of being a Stowne spy snooping around your quarters."

Outrage flashes in Enola's brilliant lapis lazuli eyes.

"She's lying to cover herself, Sylvan. I hope you realize that."

"This incident still needs to be unraveled. According to Nadya, Selaine didn't even try to use her Fire magic."

"Because she was terrified, or maybe Nadya's Air magic blocked her from defending herself. She's young, inexperienced—"

"Or Powerless?"

"Sylvan…"

"Patience. We'll get back to this matter after we've dealt with this one," I remind her, tapping a finger on the assassination contract spread out on the table before us.

Seized by a need to move, my wife rises from my lap and begins pacing a short distance away, arms crossed tightly over her chest. I stand to join her.

"Your stepmother might be in league with your uncle, Sylvan."

"Nadya's been locked in her suite with your old collar around her neck and guards at her door. She's not a threat to anyone at the moment. It's him we need to deal with first."

"You also need to free Lia and Belise."

"I still need to think about it," I reply, catching her by the elbow so she can nestle back into my arms.

"Where are they?"

"They're not exactly in Astranis."

"It doesn't matter; I want to meet them," she says with firm resolve, tugging on the collar of my tunic.

Raising an eyebrow, I take her hands in mine, move them from my neck, and press them against my chest.

"For what purpose?"

"Because I care, that's why. Take me to see them. Tomorrow."

"And if I refuse?"

"If you refuse… I I'll make sure you don't touch me again, and you'll be back sleeping in your old bed, Sylvan Ren-Fuegis," she declares, lifting her chin with that imperious defiance.

It's the first time a woman has dared to blackmail me this way. I burst out laughing, which only annoys her more; a severe line creases the blue-tattooed mark of Glace royalty on her forehead. I let go of her delicate fingers to cradle her soft, sculpted face between my hands. She lets out a small, charming sigh as my thumbs caress her cheekbones with a tender, languid touch.

"You forget I'm a soldier, Enola. During military campaigns, I'm well-accustomed to long stretches of abstinence. You'll have to come up with something else."

"I won't beg on my knees, you Fuegis idiot."

"What a shame. I'd love to see you on your knees, but not to beg me," I murmur, leaning in closer to her.

My mouth hungers for hers, those two rose-petal lips glistening invitingly. I ache to bite them, to kiss them until they yield sweet moans. My wife's breathing quickens, and her eyelids grow heavy.

"Sylvan, you are—"

A loud crunching sound, followed by an exaggerated clearing of the throat, interrupts us from behind, igniting a spark of anger that stirs my Fire magic.

Damn elfid, I think, turning toward the intruder who is…

… lounging arrogantly across my second throne!

With one leg draped over the armrest, Beladyn nonchalantly bites into a green apple. Fighting to contain my fury, I scan the room. No sign of his father nearby to rein him in. This cocky Clepsydrian is about as welcome as a fishbone caught in one's throat.

"Oh, don't stop for me; carry on," exclaims the assassin, waving his half-eaten apple at us. "You were saying you'd love to see her on her knees—I'm dying to hear the rest! Finally, something juicy to bite into in this kingdom," he snickers before taking another bite.

"Where's Jerys Targam?" I growl, barely suppressing my murderous impulses.

Beladyn takes his time to respond. Watching Enola and me with a lazy, predatory gaze, he chews loudly, then swallows.

"He had to go home," he finally explains. "Some urgent business in Clepsydra required his attention. One of our assassins was gutted by a competitor on a mission. Occupational hazard; may his dark soul rest in peace! Anyway, my father will return to Astranis as soon as possible. Not to worry; I'm more than capable of handling the situation."

This news actually worries me quite a bit…

"But how can you move so quickly?" whispers Enola, mystified.

"My little snowflake, I'll tell you but keep it to yourself. My dear old father's Gift is teleportation."

"Oh! I thought he had telekinesis," my wife says, surprised.

"Telekinesis *and* teleportation, in fact. We have more than a few tricks up our sleeves. Still, we avoid announcing it to the world to keep from attracting even more enemies and critics than we already have outside the Brotherhood."

"So, you have a Gift of teleportation, too?" she asks, glancing at the half-open door.

"No, not me. But I'm more stealthy and quiet than a shadow."

"What are *your* Gifts?"

The gift of annoying everyone he talks to, without a doubt.

Beladyn shoots me a mischievous glance before turning his attention back to Enola.

"I could reveal one, but are you sure you want to know? Most people react… unpredictably when they find out."

"Go on, try us," I grumble, ready for anything.

His enormous grin reveals teeth that gleam against his dark complexion. He sets his apple down on the table near the contract.

"Sylvan Ren-Fuegis, you're as cranky as a constipated dwarf. Perhaps you should bring in a palace doctor to prescribe an herbal cure to get things moving. And rest assured, I won't make any improper moves toward your lovely wife during our training session. I'd be mortified to have to beat you senseless if you tried to emasculate me with plans to toss my severed parts to your hounds. And I don't need any Gifts to annoy people—it's an innate talent I've been perfecting since long before you were born."

I'm dumbfounded.

"You… you've been here this whole time."

"Not at all; I just walked in. Want to venture a theory?" He glances at my wife, his mocking eyes alight. Suddenly, he claps his hands. "Bravo! She got it! She's far quicker than you, Sylvan."

"Enola…?"

"Telepathy, Sylvan," she murmurs, staring at him in shock. "He… he's a telepath."

"That's right, my dear," Beladyn confirms. "And I'm going to use that Gift on your uncle in less than a minute because I can already sense his thoughts. I'm a walking truth serum—good news for you, isn't it?" A masculine voice echoes in my head. Enola and I start in surprise. *"Ah, he's almost here. Wouldn't want him to get too scared seeing me in the room, so I'll post myself over there to give him a little surprise."*

And now this assassin is speaking inside our heads!

"I can sing too. I have a magnificent mental voice," the High Master chimes in our thoughts as he heads toward the wall beside the door.

So, if I think—

"I can hear you thinking, champ," Beladyn finishes mentally, giving me an oblique, mischievous look. *"Your logic is absolutely staggering. Focus, Leonal is not a small player."*

By the gods; I'm going to have to be extra careful with my thoughts.

"Tell me about it," the Shadow whispers, leaning back against the wall beside the door and giving Enola a wink.

My uncle strides into the meeting room with a military gait. His gaze lands on my wife holding onto my arm, then on me. I steel my mind and my heart. My impassive expression betrays not a flicker of the deep-seated hatred twisting within me.

"What's going on, my nephew? Why did you summon me so

urgently? I thought I made it clear through a valet that we'd recalled both of our military detachments to Astranis," he declares, his voice tinged with annoyance.

"Your dedication and commitment speak for themselves, Uncle. You always seem to adapt to any situation."

"I do my best to serve our people's interests."

"Our people's interests—or yours, Leonal?" Enola's voice is as icy as mine.

"You should stay out of our kingdom's politics, Your Majesty," my uncle replies imperiously. "We do not conduct ourselves like Glace dignitaries."

Leonal hasn't noticed Beladyn standing just a few steps behind him. I have to admit, the assassin is discreet beyond reproach. He doesn't even blink; his breathing is imperceptible. He resembles a dark statue, barely distinguishable from the wall. If he weren't in my line of sight, I'd almost forget he was there.

"I truly admire your sense of self-sacrifice and family loyalty," I say, letting my burning gaze meet my uncle's. "You always supported my father, despite your occasional disagreements, Leonal. How many men would have resisted the golden rope of power hanging right in front of them?"

"Sire, your insinuation confuses me," he replies with unsettling calm.

"This belongs to you, I believe," Enola cuts in, holding up the parchment.

"What's that document?"

"An assassination contract on Sylvan and me. Written and signed in your hand."

"This is utterly absurd! Someone must have forged my handwriting," my uncle denies immediately, eyeing the parchment with feigned shock.

"The egghead Fuegis is lying," Beladyn's voice affirms in our minds.

"Who gave you this contract, Sylvan?" Leonal demands, bristling.

Close the door, I think.

The assassin obeys, pressing his fist against the door to shut it. The loud click makes my uncle flinch. He whirls around to face the fourth person in the room.

"Me, Leonal Ren-Fuegis."

At the sight of the elfid figure clad in black and red armor, my father's brother begins to betray signs of panic.

If he's anxious, it means he's got things on his conscience.

"A Shadow in our palace, Sylvan?" Leonal roars, stepping back with clenched fists at his sides. His composure is starting to crack.

"And yet, that's exactly what you wanted—a Shadow to infiltrate the palace and eliminate my wife and me. You didn't want to dirty your own hands this time, so you turned to Clepsydra's Guild, the best assassins on the Continent."

"You're out of your mind, nephew! I'd never harm you! I'm your uncle, your most loyal subject!"

"He's lying again," Beladyn says, observing Leonal closely. "He despises you as much as he despised your father, Sylvan. He thinks you're weak and foolish."

"You poisoned your own brother," I growl, seething with rage. "Why, Leonal?"

"I… I didn't do that, Your Majesty! It wasn't me, and you know it! It was Idric San-Stowne, Cyriel Ler-Aeria, and *her*!" he cries, his finger shaking as he points at Enola. "Alena Kan-Glace. But you forgave her! You pardoned her! That woman has bewitched you!"

"No, I'm clearer than ever. My wife is innocent, just as Idric and Cyriel were. You manipulated me to shatter alliances and sow chaos across Symbiosis. You betrayed my father in the worst possible way. I trusted you completely, Leonal, as you led me to the brink of a precipice!"

"I loved your father. I was as devastated as you by his undignified death!"

"You celebrated," Beladyn contradicts him calmly, probing his mind with telepathy. "You congratulated yourself for finally having the courage to pour poison into Saradin's wine after keeping it in a chest in your quarters for three years." My uncle steps back, swallowing hard. "In that moment, you thought you should have done it sooner, convinced that your young, impulsive nephew drowning in grief would be far easier to control than his father, making him the perfect pawn for your secret ambitions. With him, you could wield power without anyone realizing, not even him. And what better way to execute your schemes than by pushing Sylvan into a war of vengeance against the other kingdoms? You always considered the Renegades, Glaces,

Aerias, and Stownes beneath the Fuegis, Leonal. You'd long wanted to subjugate them, but Saradin would never have allowed it. You could have poisoned your nephew along with his father to seize the throne yourself, but you needed a scapegoat for the war you planned to launch. Too cowardly to rule openly and face the consequences of your actions, you're a megalomaniac, hungry for power without the courage to claim it. So, you turned Sylvan from a martyred orphan into a ruthless despot in the eyes of Symbiosis, as planned. While everyone's hatred shifted to him, you basked in admiration in his shadow. After the chaos, you plotted to have Sylvan killed by a third party and claim his crown. You'd blame a rebel and cast yourself as the pacifier who restored order after you yourself had fractured it… But then, this young Glace woman arrived in Astranis and unraveled your plans," he adds, glancing at Enola, whom I hold by the waist. "Because you saw, to your dismay, that you were losing your hold over Sylvan… as he fell in love with her, and she gradually opened his eyes. So, you decided to eliminate your nephew and his wife ahead of schedule. It would incite the Fuegis to a frenzy, making them fight with unmatched fury against their enemies to avenge their murdered king."

A deathly silence falls over the room. Pale and shaken, Leonal has been shaking his head throughout Beladyn's speech. His panicked eyes dart between the three of us, monitoring our every move. He's on edge, like an animal cornered.

"Did you alert the Stownes to attack us at Raockar, Uncle?" I ask, my jaw clenched so tightly my teeth ache.

"No, it wasn't me!" Leonal snaps fervently. "I demand you call the High-Fuegis immediately"!

"This time, he's telling the truth," Beladyn confirms telepathically. *"He doesn't know who did it."*

"Could there be another traitor?" I think, stunned.

"Most likely, Sylvan."

"Is Nadya Ler-Aeria his accomplice?"

The High Master of the Guild of Shadows studies Leonal thoughtfully for a moment. I dread his verdict; there's already so much to take in…

"No. He has no accomplice. He acted entirely alone. Even the other High-Fuegis aren't aware of his betrayal. If there's a spy in the palace, they're unaffiliated with your uncle and likely working for the opposing side," the elfid says.

"I want to hear his confession about my father's death, Beladyn."

"Leave it to me," he assures me, then fixes a sinister, intimidating smile on my uncle. "Leonal, I read your thoughts. Your twisted mind is as legible as an open book—a bad book, at that. You have no way out. If I were you, I'd confess without delay and beg your king for mercy. Tell us the truth."

"The truth, Shadow?" A dark, mocking laugh escapes him. "The truth is that you're in the pocket of that Glace witch, and the two of you have brainwashed my nephew! This man doesn't read my thoughts, Your Majesty. He's made up this entire story. I wasn't the one who poured *The Kiss of Death* into your father's wine cup. That was an agent of the harlot who clings to your arm like a vile leech!"

Enola tenses, recoiling from his venomous words. I pull her closer, shielding her as best I can.

"Leonal," I murmur, locking my fiery gaze on my uncle's, "how do you know the poison that killed Saradin is called *The Kiss of Death*?"

He freezes as he realizes the magnitude of his mistake.

"The… the elfid said it," he replies, voice faltering.

"No, Uncle. The elfid never said the poison's name to you. Neither did I. In other words, you've just confirmed all our suspicions."

"Sylvan, this is utter madness! I'm your uncle, your flesh and blood!"

"And my father was your brother. YOUR BLOOD!" I erupt, as fiercely as a volcano.

Leonal is speechless. I've never seen him this terrified in his life.

And it fills me with a dark satisfaction.

I close my eyes for a moment to regain my composure. Enola strokes the tense muscles of my chest in support. Her touch is as gentle and calming as a light drizzle after a storm.

"In Saradin's memory, I'll give you one chance, Leonal. It's time to prove your courage, if you have even a trace of it left. Beladyn?"

The assassin swiftly draws his two elven blades and tosses one to the ground at my uncle's feet. Leonal stares at the weapon, baffled.

"What is—"

"Fight the elfid blade to blade, without using your powers," I cut him off. "Like an honorable Fuegis warrior. If you manage to win this duel, I'll spare you; you have my word. You'll live out your days in prison, but you'll live. But if you resort to using your Fire magic, I'll respond with mine, Leonal. And Beladyn could fry your brain in an instant with his telepathy."

"Oh, absolutely," the assassin grins broadly. "One wrong move, egghead, and you'd turn into a vegetable."

Leonal slowly picks up the sword, his despair peaking as I deliver one final, icy warning, "Oh, one last thing, Uncle… I suggest you stay on your guard at all times, because you won't have room for a single mistake. Your opponent had the courtesy to coat his blade's tip with a few drops of the Kiss of Death. So even the slightest cut will condemn you to the same agonizing end as Saradin Ren-Fuegis." Leonal lets out a strangled gasp. "Good luck—you'll need it."

Justice shall be done.

For my father.

And for Symbiosis.

CHAPTER SIXTEEN

THE KISS OF DEATH

SYLVAN

I step back, pulling Enola close to me as we move away from the impending duel. Hand in hand, we retreat, our backs against the wall of the meeting room.

In his younger years, my uncle was a skilled swordsman. He fought alongside my father against the Renegades more than once. Though it's been years since he's fought a battle to the death, he's kept himself fit with regular training. We've sparred countless times, even after my father's death. I know he can hold his own. The question is: will that be enough against the Grandmaster of the Guild of Shadows?

It takes only seconds to know the answer.

I study Beladyn Targam. His body language is unmistakable. He's clearly unsettling Leonal, who holds his sword, his eyes flashing with nervous intensity.

The fight has yet to begin, but I can already tell I misjudged him—this Shadow is not a show-off.

I've never seen anyone so calm and self-assured in such a situation. He doesn't flinch, nor does he raise his poisoned sword. He simply stands there, head slightly tilted, his breathing barely noticeable, his gaze piercing and unyielding. There's no hint of the casual attitude he usually shows. The shift is stark. He's now showing the most dangerous side of his nature: that of a disciplined, seasoned assassin…one likely much older than he appears. His unwavering confidence and marble-like expression can only mean one thing: he's amassed decades, maybe centuries, of field experience. I have the distinct feeling he's killed far more men than Leonal, my father, and I combined. He resembles a predator lying in wait, ready to strike at the perfect moment. He assesses his opponent from every angle, mentally noting every useful detail for the fight ahead—a hunter strategizing his pursuit in real-time, not a soldier following orders on a battlefield.

I wouldn't want this elfid as my enemy.

"Sylvan, don't do this!" my uncle pleads, his eyes never leaving Beladyn, reflecting desperation, fury, and frustration. "If this man can read my thoughts, he'll anticipate every one of my moves. This fight is unfair, it's an execution!"

"Don't question my honor, High-Fuegis," the assassin retorts, answering before I can. "I won't use my telepathy. I swear it on Death. Your nephew has forbidden you from using your magic, so I've silenced my psychic powers to level the playing field. Otherwise, it'd be far too easy. In that same spirit, I'll grant you ten attacks without retaliating to give you a chance to defeat me. After that, I'll go on the offensive."

Ten potentially fatal strikes without using his telepathy. That's a huge risk—one I wouldn't take myself, especially not with my uncle.

My father didn't get ten chances.

But this is Beladyn's choice. I suppose he knows what he's doing.

Hearing these terms, Leonal regains a touch of confidence. He attacks.

Beladyn waits until the last second, then sidesteps my uncle's powerful thrust with stunning speed, bending his knees and tilting his head to the side. The blade slices the air just above him.

First strike.

Leonal raises his weapon and brings it down, aiming for the assassin's torso. Beladyn springs back with the agility of a wildcat. The tip of Leonal's sword barely grazes the chest of his armor.

Second strike.

My uncle then aims for Beladyn's legs, testing a new angle, a different type of attack. With no apparent momentum, Beladyn leaps over the blade, which sweeps the ground like a scythe through wheat.

I raise an eyebrow. I've never seen anyone propel themselves so high; the elfid has the reflexes of a young panther.

Third strike.

The fourth blow is parried with what looks like casual indifference, as if Beladyn's already grown weary of dodging. Their elven blades clash in a metallic ring. Leonal grips his sword with both hands to keep from being disarmed, such is the force of the block. A look of panic briefly crosses his face when he realizes he's outmatched. But Beladyn keeps his word; he doesn't counterattack, only defends.

For now.

My uncle resorts to a dirty trick, aiming a punch at the assassin's midsection. I scowl in anger at his dishonorable move.

Yet Beladyn counters this fifth attempt with a swift, precise kick to Leonal's forearm. Leonal staggers back, grunting in surprise and pain.

Impressive. This elfid keeps a sharp eye on every move his opponent makes, and his reflexes are remarkable. If he weren't an outsider assassin, and if he weren't so insolent, I'd consider inviting him to join my royal guard—or even to train my soldiers with his unique techniques. In any case, he's climbed a few rungs in my esteem.

Pale and breathing unevenly, Leonal is starting to lose his composure—a novice mistake against someone as skilled as this Shadow. His sixth strike is clumsy and poorly aimed. With a simple twist of his blade, Beladyn deflects it effortlessly. The seventh and eighth strikes also miss.

Only two strikes remain before the counterattack.

I glance briefly at my wife, who squeezes my hand, her breathing slightly tense. Her eyes dart with each motion, following the fight closely. She looks nearly as tense as Leonal, though for different reasons. I see her inner turmoil in her anxious expression. On one hand, she wants justice. On the other, she dreads the pivotal moment when the executioner will strike. Nevertheless, I'm sure she won't interfere—not out of respect for me. She wouldn't have responded the same way in my place…yet she respects my choice and my judgment.

The ninth strike misses its target once again. With a forceful shove, the assassin pushes Leonal back, and he staggers five steps in retreat. My uncle's fingers tremble on the hilt of his sword, his gaze darting to the closed door behind Beladyn, who advances steadily toward him, expression unforgiving. Leonal's feverish black eyes flick over to me, silently pleading for me to end the duel. I meet his panicked stare unblinking.

I told Enola this more than once—I have no pity for my enemies.

Suddenly, Leonal charges at Beladyn with a roar. But he isn't holding up his sword. He raises his free hand... and hurls a fireball toward the assassin before I have time to intervene against his treachery.

For a moment, I think the elfid is done for. But then Beladyn raises his own hand.

The fireball halts in mid-air, hanging there between the two men.

Enola lets out a gasp of shock, and I mutter a low curse.

That explains why *Nesayan's* blade heated up when it touched the Shadow in my quarters.

He has some form of Fire magic... similar to ours but different enough that I didn't sense it.

Could he have Fuegis blood?

Beladyn smirks slightly, and with a closing fist, he shrinks the fireball down... until it fizzles out right before my uncle's stunned gaze.

"A man who has never known honor in his life will not find it in his final hour," the assassin declares, his voice low and grave. "Your time is up; that was your tenth strike."

My father's brother isn't fast enough to dodge or block.

With a swift, gleaming arc, Beladyn's blade strikes, knocking Leonal's sword from his grip. The elven sword whirls through the air and lands on the table. I realize in that moment: the assassin could have disarmed him at the start.

A second later, the poisoned tip of Beladyn's sword draws a bloody gash across my uncle's temple—precisely where my own facial scar lies.

Leonal screams, more from terror than pain, wiping his face with his sleeve as if that could stop the poison from seeping into his veins. He stumbles toward us, using the table for support, his breathing ragged. I position myself in front of Enola, gripping the pommel of my sword.

But my uncle never reaches us. He collapses halfway there, vomiting a spurt of blood, and then another. His hands blacken just as my father's did. *The Kiss of Death* is claiming him with brutal swiftness.

His bloodshot, terrified eyes fix on something in the corner of the room. I follow his horrified gaze, my brow furrowed, but all I see is the shadow on the wall. A cold draft prickles the hair on my arms.

Enola holds her breath, crushing my hand in hers. The temperature has dropped.

Something has entered the room. I have no idea what it is, but a fear unlike anything I've ever felt surges within me. I don't dare to move, paralyzed. My wife trembles beside me, murmuring my name.

Leonal *sees* this thing.

We don't.

Beladyn sheathes his sword, stepping around my uncle's body as he summons the last of his strength to crawl toward the door, desperate to put distance between himself and the… dark, invisible creature.

"Do you know the motto of the Guild of Shadows, Leonal Ren-Fuegis?" asks the assassin, his tone almost cordial.

With froth gathering at the corners of his mouth, Leonal writhes in agony, curling in on himself, convulsing like a dying spider. The end is near. I force myself to watch the macabre scene. Unable to bear my uncle's suffering, Enola buries her face against my chest, her arms wrapped around my waist.

Beladyn sits on the edge of the table, watching his target, who is now nearly motionless. With an unsettling calm and softness, he recites the motto of his guild, "*We are all destined for the Kiss of Death. Only gods are immortal.*"

Leonal exhales his final breath in a painful spasm. Relief washes over me immediately. Moments later, the temperature in the room returns to normal, and the icy weight crushing my insides vanishes.

The strange threat has left.

I believe it came solely for my uncle.

"Damn it, Beladyn, a little warning would have been nice. What was *that?*" I growl, my heart still pounding.

"I can't always predict when *it*'ll appear," the assassin replies thoughtfully, his gaze fixed on my uncle's corpse. "Sometimes, when the time comes, it arrives in person to claim certain souls. Those of all the Shadows, of course, but also mortals who have disrupted the world's natural Balance. Mass murderers, usually. Leonal intentionally incited a war on Symbiosis. Thousands of innocent lives were lost because of his schemes."

"That doesn't answer my question. What just happened here?" I insist firmly.

The High Master looks deeply at Enola answering in a solemn

tone, "The Kiss of Death, Sylvan."

And from the weight of his words, I understand he isn't referring to the poison's name.

CHAPTER SEVENTEEN

THE ORIGINAL MAGIC

SYLVAN

I offered Beladyn a place to sleep in the palace tonight. I would have given him a comfortable suite, keeping his presence a secret from the staff. But he declined, braiding his ebony hair back, revealing his long, pointed ears adorned with silver rings.

"Are you kidding? I'm going to take advantage of this beautiful night to soak up your culture. I came prepared; I brought some of my savings to spend here. I'm not missing the chance to tour the brothels of Astranis and enjoy the fiery charms of the Fuegis courtesans."

I frown at his risky plan.

"That's a stunningly stupid idea. Forget it. You draw way too much attention with your skin color, armor, ears, and… everything else. No woman in this city would want to sleep with an elfid; you must know that your people have a reputation as criminals on Symbiosis." The fool of an assassin smirked, puffing up as if I'd just given him the highest compliment. "Anyway, long before that, the Fuegis will call the guard the second they see you lurking in the streets. It'll be chaos, and I have more important matters to deal with."

Of course, he is not listening to me.

"Don't worry about that—I'm the emperor of disguise and infiltration. A real chameleon; they won't suspect a thing. I'll bet you a million crowns that I'll have bedded the most sought-after courtesans of Astranis before sunrise. I never do things halfway." He turned to Enola. "My snowflake, see you at first light in the training room."

"Got it," replies my wife with a hint of amusement.

"Beladyn, by all the gods, don't stir up any trouble in my kingdom!" I shout as he walks away.

"You can count on me, Your Scarred Majesty!" he says, laughing over his shoulder before vanishing.

Hopeless.

After he left, I gathered the High-Fuegis Council to inform them of Leonal's betrayal, evidenced by the assassination contract, and his death. My advisers are dumbfounded to learn that he had poisoned his own brother and tried to have my beloved and me killed by Shadows. Most are approving my decision to execute him, except for two of my uncle's old friends, who are more reserved on the matter. I'm not surprised; one can't expect unanimous support in such circumstances, especially when presenting the Council with a fait accompli.

I allow them time to process this harsh news before revealing that my queen is not Alena Kan-Glace and that she is none other than the Rose of the Elements. Skipping the steps would have been a tactical error in our delicate situation.

I'm hoping to avoid the siege of Astranis by arranging an unofficial meeting with Alena, with the aim of discussing the possibility of a peace treaty. Enola will accompany me; her help could be crucial in reasoning with her sister. Without hesitation, my wife told me she will renounce her blood rights to the Glace throne if it would help to pacify things with Alena and the rebels. She argued that if we all made concessions and negotiated the terms of a potential alliance properly, we'd have a good chance at defusing the threat of war.

I haven't told Enola yet, but I'm not feeling particularly optimistic about it.

✳✳✳

ENOLA

Love is a tale woven with a powerful magic that has ruled the world since the dawn of time.

This enchantment binds two hearts, two souls, two spirits residing deep within two bodies lost in darkness—searching without knowing it, only to miraculously find one another. We bloom in its sublime embrace, healing deep wounds with pure tenderness. Through kisses and caresses, we absorb each other's emotions, binding them endlessly across familiar lands and beyond. Violence, fear, and death are banished from our world. Love holds the most essential place in the heart of our new story.

The union of bodies. The destiny of souls. Until now, these terms were abstract to me. They meant nothing.

He made them real. They became my everything.

I open my mouth to let his tongue tell our story in the dialect of passion, a word I redefined since our first time together in the Red Desert. His lips spell out indulgent syllables against mine, stifling my responses, stealing my laughter; he literally takes the words from my mouth.

We write the bold strokes of our tale on the surfaces of our bodies. My saliva, like invisible ink, pens sweet words on the silky, golden parchment of his skin. He draws both our names with his fingertips on my bare flesh, intertwining the letters so they merge. I whisper celestial promises in his ear that belong only to him, ones I could never share with another. His mouth traces the contours of my body, sending sparks through my veins like tiny stars igniting within. We craft our own story with tender words, inventing a delightful language, in no rush to bring these unspoken exchanges to an end. I begin to speak an unspoken vow as I kiss the pulse beating in his neck; he finishes my sentence with a languorous touch along the inside of my thigh.

I savor each of his smiles like sweets, brushing them with my insatiable lips. He bites my chin, my jaw, my ear, and my shoulder, breathing my name in a rough, prayerful whisper: "Enola. Enola. Enola. Enola." His loving voice and feverish gaze already possess me, so much so that I could beg him to reveal the rapturous end of his story. I want him so fully, so deeply within me, to reach the eternal fire that burns at the core of my being…

Tonight, I'm indifferent to wars, deaths, schemes, enemies, worries, the past, the future. Sylvan Ren-Fuegis is my everything, just as I am his, and nothing else matters but the present we're creating together in this room.

Sitting on cushions on the floor, our legs and arms entwined, skin to skin, we face each other, fully savoring these moments of closeness before the union we've both longed for.

"I was thinking of issuing a royal decree," Sylvan murmurs between soft kisses at my neck.

"Mm?"

"Three days of holiday starting tomorrow across the kingdom."

"And why this decree?" I smile, relaxed in his arms as I run my fingers through his dark hair.

"To celebrate the Rose of the Elements, the daughter of Nature. That way, I could personally honor you for three days, making love to you with all my devotion, and wouldn't have to explain my absence to my officers," he says, gently rubbing his bearded cheek against my Fuegis mark on my chest.

I burst into laughter. My husband truly thinks ahead.

"Three days? You should extend it to three months. The whole spring season. Then you could honor me morning, noon, and night."

"You're not a demigoddess; you're a full-fledged demon," he mutters, tracing a soft line along my pleasure point with the knuckle of his index finger.

"Let me honor you first, my king," I whisper, sinking my teeth playfully into his full lip.

A shiver escapes him, landing on my face as my hand closes around his arousal, feeling more enticing than ever. Sylvan's hips buck forward reflexively, and my fingers slide to his base.

"And how would you like to be honored, Your Majesty?" I murmur, stroking him, feeling him grow even harder in my hand. "With my hand… or my mouth?"

"Your mouth," he says without hesitation. "Honor me with your mouth."

I smile, a bit shyly. I've never done… this before, but it can't be too difficult.

Kneeling between his legs, I trail kisses down his sculpted torso. Sylvan leans back on his hands, his chest heaving as he watches me intently. My curious gaze falls on the glint of gold at the tip of his erection, a small piercing that crowns him like a scepter. The tiny metal bead on the right feels warm beneath my lips. I tease it with my tongue and catch it lightly between my teeth, letting it move over his skin as I savor his taste. His hips jerk in response, a rough, nearly desperate sound escaping him as his hand knots in my hair at the back of my head. Clearly, he's very sensitive here, and my playful explorations have quite an effect on him. I look up at him with a mischievous grin. His cheeks are flushed, his scar creased in tension, and his eyes have darkened to a forest green.

"Are you done teasing?" he asks in a husky tone, a blend of desire and frustration.

I shake my head, smiling at him. *I'm only just beginning.*

I capture the small piercing between my lips, tugging lightly on his skin. Sylvan throws his head back with a long, deep moan. In my hand, his arousal swells and throbs as if it's alive. I take the head of him into my mouth, rolling it with my tongue, thrilled by his reactions—they reassure me that I'm doing this right. His piercing taps against my teeth, slides against the inside of my cheek, and nudges my palate in rhythm with my movements. Sylvan surrenders entirely, to my immense satisfaction. My hands roam up to his chest, massaging his tensed muscles as I take him deeper between my lips. Though I can't manage all of him, it seems to be more than enough. His fingers dig into my scalp, tugging at my hair, but I don't mind. Guided by instinct, I suck him as intensely as I can. His hips roll slowly under my face, his lips whispering my name over and over. His body trembles, and then, suddenly, he tilts my head back, making me release him.

"Did I hurt you?" I ask, a bit dismayed.

A playful smile shapes his lips. He's breathtaking when he smiles… and I'm almost certain it's the first time I've seen him blush.

"Far from it, my love. I'm this close to coming."

"Well, if you want, you can… I mean…"

"No. I want to finish between your thighs."

"Then come, my love."

"Soon, Enola. We have all night. Now, it's my turn to play with you," he whispers, laying me gently down on the cushions in a way that melts me.

He rains kisses over my body, nipping at my collarbone, teasing the tips of my breasts, tracing his tongue down the curve of my belly… then he nestles his head between my parted thighs. The firm brush of his tongue against my center makes me jolt. I let out a long, satisfied moan as he worships me there with his mouth, drinking in the essence of my femininity with the passion and tenderness of a man utterly in love.

Minutes later, after bringing me to a stunning release, Sylvan lies on top of me, breathless. He kisses me with a raw, wild intensity, yet, paradoxically, he enters me with delicate care. I welcome the heat of him into my drenched sanctuary with a sigh of pleasure, clenching my inner muscles around him and wrapping my legs around his hips to hold him as deep as possible. We shiver in unison. His magic, blazing like fire, flows into me, mingling with my own powers in an erotic dance that heightens every physical and spiritual sensation. His soul pours into mine like a cascade of flames, igniting my spirit further with each thrust. Our four elements merge as one. Tears of joy bead at the corners of my eyes.

Yes, love is a tale infused with a magic so powerful it has governed the world since the Dawn of Time.

In this moment, ours echoes through eternity.

Sitting cross-legged on my bed, alone in my chambers, I read. I don't know who taught me to read, but the words on the pages do have meaning. It's a novel about a tragic love between two people separated by all odds. Two soldiers—one Stowne, the other Aeria. Their Clans are at war. Enemies, despite themselves, the two men must hide to love each other. Enemies despite themselves, the two men must hide to love each other. The emotions in the story pierce my heart and fill me with a deep sadness. My fingers tremble on the cover. I'm not sure if I'll be able to continue. My pain is too vivid.

I sense a familiar presence moving through the hallway—a comforting aura that always soothes me. The ache of my sadness fades a bit, swept away by a wave of love and warmth. A smile creeps onto my lips just as the door cracks open.

A tousled head appears in the doorway, checking if I'm asleep. I close my book, noticing the flame flickering in the hollow of his palm to light his path through the dark corridors of the Astranis palace. My own Fire magic hums in recognition of his; they know each other.

"Come here, my little love," I invite, patting the bed.

He had a nightmare. It's been happening frequently lately.

The child closes the door behind him and hurries over to curl up in my arms. I rock him against my chest, pressing a kiss to his forehead tattooed with a red sun, then gently cup his face to lift it up and meet my gaze. I look into my son's sapphire eyes, stroking his silky black hair. He's five years old, my most priceless treasure.

"What was it this time?" I ask softly.

"A giant flying insect was chasing me, Mom. It wanted to drain my blood with its stinger," he mumbles.

I smile and glance toward a moth resting on the wall. I extend a hand in its direction, summoning my Earth magic to communicate with the tiny creature. The insect flutters and lands on the back of my hand. My son draws back, his eyes wide with fear, but I hold his wrist gently.

"Fear is your greatest enemy, my little love," I reassure him, showing him the moth's trembling wings. "See? It's harmless."

I place my hand against his, and he bravely resists his fear as the insect crawls onto his skin.

"Hey, it tickles," my son observes, relaxing.

The moth takes off, flying out through the open window, disappearing into the starry night.

"You're not sleeping either," he sighs, casting a forlorn look at the empty spot beside me, understanding the reason for my sleeplessness without me having to say it. "What were you reading?"

"A beautiful love story, for grown-ups."

"Can you tell me a story so I can go back to sleep, Mom?"

"Of course, sweetheart. Any particular one?" I ask, already knowing which he'll choose.

"The one about Rascal the dragon," he says eagerly, snuggling against me.

I breathe in his scent, soaking in his warmth. Without this child's love, I might have faded away. He is my salvation.

"Once upon a time, there was a young, fearless prince named Saradin Ren-Fuegis who one fine day found a massive dragon egg in the Red Desert—"

***

I open my eyes in the darkness of our room, slowly surfacing from my unsettling dream.

I'm lying on my back, a weight on my abdomen drawing my gaze downward.

Sylvan is asleep, nestled deeply against me. My thighs, parted, frame his shoulders. His head rests on my belly, rising and falling with each of my breaths. My hand is lost in his dark hair, so similar to that of the child from my dream. His beloved features… are the same as those of our son.

The Prince of Symbiosis.

Named Saradin, in memory of his grandfather.

This isn't the expression of a longing for motherhood.

It's another premonitory dream.

For I can already feel it within me, a tiny seed sheltered deep in my womb. Nature has crafted its finest work within my body. My king's essence has seeded new life within me.

I'm pregnant.

I should be happy, but I can't be. Something cruel is stopping me.

Because I just realized, no matter what I do…

I am destined to lose Sylvan.

CHAPTER EIGHTEEN

NEW ACUITY

ENOLA

"Enola Ren-Fuegis."

My eyelids lift at the sound of my name. My tired gaze locks onto my instructor's eyes before drifting down to my own helpless hands. They're so pale I can see the network of bluish veins beneath my skin, like tiny streams branching out. *A map leading nowhere.*

"What's the first thing I told you, Enola?" Beladyn asks calmly.

He isn't scolding me. He's maintaining his composure, extraordinarily patient despite my struggle to summon any magic at all for over an hour.

We're kneeling across from each other in the center of the room. Between us lies a simple olive branch on the floor, about as long as a forearm. As ordinary as it is, this branch—picked up in the palace gardens—is giving me no end of trouble. My powers are hibernating; they refuse to awaken.

"To focus my mind on this branch," I sigh, dispirited.

"And then, what else did I tell you?"

"To clear my mind of all thoughts but this branch, letting them go one by one as I exhale. As I physically breathe out, I mentally sweep away," I recite mechanically.

"Did you sweep away every intrusive thought?"

"I… I can't. Are you reading my thoughts right now?"

"No, Enola. I respect the mental privacy of those I trust. Do you also trust me?"

I nod. Odd as it may seem, I do indeed trust this assassin as if we've known each other for years. I feel a kind of friendly kindness in him toward me.

I glance at Sylvan for what must be the hundredth time. Seated on a bench across the room with his arms folded over his chest, he watches our session. Though he's silent, I can't seem to ignore his presence. He must be bored, but he remains quiet and stoic to avoid disturbing us.

Beladyn follows my gaze, puzzled.

"Sylvan, please leave us."

My husband straightens his back, visibly bristling at the request.

"And why would I do that, Beladyn?"

"Because you're distracting my student."

"Nonsense! I haven't said a word in over an hour."

"You don't need to speak to disturb her emotions, Your Stubborn Majesty. She needs to free herself from every constraint. We won't make progress if you don't leave."

"He's right, my love," I add gently, giving my husband a peaceful look. "Please, listen to him. It'll be fine."

Disappointed by my request, he hesitates.

"Enola, you don't—"

"I'll watch over her as the apple of my eye, Sylvan," the High Master interrupts firmly. "If we don't make a few concessions, we won't get anything beneficial. And by *we*, I mean *you*."

"Consider this a warning, Beladyn! If you—"

"Touch her, you kill me," the assassin finishes in an exasperated tone, waving a hand dismissively in Sylvan's direction. "I get it, noted, acknowledged, petrified. Farewell, Majesty!"

I offer Sylvan a reassuring smile as he stands, looking none too pleased. He shoots a menacing glance at the elf for show, then reluctantly leaves the room.

"Love really does make some humans foolish and narrow-minded," comments Beladyn with a grimace. "I couldn't stand a woman being so possessive and suffocating. Does he escort you to the latrine, too?"

"Oh, stop it. I find him endearing."

"Because you love him, you're as foolish and narrow-minded as he is in this respect."

"I take it you've never been in love."

"You'd be correct. Freedom and cynicism are two concepts incompatible with romantic love. A wise man once said so."

"And which man was that?"

"Me, of course." He becomes serious in an instant. "Enola, tell me what's troubling you and preventing you from concentrating so that we can focus fully on the exercise. Whatever you tell me will stay between us."

I rest my hand on my stomach, wondering how to broach the subject. My skin feels warm under the thin fabric of my dress, while my hands are so cold they go numb at the touch, as if experiencing a small shock.

"Yesterday, at the top of the Tower of Eternal Flame, your father mentioned the dragon's Vision of Finality during your war on the Continent," I murmur. "Why didn't he try to… change that fate before it happened?"

Beladyn pulls his knees to his chest, rests his elbows on them, and runs a hand over the back of his neck. It feels like a gesture of slight discomfort, which is surprising coming from him.

"Visions of Finality always come to pass; they are inevitable. Death itself sends them to choose mortals. The dragon accepted his fate, knowing he couldn't avoid it. It was a necessary sacrifice to win the war and restore Balance on the Continent. Why are you asking this?"

"I… I had a Vision of Finality last night, I think. It was altered."

"On your own death?"

"No. Of Sylvan's," I confess, sadness weighing heavily in my words.

"What do you mean by *altered*?"

"I… I saw my future. Without him."

"That's not what it was, Enola. Visions of Finality reveal the exact moment of a death. You probably had a hypothetical future vision, which isn't in the same category."

"What's the difference?" I ask, lost.

"Hypothetical future visions are potential paths, parallel roads. Nothing is set in stone there. Some unfold completely, others partially, some… not at all." He pauses and clears his throat. "We have to be cautious in interpreting these visions and take a step back. I give them only relative weight. I've been predicted things that never came to pass or happened indirectly."

"So Sylvan isn't… isn't doomed to die?" I say, hope returning.

"No, Enola. Only Visions of Finality are unavoidable. However, I'd like to caution you. When you focus too intently on a hypothetical future vision, you can lose sight of the present, and what ends up happening may be worse than the original vision. The Balance of natural forces nearly always wins in these games, especially since many factors lie beyond the control of those involved."

"What do you mean?"

"Well, if one life is saved, another might be taken in its place, maybe even more than one. This the Fireades call it the *butterfly effect*. A tiny flap of wings in Land of Fire could trigger a devastating snowstorm in Symbiosis. This is why free will is so important. We're all responsible for our choices and actions, but their consequences are sometimes unexpected. Personally, I've never liked the word *destiny*. It exasperates me. My father, who swears by the Weave of Fate, would tell you a very different story, but he and I don't see the world the same way."

"So, in fact, you're saying I shouldn't take this vision into account?"

He lets out a long sigh. "Enola, it's not for me to tell you what to do; act as you see fit. Your anxiety about the future is understandable, but you mustn't let it consume you, especially in these troubled times. Especially in your condition."

His last words make my heart skip a beat.

"Beladyn, you promised you wouldn't read my thoughts!" I exclaim, blushing.

"I didn't, my little snowflake. But you keep touching your belly since your scarred king left. A small, telltale gesture."

"Oh. Forgive me for raising my voice. I… I jumped to conclusions."

He chuckles, shaking his head. "It's nothing. My congratulations. Do you plan on telling the future father soon?"

"No, I'm going to wait. His protective instinct would go against my wishes. He'd lock me in a tower to keep me safe while he went off to see my sister, knowing him. That's not what I want; I intend to accompany him."

"Don't wait too long to tell him, though. If I were in his place, I'd want to know as soon as possible. Shall we return to our lovely olive branch now?"

"Beladyn, one last question… If we can't prevent the war in Symbiosis War, will you stay and fight by our side?"

"No, Enola, because this isn't our war," he says softly, his voice filled with a gentle solemnity. "My father will come to retrieve me today, and we will return to Clepsydra. We've done what we needed to do here, to make amends for the poison that killed Saradin Ren-Fuegis and to guide you on the path to your own truth. It's up to you to write the next chapter of your story… This one isn't ours."

With my eyes closed, I focus my mind, breathing deeply. I studied every detail of the branch before shutting my eyes. Now, I recreate it, drawing it in my memory. Its roughness, its angles, its colors. I visualize it until it becomes part of me. I can feel its microscopic vibrations, imperceptible to an ordinary human. Its energy melds with mine.

Though Beladyn's drawling voice is nearby, it feels as if it comes from a great distance, like a thick fog separates us. Still, I catch every intonation without letting my concentration waver. My heartbeat is slow. My breathing is calm. My muscles are relaxed. Everything flows, ethereal. My emotions are steady.

"Connect with the element. Follow the invisible thread that binds you to it. Welcome this bond with calm. Open your senses. Listen to your instincts. Sharpen your perceptions. What do you feel?"

"The air around us. It's tangible. Its smell. Its taste. Its… texture," I murmur, surprised by the words coming out of my mouth.

I can't fully describe it. It's unlike anything I've known. New words would need to be invented. It's absolutely… beautiful. I've established a connection with nature. It fills me and transcends me. At this moment, I can see beyond *everything*.

"Well done, Enola," the assassin approves, a smile in his voice. "You've reached the higher level of sensory trance. Describe everything you feel."

"Organic materials. Mineral. Plant. Animal. Oxygen. Sand. Wood. Steel. Leather. Pollens. Scents. Variations in warmth, in light… The water sources… There's… there's a multitude of insects under the floor and behind the walls. I can sense them, like points of light. There are nine fireplaces and about a hundred candles lit on this floor. I can feel the Fire magic of all the nearby Fuegis. There's stagnant water in the bathroom of the next room; the basin wasn't fully emptied. Outside, the desert wind changed direction less than two minutes ago and has weakened. It's warmed up. This plant…" Without opening my eyes, I point to a potted lemon tree giving off a faint tangy scent in the corner of the room. "… hasn't been watered in a long time and is drying out, bit by bit. And I could go on like this for hours."

"Impressive, my little Rose of the Elements. You're on the right path. Now, bring your focus back to the olive branch. Imagine lifting it, touching it with your mind. Stretch the thread that connects you to it, meld into the air, ground yourself in the earth. Breathe deeply. Fully feel it. Levitate the branch, Enola."

A sudden wave of anxiety fills me at his command.

"I…I can't do it."

"Yes, you can. Believe in yourself. Say you can make the branch levitate."

"I can make the branch levitate," I repeat weakly.

"Your words are empty. You're lying to yourself. Stop lying and underestimating yourself. Draw on the best part of your emotions— the part that lifts you up. Fill this statement with faith and conviction. Not only can you do it, but you *will* do it. Because, for you, the Rose of the Elements, daughter of Nature, it's inevitable. It's natural. It's simple. Accept it, Enola Ren-Fuegis. Accept your power. Embrace your divine side. Say the words again: *I can make the branch levitate.*"

I'm going to do it.

Not because I have to.

But because I want to.

"I can make the branch levitate."

"Again."

"I can make the branch levitate!" I exclaim, my voice strong and resolute.

Silence settles in the room. Then, calmly, my teacher speaks again.

"Open your eyes. The hardest part is behind you now."

I gasp I open my eyes.

The olive branch is suspended in the air, just inches from my face, between Beladyn and me.

I move my hand, marveling like a child. The branch follows my fingers, twirling with an effortless grace.

"You used Air magic. Now call on Earth magic. Make it sprout."

I focus again on the branch. A second later, tiny green leaves emerge from the wood like emerald jewels.

Marvelous.

"Water magic," Beladyn encourages.

Drops of water gather on the leaves and gently detach one by one. They begin to whirl around the levitating branch, sparkling like raindrops… that don't fall.

"Fire magic," the assassin concludes.

My heart tightens. Destroy this beauty I've just created? No, I can't…

"All life ends in death, Enola," Beladyn insists. "This, too, you must accept. It's the law of nature and the foundation of Balance. Burn the branch."

I sigh, nodding faintly.

The branch ignites in a crackling blaze. Tiny, charred particles drift down to the floor. Moments later, all that remains is a small pile of ash. I run my fingers through it.

Even in death… there is life.

With serene joy, I summon a new sprout to rise from the ashes. I look up, my eyes misty with emotion, and meet Beladyn's gaze. He takes my dust-covered fingers in his own.

His gray skin feels like a furnace, his power hitting me like a thunderclap.

He places a gentle, approving kiss on the back of my trembling hand.

"There, I have nothing left to teach you, Your Majesty. You've understood the principle. You've found the key that unlocked your own balance."

I fix my shocked gaze on his, both captivated and shaken by what I see deep within his dark irises, beyond his outer shell.

His true nature.

It echoes the first rule of the Guild of Shadows: *Don't trust appearances.*

"I… I can see you, too, Beladyn. You're not… you're not an elfid."

An ironic smile spreads across his lips.

"No, my little snowflake. I never was. This will stay between us, won't it?"

I return his smile, sealing our unspoken pact.

"It will stay between us," I murmur, inclining my head toward him in gratitude.

Chapter Nineteen

Evening Encounter

Sylvan

in the searing heat of the Red Desert, leaving behind the towering dunes that consume the outline of Astranis. Each time I leave my homeland, a pang of emotion tugs at my heart. Every time I set out for war or a mission, the question echoes in my mind: *Will I see it again?*

"You're unusually quiet," I remark to Enola, who sits behind me on the saddle.

Her arms wrapped tightly around my waist; she has rested her head between my shoulder blades. I almost thought she'd fallen asleep until I felt her delicate fingers intertwine with mine on my thigh.

"I'm just tired," she replies in a weary voice. "This morning's training drained me of all my energy."

"There's still time to turn back, love. If you're not feeling well, we can postpone this visit."

"No, don't worry. Beladyn explained it's just a side effect that'll fade in a few hours, once my magic replenishes itself. Are you nervous about your three wives meeting each other, Sylvan Ren-Fuegis?" she teases, lightly scratching my thigh with her nails, sparking a pull of desire within me.

She guessed my worries. I am, in fact, a bit anxious. I'd have much preferred to avoid this awkward situation. But I'd never admit that, not even under torture.

"You are my one and only true wife." At that precise moment, my mare shakes her neck and snorts. "Jada, don't be jealous; that's childish."

Enola's amused laughter spreads through my chest and belly like warm honey. My affection and tenderness for this woman grow stronger by the hour, seemingly boundless. I never thought it possible to cherish someone so profoundly. Now, I understand what my father meant when he spoke of his unconditional love for my mother. I also fully grasp the depth of pain he must have felt at her death. When the young Glace is out of my sight, a wave of uncontrollable anxiety crashes over me. I fear for her safety, fear losing her. Yet, when I hold her in my arms, I feel invincible.

"I knew you were hiding your first wife, Fuegis!" she jokes between giggles. "The king of Symbiosis married to his horse; imagine the court scandal! Have you secretly married your sword as well?" I shake my head, groaning, though a smile tugs at my lips at her playful cheekiness. "Your armor? Your crown, maybe?"

"You're the one exhausting me right now."

"Hmm, your throne, Sylvan."

I lean back in the saddle to whisper so that Daegan and Anetos, riding ahead, won't overhear us.

"If you don't stay quiet, I'll take you on that throne as soon as we return to Astranis."

"No way, my devious husband. I prefer the bed; it's more comfortable." She gives me a playful nudge in the shoulder. "A minute ago, you were scolding me for being too quiet, and now you're saying I talk too much. Make up your mind."

What I really want is to silence her mouth with mine, but our current position doesn't allow for such a move. I'm no contortionist and trying that would likely end with me falling off the horse.

✳✳✳

ENOLA

After an hour's ride, we dismount in front of an agricultural estate nestled between rocky hills. The climate here is somewhat milder compared to the rest of the Red Desert. A few Fuegis guards patrol the perimeter.

"Who owns this farm, Sylvan?" I ask as my husband hands Jada's reins to my bodyguard, Anetos.

"It belonged to my old nursemaid. She didn't want to live in the city anymore, so my father gifted her this land. She passed away shortly before he did. Her daughter, Raïa, inherited the farm," he explains, waving to a Fuegis woman in her forties holding an amphora.

With a smile, the woman nods in our direction as she brings water to an old soldier sitting on a bench.

"Has Raïa been taking care of Lia and Belise since the war began?" I ask.

Sylvan nods, leading me toward the farm entrance.

"Lia's easy to manage, but Belise drives her crazy, from what I hear."

"Have they ever tried to escape?"

"Lia would never dare. Belise, on the other hand, is more stubborn. A few weeks ago, she tried to make her way back to Stalagmis on her own. She knocked out a guard and stole his horse while Raïa was asleep. But my men caught up to her in the desert after a ten-minute chase."

"She didn't use her powers?"

"They both wear an artifact around their necks like the one you used to have. I'm the only one who can release them."

"What? There are more of those collars?"

"I have four at my disposal."

"And you're only telling me this now!"

"You never asked," he points out with a sly smile, pushing the door open.

We step into a large, simply furnished room. The first prisoner I see is Lia Ler-Aeria, Cyriel's daughter. Sitting on a cushion by the window, she holds a book in her hands. Dressed in a plain peasant's dress, she bears a slight resemblance to her cousin, Nadya, though she is younger, smaller, and gentler. Long blonde hair is braided over her shoulders. The Aeria tattoo, a silver feather, marks her forehead above her wide, childlike eyes. She is as lovely and delicate as a porcelain doll.

Belise emerges from another room when she hears the front door open. Idric San-Stowne's sister is older than Lia and me; she must be around thirty-five. Her mahogany hair, streaked with gray, is cut to her thin shoulders. Her face is unremarkable, but her pride and noble bearing make it clear, even without the green oak tattoo of her Clan on her forehead, that her royal lineage is undeniable. Her cinnamon-colored eyes dart to Sylvan and then to me.

We all share one thing in common: the Fuegis mark on our chest. It painfully reminds me of how my husband etched it into my skin during our wedding. Though I have forgiven Sylvan, a surge of empathy for Lia and Belise washes over me.

The same expression of shock spreads across the faces of the two other wives as they see me holding hands with their captor—without a collar—and most importantly, alive. Lia turns pale, slowly closing her book. Belise's expression hardens, full of disdain, bordering on disgust.

"Alena Kan-Glace," whispers the Aeria Princess in a small voice.

"No," the Stowne counters, narrowing her eyes at me. "This woman is not Alena, Lia."

"What makes you think that, Belise?" Sylvan asks, maintaining his calm demeanor.

"I never forget a face, and I met Alena twice in my life. She's taller than you, her eyes are lighter, and her mouth is thinner. You look a lot like her, but you're not her," she states, staring at me intently.

"I'm her older sister," I reveal softly. "My name is Enola."

"You're lying, Glace. Alena has no brothers or sisters," Belise retorts, unfazed by my confession.

"She doesn't know. I am her father's daughter, but… with another woman, not her mother. I was raised by my adoptive family far from Oceanar."

Lia and Belise exchange a brief glance.

"You're saying you're a royal illegitimate child? What proof do you have of that claim?"

"We don't owe you any explanations, Belise," Sylvan cuts in before I can respond.

"*We?*" Idric's sister repeat, her tone filled with contempt. "I see what kind of woman you are. A shameless opportunist. Alena would never have betrayed her kingdom for the tyrant who laid it to waste."

"You don't know me, Belise," I retort coldly. "Nor my sister. Nor Sylvan."

"Then where is Alena Kan-Glace?" asks Lia, rising with a rustle of her skirts. "Is she alive?"

"Yes. She has raised an army against our kingdom," my husband informs her succinctly.

A sarcastic laugh erupts from Belise's throat.

"You reap what you sow, Sylvan Ren-Fuegis! Why are you here with your new bastard queen? Have you come to execute us after all?"

Grumpy. The word suits her perfectly. Yet, I can understand her bitterness given her circumstances. Sylvan killed her brother Idric before imprisoning and forcibly marrying her. Although he spared her life, she still sees him as her enemy. Lia, on the other hand, appears slightly less hostile than Belise. She seems more subdued, resigned, and afraid. The young Aeria watches Sylvan out of the corner of her eye, as if expecting him to draw his sword and strike her down at any moment. She stirs an almost maternal protective instinct in me. I want to reassure her, to promise that everything will be all right and that we won't harm her.

"Of course not," Sylvan assures, making an exasperated gesture with his hand. "This charade has gone on long enough. I will free both of you very soon."

Lia gasps in astonishment. Belise frowns, wary.

"Free us? Under what conditions?"

"None. You will soon be escorted by my men to the borders of your respective kingdoms. I will have our marriages annulled. I intend to try to negotiate a peace treaty with Alena Kan-Glace. Your release is a gesture of goodwill on my part and..." He closes his eyes for a moment before reopening them, swallowing his pride. The intensity of his remorse tightens my throat. "A way to make amends with you two. Even if it doesn't erase what I've done, I... apologize for the harm I've caused."

"You burned my brother and his father alive, Sylvan," Belise reminds him, gesturing to Lia, who looks distraught. "You branded like livestock with your Fuegis seal. You can *never* make amends. Whether your remorse is genuine or not doesn't change the facts. Your apologies mean nothing."

"You're right. My apologies won't bring back Idric and Cyriel. Things are what they are," admits my husband, his expression dark.

"We all have a vested interest in preventing the war from continuing," I murmur sadly, watching Sylvan's other wives. "To rebuild unity on our island, we must be willing to learn from our mistakes. We need to look forward and choose life over clinging to the past and death. Symbiosis has suffered enough, don't you think?"

My question hangs in the silence. Lia presses her lips together, lost in thought. Belise remains silent, arms crossed over her chest.

"Whatever happens, our influence is limited, and we aren't the decision-makers," she finally says with an edge. "But I believe that, at this stage, only one sacrifice might convince our three kingdoms to abandon the idea of destroying yours."

My husband raises his head to her, a fragile hope flickering in his eyes.

"What sacrifice, Belise?"

"Your death, Sylvan."

He takes the blow in silence. My hand instinctively rests on my belly, where the gift of my beloved grows. I hope with all my heart that Belise is wrong.

"I would like to tell you a story, if I may," I sigh, gently stroking my husband's tense back.

"About what?" mutters the Stowne, slightly confused by my request.

"About a young king, blinded by grief and betrayed by his uncle, who seeks redemption as he tries to atone for his sins…"

✳✳✳

Upon our return to Astranis, Sylvan escorts me to my quarters. Before sunset, he must conduct an inspection of the Fuegis troops' barracks with Daegan to assess supplies and begin organizing the city's defenses in case our plan fails. After kissing me deeply and promising he would return to my arms as soon as his duty was done, he leaves reluctantly.

My solitary dinner in my quarters is interrupted by a maid who informs me that Selaine has requested to see me outside the Temple of the God of Fire. The courier adds that my young attendant has crucial information to share regarding Lady Nadya. My heart leaps in my chest.

I hurry down to the palace gardens, instructing my bodyguard, Anetos, to stay back so Selaine won't feel uneasy about revealing confidential matters in his presence.

I approach the temple. On its closed doors, the glowing hues of twilight and the shadows of the tree branches intertwine like lovers.

Selaine is not there.

I call out for her, walking around the area bordered by bushes and palm trees, my hands cupped around my mouth.

A creeping anxiety starts to set in.

Has someone harmed her?

This silence… it's not normal. I should be able to hear the animals and insects, sense their presence through my magic. But there's nothing.

A cool gust ruffles the hair on my arms and makes the flames of the torches on the temple's façade flicker.

Danger, whispers the wind in my hair.

Threat, crackles the fire dancing before me.

Trap, sings the water from the nearby fountain.

Death, rumbles the earth beneath my feet.

I back away, like a deer on high alert, breath shallow, scanning the desolate surroundings. A shiver runs through my entire body. My focus wavers under the grip of fear. *Refocus your mind, Enola Ren-Fuegis*, echoes Beladyn's voice in my mind.

But I can't. My mind spirals in all directions.

"ANETOS!" I scream at the top of my lungs, calling for my bodyguard's help.

That's when something shifts behind me.

I whip around, frantic.

A vine coils around my neck at lightning speed and lifts me off the ground. I flail my arms and legs wildly, completely panicked, suspended several feet in the air. A strangled rasp escapes my throat, compressed by the living vine, animated by Earth magic. I try to command the treacherous vine, but it resists me. My chaotic emotions block the flow of my powers.

"I regret to inform you that Anetos is dead, Your Majesty," a familiar voice announces calmly below me. "But that's not a bad thing. This way, we won't be disturbed."

Oh no.

I look down, in shock.

And I meet Selaine's amber gaze.

Chapter Twenty
Strength and Fragility

Enola

I'm suffocating. My feet kick frantically in the empty air. The vine tightens its lethal grip around my throat, crushing my bruised flesh with calculated slowness. My vision blurs. My ears ring. A strangled cry escapes me.

Above all, I am terrified of dying because it would mean my son will never be born. My innocent child, my most precious treasure, the fruit of the love I share with Sylvan.

"I will loosen my hold on your neck so you can answer my questions, little Powerless Glace," Selaine says from below. "If you call for help, you will die. If you lie to me, you will die. However, if you cooperate, I will spare your life." The icy tone of her voice contradicts this last statement. "I suggest you make wise choices, Enola."

She knows the truth, at least partially. She called me by my name. She referred to me as *little Powerless Glace*.

Her voice is cold, confident, and detached, unlike the Selaine I know—or thought I knew. This girl is a Stowne spy who has stolen Selaine's appearance.

Just as Nadya claimed.

So why didn't I sense her deceit earlier with my divine perceptions?

The vine loosens slightly, allowing me to breathe again. I stare into the traitor's amber eyes. That's when I catch something, a subtle detail I hadn't noticed before because I trusted her completely. *A crossbreed.* This girl has both Fuegis blood, but her powers manifest through Earth magic.

"Who… who are you?" What have you done with Selaine?" I croak, my voice raspy.

"I'm the one asking questions here, Enola. Let's start with the first one. I've learned that Leonal Ren-Fuegis was executed for high treason. Why?"

"I have no idea. Sylvan didn't tell me, and I wasn't there."

"Wrong answer."

As punishment, the vine tightens around my neck. I try to grab it with my hands, but two more vines coil around my wrists and force my arms apart. The three binds pull me backward, slamming my back against a tree and scraping my skin against its rough bark. My eyes roll back. My oxygen-starved organs scream in agony. My heartbeat slows.

After ten excruciating seconds, my tormentor slackens the vine again. I fill my lungs with air. My heart races.

"Don't take me for a fool, Enola," the girl hisses. "You became his confidante and accomplice. The bloodthirsty despot spared you because he fell in love with you, and I'm certain that despicable love is mutual. You are no better than that tyrant. You were supposed to die to buy Alena more time, not fall in love with our enemy."

Lying to survive. To buy time. To uncover the truth.

"I'm not in love with him, stupid Stowne!" I snap hoarsely. "I made him believe I was. I've been waiting for the perfect moment to kill him. Since I have no powers, I have to get the job done with a blade while he's asleep. So far, he hasn't completely let his guard down, despite his feelings for me. For weeks, I've been working to earn his trust. I'm on your side—set me free!"

She frowns, her face full of distrust.

"Stop the nonsense, Enola. You love him. I've seen the way you look at him, and it's disgusting."

"I'm an excellent actress. Like you, apparently. You're working for Alena, aren't you?" She doesn't answer, but her gaze darkens. I'm sure I'm right about that. That's how she knows my true identity. "So am I. I've always been loyal to my queen."

She grimaces with skepticism.

"Then why haven't you contacted Alena to tell her about your plans?"

"Because I'm constantly watched by the Fuegis guards. Besides, I couldn't have sent her a message anyway—I can't write. You ruined my plan when you killed my bodyguard! How am I supposed to explain that to Sylvan?"

"That's the least of my concerns, Glace. I'll give you the benefit of the doubt only if you tell me where Belise San-Stowne and Lia Ler-Aeria are. I found out they're not dead from that idiot Daegan. I know they're being held somewhere else, because I've searched every room in this palace since you arrived."

Since my arrival. That time frame meant I had only ever dealt with this Stowne, never the real Selaine. She infiltrated the palace when I was captured in Oceanar. She posed as a gentle, reserved, and innocent girl to better fool everyone. She must have been passing information about Sylvan to Alena Kan-Glace so Alena could adjust her rebellion plans against the Fuegis forces.

Keep her talking, my reason urged.

"I'll tell you if you tell me what you did to the girl whose appearance you stole. Is she alive?"

"Yes," grumbles the girl. "I don't kill innocent children, unlike your husband. She's become Alena's servant."

You mean her slave, I think, torn between relief and worry. Selaine had been taken right under the noses of the Fuegis and replaced by this Stowne spy within the palace of Astranis.

Refocus your mind, Enola. Fear is your greatest enemy. Trust yourself.

"You're quite the hypocrite," I say quietly, gradually regaining control over my emotions. "You're responsible for the massacre at Raockar. Innocent children, specifically, died because of you."

Including Kara, my little Fuegis taken far too soon by the madness of men.

"I didn't kill them myself!" the spy protests defensively. "It was Sylvan who started the initial conflict, don't forget that. He should bear the weight of those children's deaths on his conscience, but he has none! He will pay dearly for all the harm he's caused, and Alena will personally make sure of that. Where are Belise and Lia, Enola?

Speak!" she demands fiercely.

There it was. I had reached it—the source of power buried deep within me. That calm reservoir surrounded by earth and fire, brushed by the wind, standing in contrast to the inner turmoil of the Stowne, increasingly disturbed by the direction of our conversation.

Just as I had done with the red tiger, I established a mental connection with the vines, followed by a second one with the forces lying beneath the ground.

It's time to turn the tide.

"You're mistaken," I whisper, holding gaze, as hard as stone.

"About what?"

"I'm not Powerless."

Dozens of roots erupted suddenly from the grass around the Stowne and struck her all at once. She shrieked in surprise and fear as the plants bound her arms, legs, waist, and neck. The three vines that had imprisoned me slithered down and placed me gently on the ground before releasing me. I rubbed my sore neck, watching the spy struggle uselessly, ensnared in a tight cocoon of greenery she couldn't escape. My powers were far greater than hers, and from the look on her face, she was realizing it. With a flick of my mind, I forced the spy to reveal her true form. Her face shifted, transforming into that of a woman in her thirties, with short chestnut hair and freckled cheeks. Her wide, stunned eyes locked onto mine.

"W-what are you?" she stammers, her voice shaking.

"What am I?" I repeat thoughtfully.

A few days ago, I wouldn't have known how to answer that question.

I roll up my sleeves, showing her the marks on my wrists. Her eyes widened, and her breath caught in her chest.

"I am the Earth you walk on. I am the Air you breathe. I am the Water you drink. I am the Fire that consumes you." Leaning down, I brush my fingers over a twisted root, and a brilliant white orchid sprouted and blossomed at my touch. "I am the Rose of the Elements. And I will not allow any more innocent children to die in this war."

✳✳✳

SYLVAN

With my heart heavy with bitterness and my stomach knotted like lead, I buckle the bewitched necklace around the neck of the Stowne spy I had just knocked out with a punch to the temple. I need to free Nadya as well and offer her my sincerest apologies for this grave misunderstanding.

"She strangled Anetos to death, Sylvan. We shouldn't show any mercy to this scum!" Daegan barks on edge, pacing behind me. "And my daughter—"

"We won't get your daughter back if we act that way, my friend," I cut him off, stepping toward him and placing my hand on his tense shoulder. "We will ask Alena to release Selaine in exchange for Belise, Lia, and this woman before we begin negotiations. She will accept our proposal, if only to satisfy her allies."

Enola and I shared the entire truth with Daegan. He didn't question our claims for a second. Now, he looks at my wife differently, with a mix of fear, respect, and confusion.

"Let me make this clear, Your Majesties! If she so much as laid a finger on Selaine, I'll kill that Glace witch, negotiations be damned!" my captain spits out, his voice raw with desperate intensity, before storming off into the palace gardens.

I step closer to Enola, who is staring at the spy's lifeless body. I need to pull her away from her dark thoughts. Cupping her face in my hands, I lift her head. She exhales deeply. My heart aches as I trace the purplish mark left by the vine on her neck with my thumb. I'll personally apply a healing balm to ease her pain.

"God, I almost lost you again… That's it, from now on, we don't separate until this cursed war is over."

"I managed this situation without you, didn't I," she points out, adjusting the collar of my doublet.

"You're powerful, my love, but you're not invincible any more than I am. It would take so little for death to tear us apart."

She blinks, crystal tears gathering at the corners of her eyes, as if my words cut especially deep. With a tenderness that stirs me to my core, she touches my jaw, my cheek, the scar at my temple, before burying her fingers in my hair.

"I want this whole ordeal to end, Sylvan. I can't take it anymore."

"I know. I know, Enola…" I press my forehead to hers. "Me too. I'll do everything in my power to keep the worst from happening on all fronts. But it doesn't only depend on me."

"Promise me… promise me that everything will be okay."

"Alas, I can't promise you that, because I don't know."

"Then lie to me. Please. I need to hear it," she pleads, her tear-filled sapphire eyes meeting mine.

So strong and so vulnerable at the same time.

A joyless smile tugs at my lips. I steal a gentle kiss and murmur solemnly against her mouth, "I promise you everything will be okay, my love."

Chapter Twenty-One
The Birth of a Queen

Enola

All eyes in the court are fixed on Sylvan and me as we walk side by side through the throne room. Anxiety twists my stomach into knots. My queen's tiara feels twice as heavy as usual, and the corset of my crimson dress squeezes my chest, which is already more sensitive due to my pregnancy. An oppressive atmosphere hangs thick in the air. The faces of the Fuegis are tense, somber, and attentive.

Jerys Targam told us at the top of the Tower of Eternal Flame that the Ocean Goddess was a female dragon named Crystal, a hydro who entrusted me to the care of my adoptive mother, Bleuène. I don't know if this extraordinary creature can hear me, but right now, I send all my prayers to her in mind.

My husband and I ascend the royal platform. For the first time, I see my throne, and a shiver runs through me. It is smaller and more delicate than the one belonging to the monarch of Astranis. Made of cedar wood, it is adorned with golden filigree forming intricate patterns on the backrest and features a cushioned seat of red velvet. This was Sylvan's mother's throne. After her death, it was stored in a room with her personal belongings. Recently, it was dusted, cleaned, and polished by a carpenter before being placed to the right of my husband's throne at his order. I sit down slowly, my back straight, my hands resting on my knees, as Sylvan takes his place beside me. Our eyes meet briefly. He gives me a small, reassuring smile that makes my racing heart soften. Then he resumes his impassive demeanor and begins to speak before his—*our* court.

"I'll get straight to the point. I wish I had better news to share, but if I've called you here today, it's primarily to confirm your fears and update you on our current situation. The rumors you have heard are, unfortunately, true. The other three kingdoms have allied with the Renegades with the intent to rise against us." Troubled murmurs ripple through the room. Sylvan raises his voice to cut through the noise. "Our scouts have just returned to Astranis with reports from Symbiosis. Stalagmis, Oceanar, and Eolan have fallen to our enemies."

Cries of dismay erupt from the crowd at his last statement.

"All three cities, Your Majesty?" a man in the front row exclaims, stunned.

"All three cities," Sylvan confirms without breaking his composure. "The garrisons we left there have been wiped out one by one." A young courtier lets out a wail of grief. I swallow hard. The worst is yet to come. "The enemy forces are marching toward Astranis. According to our estimates, they will be at our gates in less than a week."

A cacophony of voices fills the throne room, the uproar deafening. Several nobles begin to stir restlessly. I clench my fists on my lap, just as shaken as they are. My husband, however, drums his fingers on the armrests, his expression dark. His patience is wearing thin.

"May the God of Fire protect us!" an elderly woman laments.

"Astranis will not fall!" retorts a High-Fuegis fiercely. "Let them come; we'll fight with all our might to defend our kingdom! We are a people of warriors; we don't fear a bunch of peasants waving poorly made blades!"

"You forget their powers!" counters another man, just as vehement, gesturing wildly.

"We have our Fire magic. We have our walls. We have our experience in war. We are not defenseless!"

"SILENCE, FUEGIS!" Sylvan roars suddenly, his voice as powerful as a clap of thunder.

The throne room falls silent immediately. All eyes turn once more to the young sovereign, who sweeps his gaze over the faces of the courtiers in the front row.

"Succumbing to panic is the surest way to splinter us," he notes acidly. "We sent an emissary to the leaders of their armies to propose a meeting. We will attempt to negotiate an armistice, so Astranis won't face a siege. If we can end this war without violence, we will. As members of the court, you must set an example for the people of our kingdom. Stay united and confident. Don't get lost in the maze of terror or rage. We have leverage for peace."

"What kind of leverage, Your Majesty?" asks a soft, familiar female voice.

Sylvan and I both turn our gaze toward Nadya, who is standing near the wife of a High-Fuegis.

"First, Lia Ler-Aeria and Belise San-Stowne have not been executed. They are alive, and I intend to return them to their kingdoms," declares my husband.

New murmurs of surprise ripple through the assembly. I keep my eyes on Nadya, whose radiant smile speaks volumes. It's genuine. Emotional. Even grateful. Her young cousin is alive, and she's truly relieved.

This woman is not without her flaws, but she is on our side. I'm certain of it now. Beneath her hard exterior and sharp demeanor lies a heart. Once again, the first rule of the Guild of Shadows proves to be right. *"Don't be fooled by appearances."*

I gradually absorbed this lesson through Sylvan, Daegan, Beladyn, Selaine, Nadya… and myself.

I may never be friends with Nadya Ler-Aeria, but I now realize she isn't my enemy. Like me, she wasn't born in this kingdom. Yet, like me, she has made it her own without renouncing her roots, her homeland, or her family.

"Secondly, we have the most powerful symbol of unity in the history of Symbiosis," Sylvan continues in a calmer tone. I take a deep breath, my cheeks burning. "The woman sitting to my right. My beloved wife."

Hundreds of eyes fix on me at once. I wish I could be anywhere but here. My heart pounds against my ribs at an impossible pace.

I feel Sylvan's warm, long fingers cover mine on my lap. I turn my head toward him; he gives me a small, encouraging nod. His bright eyes, filled with love, support, and confidence, give me the strength to face the trial ahead.

"My wife," he continues calmly, holding my gaze, "is not Alena Kan-Glace."

"Don't deny your name, my little sapphire. Your identity, like your roots, is anchored in your soul for eternity."

My mother's words now hold their full meaning.

The Fuegis exchange confused looks. Out of the corner of my eye, I see Nadya stifle a cynical laugh, nodding knowingly. Her suspicions about me have just been confirmed by the King of Astranis.

"Introduce yourself to your people," Sylvan whispers, squeezing my fingers.

Legs shake beneath my gown as rise from my throne.

"My name is Enola," I say, my voice unsteady, failing to carry as far as my husband's.

"Who?" someone mutters in the crowd.

"Enola," I repeat louder. "I am the double of Alena Kan-Glace. And more importantly, I am her older sister."

Several Fuegis glance at Sylvan, their expressions incredulous, as if suspecting a cruel joke. He remains silent, allowing me to speak for the first time in public.

"I lived away from the Glace court for twenty-six years, raised by a modest fishing family," I continue mechanically, trying to ignore the conspiratorial murmurs from the assembly. "I took Alena's place during the siege of Oceanar to become the war captive of your king. I was born Powerless, but Sylvan and I have discovered that I am the Rose of the Elements, as foretold by the ancient prophecy of Symbiosis."

I'm unsure what else to say. I'm usually far more eloquent… in smaller circles.

Four or five muffled laughs ripple through the crowd, throwing me off balance. I glance over my shoulder at Sylvan, who arches his eyebrows, his green, shining eyes sending me a message. *Show them, my love.* I draw strength and courage from him. And from the tiny life growing within me.

Yes, my love. I will show them.

Calming the storm that had been churning in my chest moments before, I step to the edge of the platform and slowly spread my arms, opening my hands.

"And I am no longer ashamed!" I declare, my voice so firm and proud I barely recognize it. "I am no longer ashamed of being born Powerless. On the contrary, I proclaim it loud and clear! I am not ashamed of growing up in a home that was poor in gold but rich in love. My adoptive family made me the woman I am, and my husband has helped make me the queen you see before you. Today, before you all, I challenge the outdated motto of my Element Clan. *Facing his enemy, a Glace sheds no tears, and never relinquishes his weapons.* Because our tears are not a weakness. Because our enemies are not always who we think they are. Because our sharpest weapons are not always forged from steel. Our tears strengthen us. Our fear is our greatest enemy. Our weapons should serve to restore peace and balance, not to shed blood! Love. Unity. Equality. Forgiveness. Kindness. Mutual support. These are the weapons that will save Symbiosis. These are the weapons we must wield together so that our five peoples become one on this island. Fuegis. Glaces. Aerias. Stownes. Renegades. We can change. We can live side by side. We can allies. Sometimes all it takes is a breath of goodwill…"

A warm breeze rustles through the crowd, tousling their hair. Reflexively, the courtiers turn toward the door and windows, amazed to see they are all closed.

"… with a tear of selflessness…"

A fine rain begins to fall from the ceiling, sprinkling the Fuegis, who all lift their heads in astonishment.

"… a tremor of forgiveness…"

A slight tremor ripples beneath their feet. A few gasp in surprise. I hear the elderly High-Fuegis Andreas, murmur from the front row, "She exists."

"… and a spark of hope," I finish, bringing my hands closer to summon a ribbon of fire that dances from one palm to the other, forming a crackling arc.

I meet the amazed, reverent eyes of several court ladies. I nod to Nadya, who, after a few seconds of hesitation, returns the gesture.

In the hushed silence that envelops the throne room, Sylvan steps up beside me at the edge of the royal platform. His hand fits into the curve of my lower back. When he presses a lingering kiss to my temple, the flames I conjured flicker in his admiring eyes.

"My name is Enola Ren-Fuegis, and I'll never hide again," I declare softly, as every member of the court kneels before my husband

and me.

For the first time in my life, I truly feel at home.

In this kingdom. Beside the one I love. In harmony with my true nature. Offering my unguarded truth to my people.

For the first time in my life, I truly feel like a queen.

CHAPTER TWENTY-TWO
A WELCOME RESPITE

SYLVAN

As I quickly finish my evening wash, running a cloth soaked in warm water over my skin, I watch my wife, who is kneeling naked on a cushion. She is making small creations of fire and ice appear and vanish one by one. At this moment, two fiery creatures dance in her palms, casting a glow over her focused face. A lamb and a wolf are circling each other.

Us.

The two figures inch closer, brushing against each other, sniffing, pulling away, caught in a mystical dance of seduction. It's mesmerizing. I wouldn't be able to replicate anything so fluid and detailed myself; my own attempts would end up as shapeless blobs of flame. But nothing seems out of reach for Enola. She has gained remarkable control over her powers in such a short time. I suppose her divine half has something to do with that.

Setting the cloth back in the basin, I sit across from her to better enjoy the scene. My wife places the fiery lamb and wolf on my bare shoulder. I extend my arm, amused. The tiny animals scamper down my arm—the lamb, ironically, chasing the wolf—until they meet on the back of my hand. They nuzzle their smoking heads together before evaporating into the air.

Enola smiles at me, her eyelids half-closed. Every day, she grows more beautiful and radiant than the day before. She's incredible.

She presses her palms together as if in prayer and then opens them. A blue orb flecked with iridescent specks forms between her fingers. She begins shaping it with her will, stretching and refining it right before my eyes.

"Tell me a story."

Her request catches me off guard.

"I don't have your imagination or your gift for spinning elaborate tales."

"Try. I won't judge, I promise. Surely the fearsome Sylvan Ren-Fuegis won't turn down such an easy challenge?" I shrug. "Maybe you need a bit of inspiration…"

With a playful look, Enola crafts an ice rose, the size of her palm, its translucent petals glistening and its stem dotted with thorns. She drags the flower along the base of her neck, leaving a damp trail above her Fuegis mark. Heat surges through my veins. If she keeps teasing me like this, the story will end before it begins. I slide my hands over her creamy shoulders, gently lowering her onto the cushions, then take the ice rose from her fingers and trace it across the top of her chest.

"So, once upon a time—"

"What a *sadly conventional* opening."

"Be quiet, Enola."

"It's a bit annoying when the person you're telling a story to interrupts, isn't it?" she teases, pinching my chin between her thumb and index finger as if I were a child.

Ah, she's holding a grudge! I tease her pink nipple with the tip of the flower, making it harden. With a flick of my tongue, I taste her sensuous coolness.

"I'm hungry for you, my queen."

"And what about my story?"

I trail the rose across her stomach, below her navel, to the edge of her pubic area. Goosebumps rise on her skin as the icy flower brushes over it. Her eyes, blazing with passion, lock onto mine. This little enchantress has me so worked up that I can't think straight anymore. I kiss her upper lip, then nibble on the curve of her lower lip.

"I'll tell you a thousand and one stories after making love to you a thousand and one times."

"More like, you'll fall asleep like a log after making love to me just *once*."

I laugh, sliding the rose between her slightly parted thighs, cooling her heated skin. To my delight, she shivers, pants, moans, squirms, and begs as the ice traces circles over her most sensitive spot. Setting the rose down to end her torment, I lower myself onto my wife. I deepen the kiss so I can taste her sweet tongue. I'll never tire of the flavor of her mouth, her nails in my neck, her breasts against my chest, her body against mine. With a sudden thrust of my hips, I press my aching hardness between her slick folds.

"Ah, you're crushing me, Sylvan," she protests, pulling away from my lips.

I shift my weight onto my elbows and knees so I'm not pressing down on her too much.

"You usually don't mind."

"My breasts and belly are sore tonight. I'm about to have my period," she explains, looking down with her cheeks charmingly flushed.

"If you don't want us to—"

"That's not what I meant," she corrects me with a tender smile that eases my momentary disappointment. "I want you just as much, my king. A different position would probably be more comfortable, that's all."

"I'll move gently," I promise, taking her by the hips and shifting her onto her right side.

I nestle against her smooth body, her back pressing against my chest, her hips aligned with mine. With my mouth pressed to her shoulder, I guide myself to her entrance and slowly push into her warmth. She arches against me, sighing with pleasure, her hand gripping my hip, eyes rolling back.

"By the way, would you do me the great honor of marrying me?" I whisper in her ear, my hand cupping her breast, massaging it gently.

"I'm already your wife, you absolute fool," she says with a laugh as I withdraw, only to return with deliberate slowness.

"If you agree, I'd like to renew our vows when everything is over."

"Why is that?"

"Because I was obligated to marry a woman named Alena, whom I didn't love. I want to marry, by choice, a woman named Enola, whom

I love more than life itself."

She turns her head suddenly, her gaze so intense I could drown in it. Her pupils are wide, and her irises are the color of the Endless Ocean in the middle of the night.

"Yes. Yes, you're right. But let's not wait, let's not waste any time. Let's do it now."

"Now?" I pause in surprise, stopping my movements.

"I, Enola, take you, Sylvan Ren-Fuegis as husband and my king. I swear before all the gods of Symbiosis to keep the sacred flame that binds us until death parts us," she declares with palpable emotion, her eyes locked deeply with mine as our bodies are intertwined.

"I, Sylvan Ren-Fuegis, take you, Enola, as my wife and my queen. I swear to all the gods of Symbiosis to keep the sacred flame that binds us alive until death parts us," I hoarsely recite, my free hand caressing her belly.

We kiss with wild passion, sealing our private vows, marking each other with our tongues, lips, and teeth. She is as much mine as I am hers. Her fingers tighten around my neck, slide up, and tug at my hair. A primal growl rumbles in my throat as I resume moving within her, contracting the muscles in my thighs and hips with each thrust. Fiery heat licks at my lower back. She chants my name between gasping breaths. My heart races against her back as hers thuds wildly under my palm. I wrap my arms tightly around her trembling body, holding her firmly to me, keeping her captive as she holds me captive within her.

If I had the power, I would make sure dawn never came and our night lasted forever.

When we reach our peak together a few minutes later, our arms and legs tangled, I vaguely notice through hazy vision that the ice rose has melted completely on the floor.

***

The next morning, I wake to Enola's lips showering my face with kisses. She announces she wants to do something *unusual* this morning. I whisper a suggestive idea in her ear that makes her laugh and blush at the same time. Shaking her head and calling me a fool, she explains she wants to go mingle with the crowd. Today is the last market day in

Astranis. We're in the middle of military protocol: fortifying defenses, making extra weapons, bringing the inhabitants of the Desert Red villages back into the city, and stocking up on food before we shut our gates. So, starting tomorrow, the market will be suspended for an indefinite time, and we'll need to ration our supplies.

Strolling through Astranis's market like any other Fuegis? I've never done such a thing. To be honest, I've never even *thought* of it.

Worried for her safety, I spend nearly half an hour trying to dissuade her. My wife patiently counters all my arguments. She starts by saying that we need to be close to our people and adds that they need to see for themselves that I care about them and am not the tyrant some believe me to be. When I retort that I have more pressing priorities than managing my public image, she claims that our presence will reassure them regarding the potential siege of Astranis and that it's even more important to make time to show concern for our people. Batting her eyelashes, she finishes by whispering that she really wants to spend my money on fabrics and jewelry.

I married the most stubborn woman in Symbiosis.

With reluctance, I finally gave in.

ENOLA

In the winding streets, exotic goods are displayed on countless stalls beneath large, light-colored tarps strung between the buildings to shield us from the searing sun.

Bags of spices, shimmering silks, decorative wooden trinkets, silver jewelry, oil lamps, rich perfumes, fruits, and vegetables… I am overwhelmed by the eclectic sensory whirlwind that pulls me deeper into its vibrant depths. The market bustles with life, warmth, sounds, smells, and colors. My hand in Sylvan's as I guide him through the colorful crowd—he lags behind, scanning our surroundings with his other hand resting on the hilt of his sword under his dark cloak—I savor every moment, delighted. I soak in the joyful shouts of children marveling at the fire-eaters and belly dancers, the laughter of women exchanging neighborhood gossip, the grumbling of men haggling with artisans. We're not trying to hide, but we've dressed simply and, of course, aren't wearing our crowns.

At first, most people don't notice us: focused on the stalls, they chat among themselves. But then the passersby we meet begin to recognize us. They step aside and bow hastily, making me wince. It's true that my white hair doesn't go unnoticed, as I am the only woman in the kingdom with such a mane. The news of our presence in the heart of Astranis's market spreads like wildfire. Astonished glances accompany our progress. Sylvan is tense, paranoid, almost uneasy, as if unsure how to act in this unprecedented situation for him. With a closed-off expression, lips pressed together, and constantly on guard, he gives curt, dry responses to the nods of acknowledgment from the city's citizens. Having witnessed it in Raockar, I know he can be friendly and warm toward people he's known for a long time, like the late Talbêk-Elir and his son Metân. Sometimes, he also lets his royal mask slip in the palace, showing kindness and camaraderie to Daegan and his soldiers.

But I want that to change. I want *all* Fuegis to see that their king is a good and remarkable man, just like his father, and to see him the way I see him. I want them to learn to love and trust him because he deserves their positive feelings. I believe I am also here to bridge the gap between Sylvan and his people, and this mission is particularly close to my heart. I slide my hand under his cloak to grasp his wrist and release his clenched fist from the hilt of his sword.

I lead him to a stall of colorful and tempting pastries. After exchanging a few polite words with the friendly vendor and giving her four gold coins, I pick up a fruit cake, break it in half, and offer one piece to my husband. He eyes the sweet offering with suspicion. Typically, Jall tastes all our food first, in case it's poisoned.

"Enola, that's not—" Without warning, I take a bite of my piece of cake, smiling. "Safe."

"You didn't have breakfast this morning."

His green eyes sparkle. He opens his mouth and takes a bite of the pastry too, under the proud gaze of the vendor. He swallows before addressing her, "It's delicious."

"Thank you, Your Majesty. I'm delighted you like it."

He even grabs another to eat as we continue walking. As the minutes pass, he realizes there's no danger and finally begins to relax.

Further ahead, a beautiful little girl offers me a desert flower with a shy smile. I thank her, patting her head and inhaling the fragrance of the petals before holding it up for Sylvan to smell. We hand out a few coins to young children so they can buy toys. They skip around us in joy, making us laugh together. We linger in front of a fabric and clothing stall, chatting with the elderly weaver. I buy two beautiful red and gold scarves. I give the rest of my money to a beggar sitting on the ground who needs it far more than I do.

A group of men approaches us, asking Sylvan for updates about the war. He responds to their questions with pragmatic ease. Without going into technical details, he outlines several precautionary measures for the city's defenses and stresses that we hope to negotiate a truce with the opposition. We also listen to several residents describe the disrepair of their homes, some of the oldest buildings in Astranis. My husband promises them he'll have their homes renovated as soon as peace returns to Symbiosis. I know he'll keep his word.

When we return to the palace two hours later, Sylvan has a smile on his face and a distant look in his eyes. He presses a kiss to the back of my hand.

"I'm glad I went to the market with you. It was enlightening."

"*Enlightening?*"

"And rewarding."

"In that case, we'll do this every week"

"At this rate, you'll bankrupt me."

"Isn't that every wife's goal? Ah, Daegan, you're just in time."

The armored warrior descending the staircase raises an eyebrow as he looks us over.

"I was looking for you, Your Majesties. We received a message in your absence. Alena Kan-Glace and her allies have agreed to meet with us."

"Good. It's a first step," Sylvan says in a neutral tone.

"By the gods, where were you?"

"I was taking a walk in the market."

"What, without an escort?"

"I'm his escort!" I joke, linked with my husband's.

"Well, that explains why you smell like old lady perfume and saffron, my king," the officer grumbles, wrinkling his nose in disgust.

"Direct all complaints to my wife, Captain," Sylvan replies, weary.

I wrap my new red and gold scarf around Daegan's thick neck, catching him off guard. Blushing, he stammers, "But... but... my queen... what..."

"I brought you a gift," I say cheerfully, standing on my tiptoes to plant a kiss on his scarred cheek. "You can give it to your daughter when you see her. Or keep it for yourself if you'd like. It suits your tan."

With an awkward gesture, Daegan touches his cheek with his gloved hand, staring at Sylvan with wide eyes as if he can't believe I just kissed him. And I laugh until my sides hurt.

CHAPTER TWENTY-THREE

TWO SISTERS, ONE CROWN

ENOLA

Fear claws at my insides at the thought of seeing her again. I massage my stiff neck absentmindedly, my eyes lost in the darkness of the night as Jada leads us to the meeting place. I feel Sylvan's fingers slip under my hair to take over from mine. With his thumb, he presses against the tiny knots formed by my tense muscles to ease them.

"Do you know when I first started falling in love with you, my Glace?"

His whisper caresses my ears and pulls me away from the shadowy unknown ahead, bringing me back to the light of the torches carried by our soldiers.

"No, my Fuegis, but I imagine you're going to tell me."

"Try to guess."

My husband is clever. He's trying to distract me during the journey, so I stop brooding.

"The first time we made love in Raockar?" I suggest.

"Wrong. It was before that. The day I took off your slave collar. That's what made me decide to remove it. I hadn't planned that public gesture on the terrace of the Tower of Eternal Flame."

His answer throws me completely.

"At what exact moment did you become aware of your budding feelings for me?"

"When my uncle came before I announced to our people that I was pardoning you and that you were my rightful queen. He tried to convince me to delay the event and consult with the High-Fuegis. He scolded me as if I were a brainless child. You stepped in. Do you remember what you said to him?"

"I brought up his harsh words in the garden."

"That happened afterward. He made a reference to one of my father's sayings about the unity of our kingdom. You stepped closer to me, placed your hand on my arm, and spontaneously offered your support. I've remembered every word you said. 'What symbol of unity would be more powerful than a king who chooses to spare his enemy and take her as queen? It shows the compassion, mercy, and moral strength he possesses. The ability to forgive is a rare virtue. The Fuegis people need hope, Leonal. They need to believe in their king. Your nephew knows this well. He made this deliberate choice with that in mind: to strengthen the unity of his kingdom.'"

Overcome by this memory, I nestle into his arms. I hadn't realized my small speech had made such an impact on him. He brushes my hair aside to place a gentle kiss at the nape of my neck.

"You didn't say that just to oppose him," Sylvan continues. "You truly meant it; I could see it in your eyes. It wasn't a lie. You spoke with such confidence and conviction, as if you had been my queen for years. You were already fighting for our shared values. You began to have faith in me at that precise moment, despite everything I had done to you, Enola. You seemed convinced that I could become a better man and a better king, even when I believed I was doomed by my actions. Your words hit me with full force. Ah, my heart had never beaten so fast and so hard; it ached in my chest." A smile spreads across my lips. "And I thought, 'I have faith in her, too. I'm going to remove the collar. Because the woman who inspires such feelings in me cannot be my captive.'"

I nod thoughtfully, touched by his unexpected confession.

"I realized I loved you during—"

"During the Fire Dance in Raockar," he completes softly, intertwining our fingers. "You watched two soulmates bond through the fire, Metân and his wife, and you knew that our souls had already found each other. That's why you gave me your virginity that night. You understood we were meant to be together."

"Yes, Sylvan, that's… that's it."

"One day, you'll tell our story to our children," he whispers with an emotion that stirs a deep resonance in my chest. "You'll tell them that hatred often comes from misunderstanding, and that even two people who started as enemies can recognize themselves in each other and love despite their differences. And when you finish, I'll tell them that it wasn't I who granted you royal grace, but you who honored me with your divine grace."

I close my eyes, soaking in his words that fill me with both joy and an aching tenderness. His embrace tightens around me.

"I love you, Sylvan."

"I love you, Enola."

A few minutes later, we arrived at the meeting point.

Alena Kan-Glace.

The last time I saw her at Oceanar, she was my queen.

Tonight, in the Red Desert, she becomes my sister.

She has arranged an elaborate scene that feels surreal against this backdrop, as if she had already conquered these lands with her mere presence. Surrounded by dozens of tall torches casting golden, flickering light across the sand, a massive white tent with its sides drawn up stands in the center of the dunes. The Glace royal banner, adorned with twin blue waves, flutters before the tent. In the distance, a long line of soldiers, barely discernible silhouettes, melds into the shadows. Like us, Alena has not brought her *full* army, as agreed upon in writing. But there must already be hundreds.

In tense silence, we leave most of our military escort behind and approach the tent: Sylvan, Daegan, Metân-Elir, Lia, Belise, and our prisoner Stowne, her hands bound. Thirty Fuegis guards follow us— no more, no less. They position themselves around the tent, mirroring the thirty Glace soldiers stationed by Alena, forming an unbreakable circle of steel between both sides.

Alena sits on an imposing throne of transparent, intricately carved ice, kept solid by her elemental magic. The throne itself is a display of her power: it doesn't melt, even in the sweltering heat of the Red Desert. She wears an ivory bodice with a plunging neckline that accentuates her slim waist and a double-layered turquoise satin skirt, slit at the thighs, revealing her long, crossed legs. Her crown, which I find even more hideous than my husband's, is an onyx serpent winding around her head, encrusted with sapphires, diamonds, and aquamarines. It contrasts sharply with her platinum-blond hair that cascades over her shoulders, slightly shorter than mine. This crown is an exact replica of the one I wore when Sylvan captured me in Oceanar—destroyed before my eyes in the throne room by his magical flames. Alena must have had this new crown forged in Stalagmis, where she took refuge after the fall of her kingdom. Her icy blue eyes, as cold as her Glace powers. They dissect me as though I were an animal being skinned, exposing my very soul.

From the corner of my eye, I see Sylvan glancing between us, his expression darkening. He's noting our striking resemblance.

Standing next to Alena's throne is the detestable Vidal. Her shadow, her lover, her commander, her weapon. With handsome features, short-cropped blond hair, and topaz eyes slightly darker than my sister's, he exudes an air of menace. His silver armor gleams, hands clasped behind his back, and a half-smile perches at the corner of his lips. Or perhaps it would be more accurate to call it a sneer, as it holds no warmth. It's a cold, cynical, and malevolent smile that fills me with disgust. He groped me more than once without consent during the lessons he gave me to perfect my imitation of the queen. If he appears as I described him physically to my husband in my first tale, his fictional counterpart, the good King Vidal, is his opposite in terms of character.

My gaze darts around them. Among her allies, I spot two High-Aerias, including a young officer, and a High-Stowne. There are no Renegades in sight, not even among the guards.

"Once they've used you, they'll throw you into a mass grave! They only came to recruit you for the sole purpose of sacrificing you in droves at the front," Sylvan told the Powerless sentry before executing him. He was right, it seems. The Renegades are here only because they outnumber the Glaces, Aerias, and Stownes soldiers combined, but they have no say in this campaign. They are cattle, plain and simple. It's infuriating.

Then I spot her. She stands behind Alena's ice throne. Selaine. The young Fuegis girl doesn't seem mistreated, but she watches her father with tear-filled amber eyes, her lower lip trembling. Daegan's jaw is set tight, barely containing his rage and resisting the urge to rush in and save his daughter. Sylvan places a calming hand on his arm and whispers something in his ear. The captain stiffly nods, forcing himself to hold back from taking any rash actions.

The little scene does not escape Alena's notice. She eyes my husband and then the captain with a knowing smirk.

"So much violence contained within one man," she comments, her voice sharp and clear. "Daegan, isn't it? Selaine has spoken of you. The foolish girl claimed her father was as fearless as the king he served. And yet, right now, you seem paralyzed by the fear of losing your only daughter, Captain Fuegis." Daegan clenches his fists, glaring daggers at her. "In other words, even the bravest warriors…" Her icy eyes shift back to Sylvan. "… have their weaknesses."

And as she says this, her gaze falls on *me*.

"Some weaknesses are actually strengths, Alena," my husband replies in a calm voice. "True weakness is being too arrogant to recognize them when they're right in front of you."

"You inherited your father's unsubtle rhetoric, Sylvan Ren-Fuegis. I hope for Enola's sake that you haven't also inherited his brutish haste in taking a woman like a drunken lout, without a thought to her pleasure."

My throat goes dry. By the gods, did Saradin sleep with Alena? I glance at my husband. His severe expression confirms my sister's defamatory words. He bears the insult to his deceased father with difficulty, fully aware that she is baiting him to make him lose control in front of the others.

I am aware of it too, but I can't allow her to tarnish Saradin's memory, the grandfather of my son, without response.

"Alena, the hallmark of narcissists is that they can only find satisfaction with themselves," I retort coldly. "Next time you seek pleasure, I suggest using your right hand."

An outraged expression spreads across my sister's porcelain face. I feel Sylvan discreetly touch my hip in approval and see Metân-Elir biting his lip to keep from laughing.

"Goddess of the Ocean, you've become as crude as a Fuegis

courtesan," Alena hisses, shaking her head. "We should have taught you better manners."

"It wouldn't have made a difference, Your Excellency," Vidal interjects. "It's not about upbringing; it's in her nature. Even a crown and throne cannot transform a harlot into a queen."

"Silence your jester, Alena Kan-Glace!" Sylvan demands, his gaze heavy with menace and danger. "If he disrespects my wife again, I will cut out his tongue and burn it before his eyes."

My sister's lover lets out a harsh, mocking laugh. The Queen Glace smiles indulgently.

"Vidal, naughty, unruly boy—you manage to upset our delicate guests with just one word," she scolds with irony, turning her attention back to us. "Let's proceed with the hostage exchange before we move on to the heart of the matter. Selaine?"

The young girl steps forward three paces.

Sylvan removes the enchanted collars from Belise and Lia. The former remains silent, feigning indifference. Lia gives him a tight smile, as if torn between cursing him and thanking him. My husband then removes the collar from the Stowne spy, whom Alena is watching intently. Metân-Elir collects the power-infused objects. The three women walk towards the opposing camp. On Alena's command, Selaine crosses to our side and falls sobbing into her father's arms. Relief swells in my chest. She is safe.

Murmuring something, Lia runs to the High-Aeria officer, who opens his arms to her. She kisses him, wrapping her hands around his neck. Her fiancé… They hold each other tightly, trembling with emotion. The sight moves me as much as the reunion of Selaine and Daegan. That soldier thought she was dead until recently. I also know that Aerias do not take engagement lightly. Dowries are never part of their Clan's tradition. When a young man asks for the hand of his beloved, regardless of status, he must earn it by proving the strength of his powers. With arms outstretched, he leaps from a mountain peak before the eyes of his family and the woman he desires. If he manages to levitate, the bride's father grants his blessing through a sacred song. If the suitor fails to fly, he falls and dies. This trial of strength, essential among them, ensures that only those with pure intentions, driven by true love, dare to attempt it.

Belise takes the hands of the High-Stowne with a warm,

affectionate smile. They bear a slight resemblance, so I deduce he is her cousin. They exchange quiet words, nodding to each other.

The Stowne spy head lowered, and hands still bound, shows no eagerness to return to her side. The furious glare Alena casts her way sends a chill down my spine and fills me with a sense of foreboding.

As if trapped in a waking nightmare, I watch my sister signal to Vidal.

A second later, a thick ice spike bursts from her lover's hand and pierces the Stowne's throat, splattering blood onto the sand. The woman drops to her knees, gurgling, and collapses to her side, convulsing.

Lia stifles a cry. Selaine's sobs grow louder. Daegan curses under his breath. Sylvan remains as stoic as Alena, though his hand tightens at the base of my back.

"Why did you do that?" I say, shocked by the senseless and brutal death.

"She failed in her mission," my sister replies as if it were perfectly reasonable. "There is no place for flawed and incompetent elements in my army. Forget her; her loss changes nothing for what's to come." Her voice hardens, and her venomous gaze shifts between Sylvan and me. "I will now lay out our terms. I will not tolerate interruptions, and I will not entertain negotiation. Remember, you requested this meeting, not me. We are in a position of strength, and our forces far outnumber yours. Either you comply with our demands, or we will raze Astranis as you did Oceanar, sparing no one. First condition: I demand your complete surrender. You will open the city gates and lay down your weapons before us. Any attempt at resistance will result in death. Second condition: You, Enola Ren-Fuegis, traitor unworthy of your Glace roots, will kneel before me, surrender your false Fuegis crown, and become my slave. Executing you would be far too lenient for your betrayal, and Vidal will be delighted to have a new toy to break." I bristle, feeling sick. "Third condition. Sylvan Ren-Fuegis, tyrant of Symbiosis, if you wish for your people and your harlot to be spared, you must pay with your blood. It is fitting retribution for all the massacres you've committed on our island. You will submit willingly, one of your collars around your neck, and place your crowned head on the block… in exchange for everyone's survival."

A deathly silence falls over the tent. In my camp, no one knows how to react. I don't think anyone anticipated her being so extreme and unyielding… except for me.

"No."

It isn't my husband who speaks. My voice cracks like a whip of fire.

"*No?*" Alena repeats with a cruel smile, as if savoring the moment.

"No to your first condition. No to your second condition. No to your third condition. You haven't even listened to what we came here to say. Sylvan is not entirely responsible for this war. He was manipulated by his uncle, who made him believe that the other three kingdoms conspired to poison his father, Saradin. Leonal was the true culprit, and we had him executed for his crime." She shrugs, indifferent to this detail. "My husband is willing to make concessions for peace on our island. He's even prepared to relinquish his crown if the people of Symbiosis ask it of him. And I, too, will give up my title as queen if necessary. But for him to sacrifice his life to satisfy your boundless madness is a concession *I* will never make. You'll have to get through me first, Alena… and I promise, I won't be the one who suffers most."

She leans back into her ice throne, running the lacquered nail of her index finger over her lower lip.

"How brazenly arrogant for someone of your social standing, Enola. Your new status has clearly gone to your head, but you're nothing more than a fraud."

"I possess powers beyond your imagination, and I won't hesitate to use them against you if you insist on laying siege to Astranis." Her smile widens. "I'm not a fraud. I am your elder sister, Alena. The daughter of your father, born a year before you. Which means I am the rightful queen of the Glace Kingdom. If you don't want me to claim your throne, it's your turn to compromise. I'll willingly let you keep your crown and your kingdom if you sign the peace treaty and disband your troops."

High-Aerias and High-Stowne exchange stunned glances behind her. But she… she doesn't look the least bit surprised or shaken by this revelation. She sizes me up with amusement.

"Oh, Enola… You dare to claim our kinship in public when you have no proof to back it up," she drawls. "Has there ever been a more pathetic lie? You're mistaking your wishes for reality. You're nothing but a petty girl reeking of jealousy. You are nothing."

A chill of horror runs down my spine. *She already knew.*

But only one woman knew my secret, apart from the Fuegis and the Shadows.

"What have you… what have you done to my mother?" I choke, clinging to Sylvan's arm as he supports me by the waist, whispering my name.

"I don't know what you're talking about. Are you sure she's even alive? I've heard she was so weak, so fragile… Maybe no one told her that your husband didn't execute you… maybe she died of grief, who knows… Your soldier brother too, probably… They both loved you so much…"

I don't scream. I don't cry. I don't wail. I don't collapse.

I roar, a sound full of hate and pain tearing from my lungs.

Alena's ice throne shatters suddenly. She leaps into Vidal's arms just as it explodes into countless fragments. A gale tears through the tent, so powerful it pulls two stakes from the sand. A flash of purple flames lights up the night, striking the ground twenty paces away and forming a smoking crater in the Desert. A crack opens between our two camps as the ground shakes beneath our feet. Most people cry out, stepping back, including soldiers. Some draw their weapons. A few run.

Sylvan cups my face with both hands, forcing me to look at him, to meet his sorrowful gaze. A red haze clouds my vision. My legs tremble. A gaping hole opens in my chest. Bent double, I moan, suffocate, burn, shiver.

"Enola, you're going to kill us all. Stop," he says gravely as the tremor grows, sending a cascade of red sand into the widening chasm.

"She… she killed my mother and my brother… Sylvan…"

"I know, my love. I'm sorry. Alena won't get away with this. But if you unleash your power in this state, with no control, your family's deaths will be in vain… and so will ours. Please, Enola… Don't abandon our cause now. If she dies this way, you'll make her a martyr, and she'll have won this battle. Let's go home; we have no reason to stay here. I need you. Our kingdom needs you. Symbiosis needs you."

And our son needs me.

I center my mind. I calm my emotions. I find my breath steadying. I draw on the wisdom of my beloved to keep myself from sinking. He is my pillar. The tremor stops, and the wind settles. My furious gaze meets Alena's, who stares back at me with a hint of fear, huddled against Vidal like a little girl. She's beginning to realize that I wasn't boasting when I claimed my powers surpassed her imagination.

"You have a choice, Alena! Either you surrender and I spare you, or you face me in a duel. Let's leave our people out of this conflict. Act like an honorable queen, not a cowardly dictator. Your magic against mine!"

"Enola, no," Sylvan growls, tensing up.

"Certainly not!" my sister retorts, pulling away from her lover's arms and shooting me a frosty glare. "I withdraw my offer; you're not worthy of it. You've just signed the extermination of the Fuegis people, Enola. We will kill them all, every last one! And Astranis will fall!"

She walks away on her side with her allies. My husband pulls me back, one arm around my waist.

She turns and walks away with her allies. My husband pulls me back, an arm around my waist. Our talks have ended in a catastrophic failure. There's no possibility of negotiation with this woman with whom I share only half my blood. She isn't acting out of personal vengeance; like Leonal in his time, she uses the anger and pain of her allies to pursue her own ambitions. She wants to annihilate us and seize the throne of Symbiosis. Sylvan, I, and the Fuegis people are obstacles in her path. Her army is just a means to her end.

I lower my tear-filled eyes to the chasm that separates us.

I realize, overwhelmed, that there can be only one fatal outcome to this conflict that tears us apart.

The death of my sister or our own.

Chapter Twenty-Four
The Siege of Astranis

Sylvan

We have been preparing for the first Astranis assault for days. I've implemented rigorous measures within my city. The Fuegis are hard at work on the ramparts and in the streets, following the orders of the officers. The help of women, the elderly, and even children has been enlisted to craft arrows, mend chainmail, and prepare medicinal ointments. We are carefully rationing our supplies in case the siege drags on. I have countless tasks to manage and little time to accomplish them. Truthfully, I have never faced such pressure since the beginning of my reign. Usually, I stand on the other side of the ramparts, leading my troops as the attacker, without second-guessing myself. This reversal of roles deepens my regret over listening to my uncle's lies and laying siege to the other three kingdoms. If only I could turn back time and erase my mistakes—a wish that belongs in the realm of fantasy.

A tension like never before has taken hold of all of Astranis inhabitants. Tempers flare frequently within my command post, among the officers, or between citizens and soldiers enforcing safety protocols. I try to stay patient and diplomatic, but I don't always manage to keep my composure. At times, I have to pound my fist on the table and raise my voice louder than theirs to restore order. Above all, we must stay united and stand together in adversity.

On a personal level, I am deeply worried about Enola. She is devastated by the deaths of her mother and brother. I wish I could be by her side more to support her, but urgent military defense preparations take precedence. Whenever I can spare a few minutes at the palace, I rush to see her in our chambers. I don't want her to be alone: Selaine stays with her, and even Nadya has taken the initiative to visit her three times. Each morning when I wake, I find my wife standing by the window, her eyes red and swollen from crying as she gazes out at the dawn. Lately, she sleeps little due to recurring nightmares and eats as little as a sparrow. The trauma from recent events has left her so shaken that she can barely keep her meals down. She's lost weight, her cheeks hollowed. When words fail to comfort her, I hold her close whenever I'm nearby. It seems to soothe her, if only for a moment.

If I could, I would strangle that witch Alena with my bare hands.

One morning, a few days after the crushing failure of the negotiations, the dreaded news falls like a guillotine. The enemy army is less than a league from Astranis. After putting on my armor, I mount Jada bareback and gallop through the streets of my city to the ramparts. People step aside as I pass. I take the steps two at a time up to the battlements and find Daegan stationed near a corner tower among other warriors. My heart skips a beat at the sight of the long, metallic lines snaking through the Red Desert. Enemy banners snap in the wind like floating threats.

Astranis is a true fortress. We've bolstered its defenses as best as we could and stored months' worth of food in our warehouses. If we were facing an ordinary army, our chances of holding out would be relatively good. But against forces larger than ours and wielding powers? Our odds drop significantly, and I think everyone knows it. That's why the atmosphere is so heavy. Hope is slim, and my men's faces are grim. Some look already resigned to defeat, even before the battle has begun. I step up onto a crenellation to catch their attention. Their somber gazes shift toward me, and a heavy silence falls over the parapet. I ponder how best to inspire them.

What would my father say in my place?

He would speak to them with heart and soul.

"I understand your state of mind, warriors," I call out in a strong voice. "I know what you're thinking. I can easily guess your worries and doubts. Right now, I am not your king. I am a soldier like you, and

I share the fears that haunt you. Death is our old traveling companion, and we are prepared to face her. But now, she looms over our homes, hovering above the heads of those we love most. Are we going to let her take them from us?" A few shake their heads, others growl a defiant *no*. "Are we going to fight with all our might to make her yield?" Several Fuegis shout a fierce *yes!* ""Let's not let our fears make us forget what matters most! We do *not* fight for glory. We do *not* fight for power and wealth. We do *not* fight for revenge. We do *not* even fight for our own lives! We fight for the lives of our families. For our sons. For our daughters. For our wives. We fight for the city built by our ancestors, the city where our parents were born, where we were born, where our children were born. We fight for the future of our kingdom. We fight for our traditions and our values." I pause, taking them in with my eyes, and gesture to the winding streets of Astranis spread out behind them. "Today, the history of Symbiosis will be written in fire and sand, in the heart of our Red Desert, with all of us as the main characters. But we will not let our assailants kill our families. We will not let them take our lands. We will not let them destroy our homes. As long as we live, we will fight with all our heart and soul for everything we believe in." My tone rises an octave and strengthens. "We will honor our motto to the death: '*The sacred fire of the Fuegis warrior is fueled by the blood of his enemies.*' Never forget that we are neither ashes nor embers, my proud warriors: we are nothing less than flames! I have one last question for you. Has anyone ever seen a Fuegis surrender before a fight?"

A thunderous roar, fierce and wild, erupts on the ramparts like rolling thunder. My men raise their weapons to the sky and pound their steel shields against the stones of the merlons. A satisfied smile forms on my lips.

I have my answer.

✳✳✳

The first volley of arrows fired by the Renegades. The rain of projectiles darkens the sky with a whistle. Daegan shouts, "TAKE COVER!" We crouch behind the merlons, lifting our shields over our heads. Half of their arrows shatter against our walls. Unfortunately, a few find their way through the gaps. A Fuegis struck in the throat who wasn't well-protected enough, cries out in pain and tumbles over the edge, crashing into the street below. Another next to me is hit in the leg. At my command, two Fuegis drag him along the battlements to the guard tower. He will be evacuated as soon as possible and taken to the infirmary on a stretcher.

We fight back. Raising my sword high, I shout, "FIRE!" At my command, our men unleash fireballs. Dozens of Renegade infantrymen in the front line of the enemy army fall, their shields of boiled leather no match for our flames. Charred bodies collapse onto the sands of the Red Desert.

A second volley of arrows from them. Then, our second counterattack. This alternating exchange continues for four more rounds until I notice that the magical energy of my Fuegis is depleting rapidly. Their fireballs shrink in size and vanish before reaching their targets. Enraged by this realization, I step over a body sprawled across the battlement path and rush to Daegan, who's about to order another offensive.

"Wait, stop!" I exclaim, grabbing his arm.

"What? But we have the advantage, Your Majesty, we're slaughtering them!" protests the captain, pointing at the numerous Renegade corpses lying in the desert at the foot of our walls.

"Alena and her allies are outsmarting us, Daegan! This is a war of attrition. They're sacrificing the Renegades just to drain our energy fighting them. At this rate, our men will soon have no magical reserves, and the most dangerous units in their ranks will strike when we're weakest!"

He curses under his breath as he realizes I'm right.

"What do we do, Sylvan?"

"Our warriors must conserve their power." I roar to the troops, "Take up your bows! Save your elemental magic for countering the Glaces, Aerias, and Stownes!"

We begin firing our arrows. I join my defenders, notching an arrow and drawing the bowstring back before releasing the shot toward our foes. This attack is less devastating than our fireballs but manages to take down a few Renegades, creating new gaps in their lines. An enemy officer yells out orders, waving his hands. They've realized we've uncovered their strategy and adjust their plan accordingly. The archers in the front retreat to the ranks behind: Aeria soldiers carrying tall ladders. They don't need grappling hooks or ropes to hoist them up to our walls. Using Air Magic, the wooden structures rise horizontally and slam onto our battlements. While my Fuegis shoot arrows at the attackers to dislodge them, I wait for several enemies to start climbing one ladder before jumping onto a crenel and setting the top of a post ablaze with a touch of my hand. The entire structure ignites instantly, along with the men climbing it. Burning bodies tumble into the void.

"SYLVAN, WATCH OUT!" Daegan shouts behind me.

I duck just in time. An ice projectile as large as a raven skim over my head. Without my captain's warning, I would have been dead. I squint toward the battlefield, searching for the Glace responsible for the shot. There is only one in the front line. I recognize Vidal, Alena's lover, astride a warhorse. He gives me a mocking wave, laughing. In retaliation, I hurl an enormous fireball at him. But the High-Glace retreats at a gallop, and my magic projectile kills three soldiers behind him who didn't have time to get out of its way. It's not over yet: if I get the chance, I will kill that scum Vidal with my own hands.

"Thanks, Daegan, I owe you one!" I say to my friend.

A few minutes later, as we continue to push back the ladders and attackers while dodging the arrows raining down on us, an earthquake shakes our battlements. The High-Stownes have joined the battle.

Bent over, we cling to the merlons, praying that the walls hold.

Unfortunately, one of our watchtowers collapses with a deafening crash, taking a section of the wall down with it and creating a significant breach. Through the cloud of dust from the collapse, the first invaders pour into Astranis, shouting war cries. I rally a group of soldiers for reinforcements and rush to the battle, drawing my sword, which ignites in flame. Consumed by battle fury, I slash, maim, leap, parry, block, and spin. I strike over and over, breaking bones, tearing flesh, piercing organs, and charring bodies. I attack anyone who isn't a Fuegis, without discrimination. I save some of my men by cutting down their assailants, only to see, moments later, that others have fallen to new enemies while I was fighting elsewhere. Ice spikes burst in our direction. I lift my metal shield, taking hit after hit, my entire body jolting with the impacts. Magical blasts hurl my soldiers against the walls. Our fireballs light up the base of the battlements. The enemy surges like a relentless torrent into the breach, and our line of defenders weakens by the minute. Corpses pile up around us—

dozens, then hundreds. Fuegis, Glaces, Aerias, Stownes, Renegades. A growing mass grave.

Amid the chaos, a familiar cry of pain chills me to the core. I turn, wild-eyed. I see Vidal standing before Daegan, who is on his knees. He's been disarmed, his helmet lost in the fray. The Glace's icy sword is lodged in my captain's throat, his eyes rolled back and lips bloodied.

"DAEGAN!" I roar, devastated.

Vidal pulls his blood-stained weapon from my friend's torn flesh, and Daegan collapses face down, limbs slack, eyes lifeless.

Blinded by fury, I unleash my flaming whip and charge at Vidal. He pivots to face me, brandishing his ice sword. My burning ribbon coils around his blade and rips it from his grasp. The High-Glace hurls another ice shard at me, which I dodge with the agility of a leopard. I swing my arm back and strike a brutal blow with the whip that severs my enemy's head clean off.

Vidal is dead.

But so is Daegan.

I was too late to save my friend, my brother-in-arms, my captain. Tears of grief burn in my eyes. Through my blurred vision, I see a frail female figure stepping boldly toward the fray. An unnamed terror and horror wash over me.

She's here.

No.

I sprint toward Enola as fast as I can. My panic doubles when I see a Aeria soldier aiming his spear at her, just a few steps behind. Just as I'm about to hurl a fireball at him, he throws his weapon toward my wife's back. I shout her name in a panic.

"ENOLA!"

She doesn't turn toward me. I've never seen her so calm and confident.

The spear bounces off the thick ice shield she suddenly conjures.

And she doesn't stop there.

Clouds darken the sun. With her hands raised, she summons a crimson tornado from the sky. The thin column catches our enemies one by one, tossing them back over the breach, hurling them into the advancing forces trying to enter the city. The supernatural whirlwind sweeps up only our foes because hundreds of roots emerge from the ground, holding the ankles and wrists of the Fuegis soldiers to keep them steady. With stunning ease, the tornado drives all of our adversaries beyond the walls and then stands guard at the breach.

Like a divine architect, Enola takes the opportunity to rebuild our tower with her powers.

Her fingers draw intricate, cryptic patterns, sketching invisible runes. Under the awestruck eyes of my warriors, stones float into the air, dance, and realign, cemented together by ice that won't melt anytime soon. Water magic is even more potent in my wife than her other three abilities, due to the royal Glace blood that runs in her veins.

When she finishes her work, the tornado dissipates into the sky, and the clouds vanish. The tower and wall are whole again, likely even stronger than before.

Thanks to Enola, we've gained precious time.

However, we're far from victory, and the losses are heavy.

When night falls, offering a brief reprieve, the fighting ceases until dawn and the enemy sets up camp in the Red Desert. After organizing the night watch shifts on Astranis's battlements, I return to the palace, exhausted by the harrowing day and weighed down by the loss of Daegan. Selaine wept bitterly in Enola's arms when I broke the devastating news to her earlier. My captain's body has been wrapped in a red and gold shroud and taken to the Temple of the Fire God alongside those of the other fallen Fuegis officers. Damn, I can't believe my loyal captain is no longer by my side... He's been there since my teenage years, an unwavering support I could always rely on. He saved my life countless times. His courage inspired me when I was younger, just like my father's. I feel hollow, as lost as a child in the dark.

A quarter of our defenders perished today, according to my general staff's estimates. That means many widows and orphans. Not to mention hundreds of wounded. It's a disaster. Without Enola's timely intervention, the city would probably have fallen before nightfall. I haven't told any of my men to avoid demoralizing them further, but this time, we're outmatched. I've fought in enough battles in my life to know when defeat is staring us in the face.

It's only when I'm alone with my wife that I allow my despair to surface. I collapse onto the floor of our quarters, my legs pulled up to my chest, head buried in my hands, my mind clouded by the shadows of death. She kneels beside me and holds me close, her fingers stroking through my hair, sticky with sand, dust, and dried blood, in an attempt to console me.

"Sylvan, my love…"

"You could have been killed, by the gods. What were you thinking?" I spit out through clenched teeth.

"I wanted to help you," she admits, her voice a mixture of gentleness and sadness. "I couldn't just stand by and do nothing, waiting for the worst. When I saw the tower fall, I knew I had to act."

"I can't lose you. I. Can't!"

"And I can't lose you, Sylvan. Try to put yourself in my shoes for a minute. I was so terrified you wouldn't come back to me."

"We won't hold this siege for long. After today's battle, I'm sure of it. There are too many of them," I say darkly.

"I will fight at your side with my magic."

"It won't be enough. Unless you plan to turn into some malevolent goddess and annihilate every last one of them with your powers, but that's not what we want."

"No. There has to be another way to bring back peace…"

"There is, Enola," I say gravely, lifting my head to look at her.

She stares at me, eyes wide. I don't need to say it aloud. Her stricken expression and tear-filled eyes tell me she understands what I'm thinking. She steps back, shaking her head feverishly. She doesn't want to hear it. I grasp her wrist and hold it tightly so she can't run from this conversation. Her arm trembles under my fingers. Her skin turns pale, her gaze pleading. Her pain deepens mine, but I cannot waver now. She must grasp the reality of our situation.

We've lost too many loved ones. This must end.

"I started this war, Enola. It's up to me to end it."

"No," she whispers, voice breaking. "I forbid you to surrender to the enemy."

"You can't forbid me. I've made my decision."

"Your… your sacrifice wouldn't change anything. She won't give up her plans. She wants to destroy the entire Fuegis kingdom; she told us so!"

"Alena isn't alone in this army. Her allies are more reasonable. They'll accept my offer, and she'll be forced to go along with it. I wish there were another way, but this is our last option, our only alternative. It's the right choice, the most logical one. My life in exchange for peace. I won't let my people die for my failures as a king, Enola. I won't let you die for my failures as a man."

"NEITHER WILL I, YOU FOOL!" she screams, grabbing a fistful of my cape and pulling me closer. "If I have to become as ruthless as my sister and kill every last one of our enemies so that you survive, I will! I'll damn myself for you, Sylvan Ren-Fuegis! I'll defy that stupid prophecy that makes no sense! I'll laugh in destiny's face!"

"I will never allow that, Enola. It's fear, anger, and grief speaking for you; you don't mean what you're saying. But you aren't like Alena, anyway. You're not like me. You're stronger than both of us because you see the world more clearly than we ever could. That's why you must live. You are the Rose of the Elements. You show the way for others. You're a light, a gift to Symbiosis, my love. You always have been," I finish, softening my tone.

A wail of grief escapes her lips, cutting into my chest like a blade.

"I've made terribly bad decisions in the past. I blindly believed my uncle who conspired against my father. I waged war on three kingdoms without questioning what Leonal assured me. Thousands of civilians, including children, died because of my impulsiveness. And two kings, who were innocent of the crime I accused them of. Later, I almost ordered the execution of my soulmate: you. If you hadn't spun those ridiculous stories to delay your death, I would have killed you, mistaking you for Alena, believing you responsible for my father's death." With a heart weighed down like lead, I gently caress her face. "But giving my life to ensure the survival of my people and my wife? That's a decision I know is right, without a shadow of doubt. I'm not doing this for redemption or any nonsense like that. I'm doing it because a king without honor or principles is nothing but a tyrant, and I refuse to be that any longer. I'm doing it because a ruler who doesn't care for his people doesn't deserve his crown. I'm doing it because a man who values his life over that of the woman who means everything to him… is nothing. Ultimately, I'm doing this for love in its broadest sense. Because you taught me how to love again, and you are the most beautiful thing that has ever happened to me, Enola. That's why I'm asking you to prove your love by respecting my choice."

"You don't have the right to leave us, Sylvan! I… I'm carrying your son!" she cries, collapsing in tears in my arms.

I freeze.

She's pregnant.

For a brief second, I wonder if she's lying just to keep me here. But then I see the truth in her eyes, and reality crashes over me.

My wife is expecting our child.

A wave of emotions, each as powerful as the next, surges through me. Happiness. Pain. Love. Anxiety. Pride. Frustration. Gratitude. Sorrow. Hope. Despair.

Unable to express them to Enola in words, I crush my mouth against hers. Her salty tears seep onto my tongue as her lips quiver under mine. This kiss is more intense than any we've shared before, because it might be the last. She returns it with frantic passion. She bites my lips, groaning like a wounded animal, pressing my cheeks between her hands and digging her nails into my skin. She's as shattered as I am.

After several minutes, she pulls back, her sapphire eyes, wet with tears, pleading with me.

"Alright, alright," I murmur, placing my palm on her belly. "I'll stay with you. A boy, you say? Are you sure?"

A relieved smile blooms on her lips, tightening my chest. She nods slowly.

"If it's alright with you, I'd like us to name him—"

"After your father," she whispers. "Saradin."

"Yes," I reply in a hoarse voice, taken aback by her perceptiveness. "Thank you, my love. I am honored. It's the greatest gift I have ever received."

My son. My heir. Saradin Ren-Fuegis.

With a deep sigh, Enola nestles against me, resting her head on my chest plate. I wrap my arms around her, my gaze fixed on the wall. I never knew it was possible to feel boundless happiness and profound sorrow at the same time.

Her being pregnant only strengthens my resolve and solidifies my decision. It shatters me into a thousand pieces, but I had to lie to her to calm her fears. I want my child to be born. I want my wife to live. I want my people to be spared. I want my death to have meaning.

So, once Enola falls asleep, I will surrender myself to the enemy to be executed.

I hope that one day, she will understand my choice and forgive me.

CHAPTER TWENTY-FIVE

SACRIFICE

SYLVAN

One hour before dawn.

After making sure she is sound asleep, I give her a gentle kiss on the lips and press another on her belly. In my mind, I tell them both that I love them. The last thing I want to do is leave this bed, but I must. I put on simple, humble clothes—a tunic and pants—without taking my melancholic eyes off Enola's face. I imprint every detail into my memory to summon the strength I need to follow through with what I have set out to do.

Her silvery hair spread like a crown on the pillow. Her closed eyelids. Her mouth. Her breathing. Her curves. Her beauty. Her gentleness.

Leaving these apartments, leaving her behind, is the hardest thing I've ever had to do.

Quickly, I draft two documents and carry a third one with me.

I do not take *Nesayan*. I lay it down on the chaise. My son will inherit it when he is old enough to wield a sword.

Silently, I close the door behind me and lock it from the outside. I hand the key to the two Fuegis guards in the hallway. I give them strict instructions: do not open it before noon tomorrow, no matter what their queen says or does from inside, even if she pounds on the door, even if she threatens them, even if she pleads, even if she cries, even if she screams. They nod solemnly, wordless and without questions. I give them a letter containing directions on how to manage the kingdom, which they will deliver to the High-Fuegis.

At the stables, I mount Jada for the last time. She is restless; she senses something is amiss. I soothe her with gentle words and strokes. We pass through Astranis's darkened streets. I think of the families behind the windows of these houses, the mothers cradling their frightened children to their chests, the watchful fathers sleeping lightly with weapons within reach. My people. My Fuegis brothers.

I dismount in front of the city gates. Three sentinels approach me. I pat my mare's neck and hand her reins to one of the guards. She whinnies and paws the ground.

"Your Majesty? What are you doing here at this hour?" one of the men asks.

"I have something crucial to do. Open the gates and close them behind me."

Their features tighten with tension, and they exchange looks as if they have misheard my command. One mutters, "Alone?"

"Open the gates, soldiers," I repeat in a firm, unyielding tone.

They comply.

Minutes later, I am walking across the sands of the Red Desert toward the enemy camp, eyes fixed straight ahead, Astranis at my back. I do not look back. There would be no point; it would only feed my regrets. I feel dozens of emotions; strangely, fear is not one of them. I do not fear my own death; I fear the deaths of those I love. I wouldn't go so far as to say I am calm and confident, but I am deeply convinced that I am making the right choice, staying true to the principles my father instilled in me from my earliest days. At last, I am in harmony with my ideals.

"A ruler's honor is reflected in his deeds far more than his words."

"A true king must never hesitate to dirty his hands for the good of his people when necessary and must sometimes act as any other man to share in the sufferings of his people."

I understand now, father. I finally understand.

Figures holding torches quickly surround me, weapons raised: arrows notched in bows, spears, swords. Renegades. I look at them, calm and unmoving. One of them utters a surprised exclamation when he notices the red sun-shaped tattoo on my forehead.

"By the blood of the woods, look at this—it's the tyrant Ren-Fuegis!"

Instinctively, I address the eldest among them, "I I've come to negotiate my surrender. As you can see, I am unarmed and..." I carefully pull back the collar of my tunic. "...I am wearing an enchanted collar that neutralizes my magic." The older man raises his bushy eyebrows. "I have two documents to show your leaders; they're in my pockets. Do you have a clan leader, Renegade?" After a moment of hesitation, he shakes his head. "A representative then? A spokesperson?"

"Yeah, we've got one."

"Then take me to him."

"That's not protocol, Ren-Fuegis. We're taking you to Queen Alena. She's in charge."

"Alright, but I want your spokesperson present, as well as the leaders of Clan Aeria and Clan Stowne."

"Why?" the Renegade asks suspiciously.

"Because I want to speak to all of them. I think the request is reasonable, considering my vulnerable situation."

"It could be a trap," hisses one of the men, glancing over my shoulder as if expecting a horde of Fuegis to appear in my wake.

"We should kill him right now," adds another. "She'd be glad if we brought her his corpse, Glace Queen. And we'd be rewarded handsomely."

"No, it's not for us to decide his fate," the older Renegade declares, scrutinizing me with a puzzled expression. I'm relieved I addressed him; he seems less hot-headed and more thoughtful than his younger comrades. "You, search him and tie his hands with rope. You two, go wake all the officers. Sylvan Ren-Fuegis, follow us without causing trouble. Any sign of rebellion, and you're a dead man."

He doesn't grasp the bitter irony of his words. I do.

✳✳✳

Flanked by sentries, my wrists bound, I walk down the main path that splits the enemy camp in two. Sleepy, disheveled soldiers emerge from their tents as I pass. Most are puzzled by my presence. Some are gleeful at the sight of me as a captive. The most hostile spit on the ground or hurl insults. Their animosity means nothing to me. I'm used to it.

They lead me into the command tent. The leaders of their army are already gathered there. Including Belise and Lia, as I hoped. Three individuals I haven't met in prior negotiations are present: two High-Glaces and the Renegade spokesperson, a muscular man in his thirties with a shaved head, a thick beard, and raven-black eyes. All eyes are locked on me. Alena steps forward, a delighted smile on her lips—she should enjoy it while it lasts, because I'm going to make sure that smile disappears. She wears a white velvet night cloak, blending with her moon-like hair so similar to my wife's.

"What a delightful, unexpected gift! The proud warrior king Sylvan Ren-Fuegis, preparing to grovel to beg for our mercy. If I weren't seeing it with my own eyes, I'd find it hard to believe."

"No need to gloat. I'm here neither to grovel at your feet nor to beg for mercy. I've come to negotiate," I reply curtly.

"Negotiate! You must be in utter despair. Didn't the outcome of our last discussions teach you anything?"

"Yes, I made a grave mistake last time."

"So, you admit it."

"Yes. I made the mistake…" I shift my gaze from hers to the others around us, "…to speak to the wrong person."

A disappointed silence fills the command tent.

"It's me you must deal with," Alena remarks icily.

"Who decided that? You? Don't your allies have a say? Without them, you'd never have reclaimed the three cities. That's the very definition of an alliance: equal power."

"We make our decisions together! As for you, however—"

"You accuse me of being a despot, Alena, yet you've acted as a dictator since the start of your uprising. Quite surprising, given that your claim to the throne is more than questionable."

"How dare you—"

"The crown belongs to my wife by birthright."

"Don't be absurd. That traitor is not my sister; you have no proof."

"If she weren't your sister, you wouldn't have executed her adoptive family, who knew of her origins. You murdered her mother and brother to ensure no one could contest your royal legitimacy. Your vile acts speak louder than any resemblance—they're proof in themselves. In fact, they're just a continuation of your despicable choices. You fled Oceanar when I besieged it, never once fighting beside your own people. You put Enola in your place, sending her to be executed by my hand to buy yourself time to stage your rebellion. You conveniently let her carry the title of Queen Glace, ready to be sacrificed on the altar of your cowardice."

Alena's allies, except for the two High-Glaces who escaped Oceanar with her, shoot her sidelong glances, clearly skeptical. I've planted a seed of discord, and it's starting to sprout. Her face flushed with anger, she searches for words, but I cut her off, "You all witnessed her powers during the negotiations and today's battle. Enola wields all elemental magics of Symbiosis. Lia, Belise, you've seen her four Elemental Clan marks; she showed them to you before your release." The Stowne remains silent; the Aeria nods slightly. "My wife is the Rose of the Elements from the prophecy. The only woman truly worthy of being Queen Glace is her. And you, Alena Kan-Glace… are nothing more than a fraud and a pretender, a bastard in the end."

Offended, the wretch loses her composure and slaps me weakly, as though she's afraid she'll break her fingers against my cheek. I laugh to myself—any child would have struck harder.

"Despite all this," I continue, looking around at everyone in the tent, "Enola is willing to renounce her rightful claim to the throne of Oceanar so that peace can return to Symbiosis. She will allow Alena to rule the Glace kingdom if we *all* sign the armistice. She cares nothing for power; all she wants, and all I want, is an end to this war. I ask you to return to your cities and leave my queen and my kingdom, as they should not die for the conflicts between us."

"You're mad, Fuegis," interjects the High-Aeria officer, who is also Lia's fiancé. "Do you think we'll be satisfied with such a meager concession from you and simply disband our troops?"

"I have other arguments. I brought documents to show my good faith," I nod toward the old Renegade soldier, who pulls two scrolls from his pocket. "First, written proof that it was indeed my uncle Leonal who poisoned my father and conspired against you in the shadows: a contract for the assassination of both Enola and me. We managed to foil it with outside help. I won't evade my responsibilities, but I swear on all I hold dear that I was unaware of these facts at the time I killed Idric San-Stowne and Cyriel Ler-Aeria. I believed my uncle when he assured me that the other three kingdoms had orchestrated Saradin Ren-Fuegis. But Leonal is now dead."

"Your proof is worthless to us!" Alena hisses, as the Aeria and the Stowne examine the contract. "The death of your uncle cannot absolve all your crimes."

"That's why I'm also offering you my life; the third condition from our initial negotiations. I've surrendered to you of my own accord, wearing this collar. We've each suffered heavy losses. All five of our peoples have suffered enough; I think we can all agree on that. In the second document, signed by me and marked with my royal seal—which I hope all of you will sign as well—I've drafted the terms of the armistice, terms meant to satisfy all factions. It includes what I've stated: in exchange for peace in Symbiosis and the withdrawal of your troops, my execution to avenge Idric and Cyriel, Enola's renunciation of the Glace crown… and the official cession of half my kingdom to the Renegades and the legalization of their status," I conclude, turning to the spokesperson for the Powerless.

The man looks stunned. His reaction confirms my suspicion: Alena only gave him verbal promises. Moreover, he must have noticed her sacrifice of Renegades en masse during the siege of Astranis. They bear the greatest risk at every level in this war, with no guarantees of achieving their aims. So, *I'm* offering them a real guarantee, hoping to persuade them and win them to my side.

Out of the corner of my eye, I see Lia whispering to her fiancé, her hand resting on his arm. He frowns and shakes his head, but she strokes his arm and says something else, leaving him deep in thought.

"We don't want your treaty, tyrant," Alena sneers, glaring daggers at me. "It's far too late to—"

"Do not speak for us," the Renegade cuts her off firmly.

All eyes now shift toward him. My heartbeat quickens. An outraged look twists Queen Glace's face, as if a bird had just defecated on her foot.

"What did you say?" she chokes out in disbelief.

"I said don't speak for us," the man reaffirms, squaring his shoulders. "You are not our sovereign, and we're not part of your

Clans. You came to find us in the Exile Forest because you needed us to bolster your ranks. You dangled promises of inclusion, equality, brotherhood before us. But from the beginning, you've treated us little better than animals. You've kept us at arm's length. You think we're fools. You showed that again today by sending my people to the front line to be slaughtered by the Fuegis as part of a strategy you didn't even share with us beforehand. Do you think I didn't see through your plan? I no longer want my Powerless to die for your thirst for power, Alena Kan-Glace. We are not your war dogs. I intend to sign this treaty, which seems far more serious than your empty promises. If your allies and you refuse to sign it, we Renegades will leave and let you tear each other apart."

A heavy silence fills the command tent. Alena turns pale as a sheet. The Powerless hold a powerful bargaining chip, given that they make up two-thirds of her army.

"Our Elemental Clan accepts this armistice," Belise says suddenly, stepping forward. "Sylvan's terms are acceptable to us. We Stownes judge that his sacrifice is a fitting tribute. His blood will be the last spilled. This cursed war must end."

"And the Aerias will sign, too!" Lia adds, holding her fiancé's arm tightly. "Sylvan will keep his word; he's a man of integrity. We can vouch for that. He spared Belise and me, and we were treated quite well during our detention. We want to turn the page and return to Eolan."

I nod in gratitude to my two former wives, and they nod back in unison. All eyes now fall on Alena, who simmers with rage.

"This wasn't the plan!" he cries out furiously to her allies. "All Fuegis deserve to pay!"

"No, Alena," Belise replies, resolute. "This is what *you* had planned on your own. We've all paid a heavy price already. There's no reason to continue taking it out on the Fuegis under these new circumstances. Their king has chosen to die for them to atone for his sins against us. It's a gesture you need to recognize for its nobility. And you will sign this armistice, Alena. Because otherwise, it would mean you want to destroy Astranis solely for your personal ambitions—to kill your sister and become queen of Symbiosis.

And I suspect no one here wants a hateful, bloodthirsty woman as their ruler, I think, understanding what the Stowne has left unspoken.

The Glace Queen lifts her chin defiantly, pulling her cloak tighter around herself. Cornered by this sudden turn of events, she has no choice but to yield to the majority's will. Finally, she asks a soldier for a quill and inkwell to seal the pact I've drafted.

One by one, they pass the quill around, signing beneath my name. A mix of relief and sorrow fills me as Lia, the last to sign, places the quill back on the table. This historic peace treaty is also my will. My victory leaves a bittersweet taste in my mouth.

"Guards!" Alena barks. "Sound the horn to wake the troops and announce the news. I want everyone to witness the execution of the tyrant Sylvan Ren-Fuegis at dawn."

***

The sun will rise in a few minutes.

The entire enemy army has gathered at the edge of the camp. Thousands of silent soldiers.

My hands still bound in front of me, I let my executioner, who is none other than Lia's fiancé, the young Aeria officer, cut my hair. In the end, he volunteered to kill me because no one else wanted the task. My black locks fall one by one into the sand at my feet, hacked roughly by the blade of his knife. My neck has to be fully exposed so that the axe's edge will encounter no obstacles. I would have preferred this ritual to be done in private, but Alena is determined to humiliate me publicly before my execution.

The Glace Queen approaches just as the Aeria steps back. I remove my gold necklace and hand it to Alena, as agreed. I keep my promises, and through the peace treaty they've all signed, they'll keep theirs. I don't trust her, but I trust her allies, who are more honorable than she has ever been. They'll ensure things go as promised.

My wife's sister runs a finger over the magic necklace, looking at me through half-closed lids. This is the one Enola wore around her neck when she arrived in Astranis. The one that was originally meant for Alena.

"Well played, Sylvan," she says softly, so only I can hear. "In the end, you got what you wanted. You're dying for your moral principles, securing your place in your people's memory as a hero of Symbiosis.

Eternal glory."

What a fool. I never wanted to leave my wife and son behind. I'm doing it because it's necessary.

"What a shame we didn't meet under different circumstances," she adds, brushing my chest with a graceful hand that makes me shiver in disgust. "You're a very handsome man. You're smart, passionate, intense. Now that my dear Vidal is gone—since you were considerate enough to behead him yesterday, just as you'll be shortly—I'll need to find a new lover. So will my sister, I imagine. She'll replace you. She'll forget you."

"Alena, order my execution right now. Listening to you is so tedious that I'd prefer death over your bland words."

She lets out a cold laugh, then sings softly in my ear, "I'll find something, Sylvan… I may not be able to annex your kingdom, but I'll kill your little Queen Fuegis Queen one way or another. Poison, perhaps? A charming tribute to your father, wouldn't you say?"

I offer a smile to my enemy, which seems to throw her off. She must have expected me to lash out, to insult her, or to try to attack her here, in front of everyone—which would have instantly nullified the armistice. But I see through her game. She's bluffing. She's too much of a coward to go after her sister alone. She's only trying to torment me, to make me lose my composure.

"Oh, go ahead and try it, Alena. You'll regret it. Enola is the daughter of a goddess and your father. You're no match for her, I can assure you of that. But you already know that don't you? After all, you refused to face her powers during the last negotiations. Now, please grant me my final request."

"What is it?"

"To go to hell."

With a scornful sneer, the wretched queen turns on her heel and strides over to her allies. She signals to my executioner, who positions himself beside the chopping block.

kneel in the sand, my gaze drifting over the first glimmers of dawn breaking on the horizon. Every thought I have is of Enola.

Her smile. Her scent. Her laughter. Her face. Her body. Her eyes. Her tears. And the child she carries within her.

My everything.

"Your Majesty, it's time," my executioner murmurs, a hint of respect in his voice.

I nod slowly, bending forward to rest my neck on the warm wood of the block. The Aeria grips the handle of his axe with both hands and plants his feet firmly beside me. He raises his weapon, taking a deep breath. Hopefully, he won't miss, or this will be unbearably painful. I savor the warm caress of the Red Desert wind against my skin one last time, soaking in its colors, its... *golden* light.

"The sun! Look at the sun!" someone in the crowd shouts.

A golden sun rises above the dunes. not the red orb that greets us every other morning. This is an unprecedented weather phenomenon in this part of Symbiosis. The sands of the Red Desert are glowing with yellow hues before our eyes.

"The red sun will turn to gold on the day of the prophecy."

A powerful tremor shakes the ground beneath my knees. An earthquake.

Ah.

Apparently, the locked door and two guards didn't stop her.

I'd bet my head my wife is on her way.

CHAPTER TWENTY-SIX
"YOU ARE MY EVERYTHING."

ENOLA

In the stories I tell, it's always the man who comes to save his beloved at the last minute.

Not in mine.

I have to get there in time. I have to make it.

My mind is linked to Jada, who gallops as if in sync with the pounding of my heart. I tear through the ranks of the enemy army like a flaming arrow. Soldiers scramble out of my way as they feel the ground shake beneath them with each of my strides. I sharpen my senses, following the warmth and unique glow of Sylvan's Fire magic. *He's alive. It's not too late.*

I burst into the central clearing just as the yellow sun drenches the area in a flood of golden light. My gaze locks immediately on the sight of my husband, kneeling before a chopping block. An Aeria raises a gleaming axe over him. Instinctively, I raise a hand in his direction. A powerful gust of wind lifts the executioner off his feet, hurling him across the square, his weapon clattering away. The slope of a nearby dune breaks his fall. I hear a woman's scream. *Lia.*

Sylvan lifts his head as I approach, shock painting his face Jada stops in front of the block, and I slide off her back. Breath ragged,

I leap at my husband, wrapping my trembling arms around him so tightly he nearly topples backward from my force. I bury my face in his neck, feeling his pulse racing as fast as my own.

"Enola, you shouldn't have come," he murmurs hoarsely as I clutch him tightly, almost enough to crack his ribs. I feel him swallow hard against my lips. "You… you're only making things more complicated. You're going to ruin everything."

Drunk with anger and grief, I fight the urge to shake him with every ounce of my strength. How could he do this to me? How can he say such a thing? I can't bear the look of resignation clouding his green eyes. I've never seen him look this defeated. That look terrifies me as much as it enrages me.

"Shut up, Sylvan," I snap through clenched teeth.

"We signed the armistice, and my death is part of the terms. Go back to Astranis, my love. I don't want you to see—"

"SHUT UP!" I shout, slamming my fists against his chest, each word hitting me like an invisible dagger.

"Get away from him, Enola!" Alena's voice rings out, sharp and threatening.

"Do as she says," Sylvan whispers, his body rigid as a board in my arms.

"No, I won't!"

"Guards, seize her!" my sister orders.

With a moment's hesitation, only one Glace steps forward, moving toward me with uncertainty, intending to tear me from my husband's embrace. The others stand frozen, too stunned by the scene we're making.

"Jada!" I call, connecting my mind with my husband's mare.

The horse sidesteps in front of us, shielding us with her body. She rears up wildly, neighing and stopping the soldier from getting too close. He draws his sword with a curse… only to drop it instantly with a scream as the metal burns his hand from the heat of my Fire magic. He stumbles back, clutching his burned hand to his chest and withdraws. I desperately hope this display will discourage the others from trying to harm us.

For a moment, I consider fleeing into the Red Desert with my husband on Jada's back, using my powers as a diversion. But my gaze drifts to the distant towers of Astranis, and the thought of escape scatters like sand in the wind. Running would break the armistice, and the enemy would flood our city. Sylvan and I won't abandon our people to such a fate. We're not like Alena.

My tear-filled eyes turn to the golden sun. Believe in the prophecy. Unite all people.

Around an act of ultimate mercy.

Sylvan is too stubborn. In his warrior pride as a king, he'll never beg for his life.

So, I'll do it for him.

Cradling his face in my hands, I kiss my husband as I stand. My name dies on his lips. He watches me, his expression tense and questioning. I gently trace his scar before stepping away from him. With all humility, I kneel in the sand before the leaders of the opposing army, including the Aeria executioner, now standing and holding Lia's hand.

"I beg for your grace and mercy," I begin, struggling to keep my voice steady. "If I could, I would give up my four elemental magics in exchange for his life, but that's impossible. What's the use of powers so strong if I can't even save the man I love?"

"Enola, stop, don't lower yourself like this!" Sylvan rasps behind me.

But I am not lowering myself, my love. I would be if I let my anger loose. I would be if I turned to slaughter. Speaking from my heart doesn't lower me. It lifts me beyond pride in the name of the love I feel for you.

"I'm not speaking to you as a queen, or even as the Rose of the Elements. I'm speaking as a Powerless. As a Glace. As a Fuegis. As a Aeria. As a Stowne. And, most of all, I'm speaking as a wife and... as a mother," I stammer, pressing a hand over my stomach. Belise and Lia exchange startled glances. Alena scowls. "Don't make me a widow. Don't make my child an orphan."

"For the gods' sake, you're utterly pathetic," my sister snaps, rolling her eyes. "You're humiliating yourself."

"I don't care, Alena. Even pride bows to death. You've never loved, I feel it in your heart. It's as frozen as ice. You don't know what it means to lose someone you love more than yourself. I know, because I lost my mother and my brother. You know it too," I continue, my gaze piercing through the other leaders. "Lia, you lost your father. Belise, you lost your brother. All of you have lost someone dear over these last months. That kind of pain—so intense it destroys a part of you forever. Do you really think Sylvan's death will lighten your grief? Do you believe vengeance will help you move forward?"

No one responds. They listen. They watch me. But no one says a word.

"Violence is not the cure for our suffering; it's the festering wound that eats away at us. Vengeance began this war, and so… only forgiveness can truly end it. Forgiveness isn't reserved solely for the gods; it's within each of us. because none of us are beyond mistakes. Because we're fallible. Because we're human. We all carry our burdens—our guilt, our doubts, our fears, our pain—as chains that make us prisoners of ourselves. Behind our facades, we fight an endless inner battle. You may think me naïve, but I sincerely believe that love, peace, and forgiveness demand far more willpower and courage than hatred, war, and bitterness. They're not easy to live by, I admit that. But… they're our greatest strengths. That's why… that's why… I forgive you, my sister," I say to Alena, locking my gaze with hers and swallowing the sob in my throat. "I… forgive you for killing my family. I believe even your frozen heart can warm, if you let someone love you. I believe you can become a better woman, and a better queen. I want to have faith in you, as I have in all of us."

Her icy blue eyes flash with fury. *I don't need your pathetic forgiveness. I don't regret my actions*, her stormy eyes seem to declare.

"I'm sorry, Your Majesty, but what you're asking is impossible," counters the High-Stowne, casting a look at Sylvan.

"No. Nothing is impossible in a world like ours."

To illustrate my words, tiny white snowflakes begin to swirl around us. A low murmur rises through the army surrounding us, soldiers tilting their heads upward, dumbfounded by the climatic marvel.

There isn't a single cloud in the sky…

And yet, it's snowing in the Red Desert.

As they look down again, they watch in awe as the melting snowflakes turn the sand into a bed of emerald-green shoots, which quickly bloom into a carpet of pure white flowers.

Hundreds of them. Thousands of them.

"One last time, I beg you; spare Sylvan Ren-Fuegis. I beg you to have faith in him. He will have to live with his guilt. I promise you that his death would only deepen your own. I assure you that justice and vengeance are two opposing forces. Don't rob Symbiosis of a great king like him. A king willing to sacrifice himself for his people. Doesn't a king who chooses peace and love over war and hate deserve forgiveness?"

My sorrowful gaze finds Sylvan's. He's deeply moved by my words, tears streaming down his cheeks as they do on mine.

Belise San-Stowne steps toward me, her expression grave. Then, she extends her hand.

"Stand up, Enola," she commands in a low but resolute voice.

I slide my trembling fingers into hers and rise, my heart pounding, my breath shallow. She holds my gaze with her shining eyes.

"A great queen like you should never kneel before anyone. You are a miracle for Symbiosis. I have faith in you. And the answer to your question is yes, Enola. He deserves forgiveness." She raises her voice, speaking calmly, "I, Belise San-Stowne, heiress to my Clan's crown, agree to spare Sylvan Ren-Fuegis."

A wave of stunned murmurs rises from the army around us.

"I, Lia Ler-Aeria, heiress to my Clan's crown, agree to spare him," adds a gentle female voice from behind Belise.

"I agree as well," the Renegade representative says gruffly. "Strike the first condition from that treaty, and let's put an end to all this."

A stifled sob escapes me. Belise gently strokes my cheek, wiping my tears with the tips of her fingers, a faint smile ghosting her lips.

"Thank you," I whisper, unable to say more.

"Go to your husband and free him, Enola Ren-Fuegis."

As I turn, I glance over at Alena. She stands rigid, fists clenched, her face a mask of stone. She won't yield. She'll stick to her stance.

But the majority has spoken. She cannot defy them without facing the wrath of her allies.

I hurry toward Sylvan, who's managed to stand. His incredulous expression might make me laugh if I weren't so shaken. I reach out to him, and he holds up his bound hands toward me.

An ominous shiver runs through me, halting me just short of reaching him. A memory jolts to life. A flash of my first dream's ending.

The golden sun.

The wave of blood behind him.

Our outstretched hands, reaching for each other.

The instant our fingers touch, Sylvan's eyes widen, staring over my shoulder, past me. My breath catches.

"Enola!" he cries in horror.

With sudden urgency, he grabs my hands, preventing me from turning toward the danger. In one swift motion, he pulls me close, pressing me against his solid body. He whirls us around with a force that stuns me before I can even grasp what's happening.

I feel the impact jolt through both of us.

I feel his flesh tearing as though my own soul is ripping.

I feel each tremor of pain reflected in his eyes, piercing into me.

I scream his name.

My voice shatters like glass.

A thin line of blood trickles from the corner of his mouth. He wavers, his weight pulling me down with him. I sink to the ground, arms wrapped around him, my horrified gaze fixed on the bloodied ice shard protruding from his back, the translucent spike meant to pierce through me. He used his body as a shield to save me and our child. Through my tears, I see Aerias and Stownes rushing toward my sister. She touches one, turning him to ice. "Stop her! Stop her!" Belise screams desperately.

With immense effort, I forgave Alena for killing my mother and brother. I made the mistake of believing she could change, could become better. She's just proven me wrong. But I will never forgive her for Sylvan's death. I will never forgive her for trying to kill my child and me.

Her life or ours.

Across the chaos, her hunted gaze locks onto mine.

"Goodbye, my sister," I say, my voice breaking.

She screams my name, a howl of rage tinged with fear. My Earth magic immediately transforms her into a statue of stone. My Air magic shatters her into a thousand pieces.

My sister, Alena Kan-Glace, is no more.

And my husband, Sylvan Ren-Fuegis, is dying in my arms, his body convulsing in pain. Several vital organs have been hit; I can feel it with my heightened senses. A kidney and a lung. Internal bleeding. In just a few minutes, he will be gone. His breath is labored, wheezing. His complexion is corpse-like. Leaning over him, ravaged by tears cascading down my face, I gently stroke his cheek with a desperate tenderness.

"You really wanted to die today a hero, didn't you?" I whisper in a voice devoid of tone.

He grimaces a faint smile and weakly nods. I close my eyes for two seconds to prevent myself from collapsing on him. Snowflakes fall into his short hair. I rake them through my fingers.

I cradle him against my chest, my heart aching with the weight of sorrow. I kiss his bloodied lips, whispering that I love him, as if it were a prayer, repeating that he is my everything.

I am already shattered. I am empty. I am dead.

Destiny, sings the wind in my ear, playing through my diaphanous hair.

I watch as countless white flowers continue to bloom around us, indifferent to my husband's agony. An image from the past overlays my present vision.

Me, burning a branch. A plant sprout emerging from a small pile of ashes.

Life. Death. Balance.

Other voices weave through my turbulent mind.

Beladyn's voice.

"Personally, I've never liked that word, destiny."

Sylvan's voice.

"So, this is the end of your story? I hope you're joking?"

Belise's voice.

"You are a miracle for Symbiosis."

Mine.

"What's the point of having such powerful powers if I can't even save the man I love?"

The beats of my heart slow, matching Sylvan's.

My mother, Nature, is the daughter of Life.

And Nature…

… is capable of healing.

Between my hands rests the secret to peace and the key to truth.

Hope.

That is the secret to peace.

That is the key to truth.

"Stop lying to yourself and underestimating yourself. Use the best part of your emotions—the one that elevates you. Infuse your faith and your conviction into this phrase. Not only can you do it, but you will. Because for you, the Rose of

the Elements, daughter of Nature, it is a given. It is natural. It is simple. Accept it, Enola Ren-Fuegis. Accept your powers. Accept your divine part. Say the words again."

I am capable of heal Sylvan.

I place my hand at the base of the ice spike protruding from his back. Using my Fire magic, I melt the projectile. My husband lets out a groan of pain as blood pours freely from his fatal wound. My palm presses firmly against the wound as I lock my gaze with his, silently commanding him to survive for just a few more seconds, to hang on. He convulses. I feel the warm, sticky blood on my fingers. I center my mind.

I overcome my terror of losing him.

I regain my confidence.

I have faith in us.

I am capable of healing Sylvan.

A source of overwhelming power condenses deep within me. All the flows of my four elements mix together. Water. Air. Earth. Fire. They form a burning river that makes me shiver all over. They disperse through my fibers. They pour into his, just as his eyes close and his head tilts against my chest.

I am capable of healing Sylvan.

The damaged tissues regenerate.

The pierced organs heal.

The blood becomes oxygenated.

Microscopic flames cauterize the wounds.

I remove my hand from his back, now whole. No scar marks his skin.

I remove my hand from his back, now whole. No scar marks his skin.

He opens his eyes, blinking, and buries them in mine. A broad smile spreads across my lips at his astonished expression and confused gaze.

A breeze of intense relief wraps around me.

"You weren't really going to insult me by falling asleep before the end of my story, were you, my love?" I whisper with a playful smile before gently pressing my lips to his, which return my smile.

I am Enola Ren-Fuegis, Queen of Astranis.

He is Sylvan Ren-Fuegis, King of Astranis.

The dawn has passed, and we are going to live for one more day. And probably thousands more.

Chapter Twenty-Seven

A New Story

Enola

"Slowly, slowly! I can't keep up with your pace!" I protest as I'm pulled toward the oasis by a swarm of energetic children buzzing around me.

The little Fuegis, Glaces, Aerias, Stownes, and Powerless pull me forward, holding onto my hands and the hem of my dress, as excited as can be. Of course, at their age, they have no patience.

"Hurry, hurry, Your Majesty!" cries a little Aeria, tapping my hip gently. "My mother and sister have served mint tea for everyone; it's going to get cold!"

I sigh I haven't liked mint tea for two months due to my pregnancy, but maybe I should have mentioned that earlier.

"It's okay," boasts a little Fuegis, puffing out his chest, "I'll warm your tea up with my Fire magic."

Laughing heartily, the girl plants a loud kiss on her friend's cheek, making him blush.

The more I watch these adorable children, the more I can't wait for my son to be born. Just two more months to wait before I can hold him in my arms and cover his face in kisses.

The villagers of Raockar have set up a chaise longue by the water and a low table surrounded by rugs. We sit beneath the long, serrated leaves of the palm trees. The children grab tea cups, bickering as they do. I call them to order with a clap of my hands, like a schoolteacher.

"I won't start any story if you keep making so much noise, you little rascals!" I warn them in a mock-authoritative tone.

Silence falls. Perfect.

I sweep my gaze over them, fondly. These past months, so much has changed on Symbiosis, which now truly lives up to its name. We've entered a new era. Alliances have been reformed. The internal borders of our island have been abolished. Every inhabitant now has the right to live wherever they choose. All the cities are populated by Fuegis, Glaces, Aerias, Stownes, and former Renegates. With equality granted, our peoples have blended together, learning tolerance and sharing; ideals we had been lacking for centuries. The climate has adapted to our evolution, thanks to the alliance of the four elements. It has become more temperate. For example, the Red Desert is less hot and arid, and it's much milder at Oceanar. The Exile Forest has been abandoned by the Powerless, who were integrated among us after the decree Sylvan and I passed.

We have mourned our dead. We have rebuilt our cities. We have reformed our laws.

In return, elemental magic is gradually disappearing from our lands. I can feel it diminishing within me and around me with each passing day. It is the law of Natural Balance, the price of our lasting prosperity. In one or two decades, our powers will be nothing more than memories, and we will be like our ancestors from the Continent; simple humans. It is not a bad thing. I think that a magic so powerful should only be reserved for those wise enough to use it properly. The gods.

And dragons, maybe.

By the way, that gives me an idea.

"I'm going to tell you a story you've never heard before," I announce to the children who are listening intently. "Another story of Symbiosis origins. You can choose to believe it or not, the decision is yours."

"And you, do you believe it, Your Majesty?" a little Powerless girl calls out.

I smile and gently stroke her cheek.

"Yes, I believe it. I believe in all my stories, even the most crazy ones." The little girl giggles. "But I But I won't force you to believe them. I will never say, 'This is the one and only truth, there are no others.' Because there are as many truths as there are people, as many stories as there are perceptions of the world. I'm simply going to share with you a different version of the traditional story your parents told you. And if you don't like it, don't blame your friends if they do… Respect their opinion, even if you don't agree with them."

"What a shame, I already know it. I wanted to hear a story of love, battles, and secrets," a teasing voice interrupts from behind me.

"Oh no, not again!" several children groan, while Sylvan sits behind me on the chaise, encircling me with his strong arms.

"We want the new story!" the Powerless girl exclaims, her little friends nodding in agreement.

"It seems you're in the minority, my king," I remark to my husband, kissing his warm, bearded cheek.

"It was a battle I was destined to lose," he replies, resting his chin on my shoulder. "But I'll recover from my disappointment."

I intertwine our fingers on the curve of my lap as he tenderly caresses it.

"I have no doubt of that, my love."

Ouch, a good one! Sylvan laughs softly, pressing his palm against the small bump formed by our son Saradin's little foot. "A future warrior," he boasts privately. "A future troublemaker, mostly," I retort every time to shut him down.

I take a deep breath as I study my dear audience and adopt my deep storyteller's voice.

"In the Dawn of Time, the goddess of Life and the goddess of Death founded the five worlds of Creation…"

Acknowledgments

After our trip to the island of Symbiosis, it's time for me to send a big thank you to all the people who made it possible to make my fantasy tale a reality through the magic of publishing.

First, I want to thank my demonic guardian angel Farah, who knows why. Your support and trust in my writing have touched my heart. My beautiful *couque*, I am delighted and honored that *The Courtesan Queen* is the second story to be part of the Fantas'ink collection alongside your magnificent *Sang des Sauvages*. In addition to all that, you were fully involved in embellishing the paperback of my story with the decorative patterns, the Symbiosis map, and your Enola fan art, and you did wonders on all levels! And to top it off, we had a good laugh along the way. Thank you so much.

My editor who rocks everything, my dear Sarah, who firmly believes in my writings, always there to answer my questions, advise me, rave between two serious subjects, and who welcomed me into her home like a member of her family… I don't think the word "thank you" would be strong enough to express how I feel about you. Running out of words, what an irony for an author! For the record, the next time we see each other, you will get a double dose of hugs. You are as professional as you are benevolent, and that is just exceptional.

My belove Marie, my good fairy with your pink wand, your passion, your naturalness, your ideas, your availability, your always fair and relevant words, which do me a lot of good in my moments of doubt… A thousand thanks for being you. I can't wait to work on the next baby because I know that a certain demonic character has a very special place in your heart.

A huge thank you to my adorable Noémie, a new author of Black Ink, who has become a friend with whom I chat almost every day. You were my half-beta (as we say between us) on that *The Courtesan Queen* given me great advice on how to polish it up before the editorial, and, by the way, claimed Sylvan loud and clear. No problem, I'll lend them to you with pleasure (I'm talking about The Fuegis King AND his famous well-placed piercing, which has been the subject of two or three improbable conversations…). I'm so happy I have met you, baby.

I also thank my sisters and my brother of… oh gee, I can't say it here, I have to behave myself. All the great and bonded team of Black Ink. I won't mention all of you; I'll be here all night since there are so many of us. By the way, you fill… everything you have to fill (starting with my heart, of course!) In short, I adore you; never change. And by the way, a marvelous thank you to Layla who gave me another sublime cover, and to Maya for this stunning trailer. You girls are real artists.

To my husband, I have not forgotten you since I dedicate *The Courtesan Queen* to you, a love story between two opposing elements that allows you to escape into another world. As we have loved to travel since we met, it seemed natural to me. But also (obviously!) because I love you, and you and our son are my everything. I know that you may not read this story because you don't like to read (I'm still waiting for you to stick to LPCE, I think I can wait for the flood!), but it doesn't matter because the main thing is here. You support me every day, reboots me and encourage me when I'm feeling down: you are my rock, quite simply.

I also thank all those who support me unconditionally: my family, especially my parents and my brother, as well as my in-laws and my friends.

Another thank you, but not least, to Mona, the author of the second Enola fan art. You draw the characters of my stories with talent and sensitivity, and you are as humble as you are passionate. I myself am a fan of your fan-arts, my dear reader.

Now you might think I'm a bit of a bulbous bore (and you would be right, I assume it), but I keep a little thought for my fictitious muse. This is one of the main characters of my *The Guild of Shadows* saga, Beladyn, my number one favorite, whom you briefly discovered here. I often joke with my Wattpad readers that Bel whispers bullshit, crazy situations, and sarcasm in my ear, but that's not entirely wrong, in a way. He often inspires me and sometimes even serves as a model or reference to build my other male heroes.

I will conclude with my driving forces… My wonderful readers! Thanks for having faith in me. Thank you for sending me these kind messages that make me so happy and encourage me, for recommending my books to your loved ones, for investing yourself so much on social media through your opinions and comments, and for following my writing in different fields where it ventures, to bring my stories and my characters to life.

Plan to sit comfortably, then let yourself be carried away by your imagination and mine… Because I, too, have a thousand and one tales to tell you.

By the way, one last thing…

As I already did for *Amour, flingues et macaronis*, I will publish a bonus chapter of *The Courtesan Queen* on Anna Triss's author Facebook page in a while.

Big hugs to you all; see you soon!

ASLO FROM ANNA TRISS

MYRINA HOLMES
DEMONS AND WONDERS
Coming Soon

**Other novels from
WARM PUBLISHING**

Scan to easily acess all of Warm Publishing books:

Join also our Facebook Group, Book Warmers, to get the lastedt updates and talk about books and more!

Falling for the Voice
by *Mag Maury*

The sexiest of surprises... and the most unbearable!

My plan was simple: Find a job quickly in order to make rent. And I found one. A waitressing job at the hottest pub in town!

Everything was going smoothly until he arrived: Matt. Sexy. Arrogant. Six feet three of muscles that drive women into a hysterical frenzy at every single one of his concerts.

This guy is really comfortable on stage and oh, so enticing. We girls can try to put him out of our minds but we end up wanting him anyway. And he knows it.

Except me, Charlotte. I say no!

Well... Maybe! After all, I have never really been good at resisting temptation...

My Hipster Next Door
by *Mag Maury*

In Liverpool, the barbershop Hipster Maniac is an institution. Run by three bearded, tattooed friends, it is the place to listen to great rock, get a trim, and have a drink.

But for Line, it also spelled trouble. For starters, when she first got to the neighborhood, she rear-ended Jordan's car, who turned out to be one of the three barbers. Then she discovered that they were neighbors in business and residence! So no way can she escape this muscle-flaunting, smoldering man who is covered in tattoos and... completely insufferable!

He draws her near only to push her away. He toys with her shamelessly. But worst of all he hates Christmas whereas that is Line's very favorite time of year!

Beneath a backdrop of festive fairy lights, intoxicatingly passionate kisses, and blistering banter... It's on!

The Cocky Heir
by *Ana K. Anderson*

She is about to get married. But not to him.

Quinn MacFayden, an accomplished expat businessman in New York, is set to return to Scotland in extremis to protect the precious family legacy. His 91-year-old grandfather is about to marry a perfect stranger sixty-six years his junior... And that is out of the question! Quinn swears it. Over his dead body will Dawn Fleming ever be part of the family!

But Dawn is not a future bride like the others. She is nowhere near the gold digger he imagined and, above all, she knows just how to stand up to him. And so a game of cat and mouse begins between them. A war with no holds barred and where surrender has never been so tempting...

My Stepbrother: A Sexual Revelation
by *Sophie S. Pierucci*

Cassie is a highly intelligent young woman... Too much so for her own good!

And she is as daunting as she is intriguing. Carl, the son of his father's second wife, would hardly say otherwise!

Carl is the exact opposite of his steady father. He is a player and a slayer. Afraid of nothing and no one. Except for Cassie when she asks him to introduce her to the pleasures of the flesh.

And when the situation gets out of control, it is too late to turn back, and the two lovers find themselves ensnared in forbidden passion. Forbidden by everyone: society, their parents, their friends.

But how to resist the desire that consumes them?

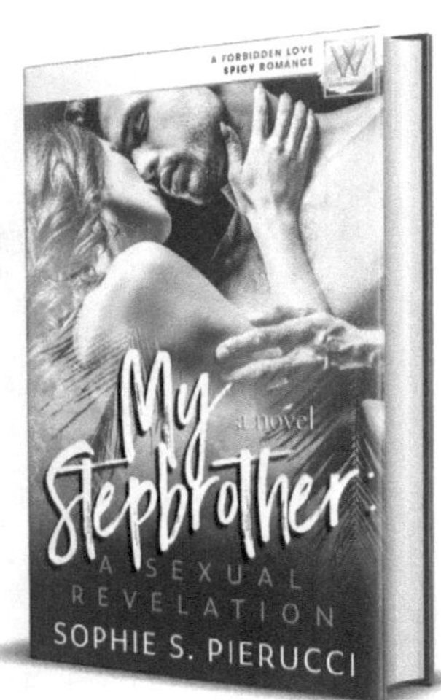

Roommate with my Boss
by *Erin Graham*

Boss, roommate, fake fiancé... real lover?

Étienne is cold, charismatic, and he never shies away from a challenge.

He masters everything down to the smallest detail... until a little accountant with an unlikely look and flowers in her hair inserts herself into his daily life.

She is whimsical, full of life, laughs at the rules and gets around them, talks all the time except about her past... and she drives him crazy. Yet, it's impossible to fire her.

She needs a job and a roof over her head; he needs a fake fiancée...

Is it a deal?

Your Power Over me
by *Missy Heart*

A family home heavy with secrets, a dangerously charismatic owner.

Will her arrival at Iron House be the end of her?

Ever since she was a teenager, Lovisa has known it: at Iron House, anything can happen, especially the worst.

However, when she is forced to return to the family home for her stepfather's funeral, her heart races: she is going to see him again, this "brother" who she never wanted and who yet turned her whole world upside down.

Now at the head of a drug cartel, authoritarian and brutal, Niklas is nothing like the teenager she knew nine years ago. At his side, Lovisa finds herself immersed in a harsh, ruthless—but fascinating—world.

Irremediably attracted to this man who wants her as much harm as good, will Lovisa manage to fight her unmentionable desires? Or will she give in to Niklas' magnetic darkness?

Touchdown
by *Sonia Birdy*

She's a runner, but the campus star quaterback runs faster than she does!

Rocky has had a chaotic life from which she concluded three fundamental things: life is a succession of problems to be solved, men are assholes to be avoided and promises are only binding on fools who want to believe in them. So, unlike the other girls on campus, boys are not a priority for her. Worse, she sees them as an obstacle to her success!

But during a student party, she meets Jude. Freshly transferred from Harvard to play on Brown's soccer team, Jude is the new star on campus. Handsome and inaccessible, he is the type not to get attached: the perfect candidate for a one-night stand.

But the chemistry is too strong. And though Rocky is determined to run away from him, he is determined to conquer her heart.

Kalliopee: A Princess's Sacrifice
by *Koko Nhan*

After years of violent battles, Kalliopee agrees to sacrifice her freedom by marrying the prince of the enemy kingdom in order to bring peace.

In a world where women are treated as slaves rather than wives, she is still delighted to be reunited with her first love, Karel.

However, life is unpredictable, and the horrors of war have transformed Karel into a tough and ruthless heir to the throne, who despises the Viridians more than anything. While he has no qualms about mistreating Kalliopee, his determination wavers when confronted with her striking eyes. In the midst of desire and animosity, schemes and plots, dreams and disillusionment, will the princess's heart endure the price of her liberty?

The Private Garden
by *Oly TL*

The most disturbing and transgressive of contracts...

Tiger Sexton seems to have it all. Charisma. Respect. Relentless business acumen. More fortune than he could spend in a life and a sublime wife. Sophia.

When Oceane is invited by Mrs. Sexton for a job interview in one of the restaurants that her husband gave her, the young French tourist knows nothing about this couple. Their name means

nothing to her, people are not her thing. She just wants a job, a place to live and to move on with her life... Sophia's proposal comes at the right time: the Sextons are looking for an *au pair*.

But by opening their doors to her, many other locks are likely to open. Is Oceane ready for this? And what about Sophia, and especially the Tiger lurking in this Secret Garden?

Keep in touch with Anna Triss
Join her social media pages
Instagram: @anna.triss
TikTok: annatriss
Facebook: Anna Triss

About the Author

Anna Triss devoured her first fantasy novel as a teenager and fell in love with this literary genre. This event marked the beginning of an unconditional passion: writing.

Enclosed in her little bubble, she escapes into her own universe thanks to her pen, guided by her imagination and madness. Publishing is a long-time dream come true.

With a degree in art history and archaeology, married and mother of a little boy, this passionate author lives ir La Rochelle, France, where she writes intense stories populated by atypical heroes, always charismatic, often badass, with developed psychology. She writes in a variety of genres (fantasy, contemporary romance, urban fantasy, dark romance) and has several bestsellers to her credit, including The Courtesan Queen, an enemies-to-lovers fantasy romance tinged with magic and secrets. In addition to reading, Anna loves art, travel, TV shows, movies, and... dragons!

www.ingramcontent.com/pod-product-compliance
Lightning Source LLC
Chambersburg PA
CBHW061535190726
48289CB00004B/1049